Home Song

Home Song

A Cape Light Novel

THOMAS KINKADE
& KATHERINE SPENCER

BERKLEY BOOKS, NEW YORK

A Parachute Press Book

THE BERKLEY PUBLISHING GROUP
Published by the Penguin Group
Penguin Group (USA) Inc.
375 Hudson Street, New York, New York 10014, USA
Penguin Group (Canada), 10 Alcorn Avenue, Toronto, Ontario M4V 3B2, Canada
(a division of Pearson Penguin Canada Inc.)
Penguin Books Ltd., 80 Strand, London WC2R 0RL, England
Penguin Group Ireland, 25 St. Stephen's Green, Dublin 2, Ireland (a division of Penguin Books Ltd.)
Penguin Group (Australia), 250 Camberwell Road, Camberwell, Victoria 3124, Australia
(a division of Pearson Australia Group Pty. Ltd.)
Penguin Books India Pvt. Ltd., 11 Community Centre, Panchsheel Park, New Delhi—110 017, India
Penguin Group (NZ), Cnr. Airborne and Rosedale Roads, Albany, Auckland 1310, New Zealand
(a division of Pearson New Zealand Ltd.)
Penguin Books (South Africa) (Pty.) Ltd., 24 Sturdee Avenue, Rosebank, Johannesburg 2196, South Africa

Penguin Books Ltd., Registered Offices: 80 Strand, London WC2R 0RL, England

This book is an original publication of The Berkley Publishing Group.

This is a work of fiction. Names, characters, places, and incidents either are the product of the author's imagination or are used fictitiously, and any resemblance to actual persons, living or dead, business establishments, events, or locales is entirely coincidental.

PRINTING HISTORY
Berkley hardcover edition / November 2002
Berkley trade paperback edition / November 2003
Berkley trade paperback ISBN: 0-425-19183-4

The Library of Congress has catalogued the Berkley hardcover edition as follows:

Kinkade, Thomas, 1958–
      Home song : a Cape Light novel / Thomas Kinkade & Katherine Spencer.
            p.   cm.
      Sequel to: Cape Light.
      ISBN: 0-425-18624-5
            1. New England—Fiction.   2. Birthmothers—Fiction.   3. Mother and daughters—Fiction.
      I. Spencer, Katherine.   II. Title.

PS3561.I534 H66 2002
813'.54—dc21

                                                                                          2002074425

PRINTED IN THE UNITED STATES OF AMERICA

10   9   8   7   6

WELCOME BACK TO CAPE LIGHT

⌒

HOME. WHAT IMAGE COMES TO MIND WHEN YOU HEAR THAT word? Do you see four walls? An address? Or do you picture a place of refuge, of comfort, and of hope?

In my paintings, whether the subject is a garden or a city street or a sailboat in the bay, my real subject is always home—the home we all wish for. The place where we feel welcomed and safe. Home is a place like Cape Light.

It was my great joy to introduce you to Cape Light and to the people who live there in my first Cape Light novel. Now I want to welcome you back.

Cape Light is still a town where friendships flourish, where people enjoy the warmth of romance, the joy of family life, and the support of the entire community. In Cape Light folks reach out willingly to lend a helping hand. They are together, not alone, yet each heart holds its own unique story and its own secret. Emily Warwick, the poised mayor of the town, still mourns the husband she lost and the daughter she gave up for adoption twenty years ago. She would never guess that her daughter is in Cape Light struggling with her feelings about the mother she never knew. Lucy Bates is following her dream—to go to college. But will her husband be able to accept her choice? Reverend Ben's gentle advice and special prayers have comforted Emily, Lucy, and nearly everyone in town, but he wonders who will comfort him as he tries to heal the hurt that wounds his own family.

Many of you have written to say that you see yourself in the people of Cape Light. I can see myself in them, too. They *are* like us—seekers who are searching for their own path to find lasting love and to face each day with grace and faith in God.

Come with me and meet again the people of Cape Light. Step into a place that sings out the joy of coming home. Come join the home song of Cape Light—you know it by heart.

—Thomas Kinkade

CHAPTER ONE

⌒✗

THE HOUSE WAS DARK, DESERTED LOOKING, EXCEPT for a small square of light in an upstairs window. Her mother's bedroom.

So she's taken to her bed. Pulling out all the stops tonight, isn't she? Emily Warwick unlocked the door, then clicked on the lights in the foyer. Her mother kept the house so dark, it was a wonder she didn't fall and break a hip.

"Emily, is that you?" Lillian called from upstairs.

"Yes, Mother. Who else would it be?" Emily climbed the stairs to the second floor and headed for the master bedroom.

"No reason to be snide," Lillian scolded.

"Sorry, I didn't mean to be." Emily entered the room, then paused at the foot of her mother's bed.

The scene was just as she'd pictured it: her mother propped

up on pillows, wearing her satin-trimmed bed jacket and a dismal expression. Despite her height and large frame, Lillian looked small and frail. The mahogany four-poster was actually too large for the room, as was most of her mother's furniture. The pieces, taken from Lilac Hall when their family was forced to leave, were better suited to grander surroundings.

As was her mother, Emily reflected.

"Did you bring the pills?"

"Right here." Emily showed her the white bag from the pharmacy. "But the doctor said to take them only if you definitely had a migraine. The medication is very strong."

Lillian shifted against the pillows. "Of course it's a migraine. I ought to know after all these years."

Emily studied her. Maybe this wasn't an act after all, a convenient emergency designed to make Emily miss her sister's engagement party. Maybe the strain of opposing Jessica's choice in a husband was finally getting to her.

"You're all dressed up tonight. Am I keeping you from something?" Lillian said.

"You know where I'm going." Emily glanced at her watch as she sat on the edge of the bed. "And I'm nearly an hour late already. Jessica must be wondering what happened to me."

"Oh, yes. The happy couple is celebrating their engagement." Lillian drew out the last word on a sour note. "I'd almost forgotten."

"Yes, I'm sure you did." Emily cast her a doubtful look.

"Your sister is throwing her life away, you know. All she's achieved so far, all she *could* achieve. She could marry anyone. But no, she picks out some muscle-bound, empty-headed laborer—"

"That's enough," Emily cut in. "You don't even know Sam Morgan. He's a good man."

"Good for someone else's daughter. Not *mine!* Not after what I went through to raise both of you. To give you every opportunity to rise above the rest of the world's mediocrity."

Lillian's voice trembled on a sharp, high note, and her cheeks grew flushed.

"Calm down, Mother. I already know how you feel about it—"

"Don't you tell me to calm down. I know you played a part in this *love* match, Emily. I know you encouraged your sister to marry him, so don't deny it."

Yes, she had encouraged Jessica, sometimes feeling as if she were in a mortal battle for her sister's soul—or for Jessica's future happiness, at the very least. Bitter experience had taught Emily the cost of giving in to their mother's imperious will. She knew she couldn't change the past, but she hoped and prayed that Jessica wouldn't make the same mistake she had, giving up the one thing that mattered to her most in the world.

"Why would I deny it?" Emily replied, unfazed. "Jessica and Sam love each other and belong together."

"Please, spare me. You sound like the back cover of a novel." Lillian looked disgusted.

Emily bit back a retort. What was the point of arguing? There was no winning this round. *Besides,* she reminded herself, *the Lord asks us to have patience, even when it isn't easy.* Especially *when it isn't.*

"Let's just drop it, Mother. This conversation isn't going anywhere."

"You know I'm right. You just won't admit it," Lillian challenged her, unwilling to back down. "Do you think it was easy for me after your father died? Salvaging what I could? Making a new life for you and your sister? And finally, old and sick and looking to my daughters for some comfort, this is the thanks I get. *Mrs. Sam Morgan,*" she concluded bitterly. "I could almost laugh if I didn't feel like crying."

An idle threat, Emily thought. She couldn't recall the last time she'd seen her mother cry. But clearly her mother was overwrought; her blood pressure was probably shooting up to a dangerous height.

"I'll get you some water for these pills," Emily said, getting to her feet. She returned a few moments later with a glass of water.

Lillian took the medication, then sank back into the pillows with a deep sigh.

"Can I get you anything else? Something to eat maybe?" Emily offered.

"I'm not hungry. In fact, my stomach is quite upset. I couldn't eat a thing. I thought you said this prescription was strong. I don't feel a thing."

"It should take effect soon." Emily sat on the edge of the bed again. Lillian's eyes slowly closed, and her breathing became slow and deep. Emily thought she had drifted off when her mother suddenly said, "How is your campaign coming along? I don't hear much about it."

"It's only September. Things won't really heat up for another month or so. Most people think I've done a pretty good job, and Charlie Bates doesn't have much to run on."

Emily had been elected mayor of Cape Light three years ago, which was still a source of great pride for her mother. If she didn't win again, Emily knew her mother would be very disappointed. Maybe even more than she would be.

"Well, don't rest on your laurels," Lillian advised. "Charlie Bates is despicable. But there are plenty of fools in this village who will vote for him, just to spite our family."

"I think Charlie appeals to a certain group of voters in town," Emily allowed. "But I don't think it has much to do with our family. That's ancient history, Mother. Nobody thinks about it anymore."

"Of course they do. You just don't want to see it, Emily. You've always been that way. You never want to think badly of people. Just like your father."

Unlike you, Mother. You never miss an opportunity. Emily let out a long breath, gathering her patience again.

"What about church tomorrow? Will you be up to it?" Emily asked.

"I don't know. I'll have to see how I feel." Lillian sat up and adjusted the covers. "Sara Franklin said she might stop by. She picked up a book I had on reserve at the library."

"Very thoughtful of her."

"She's a thoughtful girl. Full of opinions, though, especially when it comes to books. She'll argue with me until the cows come home."

"Yes, I've noticed. Good for her," Emily said with a small smile.

She liked Sara very much and was grateful for the attention the young woman showed to her mother. It was an unexpected friendship, but somehow, it worked. Seemingly shy, Sara was not the least bit cowed by Lillian's formidable personality.

Emily stole a secret glance at her watch and nearly gasped when she noticed the time. *Poor Jessica. She'll think I've forgotten her.*

"Is there anything else you need?" she asked, standing up. "I really have to get over to the party. It's getting late." When her mother didn't reply, Emily added, "I promised Jessica. She'll be very disappointed if I don't come."

"Yes, of course. We don't dare disappoint Jessica." Lillian glared at Emily, then turned her face away. "Don't worry about me. I'll survive," she added in a tight voice.

Emily knew she was being manipulated but still felt a twinge of guilt at her mother's wounded expression. "I'll stop by on my way home."

"Don't bother. You'll only wake me, probably give me cardiac arrest from the shock. I'll think a burglar is breaking in."

"Oh, Mother, really." Emily shook her head with a small smile. "I can't remember the last time anyone was robbed around here. You couldn't be safer."

"Of course you'd say that. You're the mayor," Lillian retorted. "I'm just an old woman, an invalid practically, all alone in a big house. Which reminds me, I need you to take my pearl necklace back to the bank. You know I don't like to keep good jewelry at home. It's in the bottom drawer of my dresser."

"Oh . . . all right." Emily stepped over to the dresser and found the jewelry case tucked under a pile of slips and nightgowns. The scent of lavender sachet—her mother's scent—floated up and surrounded her for a moment.

With the dark blue velvet box in hand, she turned to face her mother again. "Why don't you ask Jessica to take it back? She's at the bank every day."

"Because I asked you. If you're too busy to do it, simply say so and I'll ask someone else."

The necklace was among her mother's most treasured possessions, a family heirloom that had first belonged to her great-grandmother. Lillian had always promised her daughters that they would each wear the pearl necklace on their wedding day, and eventually one of them would inherit it to pass it down to her children.

Now the family tradition was taking an ironic twist, Emily realized. For, in fact, her mother had not worn the pearls on her wedding day because she had married against her parents' wishes. When the pearls had eventually come into her possession, Lillian had held them out to her daughters like the ultimate prize, the prize she had been denied.

And now the family history was about to repeat itself.

"You're not going to let Jessica wear the necklace at her wedding, are you?" Emily asked her mother.

"No, I will not. If she doesn't need my approval or my blessing to be married, so be it. I won't be attending the event, and I see no reason why she should wear the pearls."

Of course, it was a punishment, Emily realized. She was punishing Jessica the same way she had been punished by her parents.

"But she does want your approval and your blessings, Mother," Emily assured her. "You know she does."

"She has an odd way of showing it, then. Very odd, if you ask me." Her mother met Emily's gaze with a hard, determined stare, then turned back to her book again. "If you're going, Emily, just go. You've badgered me enough for one evening."

Emily felt so frustrated, she could hardly speak. Only Lillian Warwick could be so completely impossible and yet manage to cast herself as the injured party.

"All right, good night, then," Emily said, keeping her voice level. She put the jewelry case in her purse and slipped the strap over her shoulder. "If you need me, call the cell phone number. I'll have it in my purse."

"How up-to-date of you," her mother remarked in a dry tone. She did not say good night.

EMILY DROVE DOWN PROVIDENCE STREET, THEN THROUGH THE BACK streets of the village until she emerged on the Beach Road. As she headed toward Sam Morgan's house, her mother's harsh vow echoed in her thoughts. Would she really ignore Jessica's wedding? That would be extreme, even for Lillian; and it would hurt Jessica terribly. Although Jessica had never said it outright, Emily knew her sister was counting on her to help wear down Lillian's objections—at the very least, to persuade their mother to attend the ceremony.

I didn't do so well tonight, did I? I'll have to have more patience the next time. Jessica and Sam haven't even set the date yet. Mother will come around in time, I hope. . . .

Emily took a quick, sharp turn onto the narrow dirt road that led to Sam's house—that "rundown shack in the woods" her mother had once called it. It was actually a lovely old house on a beautiful piece of land, near a pond. It was abandoned when Sam bought it from the bank at auction a few years ago. Most people would have knocked it down and built something new on the property. But Sam saw its potential and had the know-how and skill to restore it.

Now she felt her spirits lift at the sight of the charming old house. Every window was glowing with light, the large downstairs rooms filled with movement and life. The doors were open to the cool autumn night, and the sounds of happy voices, laughter, and music floated out to embrace her like a warm, familiar hug.

Emily stepped inside and found that the rooms to either side of the small entrance were crowded with guests, most of them familiar faces. Carolyn Lewis, the Reverend Ben's wife, was standing nearby, talking with Grace Hegman, owner of the Bramble Shop, an antique store in town.

Emily was about to join them when she spotted her sister across the room, talking with the Reverend Ben. Jessica's fiancé, Sam, stood close by, his arm loosely draped around Jessica's shoulders. When Jessica spoke, Sam turned and glanced down at her, his dark eyes shining, as if Jessica was the most precious and amazing treasure in the world. There was clearly so much love between them, it made Emily's heart ache.

Her sister looked beautiful tonight in a sapphire blue satin top and loose black pants. Her long curly hair hung loose past her shoulders, one side pushed back by a glittering clip. Although Jessica was fairly tall, she looked almost petite standing beside Sam, whose dark good looks seemed a perfect contrast to Jessica's reddish-brown hair and fair complexion. They looked so happy, so right together. How could anyone object to that match? Emily wondered.

Jessica suddenly turned and caught sight of Emily. She smiled, her blue eyes wide with relief, and quickly moved through the crowd toward her.

"Sorry I'm so late. I got hung up at Mother's," Emily explained as she greeted Jessica with a hug.

"I thought it was something like that. Is she all right?" Jessica asked, taking Emily's coat.

"Just a headache. I brought her some pills. She seemed fine when I left."

"Oh . . . well, that's good." Jessica met Emily's gaze, then looked away. Emily knew Jessica had hoped that their mother would change her mind at the last minute and come to the party.

Emily handed her the two gift boxes she was carrying. "Some presents. This one is for you and Sam, for your engagement, and this is for your new house."

Jessica's smile brightened again as she took both boxes in her arms. "Emily, you didn't have to get us anything."

"Of course I did, silly. I bought both at the Bramble, so you can exchange them if they aren't right."

"I'm sure they'll be perfect," Jessica said. "Let me put these down, and I'll get you something to drink."

"Oh, I can help myself. You must have things to do. I'll find you later," Emily promised.

"The drinks and hors d'oeuvres are over there." Jessica nodded toward a long table against the windows. She turned and headed in the opposite direction. "If you see Sam around, tell him he needs to come help."

"I'll tell him," Emily answered, thinking with amusement that Jessica already sounded very married.

"There you are, Em. I knew you'd make it sooner or later." Emily turned to see her good friend, Betty Bowman. "Let me guess," Betty said. "Your mother called with a last-minute emergency?"

"Of course. What else?" Emily replied with a grin. "Lillian is nothing if not reliable."

"At least you got here. I think Jessica was starting to worry," Betty confided. She smiled at Emily with an appraising glance. "That color looks great on you. New dress?"

"Yes, it is. Thanks."

The plum-colored wrap dress wasn't Emily's usual style, but the saleswoman had pressed her to try it. The simple lines suited her slim figure, and the rich color brought out her blue eyes and short, reddish-brown hair.

"I found a great sale up in Newburyport," Emily told her. "At that boutique at the end of Lowell Street."

"They've got great stuff," Betty agreed. "And you probably need things for the campaign now, with all the appearances and socializing, I mean. How's it going so far?"

"It's a bit early to tell. As well as can be expected, I guess."

"I know you'll win it, Emily, but I'm thinking of joining your reelection committee. I'd like to help if I can."

Emily was touched by the offer. "Thanks, Betty. Are you sure you can spare the time?"

"I always manage. Besides, you know how I feel about Charlie Bates," she added quietly. "So I consider it a good investment of time."

Every inch a businesswoman, that was Betty, Emily realized. Time was a valuable commodity to be invested carefully for a good return.

"We'll be lucky to have you. Warren Oakes is the chairperson this year. I'll let him know you're joining up."

"Have him call me at the office, and I'll get up to speed. Oh . . . there's Dan." Betty's gaze suddenly shifted across the room and settled on Dan Forbes. "I need to speak with him about something. I'll catch you later, Em."

As Betty crossed the room, Emily noticed that her friend looked terrific in a slim-fitting red wool suit and black heels, her blond hair barely brushing her shoulders in a smart blunt cut. Betty was a hometown girl, who had left New England for many years before recently returning with her teenage son. But she'd never lost the aura of the most popular girl in high school—head cheerleader, even class president their senior year.

Was Betty dating Dan? Emily wondered. Betty hadn't mentioned it, but as she watched them now, talking intently, she wondered. Tall, with dark blond hair gone partly gray, Dan was attractive, Emily had to admit. Jogging and sailing kept him lean and fit. His work as owner and editor in chief of the *Messenger*, the town's local newspaper, kept his wit sharp, his conversation lively and challenging. Emily could see why Betty would like him, why most single women her age would, herself included.

But I'm not included, Emily chided herself. If there was one thing she was sure of, it was that relationships just didn't work out for her. Long ago she'd given up even trying. She had too much baggage, too much unfinished business, too many regrets that quickly smothered the spark of anything new.

Deliberately turning away from Betty and Dan, Emily went over to the table of appetizers and began making a careful selection.

"No stuffed mushrooms, dear?" Sophie Potter asked, appearing at Emily's side. "I made them myself."

"In that case, I'll take two." Emily added the mushrooms to her plate, then smiled at Sophie as she took a bite. "Delicious, as usual."

"Thank you, dear. I added a little something different this time. Not that I can tell you what, mind you," she warned.

"Of course not. I wouldn't dream of asking," Emily replied around a mouthful.

Sophie Potter was the finest cook for miles around, certainly in the village of Cape Light. Notoriously secretive about her recipes, she claimed she was writing a cookbook, though Emily had heard Sophie say that ever since she was a little girl. Emily had a soft spot for Sophie. She and her husband, Gus, had gone out of their way to show kindness and sympathy to the Warwicks during their trouble, Emily recalled, unlike many others in town who seemed almost pleased to see her father disgraced and their prominent family brought down. While her mother had never really acknowledged Sophie's generous spirit, Emily considered her a dear old friend.

"I'm glad your sister finally came to her senses and decided to marry Sam Morgan," Sophie confided. "If it's meant to be, it's meant to be. You can't fight love, no matter how you try. Like Gus and me," she added, nodding sagely.

"Where is Gus?" Emily asked, gazing around.

"Oh, didn't you hear? Gus is sick. Doctor says it's bronchitis now." Sophie shook her head.

"That's too bad. I'm so sorry. How is he feeling?"

"Not his best. But it's his spirits being low as much as anything. He feels his age finally catching up, I guess." Sophie sighed, her mouth set in a thin, tight line. "I'm just praying to get through the picking season and then the winter. When the spring comes, we'll have to see what we're going to do, I guess."

Emily knew she meant that they might give up the orchard. It was such a sad prospect, it was hard to say outright. For Emily it was impossible to imagine the village without Potter Orchard. But it was doubtful that the Potters would find a buyer for the place who would keep it unchanged. Emily knew that Betty often got calls from developers who had their eye on the land.

"Well, a lot can happen between now and spring," Emily said encouragingly.

"Quite so, dear," Sophie agreed, her expression a bit brighter. "And none of us knows what the good Lord has in store for us, do we?"

"That's the one thing that seems certain," Emily agreed wryly. She could never have imagined the course her own life had taken, so different from her dreams and plans.

Just then Jessica came toward them, carrying a platter of poached salmon. "I guess this can fit here," she said to Sam's sister, Molly Willoughby, who followed close behind carrying a platter of ham.

"I'll put the ham here, then," Molly said.

"I'll put the turkey on the end," Joe Morgan, Sam's father, added as he brushed by with another huge platter.

His wife, Marie, a small dark-haired woman with Sam's dark eyes, marched past with a large bowl of green salad and smiled a greeting at Emily.

"Can I help?" Emily asked.

"I think we've got it covered," Jessica replied. She looked back at the table and seemed to be checking off a list in her mind. "Roasted potatoes . . . I must have left them in the oven."

"Don't worry, I'll get them," Molly offered, turning back toward the kitchen with a rueful shake of her head. "Crisp-but-not-forgotten potatoes, I guess we'll call them," Emily heard her mutter under her breath.

Emily noticed Marie step up to her husband and pat his shoulder as he hovered over the platters. A professional chef, Joe couldn't resist arranging each tray just so. "Come on, Joe," Marie said. "Everything looks beautiful. Let the people have their dinner."

"All right. I give up." Joe turned to his wife and future daughter-in-law, his hands lifted in surrender. "Let them at it."

"Everything does look great," Jessica praised. "Thank you both so much," she added, turning to Joe and then Marie. "I could never have done this alone."

It was true, too, Emily knew. It was nice to see that Sam's family had gotten so involved. Whatever reservations they might have had about the match—and Emily knew even Sam's warmhearted parents had harbored a few—the Morgans seemed to accept Jessica as part of the family simply because Sam loved her so much.

How different they were from her mother, Emily reflected unhappily.

"Everything looks perfect, Jessica," Emily assured her. "The food, the flowers, the candles all around. Too bad—" Too bad Mother didn't come, she was about to say. Then caught herself. She didn't want to bring down Jessica's buoyant mood.

"Too bad . . . what?" Jessica stared at her, questioning.

"Too bad I couldn't get here sooner, to help you. Why don't you show me the house?" Emily said, wanting to distract her. "I haven't been here for weeks, and you two have obviously done a lot of work since then."

"Sure, let's go upstairs first," Jessica said, leading the way through her guests.

Emily followed her up the L-shaped staircase. "This banister is gorgeous," Emily commented, running her hand along the smooth polished wood.

"Thanks, but it's only halfway done, see?" Jessica pointed out the spot where the finished wood ended. "There are still so many bigger things to work on, I get distracted."

"It may take years before you're really finished renovating this house," Emily remarked as they reached the top of the staircase.

"Please. Don't remind me," Jessica said with a laugh. "Sometimes I worry that Sam and I will be married, and we'll still be living in our own apartments because this place will still be a complete mess."

Emily met her sister's eye and smiled. She knew how organized and particular her sister could be, her efficient personality well suited to working in a bank. Moving into this work-in-progress was a stretch for her. *But that's part of getting married,* Emily reflected, *being willing to stretch your boundaries for the sake of the one you love.*

"Sounds like I should have gotten you a framed copy of *The Serenity Prayer*," Emily teased as she followed Jessica to the center hall at the top of the stairs.

"Believe me, I already know it by heart." Jessica opened a nearby door and turned on the light, a bare bulb that hung by some wires from the ceiling.

"We haven't done much with this spare room. Just built a big closet on that wall. It could be a guest room, we thought . . . or a nursery," she added, glancing quickly at her sister.

The image of her own child rose in Emily's mind, the baby she'd been forced to give up for adoption more than twenty years ago. The memory brought a stab of pain, and she forced it away.

"Our bedroom is just about done," Jessica said, leading the way toward a larger room at the front of the house. "All we have to do to it is paint—if we can ever agree on the color."

"This is great." Emily gazed around, admiring the large room. The woodwork and floors were beautifully refinished, and a set of large French doors in the center of one wall lent an elegant, graceful touch.

"Sam finally fixed the balcony," Jessica added, opening the doors and stepping outside. "Here, take a look."

Emily gazed out at the surrounding woods, then up at the starry sky, and took a deep breath. The September night air was pleasantly cool and smelled like fallen leaves and wood smoke. "Oh, this is fantastic. I bet you'll love sitting out here, just looking at the stars."

"We already do," Jessica confided with a small smile.

Emily could just imagine it. She felt happy for her sister. Truly happy. But she felt a pang of sadness for herself as well.

She was alone and would always be, it seemed. Taking care of her mother, carrying on in her job, going to church—those duties filled her life. There was no husband or children in her future. *The role of adoring aunt is the best I can hope for now,* Emily told herself as she followed Jessica back inside.

"What about those other rooms across the hall?" Emily asked, shrugging off her dark thoughts.

"Oh, there's not much to see yet. I'm going to turn one into an office for myself, I think. But that's last on our list right now. We just want to get the main rooms ready in time. Oh, for goodness' sake. I never told you." Jessica pressed her hand to her cheek, her eyes wide. "We finally settled on our date. It's November nineteenth," she announced excitedly. "We found a really nice inn in Southport. It's right on the water, and even Sam's father approves of the food."

"But that's just ten weeks away," Emily said, a little startled.

"I know. That's the only date they had free for the next six months, so we grabbed it. Luckily Reverend Ben had the date open, too. Maybe you can go over there with me next week and take a look, help me figure things out? They have so many questions. . . . I was pretty overwhelmed," Jessica confessed. "And Sam doesn't have much interest in the small details."

"Of course I can go. I'd love to help plan the party," Emily gave Jessica's hand a squeeze.

Jessica had already asked her to be the maid of honor, and while Emily wanted to do anything she could to help her sister, they both knew that planning the reception was something Jessica should be doing with their mother.

"We don't have much time to pick out bridesmaid dresses, either," Jessica added. "But I think I found one on the Net."

Internet bridesmaid dresses? It sounded dreadful, but Emily wanted to be supportive. "You have great taste," she assured Jessica. "I'm sure you'll find something nice."

"There's just so much to do. And the house, too," Jessica said. "Sometimes I don't know how I'll ever get it all done."

"Oh, you will," Emily assured her. "One way or another." Jessica sounded worried, but happily so. These were good problems. The kind you want.

CHAPTER TWO

B ACK DOWNSTAIRS JESSICA CHECKED IN ON THE
kitchen while Emily wandered over to the buffet
table set against a large bay window. She picked up a dish and
silverware and got in line, then realized Dr. Ezra Elliot was
standing in front of her.

"Hello, Ezra," Emily greeted. "I didn't know you were
here tonight."

"I don't usually go to parties. But I didn't want to disappoint your sister."

As usual, Dr. Elliot looked dapper, in a gray wool suit and
vest, a pale blue button-down shirt, and a red-and-blue striped
bow tie. He had been their family doctor for as long as Emily
could remember and more than that, a trusted family friend. So
much like family, in fact, that Jessica had asked him to give her

away at the wedding. He was among the few in town still close to their mother and practically her only company since her stroke had kept her mostly housebound. They enjoyed their verbal sparring matches, Emily knew. Furthermore, Ezra seemed to be the only one who could challenge her mother and win.

"At my age it's good to get out and be in company," he added, glancing around. "Even if it feels like an effort lately."

Something in his tone prickled Emily's intuition. "How is your retirement going? Enjoying it?"

He looked over the platters of food, then lifted a few slices of turkey to his plate. "Frankly, it's starting to wear on my nerves. All this free time with no appointments and nobody calling me in the middle of the night. I don't even have to worry about the cottages anymore, since I sold the property to McAllister."

"How is Luke McAllister doing? I understand he's living out there now," Emily said.

"I drop by from time to time, to say hello. It's hard to say what he's up to." Ezra shrugged. "He doesn't seem to have any plans, far as I can see."

Suddenly Betty appeared beside them. "Sorry to butt in, but I just heard you mention Luke McAllister. Somebody told me they heard he was planning to renovate. Maybe build more cottages or even a motel unit?"

"Really? Where did you hear that?" Emily asked her friend.

Betty shrugged. "Just around, you know," she replied, unwilling to say. "Is it true?"

"He never mentioned anything like that to me," Dr. Elliot said. "Though I can't say I'm exactly close friends with him."

"I don't think anyone in town knows him very well," Betty noted. "Which seems to be the way he likes it."

"He's an odd one, all right." Harry Reilly stood behind Betty and now leaned over to join the conversation. "I heard he was going to sell the land again, just bought it to turn over." Harry owned a boatyard near the harbor and knew nearly everyone in town. He was a taciturn man, usually not the gossiping type. "This McAllister fellow is sort of shady, if you ask me. You know what they say about him—kicked off the police force in Boston. Who knows what he's been involved in or what he's up to."

"I heard he was shot in the line of duty and then quit due to injuries," Emily offered. Tucker Tulley, a local police officer, had been spreading that version of Luke's past, relaying information he had from friends on the Boston police force.

"That's what I heard, too," Betty agreed. "And that he had some sort of drinking problem. But when I dealt with him during the sale, he told me he wanted the land for . . . well, sentimental reasons. He said he spent the summers here as a boy, at Dr. Elliot's cottages."

"Said the same to me," Dr. Elliot added. "Of course, it could be a lot of reasons. He could have an attachment to the property and still turn it into some tacky roadside attraction."

"Or sell it to a developer," Harry added gruffly.

"I think I'll just call him and ask if he plans to sell again," Betty said, picking up a dish and silverware. "That's one way to find out."

"Yes, it is," Emily replied. She hoped Luke didn't plan on selling the land. Not until the election was over, at any rate. When Dr. Elliot had first put the land up for sale a few months ago, Charlie Bates had worked the entire town into a lather about the situation, filling people's heads with exaggerated half-truths and paranoid fears.

If Luke put the land up for sale again, Charlie would have his hot issue for the campaign.

Emily and Dr. Elliot found empty seats at a table nearby and sat down together. "By the way, where is your mother tonight?" Dr. Elliot asked. "I expected to see her here, brightening my evening with her sparkling wit."

"She wasn't feeling well," Emily told him.

"Oh? Nothing serious, I hope," he said with concern.

"Just a headache. I'm not even sure if she really had one, to tell you the truth."

"Lillian still doesn't approve of Sam?"

Emily nodded.

"Your mother is an extraordinary woman," Dr. Elliot went on. "But she can also be the most stubborn, narrow-minded creature on earth."

"Yes, I know," Emily said, biting back a smile.

"I'll stop by to see her this week, badger her a bit about missing a fine party. It will give me something to do," he noted with a sly grin.

"She'll like that." Emily smiled at him. "By the way, she has a meeting of the Historical Society this week. Maybe you should join her."

"Maybe I could shoot myself in the head first, dear," Dr. Elliot replied. "I can just imagine it. A hearty portion of gossip served up with some little cucumber sandwiches and tea. Can you honestly see me sitting with that bunch?"

Emily didn't mean to laugh, but she couldn't help it. "I suppose not," she admitted.

Ezra put his fork down and picked up his dish. "I think I'll get more of that baked ham. Not high on the health-food list but very tasty. That's important, too, you know."

"Absolutely," Emily agreed.

After politely asking if he could get her anything, Ezra left her alone at the table. But she soon looked up to find Dan Forbes smiling down at her, a plate of food in hand.

"Hello, Emily. May I join you?"

"Of course, have a seat." Emily quickly dabbed her mouth with her napkin, then realized she'd wiped off all her lipstick. *That would never happen to Betty,* she thought wryly. *Betty's lipstick seems to stay on perfectly for days on end.*

"So, how's the campaign going?" Dan asked.

"I'm sorry, but is there a sign on my back that says, 'Ask her about the campaign'?" Emily gave him a weary grin. "Sorry to sound touchy, but I was really hoping for a night off."

"Now that you mention it, I need a night off, too," Dan said agreeably. "Besides, I don't think there's too much to say either way so far."

"Pretty dull for you, I guess. No big headlines for the paper."

"True. But I'm sure Charlie will come up with something to make things more interesting for you, Mayor. Maybe at the debate."

She couldn't help smiling back. "You'd like that, wouldn't you? Meanwhile, I'm hoping for the most boring reelection race in town history."

"Sorry, that's just not going to happen. You're a fighter, Emily. You don't like folks to see you that way, but it's true," he insisted, his eyes still sparkling at her.

His casual comment sounded a lot like a compliment, and it made her feel surprisingly good.

"So, what have you been up to?" she asked. "Besides the newspaper, I mean."

"The paper is so short-staffed lately, I haven't had much time for anything else. But I'm trying to sell the house I had with Claire and the kids. I don't need all that space just for myself." He shrugged.

Dan had been divorced a little more than three years now, Emily recalled. His wife, Claire, left Cape Light for a teaching position at a university in the Midwest. Emily wasn't sure why the marriage had failed, but they seemed to have parted on amicable terms. Their two children, Lindsay and Wyatt, were both in their mid-twenties and living their own lives.

"Where will you move? Have you found a place yet?" Emily asked.

"Not quite," he admitted. "I hope to find something smaller here in town. Betty is looking around for me."

So maybe Dan and Betty were just talking over real estate tonight, Emily thought. Of course, that didn't mean they weren't interested in each other. . . .

"—She thinks she's found a couple who want my place, so I'd better find somewhere to go. Or I might end up moving everything into the office."

"You're there all night pretty often, from what I can see. It shouldn't be too big a change for you," Emily teased him.

"True enough." He smiled slightly. "I guess I could live on my boat. That would make me less of a workaholic, sort of a carefree beachcomber type. Women like that, right?"

Dan spent too much time at work. But so did she. Though his tone was light, she heard an edge of defensiveness and wondered if his dedication to the paper had been an issue in his marriage.

"Well, I've never been on your boat. But I somehow suspect you have a laptop or a typewriter stashed away in the cabin, just in case."

"I won't confirm or deny that." His serious tone was contradicted by the playful light in his eyes. "You ought to come sailing with me sometime, Emily, and see for yourself."

Emily was surprised by the invitation, but she didn't take it seriously. Dan was probably just making polite conversation.

"Sure, I'd love to go sometime," she answered. "It's hard to say when, though, with the election coming up."

"And all your other responsibilities," he added quietly.

He met her gaze with a knowing look, and Emily wondered what he was thinking. That she spent too much time caring for her mother? That probably was not something he found appealing. Dan seemed to be interested in cutting loose of responsibilities now, not getting involved with more of them.

Why am I even thinking this way? she asked herself.

Before she could come up with an answer, Joe Morgan and Molly Willoughby captured everyone's attention as they carried a large, elaborately decorated cake to the buffet table.

"Wow, what a cake," Dan commented. "Where did they get that?"

"Molly Willoughby made it," Emily replied.

"That's right, Molly's a professional now, isn't she? I like those muffins she makes for the Beanery," Dan said.

Her muffins were wonderful, but the cake was a masterpiece, Emily thought, admiring the pale yellow icing and the real miniature orchids that swirled around its sides. Across the top, written in chocolate icing, was the message *Love and happiness on your engagement and always.*

"Your sister and Sam deserve every happiness," Dan said. "I hope their life together is as sweet and beautiful as that cake."

Emily looked up at him in surprise. It was an unusual way to put it, but sincere and original. "I'll tell Jessica you said that."

As the guests gathered around the cake, Sam put an arm around Jessica. "We have a little announcement to make, everyone. We've finally set a wedding date," he said happily. "We'll be married on November nineteenth at Bible Community Church. Twelve o'clock sharp. And you're all invited to come."

"With a party after, of course," Jessica chimed in. "And I'm sending out real invitations," she added hastily.

"Real invitations or not, we'll all be there. You can count on it," Harry Reilly called out, making everyone laugh.

Digger Hegman came up beside Jessica and Sam and patted the younger man on the back. "Aren't we supposed to sing or something now, before you cut into that?" he asked them.

Jessica glanced at Sam with a confused expression. Then Digger started singing in his low seaman's baritone, "Happy engagement to you. Happy engagement to you. . . ." Before long all the guests joined in.

Digger stepped back, looking very pleased, Emily noticed. A retired fisherman and clammer, Digger was easily one of the town's most eccentric citizens. Still, he and Sam were good friends, despite their age difference—and Digger's oddities. That was something else she liked about her future brother-in-law, the way he accepted people and looked beyond appearances to the spirit within.

After the singing and applause finally died down, Sam said, "Thanks, everyone. We're happy to have you all with us tonight."

"Now for some of this delicious cake." Jessica cut a slice and handed it to the nearest guest, Digger. "Sam's sister Molly made it. Isn't it gorgeous?"

"Absolutely. Looks almost too pretty to eat," Digger said.

"But I'm sure that won't stop you. You shouldn't be eating that, Dad," Grace Hegman said quietly, coming up behind Digger.

"Oh, come on, Grace. It's a party. What's the point of living if you can't kick up your heels a little?"

Grace merely glanced at him and shook her head. Harry came up to the table. He was holding a large flat envelope in his hand, Emily noticed.

"Sam, Jessica, I thought I'd give this to you now, since you're both finally in one place at the same time."

Sam laughed. "What's this, Harry? One of those free calendars with the tide schedule from the boatyard? I've already got one down in my shop."

"You're marrying a real wise guy," Harry said to Jessica. "I hope you realize that."

"Yes, I know." Jessica grinned at Sam.

Then Emily watched Sam pull a photo out of the envelope, his eyes widening in astonishment. "It's the sailboat." He stared up at Harry. "You dog. You said it was sold."

"I didn't say sold," Harry corrected him. "I said it was no longer available. As soon as I heard you two were getting married, I put it aside as a present."

"Oh, Harry . . . you shouldn't have." Jessica leaned over and gave Harry a hug. "Thank you, so much."

"Come on, now. It was nothing." Harry ran his hand across his bristly gray crew cut and looked down at the floor.

"Thanks, Harry." Sam leaned over and shook Harry's hand hard, then slapped him on the shoulder. He glanced at the photo again. "It's a beautiful little boat. What should we name it, Jess?"

She gazed at the photograph for a moment, then pulled his head down to whisper in his ear.

"Perfect," he replied, smiling.

"Well?" Harry asked. "Now you've got us all in suspense."

"We're going to call it *Hometown Girl*," Sam answered.

Emily caught her sister's eye and nearly laughed out loud. "That *is* perfect," she said.

Emily recalled how Sam had surprised Jessica with the boat as a gift for her birthday last summer—and how Jessica wouldn't accept it. She still had plans to move back to Boston and wasn't ready to make such a big commitment to him. Sam got so angry, he jumped in the boat and took off and wouldn't speak to her for weeks. It seemed as though the relationship was over. Now it was good to see them laughing about it, Emily thought.

After all of Jessica's planning and determination to leave her hometown, she'd ended up staying here, after all—and looking perfectly content with the decision. It was funny how life worked out sometimes, no matter how you tried to plan or scheme.

After the cake and coffee were served, guests began to say their good nights, and the crowd thinned out. Emily stayed on to help clean up. She found a tray in the kitchen and began collecting empty cups and glasses.

From the front parlor she saw Jessica, Sam, and Reverend Ben talking quietly together in the foyer. Her sister looked distressed, Emily noticed. Moments later the Reverend caught Emily's gaze and beckoned her over.

"I was just talking to Reverend Ben about Mother," Jessica explained. "He's offered to speak to her."

Emily had been thinking of suggesting such a visit herself, and was glad he'd offered. "Mother thinks very highly of you, Reverend. I think she'd take your words to heart."

"Well, thanks for the compliment, Emily. But we all know how strong willed your mother is. No one is going to change her mind overnight. I'll speak to her and hope to plant a seed. Meanwhile, I think we all need to have patience. I know it's hard, Jessica. I know your feelings are hurt."

She nodded, looking on the verge of tears. Emily's heart went out to her.

"But there's plenty of time for her to see reason and change her mind," the Reverend went on. "A few prayers might help to steer her in the right direction."

"We've already got that part covered," Sam assured him. He squeezed Jessica's shoulder and smiled at her.

Reverend Ben nodded. His blue eyes sparkled behind his round wire-rim glasses. "Sounds as if we're doing all we can. Here comes Carolyn. I'll say good night, then. Thanks again for a lovely evening."

He shook Sam's hand and kissed Jessica on the cheek.

Emily resumed her cleanup work as the Reverend and Carolyn left. Even though the problem Jessica faced with their mother was distressing, Emily was glad to see how much her sister's faith had grown in the past few months. Before she met Sam, Jessica hardly ever went to church. Now she had both Sam and her faith to turn to. That, at least, was some comfort.

EMILY OPENED HER FRONT DOOR AND FUMBLED FOR THE LIGHT. HER TWO cats bounded out of the darkness and wound themselves around her ankles, purring.

"For goodness' sake, just let me in the door," Emily pleaded, laughing.

She had only had the cats a few weeks and wasn't quite used to the nightly feline attack. Still, she found it nice to be greeted by something warm and alive, instead of coming home to an empty house.

The cats followed her to the kitchen, where she shook some food into their bowls, and they settled down to eat. She checked her phone messages and found only one.

"I'm feeling a bit better, Emily, and I'd like to go to church tomorrow," Lillian said crisply. "I will expect you at the usual time. I'm going to sleep now, so don't call back and wake me up."

A quick recovery, just as I expected, Emily thought as she set her purse on the dresser. Remembering the jewelry case inside, she opened the purse and took out the velvet box. She had thought of giving the pearls to Jessica to return to the bank, despite her mother's explicit directions not to. Now she was glad she had forgotten all about them.

It was just as well if Jessica didn't think about the pearls right now, Emily decided. She would bring them to the bank sometime this week and put them in the safe-deposit box.

Leaving the jewelry case on her dresser, she started to get ready for bed. She returned from the bathroom to find the two cats already curled up on her comforter.

"At least you'll keep my feet warm when the cold weather sets in," Emily said to them. One cat narrowly opened her eyes and gave Emily a feline blink of contentment.

She was about to get into bed herself when the jewelry case caught her eye. Should she hide it, she wondered, the way her mother did? She felt downright silly even thinking about it. Cape Light was as safe as any place could be these days; she often went out without locking her doors.

But giving in to a cautious impulse, Emily opened the bottom drawer of her dresser, lifted the soft pile of old sweaters and scarves, and slipped the velvet case underneath. Pushing it toward the back of the drawer, she felt something else back there. Something hard and hidden away—a book or album.

Emily pulled it out and felt a wave of sadness wash over her. It was the journal she kept in her early twenties, when she was married to Tim and living in Maryland. She had written in it every day during their almost two years together. And later, after his death, when their baby was born. And when her mother had persuaded her to give up the child for adoption.

She didn't need to open it. She knew what was inside—the heartache, the loss, the empty place that could never be filled, the missing pieces that could never be replaced. They hadn't changed. All of it was etched inside her heart and soul. All of it she carried inside her every day.

Lillian believed that when Emily returned to Cape Light, she had resumed her "real" life, but in Emily's mind her real life had ended long ago, down in Maryland. Despite her outward appearance of success, all these long years in Cape Light had always held a peculiarly unreal feeling for her.

She studied the book in her hand, feeling its hard edges and smooth black cover. It was all in there. She wrote only a few entries after returning to New England, then put even her ambitions to be a professional writer aside forever. It was the first of many choices she made to deprive herself, knowing that she didn't deserve to be truly happy.

Emily tried not to think about her life with Tim if she could help it. But not a day passed when she didn't think about their daughter and wonder what had happened to her, where she might be right now. Raised by a loving family, she prayed, and old enough by now to have graduated college.

She had made many efforts to find her, the last time venturing down to Maryland to the agency that had handled the adoption. The adoption was sealed tight; her mother had made sure of that. All Emily could do was sign papers giving her permission to be contacted if her daughter ever tried to find her.

Putting the journal back in the drawer, she felt angry again with her mother for the way it had all turned out, the way Lillian had pressured her, manipulated her into the decision. Reverend Ben said she and Jessica should forgive their mother for the things she did that were hurtful to them.

But it was hard. Very hard, Emily thought. She tried, but she didn't think she ever really could.

She prayed for help, to find forgiveness in her heart and to someday find her daughter. It was the only thing she really truly wanted out of life.

But first she needed to get through the election and then Jessica's wedding. After that she would try again.

This time she wouldn't give up so easily, Emily vowed as she flicked off the light.

As her eyes closed she recalled one of her favorite Bible verses: "Ask and it shall be given you; seek, and ye shall find; knock, and it shall be opened unto you."

When the time is right, please help me find her, Lord, Emily prayed as she drifted off to sleep.

Chapter Three

⁓

*T*HE CLAM BOX BUSTLED WITH THE USUAL MONDAY morning crowd, customers in a rush to gulp down hot coffee, eat breakfast, and settle the check before the diner's two waitresses, Lucy and Sara, could even get out a "Good morning. What can I get you today?"

In his usual spot at the counter right behind the grill, Officer Tucker Tulley sat serenely in the middle of the rush. He took a bite of a doughnut and paged through the *Messenger* while carrying on a fractured conversation with Charlie Bates, who was pouring sizzling rounds of batter and eggs onto the grill.

"Table seven, two poached on toast—not fried and no home fries." Lucy Bates slammed down a plate at the order window.

"Here's your poached," Charlie replied in a belligerent tone. "You ran off with the order for table nine."

"Maybe because you can't tell the difference between a seven and a nine, and you put it under the wrong ticket. And now they're ice cold besides," Lucy said, looking over the eggs. A frown marred her pretty face as she pushed the plate back on the ledge again. "You better do this over."

It sounded to Tucker as if Charlie almost growled at her. Then he swiped the dish off the ledge and turned his back.

"Wow, what was that about?" Tucker said as Lucy grabbed a coffeepot and began refilling mugs.

"Didn't you hear? My wife's a college girl now. She's got opinions about everything. And she's always right, too, so don't bother arguing." Charlie flipped a row of pancakes with a deft turn of his wrist. "And she doesn't have a spare minute to help around here or help me with the campaign," he added gruffly.

"Well, she's got a lot going on right now," Tucker glanced over at Lucy, who was taking an order on the far side of the diner. "She probably needs some time to get used to school. That's pretty brave of her, going back. I don't think I could do it."

"More like insane, if you ask me. What does she need to go to college for? A woman gets some crazy idea, and a man always ends up paying for it," he insisted.

"That is not true." Lucy stepped up behind Tucker. "Not one tiny bit. I stayed up until two in the morning the other night, stuffing envelopes, hand addressing everything. You tell me, Tucker, does that sound like someone who isn't helping?"

Tucker stared at her, feeling a bite of doughnut lodged in his throat. He hated to be stuck in the middle of an argument between a husband and wife. Especially when the husband was his best friend.

"See what I mean?" Charlie shook his head as Lucy walked off with another order. "I don't know what got into that woman. One day she's as sweet as pie. The next she's snarling like a wet cat."

Tucker glanced at Lucy over his shoulder, making sure she was out of earshot. "Women get . . . moody, Charlie." He slowly stirred his coffee. "Fran got into a snit like this about a year or so ago. I could barely look at her sideways without an argument. She started redecorating the house, nearly tore the place apart. Then she got a job working for Betty Bowman. That calmed her down real fast. I think Lucy just needs a little time."

"I don't have time, Tucker," Charlie said. "I've only got eight weeks left until the election. I need an issue. I need to drum up votes. I can't wait until my wife is finished with her book reports or whatever the heck she's doing every night, when she should be taking over around here."

"How's it going with that storm cleanup issue? Getting much interest there?"

"Nothing really," Charlie admitted. "Everybody agrees the storm drains need an upgrade and the firehouse needs a substation. But let's face it. It's tough to get people to blame Emily Warwick for the weather."

Tucker had lived in town his whole life, but had rarely seen a storm like the one that hit Cape Light shortly after Labor Day. Some villagers were still cleaning up and repairing the damage. He had heard a lot of complaints that the mayor's office had not responded quickly enough and that the town was not prepared for such emergencies. But not much had come of it. People seemed to forget the crisis quickly.

"I know what you mean. A storm drain upgrade is not the kind of problem that gets people hot under the collar," Tucker said.

"That's just my point," Charlie agreed. "I need something bigger. Something that can pull in everyone. Something really—galvanizing," he said, drawing out the word.

"Galvanizing." Tucker chewed thoughtfully. "I like the sound of that."

* * *

SARA TURNED DOWN THE NARROW DRIVE THAT LED TO THE CRANBERRY Cottages, noticing the scent of fall in the chilly night air. She wasn't used to that, not in the first week of September. Down in Maryland, where she grew up, they were still enjoying summer temperatures. But fall came quickly in New England and winter would be harsh, too, she'd heard. She wondered if she would stay long enough to find out firsthand.

She parked her car and headed along the footpath toward her cottage. She felt tired from work and half-wished that Lucy wasn't coming over later that night. But she had offered to help Lucy with an English assignment and didn't want to let her down.

Sara heard the sound of wood splitting before she actually saw Luke McAllister. She slowed her steps to watch him work in the fading light.

Despite the chill in the air, he was wearing just a long-sleeved pullover, open at the neck. He was working hard, and the shirt clung to his shoulders and back, outlining well-defined muscles. He swung the ax down with a clean motion, splitting the log in one chop. The pieces fell away, and he stepped back from the block. Sara noticed how he stood slightly off balance and wondered if the exercise hurt his bad leg.

He dropped another log on the block and seemed to size it up, his strong features set in a stern expression. His usual expression, she thought. But right before lifting the ax, he spotted her. His gray eyes flashed with recognition, though he didn't quite smile.

"Hey, Sara. There's some mail for you. I'll bring it over in a minute."

"Okay. Just knock," she called back as she let herself into her cottage. He had caught her watching him, and she felt embarrassed. She dumped her knapsack on the kitchen table and slipped off her denim jacket.

She felt hungry but had decided not to bring home any food from the diner. She was getting tired of the menu there. Unfortunately, the selection in her cupboard wasn't much more appetizing. She pulled a can of chicken noodle soup out, opened it, and poured it into a pot on the stove to heat.

A moment later she heard Luke knock and answered the door.

Luke stood on the steps, his arms filled with wood. "Where do you want this?"

"Out here is fine." She pointed to a woodpile next to her door. "I have enough in the house for now."

Luke stacked the new wood neatly on top of the pile, then pulled an envelope out of his pocket. "Here's your mail," he said. "It was stuck in my box by mistake."

Sara glanced at the handwriting and return address—a letter from her parents.

"Nothing bad I hope?" Luke asked, searching her expression with his cool gray gaze.

"Just a letter from my folks. I think they're starting to wonder when I'm coming back."

Now, why did I tell him that? she wondered. They weren't exactly friends, yet somehow they were more than merely acquaintances. He had a quiet way of getting her to reveal herself, even when she didn't want to.

"Are you thinking of going back to Maryland?"

"No, not at all. Not right now anyway," she added with a shrug. "Don't worry. I'll give you plenty of notice."

"I wasn't even thinking about that." He kept his gaze fixed on her. "I'm going home for a visit myself."

"Do you miss the city?" she asked.

"No, not at all." He shrugged, looking surprised at his admission. "It's my father's birthday. There's going to be a party for him."

Sara sensed the trip was important to him. Important and difficult. She had heard a little about Luke's past, a pretty dark story about why he left Boston and police work. She had also heard that his father and brothers were all cops there and considered whatever had happened a disgrace—though she wasn't quite sure how much of that was gossip and how much was true.

"How long has it been since you've seen them?" she asked carefully.

"A few months, I guess. I haven't been back since I came here in May."

He had arrived in town about the same time she had, she realized. They were both still outsiders in a way. "Have you stayed in touch at all?"

"Just with my mother. She thought my coming up here was a good idea." Luke jammed his hands down in his pockets. "It will be tougher to see my father."

Sara didn't know what to say. He seemed uneasy but still seemed to want to talk. "Because you left the city?" she asked, really meaning "the police force" but afraid to be that blunt.

"You might say that." He leaned back against the porch rail and looked down at her, his gaze narrowed, as if figuring out how much to reveal. "My dad is funny, though. When he sees me, he'll talk a blue streak. About the weather, the news, and what kind of car I'm driving. That kind of stuff. But I can still see it in his eyes, like if he ever lets the cork out, he'll explode."

She paused and considered his words. "That's too bad," she said sympathetically. "Maybe going down there will help."

The corner of his mouth lifted in a cynical grin. "I have to go back sooner or later. It seemed as good a time as any."

"How long will you be gone?"

"I'm going in on Wednesday so I can meet up with an old friend of mine. He quit the force, too, a while back. Now he's doing some kind of counseling or social work. It will be good to catch up with him. The party will be on the weekend, so I should be back by Monday. Are you worried about staying out here alone?" he added, sounding concerned.

"No, not at all."

"That's good. I'll leave a phone number, just in case."

"Okay, if you want. I'm sure I'll be fine." She crossed her arms over her chest. She was cold, but he was gazing at her so intently, she couldn't quite find the words to excuse herself and go inside.

"I thought I might go into town later. To see a movie," he said. "There's a good suspense film playing. Have you seen it?"

"Uh . . . no, I haven't." Was he about to ask her out? She sensed her eyes widen in shock and quickly looked away, hoping he didn't notice.

"Would you like to go?" His tone was casual and light, but she could tell the question was difficult for him.

She didn't know what to say. Then she suddenly remembered. "I'm sorry, I can't tonight. Lucy is coming by. I'm going to help her write a paper. She started college, did I tell you?"

"Uh, no, you didn't." She saw a flash of disappointment in his eyes that was quickly masked by an impassive expression. "Good for her."

"Yes, it is good for her," she agreed. Sara suddenly smelled something burning. The soup! "Oh sorry, I've got to run. I have something on the stove." She ran inside, leaving the door partly open. "Good night, Luke," she called out.

"Good night." He closed the door for her, then headed for his cottage.

Sara dashed over to the stove and took the boiling pot off the flame. Saved by the soup, she thought as she poked her wooden spoon in to check the damage. It was stuck a bit on the bottom, but still edible, she decided.

She poured it out into a bowl and brought it over to the kitchen table. She took out a box of crackers and a soup spoon, then sat down to eat. She enjoyed living alone most of the time. She liked to be as messy or as neat as she pleased, and liked all the free time she had to write and read.

But dinner was the loneliest time for her. *Maybe going out with Luke wouldn't have been such a bad thing. He's different from most of the guys I've known. Older for one thing. And he's not the easiest person to get to know, not exactly Mr. Sunny,* she thought, grinning to herself. *But he's interesting and trying hard to work things out for himself. And he's attractive—very attractive.*

Maybe I like him more than I think, Sara realized. *But what's the point?*

I can't get involved with him. It wouldn't be right. I can't even tell him the truth about who I really am and why I'm living here.

Sara heard a car starting up outside, then saw the sweep of headlights through the trees, traveling up the drive toward the Beach Road. Luke on his way into town. She felt suddenly deserted, thinking she could have put Lucy off for tonight and gone with him. *Maybe living here is wearing on me,* she mused. *Maybe I should call my parents and just check in with them.* But that idea didn't appeal much to her, either. She already knew what they would ask her, and she didn't have an answer yet.

She saw her journal on the other end of the table and picked it up. She opened it to a clean page, marked the date on top, then began writing with one hand while she ate the soup with an automatic motion with the other.

My parents sent another letter and I haven't even opened it yet, but I already know what's inside. Their quiet but persistent questions: What are you doing up there? When are you coming home? Why haven't you told your birth mother the truth?

I can't explain why it's taking me so long to tell Emily Warwick who I am. I don't understand it myself.

Maybe I'm afraid that if I don't get to know her secretly, I won't get the chance to know her at all. Or my grandmother and aunt. But I do want to know why Emily gave me up. Then I get afraid to ask her, thinking maybe it's enough just to get to know her this way—as a friend. Maybe telling her that she's my mother would cause so much trouble, it would ruin everything.

I wish I had someone to talk to about this. My parents have been great, but I can't tell them much. They worry too much about me. Lucy has been a real friend. But I can't tell her, either.

Besides, nobody would really understand. . . .

* * *

Barely fifteen minutes into the movie and his hands were clenched on the armrests, his knuckles white. Luke stared at the flickering images on the screen but didn't really see them.

He sat watching another film unreel, the one that had been stuck in his mind for years now. The one he couldn't quite forget.

His mouth grew dry, and he could feel sweat breaking out on his forehead. Still, he could not look away from the dark images, the flashing lights, the sounds of sirens and footsteps running down a wet alley. He smelled the gunpowder, the blood. He heard the heart-wrenching moan of a man mortally wounded, his life spilling out second by second, with no way to stop the flow.

Another barrage of gunshots sounded through the theater, and Luke jumped to his feet and grabbed for the pistol that once sat holstered on his hip. His popcorn and soda spilled around his feet, the icy liquid on his shoes suddenly bringing him back—back from that terrible night on Delaney Street to the movie house in Cape Light. He glanced around, to see if anyone was watching him, then with his head ducked down, he left his seat and walked quickly up the aisle.

The bright lights in the lobby stung his eyes. He pushed open the heavy glass doors to the street. He stood on the sidewalk a moment, breathing in the bracing night air.

Good thing Sara didn't come, he thought. *I would have hated for her to see me like this.*

Her excuse sounded real enough. But she had that look on her face when I started to ask her—like she was scrambling for some way to get out of it.

It's just as well. I don't need that right now, he decided. *Everything in life is timing. And this is the wrong time.*

He rubbed the back of his neck as he walked along the deserted street and flipped up his collar. A damp wind blew up from the harbor and seeped into his jacket. The foghorn sounded, out on the bay, echoing through the village streets. The vintage gaslights on Main Street stood haloed in the foggy air and gave the empty avenue a surreal, dreamlike quality.

Everything was closed. Except for the Clam Box, its blue-and-red neon sign glowing a few doors down. But Sara wasn't working tonight, so what was the point? He knew the Beanery down near the green might be open. That would be a nice change, he thought. His mouth tasted like cotton. But he knew he wasn't really thirsty for coffee.

What I'd really like right now is a beer. A tall cold one. Then another, to wash down the first.

But drinking was something else he'd put behind him, and not without a struggle. Just across the street the yellow lights from a tavern flickered, and Luke paused.

He gave his head a hard shake, then turned and walked in the opposite direction. *Might as well go back home and make my own coffee. This little excursion into town wasn't such a great idea after all.*

Luke returned to the cottages and parked his Toyota 4Runner. As he started walking toward his cottage, he noticed that Sara's lights were still on, but Lucy's car was nowhere in sight. She must have come and gone already. Or was that just an excuse to get out of going to the movies? he wondered.

Then a sound in the shed near his cottage drew his attention, and he froze in place, listening, every nerve suddenly alert.

"Who's there?" he called out sharply while another part of his mind reminded him that out here, the sound was doubtless nothing more than a cat or raccoon, prowling for food.

No one answered at first, then he heard a louder sound, like a pile of tin cans falling down a hill, and then Sara's voice, sounding frustrated and annoyed.

"For Pete's sake, don't you have a light out here?"

He trotted toward the shed, reached in, and flipped a switch. A bare bulb above illuminated the scene: Sara, looking trapped by the pile of empty paint cans around her legs, holding an old blue bicycle at arm's length.

"Here, let me help." Luke rushed forward awkwardly, unmindful of his bad leg. He pulled away some of the cans so that she could get her balance.

"Thank you," she said, brushing back a strand of dark hair that had fallen across her eyes. "If you could move some of those cans aside, I just want to lean this bike against the wall. The kickstand seems to be broken."

"Sure, no problem." Luke pushed the cans to one side of the shed and helped Sara put the bike in place.

"You should have brought a flashlight. You could have hurt yourself," he said.

"I should have left the bike on my porch," she retorted. "But I was afraid it might rain."

Luke glanced at the bike. "I don't think a little rain would make much difference at this point. Where did you get that, a tag sale?"

"Lucy brought it over. I was thinking of taking a bike ride on the weekend and asked her where I could rent one. She remembered this one in her garage and insisted that I take it." Sara brushed her hands on her jeans and looked back at the bike. "I really couldn't say no. I didn't want to hurt her feelings."

The corner of Luke's mouth turned up in a reluctant smile. So Lucy had come. Sara had not made up an excuse. He didn't know why, but hearing that made him feel better.

"That's nice of you and all, but are you sure you want to ride it?" he asked doubtfully. "It looks like it needs work."

"Oh, it will be fine for me," Sara insisted. "I'm not entering the Tour de France or anything."

Luke shook his head and stared at her a moment. "You go out first. I'll get the light. Watch your step," he cautioned.

He watched Sara step carefully through the mess, then shut off the light and followed. He closed the doors to the shed and latched them, then turned to see Sara waiting for him.

"How did it go with Lucy? Did she get her homework done?"

"She already had a draft. I just went over it with her and made some suggestions. Lucy's very bright," Sara added. "Most people don't realize how smart she is."

"I don't think Charlie wants her to realize how smart she is," Luke said dryly.

"Yes, I know. It's hard for her," Sara said seriously.

Luke suddenly felt uneasy talking about the Bateses. What did he know about them anyway? He had no right—even if everyone in town, Lucy and Charlie included, gossiped about him.

"I was just going to make myself some coffee. Want some?" he offered.

At first he thought she would refuse. Was he going to be shot down twice in one night? Then she nodded. "Okay. Thanks."

He nodded back, amused at his turn of luck. He unlocked the door to his cottage and held it open for her. Once inside, he turned on the lights and went into the small kitchen.

Sara took off her jacket and hung it on the back of a chair. "How was the movie?"

He shrugged, spooning coffee into the pot. "I don't know. I didn't stay much past the credits."

"That good, huh? I thought it got rave reviews."

"It didn't do much for me," he said quietly. He turned on the coffeemaker, then turned to look at her. The truth, of course, was just the opposite. But he couldn't tell her that, could he?

He glanced at her again and felt his heartbeat quicken. If he didn't start being more honest, more authentic with people, what was the point of coming up here at all?

He stared back at the coffeemaker, watching the coffee drip into the glass pot. He wasn't sure what was driving him, but for some reason he wanted her to know more about him, who he was. The real story. Maybe just to see if she was scared off, he realized.

"You know that I used to be a cop, right?" he asked her suddenly.

"Uh . . . yes. I do. I think you told me back in the summer one time, didn't you?"

He heard her voice take on a nervous edge as he came out from the kitchen. He had told her a little about his past, but guessed she had heard even more from others.

"I think I did," Luke replied. "Or maybe you just heard it around town." He watched her. She sat on the small couch, her arms crossed, as if she felt cold. When she looked away, he said, "It's all right, Sara. I know people talk about me. Especially at the Clam Box. Lucy, Charlie, and Tucker Tulley."

"They talk about everyone," Sara said with a shrug. "The less they know, the more they have to say."

"Well, I guess they have a lot to say about me, then."

Sara glanced up at him and smiled. "You were a hot topic for a while. Now it's mostly about Charlie's election."

"So, what did you hear?" he persisted. He walked over to the wood-stove and began to build a fire. He crouched down and turned his back to her, picking out sticks of kindling. He didn't have to see her to tell that it was hard for her to answer.

"Let's see . . ." she started off slowly. "I heard that you were a police officer in Boston and that you were in a shoot-out or something. Your partner was killed, and you were shot, too, in your leg. And then you decided not to go back to police work."

He tossed a match to the wood and watched the fire spark to life. When she didn't say more, he turned to her. "That's all?"

"Basically, yes." She shrugged and leaned back on the couch.

He sensed it wasn't everything, but Sara probably felt too awkward repeating the rest. He knew some people thought he'd been dealing drugs, or taking bribes from dealers, and had been ambushed for messing around with the wrong people, his innocent partner caught in the cross-fire. Or that he'd been a drunk and found himself in a shoot-out, inebriated, unable to react. He'd heard it all, the rumors almost worse than the truth.

"I guess the gossips around here aren't half as sharp as I thought." Luke's tone was amused but edgy. He stood up and brushed his hands together.

"I did hear some other things about you," she admitted. "But I didn't take them seriously because I didn't know if they were true or not."

He nodded at her. "That's pretty smart of you. Considering how young you are."

"Excuse me? I'm not *that* young," she corrected him with a short laugh.

"Yes, you are," he countered. "But you act older," he added.

"Thanks a lot," she said.

He could see that his observation annoyed her, but he did think she was young. Maybe too young for him. He was probably ten years older than she was, and in some ways, she seemed very naive, very sheltered. A nice girl from a good home who hadn't seen much of the world beyond a college campus. But in other ways, Sara didn't seem young to him at all.

"I guess the coffee is done. I'll bring it out here," he suggested. He rose from his seat and walked into the kitchen area. "How do you take it?"

"Just black is fine," she called back.

"Like real writers do," he remarked with a slight smile.

"It's a start."

Luke brought the coffee in and handed Sara her cup. Then he sat down in the armchair across from her.

"I'm sorry if I insulted you when I said you were young. I didn't mean it in a bad way."

"That's okay." She glanced at him over her mug. "How old are you, anyway?"

"I'll be thirty-three at the end of November," he said, looking straight at her. She blinked but didn't say anything.

"I thought my vital statistics would have been common knowledge at the Clam Box," he joked.

"They don't get into the hard facts much," she countered.

"Right, the hard facts . . ." He looked down into his mug. "Okay, my version goes something like this. I was on the force about five or six years. I was promoted to detective, doing drug busts mostly." He took a deep breath and put the coffee aside, as if he had suddenly lost his taste for it.

"One night my partner and I answered a call. Sounded routine, a disturbance at an apartment building on Delaney Street. Uniforms in a squad car probably should have gone, but none were available, so we took it. We thought it was an argument between neighbors in the building. But when the apartment door opened, somebody began firing at us from inside. I saw my partner hit and I froze. I couldn't shoot. When I finally got my nerve back, my partner was down. I couldn't get near him, so I took cover and radioed for help. I tried to get back to him, but I've never really been able to remember what happened after that."

He paused for a moment, realizing that his heart was racing.

"What happened next?" she asked quietly.

"The backup found me at the bottom of a stairwell, unconscious. My partner had died at the scene. When they picked up one of the perps later, he testified that I fled when the gunfire started. I think he was willing to say anything he thought would lessen the case against him. But the official take on it was that I had left my partner in the hallway to bleed to death and crawled off to hide from the bad guys. Maybe I did. I can't remember. Posttraumatic stress syndrome, they call it."

"Will you ever know?"

He shrugged and rose restlessly from the chair. "Probably not. I couldn't stay on the force with that hanging over my head. So I quit. I had a long way back from the injury anyway. It took a few operations before I could even get out of a wheelchair."

"That sounds awful," Sara said sympathetically.

"The worst part was that I had too much time to think. I blamed myself for my partner's death. I got a lot of money from the force, because of my injury and early retirement. But that made me feel even worse. I wondered why I had ever been a cop in the first place. I decided then that I had never really even liked it." He bent down and tended the fire again. "Maybe I screwed up on purpose." He shook his head. "I don't know. Who knows?"

Sara was quiet for a moment. Then she said, "How long were you recuperating?"

"Almost two years."

"That's a long time. How did you manage?"

"I had help, my family mostly. It was hard for them, though. Especially my father. He took it the hardest." Luke stood up again and looked at her. "I think it would have been easier for him if I had died doing something real heroic."

Sara leaned back a bit to look at him. "That's a pretty extreme thing to say."

"You've never met my father. He's a pretty extreme guy."

"Didn't you have anyone—any friends, or a girlfriend maybe?"

"My mom was great. And I had a girlfriend. We were engaged. She was great to me, at first. Really sympathetic and just happy I'd survived. But I was pretty horrible. I started drinking, which made everything worse, and she left. I couldn't blame her."

"That's too bad."

"Yes, it was," he agreed. "But she's happy now, I think. She met someone and got married. I heard she's expecting a baby."

Sara picked up her coffee and took a long sip. He could see that this was more than she had expected and probably a lot to take in at one time.

After a while she said, "But you got out of it somehow. You pulled yourself together."

"You mean, I don't seem that awful now?" he asked with a sudden, surprising smile.

"Something like that," she said, smiling back.

"Well, thanks, but I have a long way to go." He didn't mean his reply to sound like a warning to her, but somehow it did. He sat up straight and rubbed his bad knee. "So, how does it compare with the Clam Box version?"

"I hadn't heard half of this," she admitted. "Why did you tell me? You didn't have to."

"I don't know. . . . I just wanted to set the record straight with you, I guess."

It was a reason, but he knew it didn't answer her question. Why did it matter to him what she thought? He didn't really care about the rest of the town. But Sara was different.

"Well, thanks for telling me. But I don't judge people, if that's what you thought. I think everyone gets knocked down, or has some problem they might be trying to work out. Even people who look totally put together," she added. "You just never know about people, what's really going on inside them."

He couldn't help grinning. "How old did you say you were—a hundred and three? You look pretty good—for your age, I mean."

"Thanks a lot—" She laughed and looked about to say something more, but didn't. "Nice fire," she said, glancing at the stove. "I can never quite get mine going that well."

"Maybe the flue needs to be cleaned. I'll check it for you."

"Thanks. When you get a chance."

"And that bike could use some help, too. Mind if I take a look?"

"You don't have to. I can bring it to a bike place in town."

"They'll charge you a fortune. It's really not worth it," he insisted. "I can at least tell if you're liable to break your neck riding it."

"Well, I guess I'd rather not break my neck, now that you mention it."

"Not on my property. You might sue me," he said, giving her a serious look.

"Oh, now I get it. Just covering yourself, are you? And I thought you were trying to be nice." She laughed and pushed back her hair with her hand.

He met her clear blue gaze and felt himself about to smile. Then forced himself not to.

"Nice?" he repeated in a mocking tone. "Give me a break. What are you trying to do, Sara, ruin my reputation in this town?"

She smiled at him. "Don't worry, I won't tell a soul." She glanced at her watch and set her mug down on the table. "Got to go. Work tomorrow. Thanks for the coffee, though."

She stood up and he did, too.

"No problem. Can I walk you back?" he offered.

"Oh, no. Don't be silly. I'll be fine." She picked up her jacket and pulled it on.

Luke opened the door for her. His gaze met hers for a long moment, and he noticed again how pretty she was, without a drop of makeup, either. He noticed her blue eyes and the way her soft brown hair framed her face. He felt himself moving toward her for an instant. Then he stopped and stood to the side of the door, clearing her way.

"Good night, Sara. I'll watch you until you get in," he said quietly.

"Oh, all right," she replied, sounding surprised. "Good night, Luke."

He watched her cross the short distance between their cottages, his mind tumbling with thoughts. Regrets about telling her his past, worry over what she thought of him now. And finally a strange sense of relief at being open with someone.

At her doorstep she turned briefly and waved to him. He waved back, watched her go in, and then closed his own door.

Yes, relief. He felt . . . better. Absolutely.

But why Sara?

Chapter Four

⌒

"Now, this one is very old. My mother and father on their wedding day." Lillian glanced at the back of the photograph, then handed it to Sara. "It has a notation, but I can't make it out."

Sara leaned over from her seat on Lillian's sofa. It was hard for her to read the faded handwriting in the late afternoon light. Finally she said, "Ruth and Albert. May sixth, 1919."

"Yes, May the sixth. Their anniversary. I'd almost forgotten." Lillian took the photograph back and studied it. "Look at my mother's gown. Wasn't it spectacular? The lace was hand-made, imported from France."

She pushed the sepia-colored photo toward Sara. It was a formal wedding portrait, probably taken in a studio. The young groom and bride looked grim and determined, as if the occasion required great moral resolve.

Lillian looked more like her father, Sara thought, with his deep-set eyes and long narrow face. But Sara could also see a strong resemblance to Jessica Warwick in the delicate features of Lillian's mother, her own great-grandmother, Ruth Merchant. They both even had the same luxuriant curly hair.

"Your mother was very beautiful," Sara commented. "She looks a lot like Jessica."

"Really? I don't see that resemblance at all," Lillian said curtly, taking the photo back. She examined it a moment, then tapped it with her index finger. "That pearl necklace first belonged to my great-great-grandmother. My mother promised that I would wear it, too, when I was married. But as it turned out, I never did."

"Why not?"

Lillian sat back in her chair and took a sip of tea, as if she was deciding whether or not to answer. Finally she said, "My parents disapproved of Oliver Warwick. They forbade me to marry him, threatened to cut me off entirely if I went against their wishes. So when I did, no pearl necklace."

"How sad," Sara said.

"I survived," Lillian replied dryly. She picked up some other photographs that were scattered on the coffee table and began to arrange them in a pile. Her hands trembled a bit, Sara noticed.

"How about your sister and brother? Did they stop speaking to you, too?"

"They were afraid to risk their inheritances, so they obeyed my parents' wishes in the matter, by and large. My sister, Elizabeth, got in touch occasionally. Of course, when trouble came, no one offered any help. . . ." Lillian paused and took another sip of tea. "I didn't go crawling back to them, either," she added stiffly.

Sara's knowledge of the Warwicks' trouble was limited to what she had heard through town gossip, but she didn't press for details, sensing that for Lillian it was still a painful subject.

"When my sister died, my brother, Lawrence, sent me the pearls and some other pieces of jewelry," Lillian continued, sitting back in her chair. "I don't believe he had any idea of its significance for me. Wait, let me find a picture of Lawrence for you," she said, rifling through the photographs on her lap.

Sara sat quietly, watching her. Had she ever heard that Lillian had defied her wealthy, aristocratic parents to marry Oliver Warwick? That was quite a twist to the family saga, which Sara was finding increasingly fascinating. The Warwicks' story sometimes seemed like an intricate jigsaw puzzle that she was trying to assemble piece by piece. Now she wondered if there was a pattern she hadn't seen before: Lillian defying her parents to marry for love, and Jessica now doing the same to marry Sam. The missing piece, of course, was Emily. What had happened with Emily that led to her own birth?

"You know," Sara said carefully, "these old photographs really are a piece of history. It would be wonderful if they were organized into a series of albums. You could do it chronologically or perhaps—" She stopped speaking as she saw Lillian's eyes narrow. Had she just said the wrong thing?

Lillian peered at her sharply. "That's not a bad idea," she allowed, "but it sounds like a tremendous amount of work. I don't even have the energy to find all my old photographs, let alone—"

"I could help you," Sara offered. "I could pick up some photo albums at Nolan's Stationery. Then it could be sort of an ongoing project that you and I could work on—whenever you feel up to it."

She waited what seemed an endless moment before Lillian said, "Yes, I think that would be a fine thing to do."

Sara felt a little guilty for tricking Lillian into telling her the family history this way. But Lillian seemed to genuinely enjoy it. This was one of the few times Sara had seen her relax and let down her guard.

"So many photographs here." Lillian sighed as she continued to search for one of her brother. "My daughters obviously don't have the slightest interest in helping me organize them. But I'm sure they'll be grateful for it once I'm dead and buried."

Lillian often referred to some future time when she was "dead and buried" and her family would finally appreciate her, Sara had noticed. As if dying were some ultimate trump card she held, waiting to toss it down just to spite them all.

"Ahh . . . here's Lawrence," Lillian said, picking out an oval-shaped portrait and handing it to Sara. "I believe he'd just finished law school when this was taken. Harvard," she added, as if that were a given.

Lawrence had his father's long nose and stern expression, coupled with his mother's curly hair, Sara noticed. He stared at the camera, his expression unsmiling, his neck rigid in a high starched collar.

"He became a judge, you know," Lillian said proudly.

It was clear that Lillian's parents were quite demanding of their children, just as Lillian seemed to be of her daughters. *And would be with me, if she ever found out I'm her granddaughter,* Sara thought.

But there were other reasons why Lillian was so obsessed with Emily and Jessica making their mark on the world, bringing recognition to the Warwick family name, especially here, in Cape Light. Sara had heard about the family scandal, how Lillian's husband—Sara's own grandfather, Oliver Warwick—had been accused and convicted of embezzling funds from his firm's accounts. Although he had never gone to jail, the family had lost almost all their money. Forced to give up the Warwick estate, Lilac Hall, they'd come to this house on Providence Street. Oliver had died soon after from a bad heart. *Or maybe a broken one,* Sara thought.

Lillian frowned as she sifted through the photographs. "There aren't any here of my sister, Elizabeth," she said. "I know I have some of all three of us, right at Durham Point Beach. We came here nearly every summer. My father loved ocean swimming, the colder the better." Her stiff fingers flipped through the pile of photos again, and Sara saw her pause, her brow wrinkling in concentration.

Lillian's memory was still amazingly sharp, nearly as sharp as her tongue, Sara thought with a secret smile.

"They must be up in the attic," Lillian said, looking up at Sara. "There's an old trunk with leather straps up there, near the small window at the front of the house, I think. It's filled with papers and things I packed up when we moved. I don't believe I've ever even opened it in all this time."

Sara knew that Lillian meant since the Warwicks moved out of Lilac Hall. That was a long time ago, she reflected, more than twenty years.

"I'll go up and get it for you," Sara said, coming to her feet.

"Oh, no, don't bother," Lillian replied. "I'm sure it's a perfect mess up there. You'll never find it, and you'll only get yourself all dirty."

"It's no bother," Sara insisted. "I don't mind at all. You should have a picture of your brother and sister for the first album. It won't be complete otherwise."

Sara was careful not to sound too eager. But the prospect of going through a trunk of Lillian's old belongings—and possibly some that belonged to her mother, too—was far too tempting to pass up.

"I suppose so," Lillian agreed slowly. "It would be nice to have a photo or two of them. . . . though I'm still not sure who I'm making these books for," she grumbled a bit crossly.

"For Emily and Jessica . . . and your future grandchildren."

Sara watched Lillian's face carefully, studying her reaction. Did Lillian ever think of her, the child Emily had given up for adoption, her first grandchild? Did she ever wonder what had happened to her?

For a moment Lillian's gaze seemed unfocused, then she stared back at Sara with a sour expression.

"Yes, if I have grandchildren, I'm sure they'll be very much in the future. And they won't be burdened with the last name Morgan, either, I pray," she added under her breath.

Knowing how Lillian felt about Jessica's engagement, Sara decided to avoid that topic. "The staircase to the attic is on the second floor, right?" she asked, starting out of the room.

"There's a door just past my bedroom, but I keep it locked. The key is in the little blue cloisonné vase on the bookcase." Lillian rose from the couch with some effort, using her cane, and walked to the staircase in the foyer.

"And don't get lost up there. I'm sure it's horribly dusty," Lillian called from the foyer, her tone suggesting she was having second thoughts about permitting Sara to go up there.

"Don't worry, I won't be long," Sara promised. She raced up the stairs and out of view. Lillian said something more, but Sara didn't quite hear her or turn back to find out.

She quickly found the key in the vase, just where Lillian said it would be. She felt her heartbeat quicken as she unlocked the attic door and it creaked open. She was immediately hit with the smell of old wooden rafters, cedar moth repellant, warm, stagnant air, and dust. Attic smell, enticing and mysterious. The narrow staircase seemed a portal to some forbidden tomb, the repository of her own mysterious past. A shaft of sunlight pierced the shadows, flecks of dust floating in the golden light that led her upward.

At the top of the stairs Sara looked around, trying to locate the trunk Lillian had mentioned. She said it would be toward the front of the house, near the small circular window where the roof peaked. Sara walked in that direction, carefully stepping around the miscellaneous flotsam and jetsam of a lifetime. There were several lamps in various states of disrepair, a ballroom chair with a carved back and a torn silk cushion, a dressmaker's dummy, and a brass mantel clock with a crack in its glass bell jar cover. A dusty black hatbox overflowed with offerings, from ribbon-trimmed straw bonnets to a gentleman's gray felt fedora. A yellow and blue felt banner caught Sara's eye. She picked it up to read the boxy letters that read "Cape Light Tigers." Just underneath she found a shoe box full of miniature china cups and saucers, perfect for a doll's tea party.

Some of this may have belonged to Emily, Sara realized. She felt a sudden tingling awareness and studied the various cartons and their blurry, almost indiscernible labels with even sharper curiosity.

Christmas decorations, several boxes of those. Books and tax records. Sara stepped around the boxes, checking the labels without finding anything of interest.

She worked her way to the small round window and found below it the trunk Lillian had described—black and battered with stamps of foreign ports and large leather straps across the top, the kind of trunk people took on ocean voyages decades ago.

The dull brass lock was open, and Sara leaned over and lifted the top back. Her nose was immediately assaulted by a cloud of damp, musty air and the scent of camphor. She pushed aside a pile of musty woolen blankets and an old military uniform. Beneath them, she found a box marked "Photographs." She checked inside and saw that it was filled with scenes of Lillian's early marriage when Jessica and Emily were very young, and then beneath those, the photos Lillian had been looking for, the ones from her childhood.

Taking the box of photographs, Sara stood up and closed the trunk. A large puff of dust set her coughing. When she opened her eyes again, she was looking straight at a cardboard carton pushed back against the wall. Its label read "EMILY—Maryland," and she felt her heartbeat speed up again.

Maryland. That was where Emily lived when she was married to my father. Sara quickly walked over to the box and pulled open the flaps. She wasn't quite sure what she was looking for, anything about her father. Or Emily for that matter. Or even her own birth.

The box was full of books. Sara fought back a surge of disappointment. She had expected something more, something—important. Still, she dug through them, quickly scanning the titles. Half of them were classics by New England writers—Hawthorne, Whitman, Dickinson, Melville, Thoreau, and Emerson. There's a surprise, Sara thought wryly. The rest were novels, all by women writers—Jane Austen, Edith Wharton, Virginia Woolf, Kate Chopin—her mother's books, Sara assumed. Books Emily had read on her own, since she wasn't enrolled yet at a college. Emily had once told her she had hoped to be a writer when she was young, but she had given it up. Well, clearly she had been trying, Sara thought.

Finally Sara reached the bottom of the box. That was it. She nearly felt like crying from disappointment. Her nose felt clogged by the dust from the decaying pages and she sneezed.

"Sara?" Lillian's shrill voice called up to her. "What are you doing up there?"

"I'll be right down," Sara called back, forcing her voice to an even tone. "I found the photographs."

Quickly she put the books back in the carton. Just as she piled the last few on top, a scrap of paper floated out of Virginia Woolf's *To the Lighthouse*. Sara turned it over. It was a photograph. A young man with thick black hair and dark brown eyes stared out at her. He wore a fisherman-knit sweater. His arms were crossed over his broad chest, and he was smiling with such affection and good humor at the photographer that Sara could practically feel his warmth wash over her.

In an instant she understood.

It was her father, Tim Sutton.

She turned over the photo and saw the notation "Tim, dock behind our house. October '78."

Sara stared down at his face and felt her eyes fill with tears. She touched his image with her fingertip. She looked just like him. The same-shaped face and mouth. The same eyes, except hers were blue like Emily's.

"Hi, Daddy," she murmured.

The face stared back at her, looking content with the world and everything in it. Surprised—but very happy to see her.

Then the image grew blurry from her tears.

"Sara, for goodness' sakes, have you gotten lost up there?"

Lillian's voice was even closer and sounded more annoyed. She had climbed the stairs from the first floor, no small feat in her condition, Sara realized, and now stood at the bottom of the attic staircase.

Sara abruptly stood up, closed the flaps of the carton and shoved her father's picture deep in the back pocket of her jeans.

"Sorry, Lillian," she called out, making her way to the staircase with the box of photos. "There are a lot of interesting things up here. I got distracted."

"I haven't been up there for years. I'm sure it's a regular disaster." Lillian sighed and stepped back into the hallway as Sara emerged.

"Maybe I could clean it out for you sometime," Sara offered.

"Why bother? It's just a lot of old, useless junk. When I go I'm sure the whole lot will be carted out and tossed in the trash."

"There are some interesting things up there," Sara said gently. "Some antiques maybe."

Lillian glanced at her, a mixture of suspicion and tentative inclination. Sara could see her trying to guess if she was really so *nice* or trying to manipulate her. But Sara was used to it.

"Well, I suppose you could go back someday and see if there's anything you want. You might as well take some things away if you could use them. It would help clear out the clutter." Lillian peered at her more closely. "It must have been horribly dusty up there. Your eyes are all red and watery."

"Oh . . . yes. The dust, I guess," Sara said, wiping her tears away with her fingertips.

Lillian stared at her again, suspiciously, Sara thought. But before she could say anything more, a sharp knock sounded on the front door.

"That must be Emily," Lillian said, moving toward the stairway. "Late, of course. She said she would be here by five."

Emily? Sara hadn't expected to see her here today. *I have to pull myself together. If Emily notices I've been crying, she'll start asking questions. And I'm liable to say anything right now.*

Sara heard the key turn in the lock and then the sound of the front door swinging open. "Mother?" Emily called out.

"I'm up here. With Sara," Lillian called back to her. She peered over the banister. "She's just been up in the attic, looking for old pictures. She's helping me put them in order."

"How nice," Emily replied in an automatic tone.

"It's the kind of thing you do before you die, I suppose," Lillian said grimly.

"Well, take your time then," Emily replied as she shut the door. "There's no rush." She glanced up at Sara and smiled. Sara smiled back and nearly laughed out loud. Then she was suddenly aware of the photograph hidden in her pocket, sure that Emily must somehow sense it there.

"Very amusing, Emily. I didn't mean it that way at all."

"Well, it sounds like a great project for you, Mother. I'd love to look at some old pictures of our family," Emily said in a more appeasing tone.

"Yes, of course. Everyone likes to look at old photos. But never enough to help sort them all out," Lillian said tartly.

She moved slowly down the steps, in a sideways crablike motion. Emily came to help her, and Sara could see the veiled tension in Emily's face as she held her mother's upper arm and guided her into the living room.

Lillian settled herself on the long, camelback sofa with an indignant sniff. Sara followed and set the box of photos on the coffee table.

"Well, sit down. Take your coat off," Lillian fairly ordered her daughter. "Or are you just here to make sure I'm still conscious and breathing?"

"I have some groceries for you in the car," Emily replied, ignoring her mother's tone. "I'll just run out and get them."

"I'll go," Sara offered. When Emily seemed about to argue, she insisted. "It's okay. Really. I could use the fresh air."

"Yes, let her go," Lillian cut in. "The girl has gotten all congested with the dust. Fresh air will do her good."

Sara ran outside, grateful for a chance to compose herself. She found two plastic bags of groceries in the backseat of Emily's Jeep Cherokee and took a few minutes in the cool air to settle herself down. But she couldn't forget the picture of her father hidden in her pocket.

Maybe it's a sign, Sara thought as she walked back up the path to the house. *Am I supposed to tell her now?*

Sara stood at the front door, summoning her courage. But when she stepped into the foyer and heard Emily and Lillian chatting in the living room, her courage began to wane.

How could she do it? she wondered as she carried the groceries to the kitchen. Finding her father's picture had just gotten her all shook up. She wouldn't be able to say it right.

But there's never going to be a perfect time to do this, she reminded herself. *Or the perfect way to tell her. . . .*

"Here, let me put that stuff away. You don't have to do that, too." Emily entered the kitchen, her words breaking into Sara's scattered thoughts.

"It's okay, I don't mind." Sara picked up a can of soup and opened the nearest cabinet. "Though I'm still not sure where everything goes, and I have a feeling that Lillian doesn't like to find things out of order."

"Yes, Mother likes her cupboards very orderly," Emily said, with a wry smile. "We wouldn't dare put a can of soup in the cereal closet. We might upset the entire balance of the universe."

Sara grinned, but her stomach was doing somersaults. *I could tell her right now,* she thought nervously. She watched as Emily turned away to put a carton of eggs in the refrigerator. *No, not at Lillian's house. That would be too much,* Sara decided.

Emily emerged from the refrigerator, holding a carton of orange juice. "Do you see a bottle of red pills on the counter near the phone?" she asked.

Sara searched the counter and found the pills. "Varex?" she asked, reading the label.

"That's the one." Emily poured Lillian a glass of juice, and Sara carried the pill bottle, and they went out again together to the living room.

"Here, Mother," Emily said, dispensing the pills. "Don't forget to take these. The doctor said that they're important."

"Important to him, you mean. I feel no difference at all, whether I take them or not."

"Just take the pills, Mother. Please?"

Lillian glanced up at Emily with the sullen pout of a willful child but grudgingly swallowed the pills.

"It's a terrible thing to get old, Sara," Lillian said, as though Emily weren't in the room. "I strongly advise against it."

Sara smiled and glanced at Emily. "I'll keep that in mind. Of course, the alternatives are not that attractive, either."

"No, they're not," Lillian agreed, sitting up straight and smoothing her skirt. "That reminds me, what do you hear from your sister, Emily? I haven't spoken with her for weeks. I could be dead and buried for all she knows."

"Mother, don't be ridiculous. It's Tuesday. We just saw Jessica, Sunday at church."

"Saw her from a distance, like a stranger, you mean," Lillian corrected her.

"Well, I asked if you wanted to go over and say hello. You said you didn't want to," Emily reminded her.

"Jessica should have come over and spoken to me. I'm not the one that ought to be doing the groveling. Ever since she met that Sam Morgan, she shows no concern for my feelings."

"Mother, you know that's not true. Jessica has called and come by repeatedly. You say such awful things about Sam, it's no wonder she's avoiding you. Think of it this way—if she hadn't met Sam, she'd be back in Boston by now, and you would hardly see her."

"If she marries that man, I just may never see her again, even if she moves in next door," Lillian threatened.

"Do you want me to fix your dinner?" Emily asked, choosing not to pursue the argument.

"I've had enough help for one day, thank you," Lillian replied without looking up. "You should both go. I need to rest."

"Can I help you to the bedroom?" Emily said.

"I'll be fine right here. I want to watch the news."

She picked up the remote control from the end table near her chair and gave the television her full attention. "Make sure the door is locked on your way out," she said. "Anyone could wander in here off the street and knock me over the head."

"Good night, Mother." Emily leaned over and kissed her mother on the cheek. "I'll speak to you tomorrow."

"Good night, Lillian," Sara said.

"Yes, good-bye. Good-bye, everyone," she said sharply, turning up the volume on the television. "Thank you for the visit."

Outside, Emily made sure the door was locked, then turned to Sara with an apologetic smile. "I'm sorry about my mother. She gets very cranky when she's tired."

"You don't need to apologize. I know how it is." Sara lifted her leather pack strap over one shoulder.

Emily walked Sara to her car, then said, "Thanks again for visiting her. I'm sure my mother never says it, but I know your company is a great pleasure to her. She doesn't have much these days to look forward to."

Sara met Emily's kind gaze and stared back for a long moment.

She could tell her right now. Her visits to Lillian weren't motivated purely by feeling sorry for a lonely old woman.

I've made friends with her because she's my grandmother, the voice in her head said. *You're my mother, Emily. . . .*

But instead, Sara said, "Lillian definitely has her grouchy moments, but I like talking to her. She told me a lot about your family today when we looked through those old pictures."

"You mean about my father, how he almost went to jail?"

"More about her own family." Sara paused, not sure what to say next. "I am curious about your father," she admitted. "Although Lillian doesn't say much about him, I've heard some stories around town."

"It seems unbelievable, but people still talk about it." Emily shook her head. "Well, let's see . . . what can I tell you? My father was basically a good man. He was loving and kind. Everyone who worked for him liked him. But he was weak, I guess, a good person who made a big mistake. I think people around here found it hard to forgive him because they felt he'd tricked them in some way. He wasn't exactly what he appeared to be."

I can definitely relate to that, Sara thought. In all the months she'd been in Cape Light, Sara had rarely felt so much a fraud, hiding her identity, as she did at that moment.

But I could tell her. There's nothing really stopping me. I could tell her right now. . . .

Emily glanced at her watch. "Oh, gosh. I've got to run. I have to drop off some campaign signs on my way home. Charlie's got so many up around town, my camp is getting nervous."

The campaign, Sara thought. *How can I tell her? It could ruin everything. People in this town would talk if Emily got a new hairstyle. They'd get plenty of mileage out of hearing her long-lost daughter showed up. Even though she was married when she had me, I'm sure no one knows she gave me up for adoption. Charlie would love to sink his teeth into that one.*

Feeling deflated, Sara pulled out her car keys and opened the door. "Well, if you ever need a spy at the diner, just let me know," she offered.

"Don't be silly." Emily laughed. "I'd never ask you to do something like that." She paused, gazing fondly at her. "The Beach Road might be foggy tonight. Drive carefully, okay?"

"Sure, I will." Sara nodded, surprised by Emily's concern.

"How is it out at the cottages?" Emily asked as Sara got in her car. "Not too lonely for you?"

"It's quiet without the tourists. But Luke McAllister is living there, so I don't feel entirely deserted."

The two women said good night again, and Sara watched Emily get into her Jeep before she drove off in the opposite direction.

Emily was right, she thought as she turned onto the Beach Road. Patches of fog clung to the curves on the road and made the short trip home seem longer. Though it was not quite seven o'clock, Sara felt drained. Actually, she often felt this way after seeing Emily, she realized. It was hard to be around Emily and not tell her the truth, but at the same time it felt good to spend time with her birth mother and get to know her better.

When will I tell her? Sara wondered anxiously. *Her campaign for mayor will last for two more months. I'll go crazy if I have to wait that long.*

She'd come here in May, not planning to stay more than a week or so. Just enough time to find Emily and tell her the truth. Now, here she was, more than three months later, feeling no closer to a resolution.

Five minutes later Sara pulled up behind her cottage and shut off the engine. She remembered the photograph in her pocket, turned on the overhead light, and pulled it out. Her father, Tim Sutton. Gazing at his image made her feel better, as if his calm, warm gaze telegraphed a message. "Have patience, Sara. It will all work out for you," she could almost hear him say.

"All right. I'll try," she answered back out loud.

Sara knew it was wrong to take the photograph without asking. But still, it was her father and she felt as if she had a right. *I think I was meant to find it,* she thought as she slipped it back in her pocket. *I think it's going to help me.*

EMILY HAD JUST TOSSED A FROZEN MEAL-FOR-ONE INTO THE MICROWAVE and fed her cats when she heard someone at the door.

"Who could that be?" The two small cats didn't even lift their heads from their dishes in reply.

Emily opened the door and felt her spirits lift as she saw her sister standing there.

"I was on my way home and wanted to drop off these platters you loaned me for the party. Is this a bad time?" Jessica asked.

"Not at all, come on in." Emily swung open the door and kissed her sister on the cheek. "I just got in a few minutes ago." She heard the microwave beep and remembered her dinner. "I was just fixing something to eat—one of those frozen, low-fat, low-taste things. Want one?"

"Uh . . . no, thanks. I already ate with Sam. You make it sound very tempting though," Jessica teased her.

Emily laughed. "It helps if you skipped lunch and you're starving. How about some coffee or tea?"

"A cup of tea would be nice." Jessica pulled off her fleece top and sat at the kitchen table. "Looks like you're going to have new neighbors soon," she remarked.

"You mean that funny-looking house down the street? It's been for sale since July." Emily filled the kettle and set it on the stove. "Betty says it's very small and needs tons of work."

"Well, somebody liked it. The sign says 'Sold'."

"Really? I didn't even notice. Leave it to Betty. She can sell anything."

Emily found mugs and tea bags and set them on the counter. "Were you working out at the house tonight?"

"Just testing some paint colors. I never thought it would be so hard to agree. Sam wants everything pale blue and green. Or maybe gray," Jessica said, sticking her tongue out. "And I'm seeing peach and rose and French vanilla. . . ."

"You know what they say, 'Women are from Venus, men are color-blind.' "

"Thanks, that helps a lot." Jessica shook her head, smiling in spite of herself as her ponytail came half undone.

Emily glanced over her shoulder. Jessica was so pretty, even when she wasn't trying. She wore jeans and a baseball-style jersey dotted with paint splatters. Nothing like her impeccable office attire of stylish suits and sleek hairdos. But this new look suited her surprisingly well. Just like Sam did.

"I like that shade of apricot." Emily pointed at a large splotch on Jessica's sleeve.

"The master bedroom, I hope," Jessica said. She looked up at Emily again. "Did you have a meeting or something tonight?"

"Not really. I stopped to see Mother, then had to take care of some campaign errands."

"How is she doing?" Jessica's voice became tense. "I meant to call her today, but I didn't get a chance."

More like, felt afraid to call her, Emily realized with a pang. "Mother's fine. Sara Franklin stopped by to visit, and they were going through old photographs. You know how Mother loves to talk about the good old days."

"Poor Sara. She's a good sport, isn't she?"

"A very good sport and an unusual young woman," Emily agreed. "Mother asked about you. She was in a bit of a snit about church. She thinks you should have come over to say hello."

"I tried to say hello to her, and she just gave me one of those—those looks. You know, like she's never seen me before in her life." Jessica gave a perfect imitation of their mother's haughty, wide-eyed stare.

"I know," Emily said, grinning. "And even she knows perfectly well what she did, but pointing it out to her doesn't seem to do much good."

The teakettle shrieked, and Emily poured the hot water into the waiting mugs and carried them to the table.

Jessica sighed and stirred her tea. "I thought it wouldn't bother me if she missed the party. But of course it did," she confessed, sounding sad and angry and frustrated all at once. "Especially when the cake came out and Digger got everyone to sing. I felt so happy—except that I wished Mother were there."

"Yes, I know," Emily said quietly.

"What if she really doesn't come to the wedding? It's hard enough that Father is gone. If Mother didn't come, I'd feel so sad. I'm not sure if I could go through with it."

"Go through with the wedding, you mean?"

Jessica looked down and nodded. "I could never say that to Sam. He wouldn't understand—he'd feel so hurt. But it's true. She's got to come, Emily. She just has to."

Emily put her arm around Jessica's shoulder. "There's plenty of time for Mother to change her mind. And Reverend Ben is going to talk to her this week. She'll come around, you'll see."

"She might listen to Reverend Ben," Jessica allowed. "She certainly won't listen to either of us."

"Just don't cut yourself off from her," Emily advised. "Mother will only use that as ammunition to prove her point."

Jessica sighed. "It's hard enough getting married, without dealing with Mother, too. Honestly, Emily, sometimes I just say to myself, why bother?"

"Don't be silly. You're going to marry Sam and live in that beautiful house on the pond, with one wall painted blue and the other one French

Vanilla, and you'll have lots of kids for me to spoil and baby-sit," she told her sister. "And Mother will come to the wedding, and she'll give you a complete critique of everything, from the flower arrangements to the cheese puffs."

"If you say so." Jessica forced a smile.

Emily wished there was something more she could say or do. Then she remembered the pearls.

"Come upstairs, I want to show you something," she coaxed her sister.

Without further explanation, Emily led the way to the bedroom. Jessica followed, looking puzzled.

Emily stepped up to the dresser, blocking Jessica's view, and took out the velvet box. "Now, close your eyes and don't open them until I say."

"Close my eyes?" Jessica sounded doubtful, but did as she was told.

Emily quietly opened the jewelry case and removed the necklace, then slipped the strand of antique pearls around her sister's neck and fastened the catch. "Don't open your eyes yet."

"What in the world—?"

Emily guided her a few steps closer to the mirror that hung above her oak dresser. "Okay, you can look now," she said, stepping back to watch her sister's reaction.

Jessica stared at her reflection, first looking puzzled and at the same time touching the necklace as if to make sure it was real. "For goodness' sake . . ." she said under her breath. She drew closer to the mirror, her gaze fixed on the necklace. "The bridal pearls. How did you get them?" she asked, turning to face Emily.

"Mother wore them to some meeting of the museum board last week and asked me to put them back in the bank for her." Emily grinned. "I just didn't get to it yet. And I thought you might enjoy trying them on."

Jessica glanced again at her reflection. She gently touched the pearls again, her bright expression clouding over.

Oh, dear, Emily thought. *Did I do the right thing?*

"I'd better take them off," Jessica said, fumbling with the catch.

"Mother would have a stroke if she ever knew I was in the same room as this necklace."

"Come on, Jessica. It's all right," Emily soothed her. "Leave them on a minute. I want to see how they look on you."

"Take a good look. This is as close as I'll ever come to wearing them," Jessica said, giving her reflection one more quick glance. Then she slipped the pearls off and placed them back in the silk-lined box. "Somehow it doesn't seem right even to try them on like this, behind her back. I know she won't let me wear them on my wedding day, not the way things are going between us."

"It's just so ironic," Emily said quietly. "I mean, Mother always sounded so hurt and bitter about the way she was denied wearing the necklace. And now she's doing the exact same thing to you. You would think she would have learned something."

"Yes, I know." Jessica took a breath, looking upset again. "I guess she didn't."

That observation seemed true enough, Emily thought, but it didn't sit well with her.

"Let's give it time." Emily touched her sister's shoulder and caught her gaze in the mirror. "I'm going to keep them here for you until your wedding day. A lot can happen by then."

"How about you?" Jessica asked. "Have you tried them on?"

"Me? Why would I ever wear them? I'm not getting married."

"You did once," Jessica reminded her. "But you didn't get to wear them. . . . Aren't you curious?"

Emily looked at the pearls, then snapped the case closed. "No . . . I couldn't. I've missed my chance. But you'll have yours," she promised quietly. "I'll make sure of it."

Jessica gazed into her eyes and smiled. "Well, I'm not going to count on it, but I appreciate you trying."

"No problem," Emily said. Older by ten years, Emily had always felt protective of her younger sister even though she knew Jessica sometimes resented it.

But Jessica needed her more than ever now, and Emily knew she would gladly play the role of both Jessica's maid of honor *and* the surrogate mother of the bride—as long as their own mother continued to oppose her dear sister's wedding.

CHAPTER FIVE

ERHAPS I SHOULD HAVE CALLED FIRST, BEN THOUGHT
as the grand white colonial came into view. *If I
show up at her door with no warning, Lillian might turn me
away, just on principle. No matter that I'm her minister. But of
course if I called, she'd have guessed my reason for coming and put
me off with some excuse.*

No, he'd done the right thing by surprising her, he decided
as he parked his car in front of the house. When it came to a
person like Lillian Warwick, a surprise attack—impromptu
meeting, rather—was best.

Ben took the small bushel of vegetables from the backseat,
then walked up the front path toward the porch. He'd always
loved Providence Street. It was one of the village's finest, with
its tall trees, deep, sweeping lawns, and majestic old homes.

He rang the doorbell and waited. He could hear the low murmur of a television or radio. Perhaps she was home but didn't hear him. He tried again and waited. Out of the corner of his eye, he saw the heavy drapes in the living room shift slightly, then snap closed.

Signs of life within after all. *I'm not giving up that easily, Lillian,* he thought, pressing the chime again.

"I'm coming. Please do stop that ringing," he heard her call out from the other side of the door.

Then the door opened and Lillian's eyes grew wide with theatrical surprise. "Why, Reverend Ben. What a surprise."

"Hello, Lillian. I was out at the Potters', and Sophie loaded me up with vegetables, as usual. I thought I'd stop by and bring you some on my way back to town."

"How nice of you to remember me." Lillian's tone was polite, despite a note of unmistakable suspicion. "I'm hardly on the way to town. I'm hardly on your way to anywhere," she pointed out.

"Well, I was thinking of you," he said with a shrug. "Shall I bring these into the kitchen?"

"Yes, I guess so," Lillian replied, stepping back and opening the door.

Ben carried the bushel through the house back to the kitchen with Lillian following slowly behind.

"Shall I put it on the counter?"

"Yes, next to the sink would be fine," she directed him.

He set the bushel down, then turned to her. "So, how are you feeling today, Lillian? You look well."

"Then I must look worlds better than I feel. I was expecting your daughter this morning for my physical therapy. But she canceled," Lillian told him, as if the Reverend were somehow to blame. "She has a bad cold. Did you know that?"

"No, I didn't," he replied honestly, feeling concerned for Rachel.

"Well, I suppose it's all for the best, since I don't need to catch it from her. But it is the second time this month," she added. She glanced at him, then pulled the edges of her sweater together and fastened the middle button.

"Well, Rachel is expecting a baby," the Reverend pointed out gently. "Maybe the pregnancy is slowing her down a bit."

"I suppose so," Lillian agreed. "Don't get me wrong. She's not a bad therapist. I've had worse."

Ben smiled mildly. He knew his daughter was one of the very best physical therapists to be found in this area. Certainly one of the most patient, if she was able to work with Lillian.

"I'll tell her you said that." He paused, wondering how to work the conversation around to Lillian's own daughter. "It's hard to believe Rachel is about to have a baby. Carolyn and I are quite excited about it. But of course, you have a big event coming up in your family, too."

"A big event?" Lillian stared at him blankly. The Reverend could have laughed aloud, if the situation wasn't so serious.

"Jessica's wedding," he prompted her.

"Oh. That." She met his gaze, her eyes narrowed with a look that said she now knew exactly why he'd come. "Don't ask me about Jessica's wedding. I don't know a thing about it." She looked away and dabbed her nose with a tissue. "Frankly, I'm not the least bit interested."

"That's too bad," Ben said quietly. "A mother and daughter usually take great pleasure in planning a wedding together. I remember the way Carolyn and Rachel carried on for months about every detail."

He paused, gauging Lillian's reaction, wondering how far he could go without getting thrown out of her house. Her mouth was pursed in a tight line, her brow furrowed.

"I think Jessica would welcome your help right now, Lillian. It's a very important time for her. She wants you to be part of it."

"Part of this ridiculous decision she's made to ruin her life? To throw herself away on a man who is totally unworthy of her?" Lillian countered sharply. "No, thank you, Reverend. That is a pleasure I can gladly forego."

"I know you disapprove of Sam, and I know I can't change your mind about him. I will say that I do believe, in time, you'll come to see that you've misjudged him."

She lifted her chin and looked the Reverend in the eye. "Sam Morgan might be the most virtuous man on God's green earth, but that still doesn't make him the right man for my daughter. All her talent and potential will be smothered by the sheer weight of his—his muscle-bound mediocrity."

It was hard for Ben to hear Sam insulted with such vehemence and by someone who knew him so little. Ben admired and respected Sam and truly believed that if God had created more like him, the world would be a far better place.

But he could talk himself blue in the face and never convince Lillian of that. Patience, he told himself. Patience and compassion. This woman is in deep pain, or she wouldn't be lashing out like this.

"You're right, it's not about Sam at all," Ben cut in before Lillian could speak again. "It's about Jessica. This is the man she's chosen to marry, Lillian. This is the man she loves. Your disapproval will hurt her. It might even break her heart. But I do believe she'll marry Sam with or without your blessings. No matter how you feel about him, you're still Jessica's mother. She needs you."

"Nonsense. Jessica appears to be carrying on very well without my help," Lillian argued. "How hypocritical can I be, Reverend? Advising on flower arrangements and table settings when, in my heart, I feel as if I'm watching her choose to be buried alive? It's not an easy thing to raise a child, to have plans for her, hopes that she will amount to something. Then sit back and watch her waste her life and all the time and hard work you've invested. It's a bitter cup, Reverend. I think you know what I mean, too," she said pointedly. "I'm not sure that you, or anyone else for that matter, would deal with this situation in a more sanguine manner."

Ben drew his breath in sharply. He hadn't quite expected Lillian to take a shot at him like that. Everyone in town knew about his son, Mark—the troubled years in high school, and how he'd dropped out of college and had been wandering the country ever since.

"Yes, it's a difficult situation," he acknowledged with hard-won patience. "I can see that. I would never say that it is not."

She stared at him a moment, then pulled her sweater tighter around her chest, looking suddenly uncomfortable, maybe even embarrassed by her outburst.

He sighed and turned to the basket of vegetables, then picked up a large acorn squash. "Here's a nice one," he remarked. "How do you like these prepared, Lillian, baked or boiled?"

"Baked. With a dab of butter and some salt. Boiled is too bland even for my taste," she added with a short, harsh laugh.

He returned the squash to the basket and glanced at his watch. "Is there anything I can do for you before I leave? Any chores you need help with today?"

"No, thank you, Reverend. I'll walk you to the door," she offered, and he noticed that she looked relieved to see him going. He wondered if anything he had said would penetrate. Or would his words run off like raindrops striking a stone?

Following her through the shadowy rooms, Ben felt deflated and ineffectual, as if he hadn't really gotten his point across. But she was so very adept at deflecting him. What else could he say?

When they reached the front door, he turned to her. "I hope I didn't upset you with our talk. But you really should take some time and think about what you're doing, Lillian. Think about the consequences," he quietly implored her.

He tried to catch her gaze, but she blinked and looked away. Still, he persisted. "Is your disapproval of this marriage really worth alienating Jessica and maybe even Emily as well? You don't have to answer me. But just consider it. Because that is what the outcome will be. I'm almost certain of it."

Lillian took a stiff step back with the aid of her cane and stared up at him, her face looking gray and hollow, he thought.

"You make it sound as if the situation were entirely in my hands, Reverend, when in fact, the choice is Jessica's. She's the one who has rejected me by agreeing to this marriage. She needs to come to her senses. That's the way I see it."

Ben gazed at her thoughtfully. She had dug into her position and would not give an inch. Not today anyway.

"Good night, Reverend. Thank you for the vegetables," Lillian added, pulling open the front door.

"Good night, Lillian." He nodded briefly as he left, pulling on his flat cap.

The heavy door closed behind him with a solid, final sound, and the Reverend stood for a moment on the front porch, buttoning his coat.

She was really impossible. He shook his head in frustration, feeling his temper rise as he walked down to his car. Seated behind the wheel, he caught himself and took a breath. He had not expected much of the meeting, yet he felt ashamed, as if he had lost some sort of important tactical battle.

That's your ego talking, Ben, your pride. He started the car and pulled away from the curb. *Patience,* he reminded himself. *Isn't that what you advised Jessica and Sam?*

A verse from Second Timothy came to mind: "And the servant of the Lord must not strive; but be gentle unto all men, apt to teach, patient."

Yes, gentle, generous, patient—and above all, trust in the Lord, "and he shall bring it to pass."

*   *   *

MAYBE IT WAS THE FEELING OF COMING IN FROM THE COLD, THE FIRST TIME so far this season. Or perhaps his visit to Lillian Warwick had taken more of a toll on him than he had expected. Ben approached the rectory—a cozy, cottage-like Cape—feeling keenly grateful to be home. The softly glowing lamplight, the sound of classical music, and the scent of Carolyn's good cooking cheered him instantly as he placed his jacket and cap on the coat-rack in the foyer.

"Ben, is that you, dear?" Carolyn called from the kitchen.

"I'm sorry I'm late." He picked up the newspaper and his mail and walked toward the back of the house. "I should have called, but I got bogged down a bit at Lillian Warwick's."

He walked up behind Carolyn, who stood at the stove, and kissed her on the cheek.

"Was she feeling ill?" Carolyn asked.

"No, nothing like that." Ben picked up a piece of raw carrot from the cutting board and popped it into his mouth.

"What's for dinner?" he mumbled as he chewed.

"Pot roast." Carolyn laughed when she saw his expression light up. "It seemed cold enough out today to enjoy it."

"Absolutely. Perfect weather for a pot roast."

"So, you spoke to Lillian about Jessica's wedding?"

Ben glanced at her. "You heard me tell Sam and Jessica I would, didn't you?"

She nodded. "Yes, at the party."

Although his conversations with parishioners were in the strictest con-fidence, it was hard to keep everything secret from Carolyn. She was, after all, his wife and totally discreet.

"So, how did it go?"

"Not well, I'm afraid. The honest truth is, I got pretty frustrated with her," Ben confessed. He felt disturbed again but forced himself to shake it off. "She's difficult. I'm not sure anything I said got through."

Carolyn cast him a sympathetic glance. "Perhaps something stuck. You never know. You tried your best, I'm sure."

"Yes, that I did." Ben took off his glasses, cleaned them with a paper napkin, then put them back on. "Luckily it's at least two months until the wedding. Plenty of time for her to give ground—and for me to pray for God's help."

Carolyn caught his gaze with a worried frown. "That bad, huh?" She shook her head. "Rachel rarely mentions Lillian, but I'm sure she's not an easy patient."

"Lillian was walking quite well today. I think Rachel has helped her a lot. Though she did complain that Rachel missed their session today because of a cold. Is Rachel sick?"

"Nothing serious. Just a bad case of the sniffles." Carolyn checked something boiling in a pot and put the cover back on. "I am afraid that she's run-down, though, working too hard. I wish she would cut back her hours. But she said they need the money."

"What does the doctor say? Does he think she should stop working?" Ben asked.

"The doctor says she's fine. But these days they want all the women out there working until they practically deliver at their desks," Carolyn complained.

"Yes, it was different when you had our children," Ben agreed. "But don't worry. Rachel has good sense." He patted his wife on the shoulder and helped her set out the silverware and napkins.

"Oh, she does. I don't think she'll risk hurting the baby. But I can't help worrying anyway," Carolyn added with a shrug.

"Let's see." He counted on his fingers. "Four months left to go. She's just about halfway through. It's going by quickly, don't you think?"

"Not quick enough for me. I wish the baby could be born tomorrow. Though I do have a few more things to buy," she said with a smile. She turned to the stove and spooned the noodles into a serving bowl. "Rachel would be so happy if Mark could come back when the baby was born. Or at least for the baptism."

"Yes, I know she would." Ben sighed and sat back in his seat. He watched his wife's smooth, efficient movements, knowing her calm demeanor masked emotions that were anything but. He saw a sorrow in her eyes that appeared whenever they mentioned Mark.

Carolyn still blamed herself for Mark's unhappiness and his breach with their family.

If anyone is to blame for not sensing that Mark needed more, for missing the signals that trouble was brewing, it is me, Ben thought. *But I was so busy with the congregation, tending to my flock, that I missed the problems under my own roof.*

"I guess he's still in Arizona," Carolyn said, referring to Mark's last postcard. "Did he ever send a new address or phone number?"

Ben swallowed hard. Dishonesty of any kind had always been hard for him, even before he became a minister. But it was especially difficult when it came to Carolyn. He had never actually shown her the postcard. Now he knew that he had to tell her the truth.

"The address . . . the name of the place where he's staying, rather," he corrected, "was on the card." He warily met her gaze. "I just never told you."

"Why not?" she asked, suddenly sounding upset.

"I'm sorry." Ben took a deep breath. "Mark is staying at a Buddhist ashram."

He watched her expression. Her blue eyes grew wide with shock. "A Buddhist ashram? You've known this for weeks and you didn't tell me?"

"Not quite two weeks," he offered in his own defense. "I got the card right after the storm, remember?" When she didn't answer, just stared at him with a tight, angry expression, he told her, "I meant to tell you, Carolyn, and I'm sorry I didn't. It was wrong of me. I knew it would upset you, and I guess I was just trying to . . . to protect you."

"You don't need to protect me, Ben," she said angrily. "You need to treat me as an equal not—an invalid. It's terribly condescending. And hurt-ful," she added.

"Oh, dear, please . . ." He moved toward her, gently catching her shoulders in his large hands. "You know I don't feel that way about you. You're more than my equal, Carolyn. You're superior to me in every way."

Carolyn spared him a glance, but he could see she was still upset.

"I was wrong to keep it from you," he admitted. "I won't do it again, I promise."

"You've said that before," she pointed out. "But somehow, it keeps happening."

The charge was true. The problem was, with Carolyn's history of depression, Ben often found himself treading a very fine line, keeping things from her that he feared would be too much for her to handle. It wasn't fair to her, he knew.

"I know and I have to stop," he promised again. "To be perfectly hon-est, I wasn't only protecting you by not talking about it. . . . I'm at a loss, Carolyn. I don't understand what Mark is doing or what the good Lord wants me to do."

"You think that Mark's rebelling against you?"

"It does seem like the ultimate rejection," Ben said, hearing a trace of bitterness in his own voice. "Or maybe it's just the latest in a long line of things he's done to put distance between us."

"We can't assume that's what he's doing," Carolyn said.

Ben shook his head. "Over the years we've seen counselors and thera-pists and smoothed over the rough edges, but I can't help feeling that the bitter seed at the heart of it all has never been rooted out."

Carolyn rested her hand on his chest. "Mark's gone through so many changes," she reminded him. "Maybe this phase will pass quickly, too."

Ben sighed and managed a weak smile. "Good point. 'And this too shall pass,' " he agreed. "The Lord moves in strange ways, and we each find our own unique path to the Lord. Maybe this is just part of Mark's journey back to his faith—and to us."

"I just hope he's not gone too long," Carolyn said wistfully. "I do miss him so." She turned to the stove. "Ready for dinner?"

"Absolutely," Ben replied as Carolyn took the fragrant platter of meat and vegetables from the oven and set it on the table.

They joined hands and Ben said a blessing over the food. *Many paths to faith*, he thought as Carolyn passed the bowl of noodles. That would be a good idea for this week's sermon. He took out the small notepad he always kept in his breast pocket and jotted it down.

"Don't you ever stop?" Carolyn teased him.

"You knew my hours when you married me," he reminded her. "And you know my Boss is always watching," he added with a twinkle in his eye.

Carolyn just laughed.

IT WAS UNUSUALLY BUSY AT THE DINER FOR A FRIDAY, SARA THOUGHT. AT five Lucy got ready to leave and Sara was sorry to see her go. They had hardly found time to talk all afternoon.

"I hope I can get the boys to bed early tonight," Lucy said, slipping on her jacket. "I have a ton of homework to do. I might have to call you later about my English paper. Did you ever read—oh, what is it called again?" Lucy squinted trying to remember. "*Portrait of the Artist as a Young Man*?"

"Only about five times," Sara replied.

"Great. You'll be hearing from me," Lucy said, looking instantly cheered.

"No problem." Sara had turned into a homework hotline the last few weeks, but she didn't mind. She was amazed at how Lucy managed to keep up with her schedule these days, working at the diner, running her household, caring for her children, and going to classes and doing schoolwork, too. She knew Charlie wasn't much help around the house, especially now with the election coming up.

"Charlie is working on his campaign tonight, so you'll have to close," Lucy added. "He's in a tizzy about that debate next week. I think they've got him practicing tonight up on stage and are even taking a video so he can see the replay."

"Really?" Sara had always known Charlie was serious about running, but this sounded almost professional.

"Really." Lucy nodded solemnly, then a mischievous look came into her eyes. "I can't wait for him to see what he really looks like, yelling his head off at somebody. I think it will be a real eye-opener."

Lucy reviewed a few more instructions for the night, then she was off. Sara gathered up all the ketchup bottles to refill.

When the phone rang a few minutes later, Sara expected it to be Lucy. But it was Emily, calling for a delivery.

Sara quickly took down the order. "This won't take long," she promised. "About fifteen minutes."

"Great," Emily said. "See you later."

A few minutes later Sara was walking quickly up Main Street toward the Village Hall. She hoped she would get to visit with Emily for a while. Fortunately, Billy, the relief cook, liked to get out of the kitchen and talk to the customers, and didn't care if she took her time getting back.

The Village Hall was quiet and dark, as it usually was when she visited at this hour. But when she approached Emily's office at the back, it sounded as though a meeting were going on. Sara walked up to the half-open door and knocked.

Emily sat at the head of the conference table, wearing her reading glasses, which had slid down her nose. She held a sheaf of papers in her hand and was carrying on an animated conversation with the woman sitting to her left. Sara recognized most of the others from having seen them at the diner—Harriet DeSoto, the town clerk; Warren Oakes, an attorney in town; Betty Bowman, a realtor; Doris Mumford, a high school science teacher; and Frank Hellinger, who ran the local fuel company.

The table was covered with papers, posters, and even bumper stickers. One was a flyer with Emily's photo in the upper-right corner. It must have been a draft, Sara realized, noticing the cross-outs and corrections in red ink.

Emily looked up and smiled at her. "Sara, come on in. We're just finishing up here." Emily turned her attention to the others. "I guess it's a wrap for tonight. We can cover the rest of this on Tuesday, right?"

"Maybe we should meet before then," Doris said as she rose and packed her briefcase. "We don't want to be caught short for the debate."

"Yeah, I agree," Warren Oakes said, following the others to the door. "I hear Charlie's camp is really gearing up. Besides, we still haven't gone over your closing statement, Emily."

"Yes, well, I'm still working on it," Emily replied. "It's almost done." She waved Sara closer as the others left. "Shut the door, will you, dear?" she asked.

Sara left the food on Emily's desk, then went back to close the door.

Emily tossed her glasses on the desk with a sigh. "My campaign committee," she explained briefly. "They mean well, but they can get a bit intense."

"They seem very serious," Sara agreed. "What do they do for you? Hand out flyers and things?"

"Oh, way more than that. They talk to the voters, try to figure out what people are thinking and what positions I should take. They help me write speeches and position papers. They do a lot, really," Emily admitted. "I certainly couldn't get through this election without them."

"But don't you just say what you believe?" Sara asked, surprised. "They don't really tell you what to say, right?"

"Well . . . yes and no, I guess," Emily replied slowly as she lifted the lid off her take-out dish. Then she laughed and shook her head. "Now, *there's* a politician's answer if ever I heard one."

Sara didn't say anything. She could see that Emily was a bit uneasy. Still, she wanted to know the real answer.

"I try to do the best that I can to be true to my ideas about issues," Emily said in a more serious tone. "But sometimes I have to be—savvy, or careful about it. Especially during a campaign. Voters tend to see things in black and white. The fine print gets lost. I have to be careful not to alienate the people I need to communicate with."

Sara felt a little startled by Emily's admission. She was basically saying that she had to compromise what she really believed in to get votes, wasn't she?

"Luckily there are no really controversial issues in this election," Emily went on. "It's been pretty easy for me, so far."

"Can I help out with your campaign?" Sara asked suddenly. *Where did that come from?* she wondered. It wasn't just that she thought Charlie would make a lousy mayor. If she had to wait until after the election to tell Emily the truth about her identity, at least she could get to know her better by helping on the campaign.

She half-hoped Emily would put her off with some polite excuse, but instead, Emily looked pleased.

"Sure, if you like," Emily said. "Let's see, what can we put you on?" She walked over to the table. "There's a draft of a letter somewhere in this mess that I mean to send to the *Messenger*. It's about the firehouse substation proposal," she explained. "Wait, here it is." She pulled out a few pieces of paper held together with a clip. "That's my letter on top. This one underneath is Charlie's. It appeared last week, so I'm trying to answer his points." She handed the pile to Sara. "But it could use some work, I think, before I send it to the paper. Want to take a look and see what you can do?"

"Uh, sure. No problem." Sara glanced down at the letters and newspaper clippings, surprised and pleased that Emily had given her such an important task. Her confidence made Sara happy. "I'll look it over right away and get it back to you," Sara promised.

"That would be great. Just call if you have any questions. The issue is a little confusing—and so are my scribbles in the margin."

"Okay, I will," Sara said. She caught sight of the small brass clock on Emily's desk and realized that she'd been gone from the diner for a long time. Too long, even for laid-back Billy.

"Oh, gosh, I've got to get back to work," Sara said, rushing off. "See you."

"Good night, Sara," Emily called after her. "Thanks again for your help."

Emily watched Sara go, thinking she looked even younger tonight than usual, with her hair pulled back in a ponytail and a red hooded sweatshirt pulled on over her waitress uniform.

Sara had seemed so shocked to hear that she couldn't just stand up and deliver every campaign speech straight from the heart. It had been almost amusing, Emily thought. But it had niggled her conscience, too.

She was that way once herself, wasn't she? Young and naive, shocked to lift the hood on the real world and come face-to-face with the greasy, clanking, broken-down mechanics that actually made things run—and in no way matched up to her pristine ideals.

Well, it was too late and she was too tired to worry about it now. *And piles to go before I sleep,* she thought, paraphrasing a favorite poem by a favorite poet.

She glanced at her overloaded in-box, grabbed a handful of folders, and took a bite of salad. Plain mixed greens and tuna fish, low-fat dressing. She paused to stick her tongue out at the sheer blandness of it. But all these campaign breakfasts, lunches, and dinners would make her gain weight.

I might be back in office next year . . . but I won't have anything left in my closet to wear to work, she muttered to herself as she unwrapped a pack of low-fat crackers.

Now, that's a problem I can do something about.

CHAPTER SIX

ARA HAD BARELY MADE IT HALFWAY DOWN THE gravel drive that led from the cottages to the Beach Road when she wondered if her plan to bike to Potter Orchard had been such a good idea.

Maybe Lucy's old bicycle wasn't up to such an ambitious trip. It was not only heavy and the seat remarkably uncomfortable, but more of the ten gears seemed to slip than actually catch. Luke hadn't had a chance to work on it; he had been away all weekend.

I really should have greased the chain a bit, she thought, glancing down at it as she rode uphill.

She checked her watch. It was nearly eleven A.M., and she had a Monday afternoon shift at the Clam Box. If she didn't ride faster, she would never get to the orchard and back in time.

Something stuck and Sara pushed hard on the pedals, feeling the entire mechanism lock. The bike wavered for a moment, and she felt herself tipping to one side. "What the—" she cried out. Branches suddenly came into view overhead as Sara crashed to the ground.

The bike came down on top of her, so that one leg was caught underneath. She lay there a moment, catching her breath. She hadn't been on a bike in years—or fallen off one, either, for at least as long. She knew she wasn't seriously hurt, but the palms of her hands stung, and she felt a little shaken up.

She heard the sound of the gravel crunching with an approaching car and looked up to see Luke's black 4Runner coming down the road. She had just long enough to disentangle herself from the bike and get up, before he stopped and waved to her.

She waved back, forcing a smile. *How dumb is this? My cottage is still in sight, and the guy finds me flat out in the middle of the road.*

"Are you okay?" he asked, getting out and walking toward her.

"Oh, sure." Sara shrugged and tugged on the bike's handlebars to lift it. "You were right, though. I should have tuned this up before I tried to take it out."

"I could say I told you so, but I won't," Luke agreed with a grin. He stood with his hands on his hips, squinting in the sunlight, little lines fanning out at the corners of his eyes.

He was good looking in a rugged way—maybe not to everyone's taste, but she definitely liked his looks.

Luke crouched down on the other side of the bike and studied it for a minute. "Chain fell off," he said simply. "Here, let me see if I can fix it for you."

He stood up and flipped the bike over so that it was balanced on the seat and handlebars, then worked on the chain, fitting it back over the sharp-toothed gears.

"I can get it on," he told her, "but it will probably fall off again."

"Don't bother," Sara said.

He flipped the bike over that so that it was right-side-up again, and Sara took the handlebars. Then he took a handkerchief out of his pocket and wiped the grease off his hands. "Where were you headed?"

"To Potter Orchard, to pick some apples. Have you ever been?"

"Yeah, sure." He nodded. "Years ago, though. The view from up there is great. You can see the whole town."

"Yes, that's what I've heard," Sara said.

He didn't answer, suddenly seeming self-conscious, Sara thought. She hadn't seen him since the night when he told her about his past. Was he feeling embarrassed about that now?

"When did you get back? I didn't see your truck before," she said.

"A few hours ago. I had some errands to do in town before coming back here."

He watched her, his gaze unnerving.

"Want to come to the orchard with me?" she asked impulsively. "I mean, if you don't have anything to do."

"Sure, why not?" He shrugged. "I like apples."

Sara smiled. "I have to be at work by three, but that still leaves plenty of time. Oh, what about the bike?" Sara looked up at him. "Should I leave it here?"

"We can just stash it in my truck," Luke offered. "We'll put it back in the storage shed when we get back."

Luke loaded the bike into the SUV, and Sara got into the passenger seat. It seemed very quiet as they drove away from the cottages. Quiet and tense, she thought. She wondered if inviting him had been such a good idea. He sat staring straight ahead, not saying a word and not looking as if he was about to, either.

Sara opened her window and felt strands of her hair lifted by the breeze. She felt she ought to start a conversation, but didn't know what to say.

"How was your trip?" she asked at last.

He glanced at her, then looked back at the road. "Interesting," he said simply.

She waited, but he didn't say anything more. She had met quiet types before, but Luke took the prize for laconic.

"So how was your father's party? Was he surprised?" she asked.

"He acted surprised, but I think he knew. It's hard to plan a surprise party for a retired detective. My mother has tried before," Luke explained. "He was surprised to see me turn up, though," he added, glancing at her for a moment. "More like shocked, I'd say."

Sara couldn't tell if he meant it in a good way or bad. She wondered if she should ask more, if it would seem too personal, then decided to plunge ahead. "How did that go?"

"Not great," Luke said quietly. "But he tried, I have to give him credit for that."

He stared out at the road, and Sara could see he felt badly about his father. There must be more to the story, she reasoned, but she didn't pry.

"My brothers were better. It was good to see them, and their kids and all. They were surprised to see me walking so well now. I guess when I left I was still limping along."

"I don't really remember," Sara said honestly.

She could hardly recall now how obvious Luke's limp had been when she first met him. It was funny how, once you got to know someone, the outer details seemed to recede and you somehow saw the person differently. More of what was inside shining through.

"I ran into some friends, too," he added. "Some guys from the job."

"How did that go?" she asked curiously.

"Good. These guys were really tight friends of mine. They never made me feel . . . I don't know, like an outcast or something. They took me out to dinner, to this steak place where we always hung out. We had a pretty good talk," he said.

He seemed happier, she thought. She couldn't quite put her finger on why; she just sensed it somehow and felt happy for him.

Sara watched the roadside with its warm fall colors sweep by, feeling content in the silence. The faded red-and-white sign for Potter Orchard came into view, and Luke turned off the Beach Road. He followed the signs to the "Pick Your Own" section and parked. There were only two other cars in the lot, Sara noticed, but several pickup trucks.

They got out of Luke's SUV, and Sara turned to admire the Potters' house, which stood some distance behind the orchard, closer to the road. The gracious old Queen Anne with its wraparound porches looked as if it had seen better days, Sara thought, but it was still remarkable.

"I love that house. It's just fantastic," Sara said.

"It really is," Luke agreed. "But check out the view in this direction."

Sara turned and gasped. From the Potters' hilltop, the town and harbor looked like a toy village set up beneath a Christmas tree.

"Wow," she said softly. She still had no intention of remaining in Cape Light, but she couldn't deny the beauty of the place.

As they walked toward the shed to pay their money, Sara noticed a group of men setting up ladders at the nearby barn. She recognized Harry Reilly, Digger Hegman, Sam Morgan, and Reverend Lewis and wondered why they were working here today. Then Sara remembered that Gus Potter was sick. They must have come to help out, she realized. A nice gesture, somehow typical of this town.

The rough wooden apple shed was painted green with white trim. Inside, Sophie Potter sat behind the counter, a stack of bushel baskets at her side. She was dressed in layers—a cotton turtleneck, a flannel shirt, and a big wool sweater that looked as if it belonged to her husband, topped with a down vest.

"These bushels are big," she said. "You ought to share one."

Luke glanced at Sara and she shrugged. "It's fine with me."

"Okay, one, then," Luke said.

He took out his wallet to pay, but so did Sara. "No, let me," she insisted.

"Don't be silly," he said, sounding almost cross.

"No, I invited you, remember?"

"What difference does that make?" Luke seemed puzzled, but finally stepped aside so that she could hand Sophie some bills.

Sara knew it was silly to argue, but for some reason she felt better paying. It felt less like a real date, maybe.

As Sara took the bushel from Sophie, she felt the older woman watching her curiously, sizing her up in some way.

"The sections are all labeled. Just check the signs at the end of each row. We've got McIntosh, Macoun, Empire, Fuji, Imperial, Granny Smith—the best selection you'll find in the area," Sophie stated proudly. "Now, do you know how to pick 'em?"

"I'm not sure. Is there a special way?" Sara asked.

"There's a right way and a wrong way to do everything, dear," Sophie observed. "As for apples, you don't need to yank them off and take half the tree with you. You just give a little twist at the stem"—she demonstrated with a slight twist of her wrist—"and the fruit will drop off right into your hand, like a lot of things in life. Yank 'em and you ruin the blossoms for the next year."

Sara nodded. She had only picked apples once before and didn't remember this tip. "We'll do that," she promised.

She noticed Luke had wandered away from the shed, taking another look at the view. His back was toward her, his hands dug into the pockets of his leather jacket. She felt that mysterious tugging in the center of her chest and realized again that she felt drawn to him. Attracted to him. There was just something about Luke. He was so different from all the others, unconventional and not easy to understand. Even now, she wondered what he was thinking about.

"Picking apples is a good way to get to know a person," Sophie said knowingly.

"Fill up this bushel, dear. You'll get your money's worth."

Sara smiled and ducked her head as she took the empty bushel. "Uh, thanks. See you later."

She walked toward Luke and took a deep breath. She didn't know him very well, that was true. And his confession about his past had made her even more curious.

There's a lot he doesn't know about me, either, she reminded herself as he turned and walked toward her.

"Ready to start?" Sara asked him.

He turned and nodded. "Sophie Potter is quite a talker," he said as they walked toward the trees.

"Yeah, but she's interesting," Sarah said. "I never knew there were so many types of apples."

Luke turned and flashed a smile at her. "I've seen you at the diner. You'll talk to anyone."

Sara felt a stab of surprise as she realized he had been watching her. She had never really thought he noticed her.

"I guess I do," she said with a shrug. She hugged the empty bushel basket to her chest with both arms. "Most people have something interesting to say—about their lives or their work or what they think of their neighbors. I find it interesting, anyway."

"Don't be offended." He rested his arm on her shoulder, and she felt keenly aware of his touch. "I think it's nice. I just noticed it about you, that's all." They walked along a few steps just that way, until he glanced at her, looking self-conscious again. Quickly he put his hand back in his pocket and gazed straight ahead.

"Is that how you get ideas for your writing?" he asked.

"Sometimes. Sometimes just by watching people or listening to their conversations."

"Eavesdropping, you mean?" he asked with a small laugh.

"I guess you could call it that. One of my favorite hobbies, actually."

They had reached the apple trees and turned down the first row. "I have the same habit," he admitted. "But mostly just from police work. They teach you to study people, to figure someone out in a glance."

"Really? Maybe you should try writing a book or something," she teased. She chose a tree and reached up to pick an apple.

He smiled back at her. "It takes more than that. You need ideas, stories."

"I bet you have loads of stories," she replied, then instantly regretted it.

"That I do." His tone was light, but his expression more serious, she noticed. She dropped an apple into the bushel, avoiding his gaze.

Finally he said, "So did the stuff I told you the other night bother you?"

"No," she said honestly. "Not at all." She had thought about it a lot over the past few days. She had thought about him. But she wasn't quite ready to admit that.

"Is there—something else?" she asked, suddenly worried that there was more he had to confess—darker, more frightening things.

Luke's mouth turned down at the corner, as if he were struggling not to smile. "No, that was it," he promised. "Ahh . . . there's a good one."

He spotted an apple, then reached for it, his arm coming around her shoulder so that she was suddenly trapped between him and the tree. He twisted it off the branch with perfect Sophie technique, then stood staring down at her. His face was so close, she could almost feel his breath on her skin. For a moment, she thought he was going to kiss her.

But he stepped back and dropped his apple into the basket. The sound startled her, making her realize she had been holding her breath.

"Today is not the kind of day to talk about the past," he said in a decisive tone.

"It isn't? Why not?" she asked.

"Well, for one thing, it's too sunny out. And for another . . . I have this idea I'm working on."

"Oh, really?" Sara could tell by the tone of his voice and the sudden light in his gray eyes that "this idea" was important to him. "What's your idea about?" she asked curiously.

He picked another perfect yellow-and-red apple and shrugged. "Well, it's about what to do with all that property I bought."

"You mean, like building a hotel or houses?"

"No, nothing like that. The truth is, when I bought it I wasn't planning on anything, really," he said, turning to her. "Then, when I went out to dinner with those friends I told you about, this guy I know who quit the force gave me this idea. There's a foundation in Boston that works with city kids at risk. You know, kids who could do better if they had more encouragement, better role models—that sort of thing."

Sara stopped picking apples and gave him her full attention.

"They have so much pressure on them in those neighborhoods to do drugs and drop out of school," Luke explained. "Even the really good kids, who have potential, get dragged under."

"I know what you mean," Sara said. "A lot of the kids in Baltimore have the same problem."

"Right. So this program—New Horizons, it's called—it gets kids out of that atmosphere for a break. They come to a place like this, and they get counseling and tutoring. They go hiking and do things they've never done and get to see the world from a new perspective. They get to see they have choices," he explained. "Maybe they also get some experience in a useful skill, like carpentry or plumbing. I mean, not every kid is going to be a brain surgeon, right?"

"I hardly know anyone who is."

"How true." Luke met her gaze and smiled at her. Small lines fanned out at the corners of his eyes, and deep creases etched his lined cheeks. She felt herself staring at him, then tried to hide her reaction, seeking cover behind a tree branch.

Yes, he is attractive, very attractive. And he hardly ever smiles, so when he does it's a little—overwhelming, she told herself. *But let's not get carried away here . . . please?*

"Well, you get the idea." Luke picked up the bushel and walked toward the next group of trees.

Sara quickened her pace to follow. She had never seen him so animated or heard him string so many sentences together. He was positively elated—for Luke, she thought.

"So what happens next?" she asked.

"I donate the land and then turn the place into one of the New Horizons centers. They have them all over the country. We could use the cottages and maybe build one more larger, central building. I've already spoken to the program director and a lawyer who will draw up the papers."

"Wow, that was quick," she said, impressed.

"Yeah, it was, wasn't it?" He met her gaze and flashed a grin. "I met with the New Horizons people twice, on Thursday and Friday. Once we started talking, things seemed to fall into place pretty quickly. The renovation on the cottages will have to start soon so the place will be ready for spring. I stopped at the Village Hall when I got back this morning and checked about building permits."

"When you get an idea, you don't waste time, do you?"

"Hey." His voice went soft with concern, and he touched her wrist. "I didn't mean you have to move out or anything. You can stay as long as you like. If you don't mind the noise, that is."

"Well." She wasn't sure what to say. "I guess I'll just have to see how noisy it gets."

She stepped up to the next tree and reached for an apple, conscious of Luke watching her. Something subtle had shifted between them, though she wasn't quite sure what. She and Luke had always had one thing in common. They were both outsiders, arriving in the village at just about the same time and staying on without any real plan.

Now it seemed Luke had found a plan and was about to make a real commitment to Cape Light. It was an even greater commitment than buying his land, which he could have sold or let a rental agent handle. With this new idea he was putting down roots, she realized. While she was still adrift, liable to sail off at a moment's notice.

"You seem really fired up about this idea," she said. "It sounds like a big commitment."

"It will be. Very big." He watched her as she leaned over to pick up the bushel. "Here, I'll carry that," he said. He bent to take it from her, and their hands met for a moment on the rim of the bushel. Sara stood still, then let go.

"How about a break?" he asked, nodding toward a bench next to a water spigot.

They walked over to the bench, where Sara took a drink from the spigot. She sat down next to Luke, wiping her mouth on her sleeve. The air was heavy with the scent of fruit that had fallen to the grass all around them, and the sky was a startling shade of blue.

"You know, I realized something when I went back home. There was a lot of truth to my father calling me a failure," Luke said.

Sara found herself instinctively rallying to his defense. "You're not a—"

"No, it's okay," he said, cutting her off gently. "I did fail at being a cop, but maybe I wasn't meant to be a cop. Maybe I was meant to do something else. This is worthwhile work. It's almost like police work, only I'm getting to the kids before they go out on the streets and get into trouble. I think I like this idea even better," he added.

"I do, too," she agreed.

He leaned back and stretched his arm along the back of the bench, not quite touching her but creating a feeling of closeness between them. Sara suddenly did feel close to him. He was trying hard to figure something out. To get up and keep going, even though he'd been hit hard and knocked down.

"I hope this works out for you," she said sincerely.

"Yeah, I hope so, too."

"You know, people around here might not be so receptive to a center like that," she mentioned, trying not to sound too negative. "You might have some resistance from the village."

He glanced at her. "I know, especially since I don't have the greatest reputation around here. But it's been done other places. Local people balk, and then they settle down. I'm going to keep it low-key at first. You're the only person I've told so far."

Their eyes met, and she felt touched by his admission. Then she felt herself blush. *He didn't mean anything by that,* she told herself. *I'm just the first person he ran into since he got back.*

"Does that mean it's a secret?" she asked him.

"Sort of." He shrugged. "The guy in the building permit office at the Village Hall knows, of course. . . . Are *you* good at keeping a secret?"

Sara thought of the secret she'd been keeping from everyone in town, Luke included. "Actually, I am. I think you'd be surprised," she added, rising uneasily from the bench.

He didn't reply, just watched her walk toward the trees again. After a moment he rose from the bench, picked up the bushel, and followed her.

"Granny Smiths?" he asked as she walked toward a tree of bright green apples. "They're too sour for me."

"They're not for everyone," she agreed. "But I like them."

"You like the unusual things, do you?" he asked, making her feel self-conscious again.

"I don't know. . . . It's not something I do on purpose."

"That makes it even more interesting."

An awkward silence fell between them. Luke finally broke it by asking, "So how is it going at the diner?"

"The usual, except Charlie's even harder to take with the election coming up."

"I noticed. Ever think of taking another job? Doing something with your writing?"

She glanced at him. "Like what?"

He shrugged as she dropped two more apples into the basket. "If this program starts up, maybe you could get involved, teaching creative writing or something like that. It would be more interesting for you than working at the Clam Box."

"I'm sure it would be, but I don't know that I'd be very good at it."

Sara knew she was making excuses. The bottom line was, despite Luke opening up to her—and despite her very real attraction to him—she couldn't get so involved with anything or anyone while she was in Cape Light. It wouldn't be fair to encourage him, she thought. She had no idea how long she'd stay, and he had no idea why she was really there.

"Just think about it," he urged her.

She glanced at him, then turned and walked to another tree, feeling she needed to put a little space between them.

"I like your plan. It's a great idea," she said carefully. "But I don't think it's something I can get involved with. For one thing, I have no idea how long I'm going to be here. I could leave tomorrow." Sara ran her hand through her hair. "I just don't know."

Surprise flickered through Luke's eyes, then his face got that shuttered look. "No problem." His voice was cool, detached. "It was just a suggestion. I didn't mean anything by it."

She could tell she had hurt his feelings.

"Look, it's not you. I really like you," she admitted in a rush. "I mean, I respect you and what you want to do here. But don't include me. My life is just really messed up right now. I know it might not look that way from the outside. But trust me, it is."

"Okay." He looked at her and shrugged.

"I'm sorry," she said, though she wasn't quite sure what she was apologizing for.

"It's all right. I get it. You don't have to say any more." He put the bushel down and looked down at her. "I hope you figure it out . . . whatever it is."

"Thanks, so do I. I'm working on it," she added.

"Good, then." His manner was offhand, yet the energy between them felt very heavy to Sara.

She glanced into the basket. "It's nearly full," she said.

Luke gave her one of his half-smiles. "You mean, maybe we should leave some apples for other people?"

"We could," she said. She checked her watch. "Whoa, I'd better get home. I have to be at work by three. I'll have just enough time to change and get into town."

"Sure, I didn't realize it was so late." He looked over at her, as if about to say something more, then just started back to the 4Runner.

They drove back to the cottages in silence.

Did I hurt him? Sara wondered. *Or did he decide that I was too young or messed up or something? I don't want to get involved with him anyway, so what am I worrying about?*

She looked up and saw that they had arrived at the cottages. Luke stopped and they both got out. He grabbed the bushel of apples in the back and carried them to her door.

"What are you going to do with all these apples?"

"Give you half?" she asked hopefully.

He laughed. "I'll take a few but not half." He picked out a few apples and put them in his pockets, then balanced a few more in his arms. "Why don't you bring them into the diner? Maybe Charlie can make something out of them."

"That would take some imagination. I don't think it would work out," she said blandly.

He gave her that smiling-in-spite-of-himself smile again and stepped back, putting space between them.

"Thanks for the apples," he said, starting back to his cottage.

"You're welcome," she called after him.

Luke McAllister was an unusual man, she thought as she let herself in. She couldn't quite figure him out, and she wasn't ready for a relationship. But she liked him. And as he had pointed out, she didn't like the usual things.

CHAPTER SEVEN

*J*ESSICA? THE TRUCK'S LOADED. ARE YOU READY YET?"
Jessica heard Sam call out to her from somewhere near the front door of her apartment. Meanwhile the
woman on the other end of the phone continued her smooth,
persuasive pitch.

Jessica could hardly follow her. It was Monday evening,
and she felt tired after starting off the work week. She sensed
Sam hovering nearby, eager to get started on their project for
the night, moving yet another load of furniture into the house.

"—and the salary is quite high, considering your experience. Probably double what you're making now."

"Double?" Jessica repeated. She wondered how this woman, a
headhunter with an executive search firm in Boston, could possibly know what she was earning. But these people had their sources.

"And the benefits are outstanding. Three weeks' vacation, full health coverage, dental, life insurance, 401(k)—"

"But I would have to be in Boston full-time, right?"

"No one's going to give you that kind of money working part-time, dear," the woman replied in an amused tone.

"Of course not. I just wanted to make sure that's what you meant." Jessica glanced up to see Sam in the kitchen doorway, a curious look on his face. She wondered how long he'd been standing there.

"So can we set up an interview? They've already seen your résumé. They're very interested," the woman assured her.

Sam was still watching her, his arms crossed over his chest.

"Uh, no. I don't think so. I'm not interested in relocating back to Boston right now," Jessica said. "But thank you for thinking of me—"

The conversation quickly concluded and Jessica hung up.

"Sorry. Some woman from a headhunting firm got me on the phone, and I couldn't get off. I'm not even sure how she got my home number."

"Headhunting?" Sam echoed. "You mean, like a job offer?"

"A bank in Boston is looking for a chief loan officer. They saw my résumé and wanted to interview me." Jessica walked past Sam into the living room, looking around for her jacket and purse.

"There must be a good salary to go with that title," he speculated.

"Very good," Jessica agreed. "Twice what I'm making now."

"So what did you say?"

She glanced at him. "I told her I wasn't interested. You heard me."

"Yeah, I guess I did," he admitted. "But I'm not sure you sounded all that sure about it."

"What are you talking about? Of course I'm sure about it. How could I take a job in Boston when I'm living out here? I'd have to get up at five o'clock in the morning to get to work on time—and who knows what time I'd get home. We'd barely see each other."

"That's not exactly what I meant." He glanced at her as she put on her jacket. "Oh, just forget it."

She wondered what he did mean. Sam was acting so funny tonight, distracted and not talking much, flying off at the slightest thing. He was usually so even-tempered, Jessica hardly knew what to make of it.

"So are you ready to go?" He glanced at his watch. "It's going to be dark in a little while. At this rate we won't be able to unload the truck."

"In a minute. I think we should talk. Is something wrong?" she asked quietly. "You seem upset."

"I'm not upset." He crossed his arms over his wide chest. "How about you? Are you upset?"

"Me? What would I be upset about?"

"I don't know." He shrugged. "Turning down that big job offer maybe?"

She felt confused. "No, not at all. I didn't even think twice about it."

"Don't say that, Jessica. You were on the phone with that woman an awfully long time. You must have had some interest."

"I was curious, that's all." Jessica shrugged. "Besides, once she got started it was hard to get rid of her. Like one of those telemarketers or something."

"Sure, it happens all the time to me," he said sarcastically. "People calling me up, making big job offers. It's hard to shake 'em."

Jessica searched Sam's expression. His eyes were dark, unreadable; his familiar features lacked their usual warmth and light. Something was wrong here, very wrong.

"Come on, Sam. What's really bothering you? That I didn't just hang up the phone the minute that woman told me who she was?"

He stared at her and expelled a long harsh breath. "That would have been one way to handle it."

"Well, I'm sorry. I was curious, I guess. The next time someone like that calls, I'll just say 'No, thank you' and hang up. Does that make you feel any better?"

"Why should you hang up? Maybe you are really interested in these opportunities. If I hadn't walked into the room right then, who knows what would have happened?"

"Oh, come on, Sam. . . ." Jessica took a step toward him. "We've been all through this. You know that's not true."

"I'm not so sure," he admitted with a shrug. "Maybe you would rather be back in the city, with all the big salaries and big opportunities. Maybe your mother is right. Maybe I am keeping you down by making you my wife—"

"Come on, Sam. Stop it. Stop it right now," Jessica snapped. She stared at him, not quite believing she had spoken to him in such an angry tone.

He was feeling insecure. Why hadn't she seen that before? Probably because he always seemed so centered and secure. This was so unlike him, she thought. For some reason the phone call had really set him off.

"You know that my career is not my priority right now. My priority is you," she added in a far quieter voice. "The life we're planning here, together."

"And you don't care what your mother thinks? You don't care that she wouldn't speak to us again yesterday in church? You don't care that she doesn't want to come to our wedding?"

"What has my mother got to do with a Boston headhunter?" Jessica asked, mystified.

"Just answer the question," Sam said tensely. "Your mother's disapproval matters to you, doesn't it? You're thinking about it and worrying about it all the time."

"Well, what do you expect? She's my mother, isn't she?" Jessica felt a hot stab of frustration rising inside her. "Why are you acting this way?"

"You feel—torn?"

"Yes, in a way," she admitted. "I want to marry you, Sam. More than anything. But can't you see how hard it is for me, dealing with my mother like this?" She pulled off her jacket and tossed it on the couch. "She's the only parent I've got, and she's so unbelievably stubborn. She won't listen to anybody, not even Reverend Ben. She's always sure she's right and the rest of the world is wrong."

"I don't like hearing that you're torn between me and your mother, Jessica. I don't think that's a match I can ever really win," Sam admitted slowly. He walked to the window and turned his back to her as he spoke. "Is that what's happening?"

"Choosing her over you? Of course not!" She took a few steps toward him, fighting the urge to put her arms around him. She loved him so much; it hurt to feel this anger between them. Still, she couldn't help feeling he was being unfair. When he didn't speak, she said, "I'm sorry, I think you're just feeling insecure for some reason, and having all these . . . doubts about me. What did I do to make you feel this way?"

"Me? Don't put this all on me. I'm not having doubts," he said, suddenly turning to face her. "You just admitted to me that you felt torn. That's what I'd call having doubts."

Jessica felt as if she had the wind knocked out of her. She could hardly believe what he was saying. "Wait just a minute. I never said I had any question at all in my mind about marrying you, Sam. I said I felt pressure from my mother. It's completely different. And you are not listening to a word I'm saying. Why can't you just stop a minute and try to understand?"

"Look, all I understand is this. You're not ready, Jessica. You think you're ready to marry me, but you're not. And I'm not going to keep acting as if nothing is wrong, when I just heard five minutes ago that you have doubts about marrying me."

"That is not what I said!" Jessica was trying not to shout. "It sounds to me as if you're the one who's absorbing all my mother's negativity. You're the one who's getting all insecure and having all these doubts about me."

Tears blurred her vision, and she covered her face with her hands. She felt Sam touch her shoulder, but she angrily shook him off and walked to her desk to grab a tissue.

Sam followed her a step or two, then turned and sat down heavily on the couch.

"So . . . what do you want to do, call off the wedding?" she challenged him.

"I didn't say that, did I?"

"That's what you implied," she pointed out in a stiff, formal voice. Inside, she felt her heart about to break in two. But she would cry later, she decided. After he went home.

Sam took a deep breath, then said, "I think we should postpone our plans. Just give it a little more time. Until you're really sure."

She met his glance, then looked away. "We'll lose our date at the inn and at the church, too, probably."

"So, we'll get another one," he replied.

He really means it, she thought. She couldn't quite believe this was happening.

"All right . . . if that's what you want, then we'll postpone it," she forced herself to say.

"It's not just me, Jessica. Be honest with yourself. It's what you want, too."

Was it? She wouldn't have said so half an hour ago, but now that it had happened, she felt oddly relieved. She would have more time to work on her mother, and that was important to her, however painful it was for Sam to hear—and for her to admit.

Elsie jumped on the desk and Jessica stroked the cat, not really noticing what she was doing.

"Three months was not really long enough to plan a wedding anyway," she said, trying to keep her voice from shaking. "And this way you'll have more time to finish the house."

Sam rose from the couch and picked up his jacket. "Yes, I will. I want us to be married, and I want you to be sure that's what you want, too. But don't make me wait too long, Jessica."

He was standing very close and she wanted to touch him. She wanted him to take her into his arms and tell her not to worry, that everything was going to be all right.

But maybe that was not how he felt at all, she realized. And she didn't know what to do or say now.

"I guess it's too late to go out to the house."

"Yeah, I think so," he agreed. "I think I'll just head home now. I'll drop that furniture off at the house tomorrow."

"Okay." She nodded. "I love you, Sam," she added, catching his dark gaze. "You know that by now, don't you?"

"Sure . . . I know."

Jessica felt awful. She wasn't going to lose him, was she? Would they go through with this wedding—or not?

Finally he kissed her quickly on the cheek, then walked out the door.

SAM HAD ONLY BEEN GONE TEN MINUTES, AND HER APARTMENT SEEMED achingly empty. Jessica paced from room to room. She turned on the television, then shut it off again. She went into the kitchen, opened the refrigerator, and stared inside. It was past dinnertime, but she had no appetite.

She sat at the kitchen table and started crying again. What had happened? What was going on? She and Sam loved each other so much. How could this happen?

The phone rang and she ran over to pick up, sure that it was Sam, calling to apologize and say that he'd change his mind.

"Hello?" Her voice croaked and she blew her nose on a tissue.

"Jessica? Are you okay?" It was Emily.

Jessica took a deep, shaky breath before answering. "Not really. Actually, I'm terrible," she admitted.

"What's the matter? What's happened?"

"Sam and I had a fight. Well, not a fight really . . . a talk, I guess you'd call it." She could hardly say what she had to next, but forced herself. "We've decided to postpone the wedding."

"Postpone the wedding?" Emily sounded so alarmed that Jessica felt her spirits sink, thinking the worst all over again. "Listen, I'm still at the office. Want to meet at the Beanery in, say, ten minutes?"

"That would be great." Jessica knew she needed to talk to someone. Emily was a godsend. "I'll see you there."

Jessica splashed her face with cold water and put on some lipstick. She hardly glanced at her reflection, feeling as if she looked totally terrible. What's the difference? she thought, heading out the door.

It was a short walk from her apartment to the center of the village, but the brisk night air helped clear her head and calm her emotions.

Emily was waiting at a table near the front door and waved to her when she came in. "Hey, how are you?" Emily asked, standing up and giving Jessica a hug.

"Sort of terrible," Jessica admitted. "But I'm really glad you called." She sat down and sighed.

Emily patted her arm reassuringly, then ordered two cappuccinos for them. "What happened? What did you fight about?"

Jessica felt her throat get tight and thought she was going to cry for a moment. Then she swallowed her tears and forced herself to reply. "We were just about to go out to the house, and Sam overheard this phone call, a job offer in Boston. I don't know why, but it really pushed his buttons. He got all worried that I'm having doubts about marrying him." Jessica shook her head. "I kept telling him I don't have doubts, but he wouldn't even listen to me."

Emily bit down on her lower lip. "Did he mention Mother?"

"That was part of it. He's the one who brought it up first, and that was when things got really bad." Jessica shook her head. "I mean, she's my mother. Of course I care what she thinks and want her at my wedding. Why can't he just understand that?"

"Goodness, that does sound bad." Emily sat back and ran her hands through her short hair, a gesture she used when she was nervous, Jessica knew. "What happened after that?" she asked.

Jessica winced and told her how they wound up postponing the wedding. "I think *he's* the one who's having doubts," she concluded. She stared into her cup, her face a mask of disbelief. "Sam acts like I have to choose— either him or Mother."

Emily didn't say anything for a long moment. "In a way, Sam is right. You do have to choose," she said finally. "He didn't make those rules. Mother did."

Jessica felt her heart fall to her knees. "You don't think she'll change her mind?"

"I wouldn't count on it. I spoke to Reverend Ben yesterday. He said he talked to her, but he didn't get very far."

"Yes, I know. He told me the same thing," Jessica replied with a heavy sigh. She didn't know what to say. It all seemed so hopeless.

"I know it's hard for you to be fighting with Mother right now," Emily said. "I know you wish she could be with you and be part of the wedding plans. But you can't let her poison your happiness, Jessica. Can't you see what Mother is doing? Divide and conquer, that's her strategy. And by postponing the wedding, you and Sam are playing right into her hands."

"We are, aren't we?" She looked up at her sister. "I'm afraid Sam doesn't want to marry me anymore," she added in a shaky voice.

"Nonsense . . . he adores you. The man is absolutely crazy about you." Emily clasped her sister's hand. "You have to go and patch this up with him. Try to figure it out together. You'll regret it if you don't. Believe me," she added in a quiet tone.

Jessica knew her sister was thinking about her own life, both the sweet and the bitter: the great happiness she stole, defying both their parents, when she eloped with Tim Sutton; and the chance she missed to raise her child by bending to their mother's iron will.

"I do believe you," Jessica said finally. "I'm just not sure I know what to do."

Emily was about to reply when Felicity Bean approached their table. Despite the low lights of the café, Felicity was unmistakable, her small, slim figure, supple and quick, matching her quick wit and bright laughter. Her long black skirt and loose, brickred top complemented her silver gray hair and looked very smart, even with the Beanery black apron on top.

"Hello, ladies. How nice to see you both," Felicity greeted them. "I was hoping to run into you, Emily," she added. "Jonathan and I were wondering how we could get some of your campaign signs. We'd like to put up a few in here."

"That would be great." Emily flipped open her Day-Timer and made a note. "I'll have someone drop some off tomorrow. And thanks. Most businesses understandably don't want to take sides."

"We think you're doing a great job. We'll proudly show our support," Felicity said.

She had a certain intensity when she spoke, energy that carried over with each word and flashed in her dark eyes. Jessica could see her sister and Felicity becoming friends—if poor Emily ever had the time to develop a new friendship, which seemed doubtful if she were reelected.

Jessica and Emily ordered refills on their cappuccinos. "And let's get a really gooey dessert," Emily suggested. "I'm on a diet, but this counts as an emergency."

"It's got to be chocolate, nothing less," Jessica agreed. "And you absolutely don't need to diet."

"Yes, I do, but sorbet just won't cut it tonight."

"Speaking of pastry . . . here comes my almost sister-in-law," Jessica murmured as Molly Willoughby entered. "Do I *have* to tell her what happened with Sam?" she asked in a hurried whisper.

"She's going to find out sooner or later," Emily pointed out, casting her a sympathetic expression. "You might as well give her your own version. Besides, she's been pretty nice to you lately."

"Yes, she has," Jessica agreed as Molly spotted her and quickly walked toward them.

"Hi, Molly. What's up?" Jessica forced her voice to sound normal, but thought that she didn't quite succeed.

"Nothing much. How are you?" Molly stood next to the table and looked them over with curiosity. "Taking a night off from working on the house?"

"Sort of," Jessica said.

"Planning a wedding is a ton of work. You need a night off once in a while," Molly said sympathetically. "By the way, I've been meaning to talk to you about that dress you picked out for the girls. I don't mean to bug you, but it's just not working out."

"Really? What's wrong?" Jessica had spent days finding those dresses and thought they would be perfect for her junior bridesmaids.

"Well, the medium is way too tight around Lauren's chest, and the large swims on her. And Jill needs hers altered, too, to the point of why even bother? And besides all that," Molly concluded, "the woman in the store says she might not even get to them in time."

"That's too bad." Jessica took a long bracing sip of her cappuccino. "But it looks like we'll have more time than we thought. Maybe I can find another dress for them," she said, not knowing how much more to add.

"More time? What do you mean? The wedding is November nineteenth. Did I get the date wrong or something?" Molly looked confused and curious.

Jessica glanced quickly at Emily, who gave her a small, encouraging nod.

"Sam and I . . . well, we were talking and decided to postpone the wedding," Jessica admitted in a rush.

"Postpone it? Until when?" Molly asked.

"Well, we're not sure yet. We just need more time."

Molly was uncharacteristically quiet for a moment, then shook her head. "Gee, that's too bad," she said finally.

Jessica didn't know what to say. Molly's sympathetic tone made her feel awful all over again. If Molly felt sorry for her, it really must be bad, she thought. But before Molly could go any further, Emily jumped in.

"Oh, it's not so bad," Emily said evenly. "Prewedding jitters. This sort of thing happens all the time. They're trying to do too much at once, I think. But they'll work it out."

Emily's calm assessment made Molly look less alarmed. Though her gaze still held a questioning look, Jessica noticed, as if she sensed there was more to this story.

"Well, sounds like you have a little time to work on those dresses, then," Molly said. She took out her car keys and hitched her handbag strap over her shoulder. "Listen, ditch mine, too, while you're at it. To tell you the truth, it makes me look like a green satin minivan."

Jessica sensed Emily trying not to laugh and avoided meeting her sister's gaze. "No problem. I'll start from scratch," Jessica promised. Molly departed with a small wave.

Jessica shook her head as she watched Molly hurry toward her car. "I'll give her twenty minutes to broadcast the news to the entire planet."

"I'd give her fifteen." Emily's blue eyes sparkled. "Don't worry. You were great, and at least you got it over with."

"Me? I hardly said a word. You're the one who smoothed it over," Jessica said gratefully.

"Oh, don't be silly. She's just wondering what really happened. Now we both deserve our treat." She slipped on her reading glasses and picked up the dessert menu. "Say what you want about Molly, but she makes a mean chocolate layer cake."

"Yes, she's a terrific cook," Jessica admitted. "It seems to run in the Morgan genes."

"And she did have a point about those bridesmaids' dresses," Emily said. She looked over the menu and grinned at Jessica. "Actually, that was something I've been meaning to mention to you myself."

"If you say so, too, I guess I *will* look for new ones." Jessica put her chin in her hand and sighed. "If there's even going to be a wedding now . . ."

"Of course there will be a wedding," Emily assured her. "I'll help you find the dresses and flowers and whatever else you need. All *you* have to do is patch things up with Sam."

Jessica met her sister's steady gaze. "Yes, I know that, Emily. I will," she promised quietly.

Emily sat there for a moment, then said, "I'll remember you in my prayers tonight. I know it looks bleak right now, but don't underestimate the Lord. He can help you work out things with Sam and even find the perfect bridesmaids' dresses."

"That would be a miracle," Jessica managed with a small smile.

Emily was right. Her courage was failing—and so was her faith. She had to hand this over to God and ask Him for help. What was it the Psalms said? "Commit thy way unto the Lord . . . and he shall bring it to pass."

That is what she would do, Jessica vowed, and silently thanked her sister for the reminder.

"MOTHER, IT'S ME. . . ." EMILY'S VOICE ECHOED THROUGH THE EMPTY rooms. "Anybody home?"

"In the kitchen," Lillian called back.

Emily followed the sound of her voice to her kitchen, where she found Lillian sitting at the table and Rachel Anderson putting on her jacket.

"Hello, Rachel. I didn't know you had a session here today," Emily said, smiling.

"Tuesday isn't our regular day," Rachel acknowledged, "but I missed an appointment last week. We're just catching up."

"Catching up? She worked me ragged," Lillian complained.

"You'll get a good night's sleep, then," Emily replied.

Rachel glanced at Lillian, and in her patient smile Emily saw the image of her father, Reverend Ben. With her rosy complexion and long brown hair pushed back from her face with two clips, Rachel seemed very young. Then she tugged her wool jacket over her rounded stomach, and Emily realized she was quite far along in her pregnancy.

"How are you feeling?" Emily asked. "Everything going well with the baby?"

"Just fine," Rachel said cheerfully as she picked up her bag. "I feel tired sometimes, but that's normal."

"When is the baby due?"

"At the end of December. I'll be taking a few months off," she added, "but I've found another physical therapist to take over my patients. She's going to call your mother and set up an appointment to meet."

Lillian's expression became markedly sour at the mention of the other therapist. Her mother didn't like change, no matter the reason, Emily knew. She probably felt deserted.

"Maybe I should meet her, too," Emily suggested.

"Yes, if you like. I'll call your office, Emily." Rachel turned to Lillian. "I'll see you Friday, Lillian. If your hip hurts later, a warm bath might help."

"Yes, thank you. I'll try that," Lillian said stiffly.

"Thank you, Rachel. Good to see you," Emily added as the young woman let herself out the back door.

When the door closed, Lillian sighed. "Thank goodness. I thought she would never go. She absolutely exhausts me."

Of course, if Rachel didn't show, her mother complained about that as well, so Emily didn't bother addressing the comment. She put the bag of groceries she was holding on the counter.

"I can't stay long, Mother. I just dropped by to say hello."

"I wasn't expecting you until this evening," Lillian remarked. "Of course, since I'm an invalid, and rarely leave the house, people do feel free to drop in whenever it's convenient for *them*." Then she went to the stove and began stirring something in a pot.

"What are you doing?"

"What does it look like? I'm heating up some soup. Occupational therapy, Rachel calls it." Lillian peered into the pot. "It smells odd for Cream of Mushroom. I wish you would try another brand, Emily."

Emily glanced at the empty can on the counter. "That's because it's Clam Chowder."

"Chowder?" Lillian picked up the empty can and stared at it. "Well, they make the labels identical. How is a person supposed to tell one kind from another? It's just ridiculous."

Emily sighed. *She can't even admit to opening the wrong can of soup. What chance do I have of persuading her to change her mind about Jessica's wedding?*

"So, why are you here so early?" Lillian persisted.

"I have to prepare for the debate tomorrow. It may go late."

"Oh, yes, the debate. That should be interesting. Ezra has offered to take me. You needn't worry."

Emily had wondered how she would get her mother to the Village Hall and still do all she had to do tomorrow night, especially since Lillian was certain to refuse a ride from Jessica.

It was nice of God to take care of these small niggling details for her when she had so much on her plate. She would have to thank Him, and Dr. Elliot as well.

The soup was ready, and her mother poured some into a china bowl on the counter. "Would you like some?" she asked.

"No, thanks. I've already had my lunch."

The table was neatly set for one with a bone china plate, a cloth napkin, and sterling flatware. Lillian maintained her standards, even when no one was watching, Emily thought with grudging admiration. Alone on a desert island, she would find a way to live like an aristocrat.

"You can bring that soup to the table for me, if you please," she told Emily as she took her seat.

Emily carried the bowl to the table, glad her mother had not attempted the task one-handed with her walking cane.

As her mother began to eat, Emily's mind returned to the reason for her visit. She had to tell her mother the news about Jessica and Sam—and somehow not let Lillian interpret it as a moral victory. Was it possible to make her mother see the hurt she was causing?

"You're very quiet today, Emily. Worried about the debate?"

"No, not at all. I'm prepared." She picked up a cracker, put it down again, then got up and poured herself a glass of water.

"What will you wear?" her mother asked with interest.

"I don't know. I haven't decided yet."

"Don't wear green or brown," her mother advised. "They make you look sallow. Navy blue is a good color for you."

"Navy blue. All right, I'll make a note of that," Emily replied distractedly.

"What about your sister? Is she coming? It doesn't look right if the candidate's own family is not out there, showing support."

"She's coming." So, here they were. No avoiding it now. "But something has happened with her and Sam." She glanced at her mother. "They've decided to postpone their wedding."

Lillian's head popped up, her eyes wide. "Postponed it? Is that a polite way of saying it's off?"

"No, it's not off. It's definitely still on," Emily assured her. "They just need a little more time to prepare."

"Oh. Something with the caterer gone awry?" Lillian turned back to her soup, looking a bit disappointed, Emily thought.

Emily was tempted not to give any further details. Her mother certainly didn't deserve them. Then she felt a pang of conscience. She couldn't be dishonest. It wasn't right.

"Jessica has been and is upset because you won't come to the wedding," Emily said. "Now Sam is concerned, too. It puts pressure on them as a couple, too much pressure."

Lillian dabbed her mouth with the edge of her napkin. "They've barely been engaged a month. I knew it wouldn't last, but this is beyond even my fondest expectations."

"Mother, please!" Emily said sharply. "Don't you have any sympathy for Jessica? She's heartbroken over this. She's miserable."

"Better for her to be miserable now than five, ten, or fifteen years from now. Wouldn't you say?"

"No, I would *not* say. She loves Sam. They belong together. But you're making it impossible for them to get a fair start."

"Me? Making it impossible?" Her mother's expression of innocence was classic, Emily thought. And totally infuriating. "I don't see that I have any part in this—change of heart. I haven't spoken to Jessica in nearly two weeks."

"And why not, do you think?" Emily asked quietly. She sat down at the table again, her hands pressed together.

"Because she doesn't care to see me," Lillian said, shrugging a thin shoulder.

"She needs to see you, Mother. She needs your help and support. Can't you put your own feelings aside and think about Jessica, about her future?" Emily implored.

"I am thinking about her future," Lillian countered. "As for putting my feelings aside for the sake of my children, *that* has been the story of my life," she stated flatly. "The only words of support I might offer to Jessica now are my congratulations for finally showing some common sense."

"There are more important things in life than common sense, Mother. Like following your heart, instead of your head. Doing something that doesn't make sense to the outside world and yet you know deep inside it's right—"

"What in the world are you babbling about, Emily?" Lillian put her spoon down carefully. "I think you've lost your mind."

Emily looked at her mother but didn't reply. She was remembering how Lillian praised her for agreeing to give up her child. For finally showing *common sense* in that matter. Now she was saying the same thing about Jessica. *Only I was in a hospital bed, a captive audience to your guidance,* Emily thought bitterly.

Abruptly she stood up and walked to the sink, turning her back to the table.

"Is something wrong? Do you feel ill?" Lillian's sharp questions cut into her thoughts.

Emily couldn't answer for a long moment. She turned on the water again and let it run, feeling the cold against her fingertips.

"No . . . I'm all right," she said finally. "I just have a lot on my mind today."

Lillian didn't reply and Emily sensed her mother watching her. "You are acting very oddly today, Emily."

I am about two seconds away from losing it, Emily realized. She willed herself to be calm, quickly sending up a prayer.

Dear God, please help me have more patience with her. Reverend Ben said I must try to forgive her. Oh, God, I really try. I just can't forget. Please help me to do better. . . .

Finally she felt calmer. She let her glass fill with water again and shut the tap. Then she returned to the table and sat by her mother again. Lillian watched her curiously.

"I need to get back to the office," Emily said.

"Yes, of course you do. I suppose I'll vegetate in front of the television for a while."

"Can I get you anything before I go?"

"No, thank you. I can take care of myself. I'm used to it by now."

She bent to kiss her mother's cheek, but Lillian turned sharply aside, so that all she managed to kiss was the air next to her downy gray hair.

"Good-bye, Mother," Emily said as she left the room. She was not surprised when Lillian did not reply.

EMILY USUALLY DIDN'T JOG LATE AT NIGHT, BUT SHE HAD MISSED HER USUAL workout routine for weeks and was determined to get back on track. Even if it meant going out for a run at nine o'clock.

Besides, I need something to calm me down, she thought as her feet pounded the pavement. She breathed deeply, focusing on the rhythm of her breath.

The night sky was clear, a deep, blue-black with pinpoints of white starlight and a silver slice of moon floating behind the treetops.

The meeting tonight with her campaign committee had been grueling, dragging on much later than she wanted. They had cornered her into a rehearsal of the debate, with Warren Oakes playing Charlie Bates, and Betty Bowman firing the questions. Emily tried to get into it, but she was tired and edgy, still upset from visiting her mother.

She was tired of feeling upset about her mother, she realized. She was forty-two years old, for pity's sake. Wasn't there some sort of statute of limitations on this?

She rounded the corner on Main Street that led back to her neighborhood, feeling winded but energized. Emerson Street was the next right, but first there was a long hill on Beacon Road, and Emily pushed herself to keep a steady pace on the incline. She suddenly heard footsteps behind her—another jogger. She glanced over her shoulder and saw Dan Forbes coming up behind her.

He smiled and fell into step beside her. "Taking your run late tonight?"

"Better late than never. . . . This last stretch is a killer," she confessed through short breaths. The muscles in her legs burned, but she pushed herself to keep pace with Dan's long strides.

Dan didn't say anything until they reached the top of the hill. "Yeah, that was bad," he agreed as they turned on to Emerson. "But I'd better get used to it."

She glanced at him. "Why's that?"

"Because I just bought that ugly little house up on the left." He pointed up ahead to the yellow cottage a few doors down from her own house. The Bowman Real Estate sign stuck in the lawn now had a "Sold" sticker slashed across the middle.

"Oh . . ." was all Emily managed. She didn't bother to deny that it was ugly.

He slowed his pace to stop in his new driveway, and she did the same.

"Welcome to the neighborhood." She smiled at him breathlessly and wiped her sleeve across her forehead.

"Thanks. It's not exactly my dream house, but it doesn't really matter. I don't plan on spending much time here."

"Oh? How's that?"

"My son, Wyatt, is finally coming back to take over the paper. With any luck, I'll be cruising through the Caribbean by Christmas."

"Oh, right . . . you told me at the party," she said, forcing a brightness in her voice she didn't really feel. "That's great. I bet you're excited."

"I love the paper, but I've put my time in. Besides, I've always wanted to take a small boat out and wander without any real plan or timetable."

"Sounds like you're planning a real adventure," she said.

"Exactly." His eyes were bright, his smile flashing white against his tan complexion.

She felt that puzzling twinge. A sense of losing out on something that could happen with him—but never would.

"Ready for the debate tomorrow?"

"Ready as I'll ever be. We rehearsed so long tonight, I feel as if I've already done it."

"I still can't imagine what you two are going to argue about," he admitted. "There just aren't any big issues. Pretty boring from a reporter's point of view."

"But pretty good from mine. Boring race favors the incumbent. Dare to be dull. That's my new campaign slogan," Emily joked.

"Come on, you know what I mean. Besides, you're the last woman I'd ever call dull."

He was laughing, but the flash in his gaze was more than friendly. She knew he was attracted to her. But he was taking off for some Caribbean island adventure, and she was signing up for another tour of duty as mayor, so what was the point in even thinking about it?

"Want to see my house? It's not officially mine until the closing. But I know where the key is hidden, and I know no one will mind."

She was tempted. But it was late and she had a big day tomorrow. And on top of that, she didn't know that it would make her feel any better to spend more time with him.

"I'd like to, but I really ought to get home."

"Sure, you need to rest up for the debate. You never know about Charlie. He might surprise you."

"If Charlie surprised me . . . it *would* be a surprise." Emily knew she wasn't exactly making sense, but when she met Dan's gaze he seemed to get it perfectly.

"Yeah . . . me, too," he agreed with a soft laugh. "See you tomorrow," he said with a wave.

"So long, Dan. Welcome again to the neighborhood." She waved back and turned to walk up the street to her house.

Dan Forbes, her new neighbor? Now, that was a surprise. . . .

CHAPTER EIGHT

*M*Y QUESTION IS FOR MR. BATES." PHYLLIS WAG-
ner, a member of the board of education, leaned
toward the microphone. "There's been some talk about passing
a law to keep skateboards and these awful scooters off Main
Street. Would you be in favor of that ordinance?"

Charlie cleared his throat, and took a sip of water. "I
believe all the children in this town should have clean, safe
facilities for recreation. And those facilities should be properly
maintained. I think that goes without saying. . . ."

If it goes without saying, then why say it? Emily countered
silently as her opponent nattered on.

The audience shifted restlessly, looking as wearied by the
proceedings as she felt. Only her mother, who sat beside Dr.
Elliot in the first row, leaned forward eagerly, following every

word. She carefully avoided meeting Emily's eye, however. Emily knew that no matter how angry her mother was, she had come both because she felt it was her duty and because she wanted to see Emily reelected. Lillian Warwick liked having a daughter who was mayor.

". . . but we cannot stand by while innocent pedestrians, going about their business, shopping in our stores . . ."

Eating at my diner, Emily filled in.

Her thoughts drifted. Scanning the audience, she spotted Digger and Grace Hegman sitting alongside Harry Reilly. Sam was not with them, she noticed, nor was he sitting with Jessica, who was a few rows back with her friend from work, Suzanne Foster. Not a good sign.

Dan Forbes sat in the last row, jotting furiously in his notebook, though Emily couldn't imagine why. "Candidates Bore Voters into a Stupor" could be tomorrow's headline. The hall had been filled at the start, but now she saw members of the audience discreetly drifting to the exits.

"You have thirty seconds to conclude, Mr. Bates," the moderator warned.

"What? Oh, right." Charlie looked annoyed at being interrupted, and seemed to lose his train of thought. "Well, we can't let these wild kids on scooters ruin our fair streets and create a safety hazard!" he nearly shouted, rushing to get it all out. "I'm surprised there hasn't been a serious accident, and—"

"That's time, Mr. Bates," the moderator cut in.

"—and some big lawsuit leveled against the town on account of it. Something ought to be done," he concluded, turning and glaring at Emily.

As if I've been out on my scooter, leading the pack, she thought, struggling to keep a controlled expression.

"Mayor Warwick, your turn to address the question."

Emily stood up very straight and looked out at the audience.

"The problem is annoying and perhaps, potentially dangerous," she acknowledged. "But I don't believe every bothersome situation should be addressed by writing a new law. Time and resources here in Village Hall are limited and must be used efficiently. I have confidence that the citizens can address and correct such issues on their own, with a minimum of bureaucratic intervention."

"There is time for one more question," the moderator noted.

At least it will be over soon, Emily thought with relief. The clock on the back wall read three minutes to nine.

Art Hecht, who owned a large insurance agency, stepped up to the microphone. Knowing he was one of Charlie's supporters, Emily steeled herself for a tough question.

"Mayor Warwick, I've heard on good authority that the new owner of the Cranberry Cottages, Luke McAllister, plans to donate the property to an organization that will set up a center for troubled teenagers there. Would you support that type of institution in our village? And if you oppose it, what will you do to keep it out?"

Emily was so shocked by the question and its ramifications that, for a moment, she couldn't react. *Set up, like a bowling pin,* she thought, catching Charlie's smug expression. *A clean strike, no spare.*

She was aware of the audience suddenly looking alert, and the buzz of murmuring voices filling the room.

"Excuse me, Mr. Hecht? I'm not sure I understood the question."

"Of course she understood the question," Charlie huffed. "She's just buying time. She doesn't know what's going on under her nose, that's the problem."

"You'll have your turn to respond, Mr. Bates," the moderator told him.

As Art Hecht repeated his question, Emily took a deep breath.

"I don't know who your sources are, but this is the first I've heard of the project," she confessed, her voice aiming at an even, reasonable tone. "But assuming it is true—"

"Of course it's true," Charlie interrupted her. "I'll bet this pot has been simmering for weeks. I'll bet Elliot knew all about it when he made the sale."

"How dare you? That is not true!" Dr. Elliot rose to his feet to contradict Charlie.

"Dr. Elliot and Mr. Bates, no more interruptions, please," the moderator warned.

"Assuming it is true," Emily continued, "what are the facts? Who would be running the facility? Who would be serviced by it? How many youngsters and counselors would be in residence?"

She paused, gauging the audience's reaction. She could see her reply was making sense to them. "Without knowing what this project entails, and what the potential impact would be on our community, I think it would be hasty and irresponsible to take any position."

"Mr. Bates, you have three minutes," the moderator said.

Charlie paused and smoothed his tie. *His dirty trick worked, and now he's basking in his moment,* Emily thought.

"We have a nice town here. More than nice, a really perfect place to live. Clean, quiet, no crime. No problems. Why invite trouble?" Charlie asked his audience.

"As it happens, I do have the full story on this situation. Even though the *present* mayor does not," he said smugly. "Like Hecht said, McAllister plans to donate the land to an outfit that helps troubled kids. I have nothing against troubled kids," he added. "But do they need to bring their troubles up here? No, sir. Do I need to study and discuss and wring my hands, wondering what to do about it? No, sir," he repeated.

"Of course, why let the facts get in the way?" Emily cut in sharply.

Charlie didn't miss a rhetorical beat. "I don't call that *irresponsible,* Mayor. It's just knowing what's what. Living in the real world," he said, glancing back at the audience. "My granddad Clifford Bates always said, 'Actions speak louder than words.' If elected mayor, I won't chitchat you to death. I'll take action and protect our town. You can count on it."

All right. Chalk one up for Charlie. And his granddad, she thought as she watched the audience's nods of approval.

"That's all the time we have," the moderator said. "Thank you, Mayor Warwick. Thank you, Mr. Bates."

Applause sounded briefly as Emily and Charlie shook hands. Charlie carefully avoided meeting her eye, she noticed, then quickly turned to greet his family.

Dressed in their Sunday best, Lucy and Charlie's two boys came up to congratulate him, followed by a crowd of his supporters. Charlie beamed, pumping hands, as if he had already won. Emily had underestimated him. He had more talent for politics—of a certain kind—than she had imagined.

Emily turned to find Betty, Warren, Harriet, and the rest of her camp circling her. Protectively, she thought, and fearfully, too.

"He got some attention at the end with that cheap trick, but he won't win on it," Betty said, her confident manner and smile giving Emily a boost.

"We didn't hear a word about that center," Warren whispered.

"Must have been Ray Farley down in permits," Harriet offered. "He has the information, and he's one of Charlie's buddies."

"We need to find out what this is all about, first thing tomorrow," Emily said. "It could be nothing—or it could be a real problem for us."

They agreed that the campaign committee would have another strategy meeting Saturday afternoon in Emily's office. Meanwhile, Betty had invited Emily's group over to her house for coffee and the recap. Emily wasn't looking forward to it now, but, of course, she had to attend.

"I'll be along in a few minutes," she promised as her group dispersed and headed out to meet at Betty's. "I just need to get my things."

Relieved to have a few moments alone, Emily gathered up her notes and briefcase. She felt deflated and even embarrassed. She had been made to look a fool in front of the entire town—or enough people for it to matter.

The hall was nearly empty. Her mother and Dr. Elliot had disappeared, but Jessica lingered, waiting for her.

"Emily, you were great," Jessica said a bit too forcefully as she walked up and gave Emily a hug.

"Thanks, but how bad was it, really? Be honest now."

Jessica's gaze was sympathetic. "Anyone could see that was a setup. Charlie was just trying to trip you up."

"And succeeded admirably, I'd say."

"Okay, you looked a little off balance for a minute or two. But you reacted quickly and your answer sounded fine. Very reasonable," Jessica added. "Charlie sounded hysterical. You'd think barbarians were invading, and you refused to close the gates."

"Spoken like a true sister," Emily replied with a small smile.

"Want to go somewhere and talk?"

Emily was touched by her offer. "I have to go to Betty's. They're all waiting for me—for the debriefing. It will be a lot of campaign talk, but I'm sure you'd be welcome."

"No, thanks. I'll just go home, I guess."

"What about Sam? Are you working things out?"

"We're trying," Jessica replied slowly. "I thought he might be here tonight. I guess he's working at the house."

Emily thought it was a bad sign that Jessica didn't know.

They really love each other, God. Please help them find their way, she prayed quickly. She suddenly realized if it didn't work out for her sister and Sam, her own heart would be broken as well. Far more in fact, than if she lost this election.

EMILY SET OUT A BIT LATER THAN USUAL FOR HER OFFICE THE NEXT MORNing. After the debate and the get-together at Betty's house, she had had a hard time waking up.

Now, rushing to work, she craved coffee badly. The line at the Beanery looked too long, and she didn't dare go into the Clam Box. She was sure that the last inning of the debate, with its surprise upset, would be the only conversation there.

As soon as she reached her office, she called the diner for a takeout order, then paged through the *Messenger* while she waited. Her eyes jumped to the headline, "Surprise Ending at Candidates' Debate," and she forced herself to skim the article.

The coverage was even-handed, as she'd come to expect of Dan's reporting, but apparently, even Dan didn't know anything about Luke McAllister's plans. *If Luke even has such plans,* Emily reminded herself.

No one at the gathering last night had any solid facts to offer, either—just hearsay, affirming that they had indeed heard a rumor or two. Well, why hadn't anyone mentioned it to her? she wondered. But finger-pointing was never the answer. She just had to find out the facts and go on from there.

Emily looked up from the newspaper and saw Sara Franklin in the doorway. "Coffee, at last. I said two cups, right?"

"You got it," Sara promised, handing her the bag.

Sara watched as Emily opened the first cup and took a long sip. "I'm sorry about last night—what happened at the debate, I mean."

"Well, thanks, but maybe I deserved it. I have been a little complacent about Charlie. Last night was my wake-up call, I suppose, though I'm still not sure what I could have done to counter it. I would have needed a mind reader on my staff to keep up with his information about Luke McAllister."

"Well, I knew," Sara admitted quietly. "Luke told me about his plans the other day. I should have warned you. But I didn't think it would be such a big deal. I never thought Charlie would find out. I'm really sorry," she said again.

"Sara, please, it wasn't your fault at all. How could you ever guess that Charlie would do that?" When Sara didn't look convinced, she added, "Even if you'd told me, Charlie still would have used it to get everyone stirred up and scared. That's his whole agenda."

"He didn't have to try very hard, either, did he?"

Emily leaned back and took another long sip of coffee. "The audience may have reacted to his tactics last night, but in the long run the people of Cape Light will do the right thing. It's just that they're not used to change. But you'll see—the people here are good at heart. If Luke's project is a worthy one, they'll give it a chance."

Sara's expression relaxed a little. "So how will you show your support for Luke's program?" she asked. "Write a letter to the *Messenger* or something?"

Emily took out her second cup of coffee and carefully removed the lid. She'd run smack up against Sara's idealism and naïveté again, like a cool, hard wall.

"If only it were that easy," she said finally.

Sara looked confused. "But you do support the project, don't you?"

"From what I've heard so far, it sounds very worthy." Emily put on her reading glasses and grabbed a handful of mail from the in-box. "The problem is, I really don't know much about it. Nobody seems to. Do you?"

Emily hadn't meant to challenge her. She was really only curious. But she could see from Sara's expression that her question had pushed Sara back a step.

"Um . . . no, not really," Sara admitted. "So what are you going to do?"

"Get the facts, for starters."

"What facts do you need?" Sara asked impatiently. "There are a lot of kids out there who need a break. Isn't that obvious?"

"Yes, of course," Emily said. "But I have to weigh the information carefully, and then find the right way to present it to the town. We have to give people time to get used to the idea."

"Does that mean you'll support it?" Sara asked bluntly.

Emily looked into Sara's measuring blue gaze, a gaze so very much like her own that for a moment, the resemblance gave her chills. "I'm not sure," she answered honestly. "Because of the election, I've got to be careful of what I say and how I say it."

Sara frowned. "Maybe you don't. I think plenty of people would support the center."

"I certainly hope and believe that's true," Emily said. "All I'm saying is that the timing is delicate. I've got to find out what the facts are and then proceed carefully."

Sara was silent for a moment. Then she replied, "That's not really an answer."

"Well, maybe not, but—" Emily started, but she cut her protest short. She could see that Sara was no longer listening. *And I've already discovered that the whistling sound is just the air rushing by as I fall off my pedestal. Second time this week, in fact.*

"You've made some good points, Sara, and I'm going to think about what you've said," Emily promised. "Honestly, I will."

She doesn't believe me, Emily realized, reading Sara's closed expression.

Emily picked up her wallet and held out some bills. "Here's the money for the coffee. Don't bother about the change."

"Thanks." Sara took the bills and stuck them in her jacket pocket. "Oh, I nearly forgot. I have that letter you asked me to look at." She reached back into her pocket and pulled out a sheaf of papers, folded in half.

Emily took it and laid it on her desk. "How did it go?"

"All right." Sara shrugged. "I made a few changes. To make the language stronger, more direct," she said curtly.

"Sounds good. Would you like to work on something else? I have to give a speech to the Rotary Club next week. I could use some help with that. I've only got a rough draft so far—"

"Uh, no, I don't think I can," Sara cut in. "I'm pretty busy right now with my own writing and helping Lucy with a paper for her English lit class."

"Oh, I see." Emily nodded and blinked. *Of course, she doesn't want to do more. I've disappointed her.* "Well, thanks for looking at the letter. I'll let you know if it's accepted."

Sara turned to leave, jamming her hands in her jacket pockets. "See you around, I guess."

"Yes, I'll see you, Sara," Emily echoed, a hopeful note in her voice.

She watched the young woman go, wanting to call her back, to say something that would redeem her image in Sara's eyes. But for the life of her, she couldn't think of what those words might be.

Lord, why did you pick me to educate this girl in the harsher realities? Or maybe I have it all mixed up? Maybe you sent her here to teach me something? she wondered as she tried to erase Sara's crushed expression from her mind's eye.

Emily sighed out loud as she once again attacked her mail.

DESPITE THE DINER BEING BUSY ALL DAY, SARA'S THOUGHTS KEPT RETURN-ing to Emily—possibly because Charlie gloated nonstop about pulling the rug out from under his opponent. "Did you see her face when Art Hecht asked the question? Did you see?" Charlie asked anyone who would listen. Only the sight of Lucy rolling her eyes at her husband's pomposity helped a bit, but then Sara's spirits would spiral down again.

Until today Emily had always seemed so straightforward, so sincere, and Sara had been baffled by the question of how and why Emily had given her up. Now, as Sara angrily dumped a load of dirty dishes in a rubber tub, she began to think it wasn't so mysterious, after all.

When pushed into a corner, Emily Warwick takes the easy way out. And if she runs scared from this situation, imagine what she will do when I tell her who I really am.

"Sara, honey? Are you feeling all right?" Lucy touched her shoulder. "You don't look very well," she said, looking her over with a mother's prac-ticed eye.

"I'm all right," Sara replied, forcing a smile.

"You look pale, sort of green around the gills. No offense," Lucy added hastily.

"I'm just tired," Sara said, searching for an excuse.

"Why don't you leave early? Go home and have a nice nap. It's okay. I'll tell Charlie it must have been something you ate."

"Don't say *that.*"

Lucy laughed. "Of course I wouldn't say that—even though it's probably true," she added, raising one eyebrow.

Charlie's food, for once, was not the cause of her indisposition, Sara knew. But she couldn't tell Lucy the real reason, much as she wanted to.

"Okay, I guess I'll go, then. Thanks." Sara grabbed her jacket and knapsack, then slipped out of the diner.

It felt good to leave work early, she realized as she drove home. Sometimes the Clam Box got to her—the noise, the smells, the constant rushing, and Charlie being his obnoxious self.

Inside her cottage she thought about the nap Lucy had advised. She was tired but felt too stirred up to sleep, and she had a terrible headache.

She took two aspirin, then sat on her bed with her journal in her lap. She flipped open the book to a clean page, marked the date on top, and began to write.

Why did I ever try to get to know Emily? I should have told her who I was before the election. Why did I wait? That was my first mistake. Now everything feels worse.

I don't know what to think about her anymore. She's not the person I thought she was. I thought she would stand up for Luke's project, but she's waffling, scared to come out and say that Charlie's wrong. It's pathetic. I thought she had more courage than that. Is that how she acted when she had to decide whether to keep me? She just handed me over without a fight?

*I've got to leave Cape Light. Why stick around? This isn't going
to work out. I can't tell her. She won't know how to handle it, and
she'll hate me. There's no point. . . .*

Sara felt so sad all of a sudden, she couldn't write anymore. She put the
journal aside, wiping away tears with her fingertips. She went into the living room, pulled her canvas duffel bag out of the closet, and started tossing
in books, papers, and the folded laundry that sat on her living room chair.

She packed haphazardly, grabbing anything in sight. The phone rang,
startling her. She felt disoriented as she stumbled toward the kitchen to
answer it.

"Sara? Hi, honey. It's Mom."

The sound of her mother's voice made Sara feel like crying again, but
she forced back the tears. "Hi, Mom. What's up?"

"Oh, nothing much. Just wanted to say hello." Her mother sounded
concerned, Sara thought, but as usual was trying to mask it with a cheerful
tone. "Did you get our letter?" Laura Franklin asked.

"Yes, I got it last week," Sara replied. But she had read it so quickly she
wasn't sure now what it said.

"Well, what do you think about our idea of coming up to Cape Light?
Your father and I always wanted to see New England in the fall. We could
drive up over the weekend, take in the foliage, and stop to see you. No big
deal," her mother added quickly. "We don't even have to stay the night
with you. We'll find some inn or something. We thought it would be
fun. . . ."

*Sure, no big deal. You're just going to drive for about sixteen hours to take
me out to lunch and look at the leaves. Just for fun,* she replied silently. *Good
one, Mom.*

"I'm all right," Sara assured her automatically. "You don't have to do
that, really."

She heard her mother swallow hard. Sara knew she was hesitating, afraid to say the wrong thing. Her mother taught high school and had always been easy to talk to. But Sara's need to confront her birth mother had pushed her mom's understanding to its limits. Although her mother tried hard to be supportive, Sara could sense her struggling. Her dad struggled, too, but avoided talking to her directly about it. In a way, that was easier.

"We really want to come, Sara. We don't even have to meet you in Cape Light—if that would make you uncomfortable," her mother added.

Sara could tell that her mother was trying to be considerate—thinking Sara might be worried they would all run into Emily somewhere and Sara would be freaked out. Well, she would be, Sara realized.

"I don't know, Mom. It seems like a long drive for a weekend," Sara said, avoiding the real issue.

Through the small glass window on her door, Sara saw Luke, stacking firewood on her doorstep. She turned away and focused on her conversation with her mother.

"We miss you, Sara."

"I miss you, too," Sara said honestly. She thought she had never missed her mother so much as she did at that very moment. Still, her need to confront and connect with Emily tugged at her. But maybe that need would never be satisfied. Maybe that confrontation would never take place, she realized.

The half-packed duffel bag caught her eye, and she felt the impulse to return home grow stronger.

"You don't have to worry so much. I might be coming home soon," she added.

"Really?" her mother said hopefully. "Why didn't you just say so? When did that happen?"

Sara heard Luke drop some more wood on her top step and saw his dark head right next to the door window.

"Oh, I don't know. I think I'm just tired of this place. I'm starting to think that it wasn't worth the bother."

"But I thought you found her and you know who she is. . . ." Her mother sounded surprised, but Sara wasn't ready yet to explain.

"I really can't get into it now," Sara said slowly. She turned her back to the door. "But I'll call you soon. As soon as I know when I'm coming back."

"Okay, honey." Her mother sounded as if she wanted to talk longer, but was satisfied to hear Sara was coming home. "I love you."

"I love you, too," Sara said. "Tell Dad I said the same," she added. Her mother said good-bye and hung up.

Sara turned and saw Luke wave at her through the window. She put the phone down, walked to the door, and pulled it open.

"Just stopped by to bring you some wood."

Sara glanced at the replenished woodpile. "Yes, I see. Thanks."

"I heard it was going to get colder. There's a front moving down from Canada," he added.

"I hadn't heard that." The way he was looking at her made her feel self-conscious. What did he really want?

"But not down in Maryland, I guess," he added, surprising her. He glanced over her shoulder at the duffel on the couch. "It will be a lot warmer down there, right?"

Sara met his gaze, feeling confused, then caught. He must have overheard her phone conversation, she realized. How long had he been listening?

When she didn't say anything right away, he added, "I'm sorry, but I was standing right near the door. I couldn't help hearing what you said."

"And you did tell me once you liked eavesdropping," she reminded him.

He shrugged. "Cop training, remember?"

She didn't know what to say for a moment. What was the use of denying it? "Yeah, well, I think I am going back."

"Your boyfriend finally persuaded you?"

"Boyfriend?" She gave him a look. "That was my mother."

"Oh." He looked embarrassed for a moment, then frowned, his thick eyebrows drawn together. "Did something happen at home?"

"No, everything's okay. I told you the other day, I had no idea how long I'd stay here."

"Yeah, you did. But this seems sort of sudden. Too sudden, I'd say."

His steady glance challenged her to deny it, and she had the urge to tell him everything. She had a feeling he, of all the people in this town, would understand. But finally she turned away and hugged her arms against the chilly air outside.

"I really wish I could tell you what it is. But I can't," she said again.

"I already told you, I don't have to know."

She waited a moment, then looked up at him. "Do you want to come in? I'm getting cold out here."

He followed her into the cottage, and she shut the door. She turned to see him staring at the duffel on the couch. He looked away and unbuttoned his jacket but didn't sit down.

"Look, you don't have to tell me anything that you don't want to. That's okay." He shrugged. "I'm just not sure you ought to take off in such a rush. Maybe you ought to think it over. Sleep on it," he suggested.

She leaned against the counter and pushed a strand of dark hair off her cheek. "Maybe if I think about it too much, I won't go," she replied.

"Well, maybe you shouldn't, then."

"What if I'm not running away? What if I've just . . . had enough?"

"Maybe you have," he agreed. "Or maybe you're just mad at something and *think* you've had enough." He moved toward her, his expression stone-serious. "I just get this feeling that whatever you came up here for is important to you. Very important. And it isn't finished yet."

She nodded and looked down at her hands. "You got that right."

"Besides, I don't want you to go, Sara." He moved closer. "I want you to stay."

A silence fell between them, and Sara felt frozen, watching his expression turn even more intense. She felt his strong hand cup her cheek, his palm rough and calloused, and then the pressure of his mouth as he kissed her, hard and brief. She felt herself leaning toward him, holding his shoulder for support as she suddenly kissed him back, surprising herself.

His hand drifted lightly through her long hair, then he pulled away. He briefly met her gaze and stepped back.

She felt stunned, couldn't speak.

"It's your call. Totally. I know that." He lifted his hands in a gesture of surrender and stepped toward the door. "Just let me know what happens, okay?"

She knew what he really meant was, please don't leave without saying good-bye. The note of need and caring in his voice touched her.

"Yes. I will."

"Okay, then. Good night." He walked out and shut the door.

Sara remained standing by the counter, as if frozen in place. The duffel, still open on the couch, odds and ends spilling out in all directions, looked ridiculous to her now. The act of someone in a state of sheer panic. Or a child having a tantrum.

Luke had been right. She felt angry and frustrated. But maybe she had to stick it out here. She had come to confront Emily, and it wasn't finished. She would at least sleep on it.

She touched her lips, remembering how he kissed her—and how she kissed him back.

Something was happening between them, even if she wasn't ready for it. They were getting involved. They were already involved.

She had to face that now, too.

JESSICA WALKED UP THE PATH TO HER MOTHER'S HOUSE WITH A POT OF mums in each hand. Halfway to the porch, she stopped and nearly turned around. Then she saw the curtain in the bay window stir. Too late. She'd already been spotted. Besides, she knew this visit was something she had to do if she were ever going to work things out with Sam.

Her mother came to the door and opened it, before Jessica even rang the doorbell. "Hello, Mother." Jessica forced a bright, natural note to her voice, ignoring entirely that they hadn't spoken now for weeks. "I picked up some mums for you. I thought I'd freshen up the planters."

Her mother gave the flowers a brief, dismissive glance. "Leave them out here on the porch," she said curtly.

Jessica set the flowerpots down near the door and followed her mother into the shadowy house. She took off her coat and hung it on the antique coat tree.

"Come into the living room," Lillian directed, using her cane to walk ahead at a slow but steady pace.

Lillian sat on her favorite chair, a high-backed armchair upholstered in dark green velvet. It often reminded Jessica of a throne, and never more than at that moment.

Jessica took a seat across from her mother on the sofa.

"I've barely spoken to you in weeks and suddenly here you are, delivering flowers, with no explanation and no word of apology," Lillian began. "What am I supposed to do now? Clap my hands and exclaim with delight?"

"Mother, I've tried to speak to you in church twice now, and both times you totally ignored me," Jessica reminded her.

"You already know why I wouldn't speak to you, Jessica. I've never made any secret of my feelings for Sam Morgan."

"But, Mother, we're engaged. We're going to be married."

"I heard that the wedding was off. The novelty had finally worn thin, I assumed. Is it on again?"

"It was never off, Mother. It's only been postponed."

"That's right, postponed. Indefinitely, I hope."

"No, not indefinitely," Jessica insisted, though in her heart she feared that was exactly what might happen.

"Mother, please listen," Jessica beseeched her, shifting to the very edge of her seat. "I know Sam is not the man you had in mind for me. He's not the man I thought I'd marry, either," she admitted. "But he's the one I fell in love with. We love each other very, very much. He's a good man, a good person, and I know we'll be happy together. I just wish you would give him a chance."

There, she had said it. She had thought long and hard about what to say and had even prayed about it. Would the words find their mark in her mother's mind and heart? Would they sway her just the tiniest bit? Jessica watched her mother's face, searching for some flicker of sympathy or understanding.

Lillian cleared her throat with a harsh, rattling sound. "You don't know the first thing about love. Or what it takes to make a marriage work," she said. "I'm certain that Sam Morgan will make you very unhappy. Clearly, he's already begun, to hear Emily tell it—"

"Emily? What do you mean?" Jessica cut in. Then she pulled back, realizing it was just one of her mother's typical tactics, trying to distract her and pit her daughters against each other. "I doubt Emily has ever said one negative word about Sam to you."

"She tells me you're miserable, broken-hearted, not happy anymore with your muscle man. The wedding is off and everyone is in an uproar."

"I'm unhappy because you won't accept Sam. You refused to come to our engagement party. You refuse to come to our wedding. You won't even give him a chance—"

"A chance to keep you down, you mean? To chain you to this small town, limiting your aspirations and your ambitions? Squandering your talent and intelligence? Is that the chance you want me to give him?" her mother asked. "Over my dead body."

Jessica sat back, feeling as if the wind had been knocked out of her. She fought for control, unable to think of anything to say to her mother that was even halfway civil.

Please, Lord, please give me patience, she prayed.

"When will you believe me?" Lillian demanded. "You're making a terrible mistake, and you'll live to regret it."

Jessica came to her feet. She had heard enough. Why had she ever thought she could come here and persuade her mother of anything? The hope now seemed absurd.

"You already told me that, Mother, weeks ago. I guess that's all we have to say to each other."

As she picked up her purse, she glanced down at the coffee table and saw some old photographs. It looked as if her mother were making an album. An image of her father caught her eye, young and handsome, his eyes sparkling from beneath the shadow of a dark fedora, the brim turned at a jaunty angle.

What did her mother feel now, looking at that picture? Regrets for having married him—or no regrets at all because she followed her heart?

"It's not the same at all as when you married Father," Jessica said, slipping the strap of her purse over her shoulder. "Just because your family disapproved and then things turned out badly for you, doesn't mean I shouldn't marry Sam. You, of all people, should understand what I'm going through."

"I beg your pardon?" Her mother grabbed her cane, her hand shaking, and pushed herself up out of her chair.

"You heard what I said," Jessica replied quietly.

"You're right, there is no comparison. Your father had means and position when I married him. Oliver Warwick was a gentleman," Lillian stated. "Now please go and take those flowers with you. I've no need for them. Or any more of this ridiculous conversation."

Jessica stared at her mother long and hard, but couldn't muster another word. Her vision blurry from unshed tears, she quickly walked out of the house. On the porch she bent to retrieve the flowerpots, then changed her mind. Let her mother keep them, a reminder that at least she, Jessica, had tried.

She hurried down the walk, feeling through her purse for her car keys. Was her mother right? Would she and Sam end up unhappy together, after all? Was she making the biggest mistake of her life? She thought of the job offer and their argument. He had felt so threatened, so angry. Jessica had felt worlds apart from him then. Would the differences between them eventually be too much to bridge, just as her mother predicted?

Jessica yanked open her car door and pushed the key in the ignition. No, she couldn't even think such a thing. Her mother's words were toxic, souring her happiness, shaking that sure solid feeling she had about Sam deep inside.

I have to get away from here right now, Jessica thought, putting the car in gear. *And I don't know if I'll ever come back.*

EMILY WAS WORKING ON THE DRAFT OF HER SPEECH FOR THE ROTARY CLUB when the phone rang, shattering the silence in her office and throughout the empty Village Hall. She kept her eyes on the computer screen, listening for the caller's voice as her answering machine picked up. Who would be calling her office at half past ten on a Thursday night?

The beep sounded, then a deep, familiar voice came on the line. "Hi, Emily, it's Dan Forbes—"

Emily grabbed the receiver. "Hello, Dan. I'm still here."

"I thought you might be," he said with a laugh.

"Why is that?" She tossed her glasses on her desk and leaned back in her chair.

"Because you're the only person in town who keeps longer hours than me."

"That's debatable," she replied, then nearly bit her tongue at her choice of words.

"Speaking of which, let me offer my sympathies."

"Well, thanks, but don't send the funeral wreath quite yet. There's plenty of campaign left."

Did she sound defensive? She didn't mean to. But she hated that Dan, of all people, was feeling sorry for her. Last night must have been even worse than she thought.

"It ain't over till it's over. Everyone knows that. And off the record, you were bushwhacked." He sounded morally outraged on her behalf, reminding Emily again of how much she liked him.

"Off the record, thanks, I was," Emily replied.

"Charlie's sly. I think you might have underestimated him."

"Agreed," she said with a sigh. "He'll get a lot of mileage out of this. He may even ride this issue right in to the finish line. It's the one he's been waiting for."

"Exactly, so get ready for a fight." Dan's voice was reassuring somehow. She pictured the hard, clean lines of his profile and his clear, blue eyes shining at her the other night.

Emily sat up straight in her chair, both shoeless feet on the floor again. "I've been painted into a corner, don't you think?" she asked quietly.

"Well, yes, you have." He hesitated, and she felt the easy flow of their banter suddenly melt away. "Does that mean you *aren't* going to support Luke's project?"

She bit down on her lower lip. "Is this the paper asking—or just you?"

"Just me."

"It's complicated. I can't just hand Charlie the election. He set me up. You said it yourself."

"I said you were in for a fight. I never thought you were going to sidestep. But it's a viable strategy, I suppose."

She didn't like his tone now, distant and analytical. That subtle note of warmth was gone. She felt the chill as if someone had opened a window.

"I never said sidestep," she corrected him.

"What are you saying, then?"

"I have to figure this out, weigh the options. I can't do Luke McAllister's project any good if I'm sitting in my little house on Emerson Street and Charlie Bates is sitting here."

"Well said. Too bad this is off the record. That would have made a nice quote."

His cool comment made her even madder. Then she stopped herself. It did no good getting mad at Dan—or even Sara for that matter—when the one she was angry with was herself.

"You're disappointed in me. I've fallen off my pedestal." She shook her head. "I've got to stop doing that. I could break a collarbone or something," she murmured to herself.

"Look, Emily, I didn't mean to be hard on you. I just assumed that you would come out in support of the project."

"Dan, Charlie blindsided me. How could I support Luke's project before I had any of the facts?"

"I don't know," he admitted. "It just seemed that for the first time ever you were afraid to buck Charlie. But it's your campaign. You know how you need to play it."

Even his apology nettled her. She didn't like him seeing her as a spineless politician. *Even if I am acting like one,* she thought. "Thank you," she said dryly. "I appreciate that."

Dan didn't reply for a moment, and she thought he was getting ready to say good-bye.

"Listen, before I hang up, I really just called about that letter you sent over today, on the firehouse substation."

"Oh, right." She'd nearly forgotten. "So what do you think?"

"Not bad." High praise, she knew, coming from him.

"Someone helped polish up the writing. But the ideas were all mine, of course," she added hastily, as if suddenly everything she did was suspect.

"Of course. I just wanted to tell you it will be in tomorrow's edition. That's all."

"Thanks. I'll look for it."

I should tell Sara, Emily thought, but she had a feeling that Sara would not be eager to hear from her now.

"Emily, are you still there?"

"Oh . . . sorry, I got distracted for a moment."

"You must be tired. You ought to go home and get some rest. Return to fight another day," Dan advised.

"Or, in my case, return to sidestep?"

"Hey, I just report the news. I don't tell people like you how to make it."

"Is there someone I *can* call?" she asked.

He laughed, then his voice became more serious. "I think you're already getting enough advice. Maybe you ought to have a long talk with yourself."

She didn't know how to answer for a moment. "I'll make a note on my schedule. Good night, Dan. Good to talk to you."

"Good to talk to you, Emily. As always."

She hung up the phone, her emotions churning. Sara and Dan were both disappointed in her. *Maybe I'm just not the person I think I am—and want others to think I am,* she thought woefully.

Maybe Dan was right. Maybe she had to look inside herself for answers now, but when she did, she felt as if there was nothing there to see.

On impulse, Emily bent her head over her desk, closed her eyes, and folded her hands in prayer. *What should I do, Lord? I'm so confused. I've lost Sara's respect, and even Dan isn't thinking well of me tonight. Have I changed so much—replaced my moral compass with a popularity meter? Please help me find the way out of this dilemma, Lord. . . .*

Emily remained with her head bowed, trying to hear a clear voice, an answer that would ring true—the voice of the Spirit, speaking inside her.

But she didn't hear any answer, only the clatter of her own anxiety, guilt, and fear. A hollow, empty sound.

Finally she pulled herself up, slipped on her shoes, and prepared to go. She felt sad and lonely, as if even God were disappointed with her tonight.

CHAPTER NINE

*M*cALLISTER'S APPLIED FOR PERMITS. HE BROUGHT in the paperwork this morning," Harriet reported in a rush. She moved closer to Emily, sitting on the edge of her chair. "What do you want to do?" she asked in a conspiratorial whisper.

"What do I normally do about building permits, Harriet?" Emily frowned, shaking off a feeling she didn't like. "If everything's in order, the permits go through. I never get involved in it."

"Well, you could if you wanted to." Harriet sat back in her seat. "There are things the mayor can do to slow down the application, to stop it altogether—all perfectly within your rights."

Harriet gave her a knowing look. She had worked in the

Village Hall a long time. She knew all the tricks, and Emily knew what she was hinting at. The insinuation upset her.

"Within my rights as mayor, maybe, but not exactly aboveboard. That's not my style," Emily said, getting up from her desk. "I thought you knew that by now."

Harriet looked flustered. "I didn't mean to infer that you would ever do anything unethical, Emily. I never meant that at all. But you have more authority in this situation than you think," Harriet reminded her.

"More than I want to use, you mean," Emily said, slipping on her suede jacket. "Or misuse, actually."

Harriet pursed her lips and didn't reply.

"I'm going out. Do you want anything?" Emily asked.

Harriet shook her head. "No, thanks."

"Okay, see you later." Emily turned to go. As she left the Village Hall and stepped out into the crisp fall air and bright sunshine on Main Street, she knew that the only thing that Harriet and her other supporters wanted from her now was to do whatever was necessary to win the election.

It was early for lunch, but Emily found herself drawn to the Clam Box. Since the debate, she had avoided the place. But she suddenly felt the impulse to show Charlie she wasn't hiding from him. *Besides, if I'm sitting right there, he'll have to stop bragging for five minutes about how he embarrassed me.*

She walked in and took a seat in a booth near the front window. The place was quiet. She looked around for Sara, then caught sight of her in the back. Sara glanced over for an instant, then walked into the kitchen before Emily could say hello.

Emily wondered if she had been snubbed. Or was Sara just busy? *I'll try to say hello later,* she thought.

Charlie ambled out from the kitchen, carrying a huge can of tomato sauce. He dropped it on the counter with a grunt, and then spotted her. His jaw dropped a notch and Emily nearly laughed. She nodded hello instead.

"Good afternoon, Mayor," he said.

But before Emily could reply, Lucy rushed over with a menu. "Here you go, Emily. Specials are up on the board, as usual."

"That's okay, Lucy. I don't need a menu." Emily handed it back to her. "Just some cottage cheese and melon," she said, remembering her diet, "and tea with lemon."

Lucy looked surprised at the order. "Feeling okay?"

"Just trying to diet."

"Give me a break, you look great," Lucy assured her with a pat on the shoulder. "But I guess everybody starves themselves before a wedding. Did you find the dresses yet?"

"Uh . . . no, not yet. But there's still time," Emily replied.

"Weddings always seems like a mess, but it all comes together," Lucy promised as she whisked away.

This one was more of a mess than most, though. Emily wondered if her sister had visited their mother, as she had promised. Or patched things up yet with Sam.

She sighed and glanced out the window, cheered by the sight of Dr. Elliot heading for the diner. When he entered she waved to him, and he smiled and came over to her booth.

"So, not afraid to enter the lion's den, are you?" Ezra commended her.

"No big deal. But I could use some company. Have a seat."

"Thanks, don't mind if I do." Ezra pulled off his cap and sat down. "What's the latest with McAllister? I heard he's applied for building permits."

"You heard that already?" Emily was amazed. Dr. Elliot wasn't exactly part of the Village Hall grapevine. How fast did gossip travel in this town anyway?

"For pity's sakes, everyone knows it." Charlie stepped forward and slammed her mug of tea on the table. "The question is, what do you plan to do about it?"

Emily glanced up at him. She hadn't noticed him standing there. Now he loomed over them with a smug expression. She felt cornered and didn't like it.

"Block the applications, you mean?" she asked.

Charlie nodded. "That would be a start."

She felt Ezra staring at her, his thin eyebrows arching up over his glasses.

"There are no legal grounds for stopping or delaying those permits," she explained. "If the applications are in order, they'll go through."

Ezra nodded at her and sat back, his expression relaxed again. He spread his napkin over his lap, carefully avoiding looking at Charlie.

"I knew you'd say that. I just wanted to hear it from your own mouth," Charlie said, sounding pleased with her answer.

She had just handed him more ammunition to use against her, but it couldn't be helped. Then again, she hadn't really taken a position; she had simply defended Luke's rights to go forward within the system.

"You're transparent, Bates. That's what you are." Ezra peered up at Charlie. "You're making a mountain out of a molehill and hoping to scrabble up top and declare yourself king. Don't you think the people around here can see that?"

Charlie's eyes narrowed as he took in the doctor. "Of course you'd say that. You got your money. What do you care if Cape Light is going to be ruined by McAllister's project? I bet you knew about this whole mess months ago and just kept it to yourself."

"That's a lie, Bates," Ezra said angrily. "You said it at the debate, as well. Now, take that back or I warn you, there'll be consequences—"

Emily heard the bell on the door jingle as Art Hecht and Larry Carter, a local real estate broker and Betty's competitor, entered the diner. The two men were among Charlie's biggest supporters, Emily knew.

"I stand by what I said," Charlie told Dr. Elliot. "And there's a lot of people in this town who think the same." He glanced meaningfully over his shoulder at his friends.

"All right, I've heard enough." Dr. Elliot came to his feet. "You must have thicker skin than I do, Emily. My hat's off to you," he added as he pushed through the little knot of people around the table and headed out the door.

"You're wrong, you know," Emily told Charlie. "Dr. Elliot didn't know anything about Luke McAllister's plans."

Charlie looked about to reply when Lucy scooted between them, setting down Emily's lunch. "There you are. And here's some plain crackers," she added, placing a basket on the table.

"Thanks, Lucy," Emily said.

Emily stared down at her plate. She had no appetite. Charlie had wandered away with his pals, she noticed.

"Can I get you anything else? More hot water?" Lucy offered.

"I'm in up to my neck already, looks like," she murmured with a tight smile. Lucy looked puzzled but smiled anyway.

"Is Sara around?" Emily asked, looking around the diner. "I thought I saw her out here a minute ago."

"Maybe she's helping Billy in the back. Do you want me to get her for you?"

"No, that's okay." Emily felt certain that Sara was avoiding her. "Just tell her I said hello."

"Sure, I'll tell her," Lucy said agreeably. She walked off to check on another table, and Emily tried a bite of her lunch.

Out on Main Street she saw Jessica walking purposefully up the block. She was on the other side of the street, and Emily knew she couldn't attract her sister's attention by waving through the window. It was just as well, Emily thought. She had to get back to the office soon. She'd call her sister tonight to catch up, she decided.

Maybe Jessica, at least, would have some good news. . . .

* * *

JESSICA SAW SAM'S TRUCK PARKED IN THE DRIVE NEXT TO THE BRAMBLE Antique Shop. She heard the sound of power tools coming from the barn in back, where Sam had his shop. She paused, gathering her nerve. Maybe now wasn't the best time. Sam didn't like to be interrupted when he was working. *Maybe I'll try to see him later,* she thought.

She suddenly noticed Grace Hegman, crouched in the flower beds in front of the shop. Grace's yellow Labrador, Daisy, was lying on the porch, calmly watching her work.

In the height of summer the garden was a spectacular and unorthodox mix of vegetables and lush banks of flowers thriving side by side. Jessica was also a gardener—though a novice compared to Grace—and she watched closely as Grace's knowing hands prepared her beds for winter, cutting back the dried brown stalks, and planted bulbs for spring. Grace worked at a quick pace, unaware of her audience.

"Hello, Grace," Jessica said, walking up beside her. "Cleaning up the garden?"

"Just the usual. Another summer come and gone. Hard to believe it." Grace shook her head and sat back on her heels. "Every year I say I'm not going to plant so much. It's too much work. But somehow it keeps getting bigger."

"I know what you mean. I'm planning a garden for the new house," Jessica told her. "I bought about a million bulbs, but I haven't put them in yet."

"You ought to get to it then. Once the ground freezes, you've missed out. You won't have any flowers in the spring, and all those bulbs will go to waste," Grace warned her.

"Yes, I know. I've got to get to it." She had to get to so many things. . . .

Grace pulled a burr from one of her gardening gloves. "Here to see Sam?" If she had heard anything about their problems, she didn't let on.

Jessica nodded, still not sure if she wanted to go back to the barn.

"He's there," Grace assured her with a nod. "See you later," she said, turning back to her work.

"See you." Jessica walked past the building and then out to the barn in back. Sam's woodworking shop took up one half of the huge old building; the other side was an annex for the Bramble.

She felt nervous about facing him. They had hardly spoken since their argument on Monday night and had not seen each other since. Only five days. But it felt longer. Long enough for his heart to have frozen against her? she wondered.

Don't be ridiculous, she chided herself. *We really love each other, and a person just doesn't fall out of love that fast.*

She stood in front of the half-opened door and her heart ached, and she felt sure she loved him more than ever.

Jessica pushed the door the rest of the way open. The workshop was dimly lit, as usual, with low shop lights over the machinery and worktable. Sam's strong body was silhouetted by the sunlight streaming through a back window. He looked up, but she couldn't quite see his face—or gauge his reaction to her appearance.

"Working hard?" she said, walking toward him.

"Just trying to finish this chair. I promised Luke McAllister I'd go out to his place this afternoon and look over a job."

He wouldn't meet her gaze, and she felt as if he was purposely acting distant from her. Still angry. She could tell that about him by now.

She moved closer and touched his arm, then stretched up to give him a kiss on the cheek. "I missed you," she said honestly.

He glanced down at her. "I missed you, too."

She waited for him to say something more. When he didn't, she said, "I went to see my mother."

"Oh? How did that go?"

Jessica turned away. A bit of fancy molding caught her eye, and she picked it up, turning it over in her hand as she tried to find the right words for her answer. She had to tell him the truth, but she didn't want to sound too negative. "We had a talk. She still won't come to the wedding. But I feel as if I tried," she added hopefully.

"Does that mean you're ready to set a new wedding date?" he asked carefully.

She could see that he was holding himself very still, waiting for her to answer. "I . . . I want to, Sam," she said slowly. "But it's hard. I lost my temper with her. We had words, and I don't think I did a very good job of getting through to her. I guess what I'm trying to say is, I'm not ready to give up yet."

Sam shook his head and breathed out a long sigh of frustration. "If you don't mind me saying so, your mother is a piece of work, Jessica."

Despite everything, she did mind him saying so, but she didn't think it was a good idea to call him on it right now.

"She refuses to acknowledge me in public," he went on, "refuses to come to our engagement party or our wedding, and now you're taking the blame on yourself, saying *you* did something wrong. You honestly believe that the problem is you didn't say the magic words that will change her mind."

"Okay," Jessica said, trying not to get defensive. "You have a point. But no matter how my mother manages to twist things around to suit herself, when all is said and done, she's still my mother, and I still want her at the wedding. I think she just needs more time, Sam."

"Well, my folks are starting to get concerned, too, Jessica. They keep asking me why you just can't set a date. They're not sure you really want to marry me."

"Of course I do," Jessica said. "Would your family expect you to just sail right ahead with a wedding if your mother said she wasn't going to attend?"

"My mother would never pull a stunt like that," Sam countered. "Most people wouldn't."

"Well, I guess you're just luckier than I am," Jessica snapped. "I'll try to be more careful next time I pick my parents."

Sam tossed the piece of wood he was working on down on the table and rubbed the back of his neck with his hand. She could see he felt as tense and frustrated as she did and was trying hard not to blow up at her.

Dear Lord, please help us come together. Help us find a way out of this mess we're in, she prayed silently.

Without thinking, she walked over to where Sam stood and rested her hand on his arm. "I wish you would just try to understand," she said quietly.

"I am trying." He was gripping the edge of the table, and she could see he was trying hard to hold on to his temper. "Maybe we don't need a wedding date, we need a deadline."

"A deadline?" She let her hand drop off his arm.

"For you to decide if you're going to marry me or not," he said simply.

His pride was hurt. She could see it in his eyes and feel it in the tone of his voice. Still, she didn't like the sound of this at all. He was pressuring her, with no compassion and no understanding. Is this what she had to look forward to for the rest of her life? Why was she so eager to marry someone so completely—pigheaded?

"Well, that's so understanding of you." She could hear the acid in her voice—sounding uncannily like Lillian—and yet she couldn't stop herself. "It's not enough that I'm getting pressured by my mother. Now you're giving me ultimatums."

Sam stared at her, his expression tense. "All I'm saying is, it seems to me that sooner or later you're going to have to choose, me or your mother. She didn't just suddenly decide she disliked me. She never liked me. But you said you didn't care. You said you wanted to marry me, no matter what." He turned his back toward her and started working again. "Now it sounds like you do care, more than you want to admit."

Jessica summoned a last reserve of patience. How could she make him

see that this was an impossible choice? "You know I love you, Sam. . . . I just need more time to talk to her."

He looked at her for a long moment. "You keep saying that, Jessica, and I know you really mean it. You think this is all about changing your mother's feelings. But it's not. It's about knowing what *you* feel," he said forcefully.

Jessica didn't know how to answer. Was that true? She did know how she felt. She wanted to marry Sam *and* have her mother at her wedding. Was that so much to ask?

She suddenly felt so frustrated with him and the entire situation, she wanted to scream. But she forced herself not to. She glanced at her watch and swallowed hard.

"I have to get back to the office."

She turned to go but he reached out and touched her shoulder, stilling her.

"Wait, Jess." He looked suddenly regretful, his soft expression more like the Sam she knew. "Don't go like this. Don't go so upset—"

"How do you expect me to feel? You say you understand, but then you ask me to make a choice that will tear me in half." She pulled away, instantly missing the warmth of his touch.

Without looking back, she walked out of the shop and into the harsh sunlight.

LATER THAT AFTERNOON LUKE FINISHED GIVING SAM A TOUR OF HIS PROPERTY and a rough idea of the kind of construction he had in mind. Sam had taken it all in, asking the occasional question.

"So when can you start?" Luke tried, but couldn't hold down the note of eagerness in his voice.

Sam didn't seem to notice. He was still making notes on the clipboard he carried. He was a serious guy, Luke thought, and seemed somehow distracted as they talked about Luke's ideas for renovating the cottages. But Luke had heard Sam was getting married soon. Must have a lot on his mind, he thought.

"I can start next week." Sam stuck the clipboard under his arm. "If you're going to help, too, I'll just need to hire Digger to help me with some of the carpentry."

"That's okay with me," Luke told him. "The program director said he wanted to send up some kids to work here with us. Is that all right with you?"

"Sure, no problem." Sam shrugged. "The more, the merrier."

Digger Hegman, who had wandered off somewhere while Sam and Luke were talking, now returned, puffing on his pipe.

"Everyone in town is talking about this project of yours, Luke. That's all you hear about. Charlie Bates will stop you if he's able," Digger warned.

"I think he's trying to drum up some votes," Luke said. "It's just like anything else. People will talk about it for a while, until something else catches their attention. I figure, if we just start the work and they see I'm serious, sooner or later, they'll get used to the idea and give up."

Sam glanced at Digger, and Luke could see the two men were trying not to smile. "Maybe where you come from they do," Sam said. "But not around here. I'm not sure you realize what you're getting into."

"Then you're getting into it, too," Luke countered. "Are you having second thoughts about working for me?"

Sam shook his head. "Not at all. I respect what you're trying to do out here. A lot of people agree with me . . . but a lot don't. I'm just warning you that the ones that don't won't give up so easily."

"People around here take things to heart, which is a good thing usually. But not in this type of situation," Digger added thoughtfully. "When I told my daughter I was coming out here, you should have seen her face. She was fit to be tied. But I agree with Sam," he assured Luke. "And I'll do as I please without apologizing to anyone."

Luke had never really spoken with the old fisherman and was surprised at his spunk.

"Grace never liked change much," Digger added as he relit his pipe.

"Seems to me a lot of people around here feel the same as your daughter. But we start on Monday, right?" Luke said.

"We'll be here," Sam promised.

Five minutes later Luke stood watching Sam's truck disappear up the gravel drive, a puff of dust flying out from under the rear wheels as they headed for the Beach Road. He sat down on the front steps of his cottage, feeling undaunted by Sam's warnings and ready for this next phase of his life to begin.

The bright September day had darkened into a steely gray afternoon. A pale orange sun began to sink behind the pines, lighting up the bank of clouds that clung to the horizon. He thought about Sara, imagined her sitting beside him, watching the sky.

But it was too early for Sara to be back from work. At least she would be coming back, he reminded himself. She had postponed her plan to go back to Maryland. He hoped so, anyhow.

He had heard her leaving her cottage early that morning and had rushed to his window, checking to see if she was loading any suitcases or cartons into her trunk, making a secret getaway. He was relieved to see her dressed in her waitress uniform and jean jacket, looking as if she were about to start an ordinary day.

He noticed it was dark now, as if some invisible hand had reached into the woods and clicked off the light. He got to his feet. His bad leg felt stiff and sore, but he ignored it. Once he started working with Sam Morgan, it was going to feel a lot worse.

A few hours later Luke heard the sound of Sara's car pulling up to the cottages. *She needs that muffler checked,* he thought, turning down the sound on the TV. He saw her go inside, then wondered if he should go over and talk to her.

No, a bad idea. Not after last night when you snooped on her phone con-versation. She's going to feel like you're crowding her, then she'll really have a reason to take off.

He sighed and stretched out again on his couch, flipping through the channels. One hundred and three, and there was nothing on. It seemed impossible and against all mathematical odds, but it happened too many nights for him to really be surprised.

A sharp knock on the door surprised him. He shut off the television and went to answer it, recognizing Sara's silhouette through the glass win-dow. He ran his hand over his bristly short hair and tried to straighten out his shirt. *As if that will help,* he thought wryly, pulling open the door.

"Hi." Sara looked nervous, her hands in her jacket pockets. "I just came by to tell you what's happening with me. I'm going to stay."

She had changed out of her uniform and now wore jeans and a cream-colored turtleneck sweater. She looked very pretty, he thought.

"Good. That's good," he said sincerely. "Hey, you want to come in?" Before she could refuse, he opened the door and stepped aside.

She hesitated a moment, then walked in and gazed around. "Nice place . . . looks just like mine."

"It's eerie that way, isn't it?" he agreed, glancing around the large room that did, in fact, look exactly like Sara's except for a few homey touches she had added over the months. "Even the same dishes," he pointed out, pick-ing up an empty coffee cup. "I was thinking of renaming this place the Cranberry Twilight Zone."

"I don't think that would attract the right kind of clientele," she said with a laugh. She sat down on one of the armchairs in the living room area but didn't take off her jacket. "Besides, you have your new plan now. No more tourists."

"Absolutely. Renovations start Monday morning, bright and early. Sam Morgan is going to do the work."

"I didn't hear that." Sara shifted in her seat and crossed one long leg over the other.

"What did you hear? Plenty, I bet, in the diner."

"I heard you applied for the building permits. Charlie Bates told the mayor she should try to hold you up. But Emily said she wasn't going to," she reported.

Sara had felt a little better about Emily when she heard her standing up to Charlie—but not enough to come out from the kitchen and speak to her.

"Good work," Luke said, sounding impressed. "You really are a champion eavesdropper."

He saw two spots of color appear on her cheeks.

"I was right there. I couldn't help it," she protested. Then her tone became more serious. "Dr. Elliot is taking some heat, too."

"Yeah, I know. That's too bad. He's a nice guy," Luke said with concern. "Maybe I'll try to go see him."

He pulled open a cupboard. "I have nothing to feed you but microwave popcorn and diet soda."

"As long as it's not a clam roll, or in any way resembles a clam roll, I'll take it," Sara said.

Luke tossed the popcorn package into the microwave and pulled out a bowl. "Sounds like I was smart to stay out of town today."

"If I were you, I'd stay out of the Clam Box indefinitely. Charlie is practically frothing at the mouth."

"I'm sure it's hard to listen to, but so far it's just talk," Luke assured her. "The work is going to start Monday, and next week, I meet with the attorneys to wrap up the details."

The sound of breaking glass shattered the deep silence of the night. Sara got up from her chair as Luke walked quickly into the living room and pulled open the door to look outside. "Stay back, Sara," he said curtly.

Sara stayed where she was, noticing how he stood with his body behind the doorframe, like the detectives she had seen on TV shows. His tense, alert attitude alarmed her. Just as quickly, he shut the door and stepped inside again.

"What happened?"

"Looks like somebody threw a rock through my windshield." He sat on the couch and pulled on his hiking boots.

"What are you going to do?" She followed him to the door.

"Wait here," he told her as he headed outside with a flashlight. "I'm pretty sure they took off, but I want to make sure."

Sara watched through the window as the beam of Luke's flashlight darted around the property, illuminating the deserted cottages and the thick fringe of trees.

At last Luke circled back to his truck. The windshield was completely smashed. He opened the driver's door, looked inside, and took something from the front seat.

A few minutes later Luke returned to the cottage. He set the flashlight on the kitchen table, along with a big gray rock. The rock had a note tied to it with string. As Sara watched he pulled it out and unfolded it.

" 'Quit while you're ahead. Before somebody gets hurt,' " he read aloud. He nodded. "Very original." He turned to Sara. "I can't say I'm surprised."

"You're not?" She heard a thin note of fear in her voice and felt embarrassed.

"Sara? Hey, it's okay." He rested his hand on her back, under her hair, and rubbed in a small, soothing circle. "Whoever did this is just—an idiot. I'm not going to be scared off by a broken windshield."

Luke picked up the rock, testing the weight in his hand. "The cops in town will like this. It's a nice hefty piece of evidence, though it may not do them much good."

"I guess it would be impossible to trace," Sara agreed.

He still stood with his hand on her back, and when she turned toward him she felt his arm curl around her shoulder. She found she didn't mind at all. She felt calmer, though still a little nervous.

"You will call the police, right?"

"Right away," he promised. He gazed down at her. "But what about you? I don't like the idea of you sticking around here with some jerk tossing rocks through the windows. Maybe you should move off the property, find a place in town."

His concern touched her. She was shaken but had never thought of leaving. "I don't need to go. Why give the guy the satisfaction? I don't want to leave you here alone," she told him. "Looks to me like you'll need all the friends you've got in this town."

"I could count them on one hand, too." Luke smiled at her and squeezed her shoulder. "There's you and Reverend Ben. And maybe Sam Morgan and Digger Hegman."

"It would help if you had Emily Warwick in your corner," Sara said. "She could dispel a lot of the negative opinion in town."

"Probably," he agreed. "But she seems to be sitting on the fence."

Sara didn't reply. She still felt angry and disillusioned with Emily for staying neutral about the issue, but she was afraid that if she said more, she'd give her secret away.

"Well, maybe she'll get off the fence," she said.

"Yeah, maybe Charlie will push her off, but I'm not counting on it."

"No, you'd better not," she agreed with a sigh.

"But you're sticking with me, huh?" he asked.

She nodded, not quite able to speak. His eyes looked bright and full of emotion. She thought he was going to kiss her again, but he only pressed his lips to her hair for an instant, then leaned back again.

"All right. We'll see what happens."

His tone was light, but she could see he was touched by her loyalty. She felt their uncanny connection, even stronger than she had the night before. Her doubts didn't seem to matter. She was getting more involved with Luke day by day. There didn't seem to be any way to stop it, and she didn't really want to.

He put his other arm around her, and this time he did kiss her. Different from the last time, the pressure of his mouth was soft and lingering. When he lifted his head, he kept his arms around her, and she pressed her head against his shoulder.

Luke held Sara close, inhaling the flowery scent of her hair. He didn't want her to think he was taking advantage of their crisis. He just didn't feel like letting her go just yet. He was worried about her, more than he'd let on. But her willingness to stay had touched him, overriding his fears. He hoped he wouldn't come to regret that.

I'll just have to keep an even closer eye on her from now on, Luke thought with a smile. *That shouldn't be too tough. . . .*

"HERE'S THE ROCK—AND THE NOTE." CHIEF SANBORN PLACED TWO PLAS-tic bags on Emily's desk. "No prints on either."

Emily picked them up and examined them. "When did it happen?"

"McAllister says he heard it crashing through his windshield a little after nine. He was in his cottage, with Sara Franklin."

Hearing that Sara was there worried Emily. She had never felt totally at ease with Sara staying on at the cottages after the summer season. Now this had happened. She wished Sara would move into town.

". . . He says he went out with a flashlight and looked around, but didn't see anything," Chief Sanborn continued. "Dixon took the call and went out there. He searched the grounds again, but he didn't find anything, either."

"What was Luke's reaction?" Emily asked.

Chief Sanborn shrugged. "Dixon says he was cool as a cucumber. Didn't seem fazed at all. But I guess he's seen worse. He was a Boston cop, you know, a detective."

"Yes, I heard." Emily picked up the rock again. It was gray with wide white stripes and some dark streaks of dried seaweed staining one side—the kind of rock anyone could pick up on the beach or might have in their garden, bordering a flower bed.

"This disturbs me," she said. "I know no one was hurt, but I don't like people in this town being threatened."

"I couldn't agree more," the police chief replied. "But I have to tell you right here and now, Mayor, we have about as much hope of figuring out who did this as finding a needle in a haystack. Unless of course, somebody starts bragging about it and we hear."

"Yes, I understand." Emily nodded and sat back in her chair. "What can we do to make sure nothing else like this happens?"

"I've already assigned extra patrols to the area. Maybe McAllister needs to hire a night watchman or some private security."

"A security guard at Cranberry Cottages?" Emily mused. "A week ago that idea would have been laughable." She pushed the rock and note back toward the police chief. "I guess we just have to wait and see what happens."

Sanborn collected the evidence and came to his feet. "Did the building permit go through?"

"Yes, I signed off on it myself."

After the confrontation at the diner, Emily had returned to Village Hall, tracked down the paperwork, then guided it through the process personally. She knew Charlie had friends in the building and zoning departments, and Luke's application might somehow get "lost" moving from one desk to another.

Sanborn didn't look exactly cheered by the news. He nodded and tucked the folder under his arm. "I'll let you know if we come up with anything more. But like I said, don't get your hopes up."

"I understand," Emily said, watching him go.

She knew it was not totally reasonable, but she felt responsible for what had happened last night. Partly responsible, at least. If she had voiced support of Luke's plans when she had the chance, maybe Charlie's hysteria wouldn't have taken hold.

She got to her feet and began pacing her office. *You can't feel responsible for some numskull tossing a rock through Luke's windshield.*

Oh, yes, I can, she argued with herself.

What was going to happen next—something even more dangerous? *A person who would do something like that won't be happy being ignored,* she knew. *They'll just go out and find a bigger rock. And the next time Sara could get hurt.*

But this isn't just about Sara's safety. Or even Luke's, for that matter. It's the principle of the thing—my own waffling principles, Emily thought grimly.

Betty Bowman appeared in the doorway, carrying a leather portfolio with a gold clasp. "Am I the first one here?" she asked.

"The very first, not counting me," Emily replied.

Even though it was Saturday, the campaign committee had scheduled a meeting; it was the only time they all had open. Emily hoped it would be quick. She still had work to do here and wanted a few free hours at home, just to catch up on real life.

Betty was dressed smartly, as usual, in a tweed suit, a burnt-orange turtleneck of fine-gauge wool, and a silk scarf. She was probably rushing back to her real estate office after the meeting, Emily realized.

In contrast Emily wore comfortable khaki pants, jogging shoes, and a navy blue and white striped sweater. Her hair, still damp from the shower, looked even more untamed than usual. Even if she spent the entire day trying, she would never look as polished as Betty, but that was all right. She was past the stage of feeling insecure about her looks. She liked her own casual style; it suited her.

"Dan Forbes bought that little cottage on your street," Betty said. She opened her portfolio and took out her thick agenda book. "Did I tell you?"

"He told me. I ran into him in the neighborhood the other night."

"We're having the walk-through today. He's closing on Monday."

"That was fast."

"He needed a quick turnaround. His house on Bayview sold in a day. Everything goes in a flash up there. Luckily, it all worked out. I think he'll be in by the end of next week."

"Really?" He hadn't mentioned anything about it when they spoke on the phone the other night.

I'll have to stop by and say hello, Emily thought. *Bring a plant or something. It's the neighborly thing to do. . . .*

Warren Oakes walked in, looking grimmer than usual, Emily thought. Then Harriet DeSoto, Frank Hellinger, and Doris Mumford.

Warren, the campaign chairman, began the meeting, addressing a list of topics he had drawn up.

"Item One: Replacing campaign signs on the access roads coming into town. I checked out there this morning, and it looks like the wind blew half of them down again," he reported.

It was an endless battle keeping the signs up, but Warren never seemed daunted, Emily thought. He was nothing, if not persistent.

"Item Two: Your schedule for the next few weeks needs work. You need to get out more, talk to more groups, drum up more support." He checked his notes. "What about your speech to the Rotary? Have you finished it yet?"

Emily nodded. "Just about." She handed out copies of her most recent draft. "It's basically the stump speech with a few extras, some praise for funding the Harvest Festival and the new equipment for the playground. Talking about our shared vision for the village. That sort of thing."

"What about this McAllister situation?" Warren asked, skimming the speech. "It's all everyone's talking about. You've got to say something."

"He's right," Betty said.

"I didn't get to work it into that draft," Emily explained. "But I agree, I need to address it."

She looked down at her hands, surprised to see them steepled together in front of her, as if she were about to pray. So she did. *Help me, Lord,* she whispered in her mind. Then she gazed up at her committee.

"I think I need to step out and support it," she said. "Maybe even before I see the Rotary."

For a long moment nobody spoke. Warren's bushy eyebrows came together over his scowling face. Betty looked at Harriet with a questioning expression, and Harriet looked down at the table. Doris seemed absorbed in twisting her wedding band on her finger.

"You can't be serious. That's a joke, right?" Frank said.

"I'm perfectly serious," Emily assured him. "I've felt uneasy about this from the start, and now something has happened. Last night at the cottages, somebody tossed a rock through Luke McAllister's windshield with a threatening note attached. No one was hurt," she added. "But it's time for me to take a clear position. Past time, I'd say. I want to support it."

"Well, then, you'd better expect a rock through your windshield next." Warren sat back in his chair and shook his head. "Can't you see, Emily? If people are so angry that they're harassing McAllister, voicing support is the worst move you can make."

"Might as well hand Charlie the election," Harriet added quietly. "He's baited the trap, and you're about to walk right into it."

"Look," Emily said, "this isn't about playing politics. It's about values and the real difference between voting for me or voting for Charlie. I've done some research, and I think this project is worthwhile and should go through. I think that once everyone has the facts, most will support it, too. This is a town of essentially good, decent people. I know they'll do the right thing."

"Nicely said." Warren extended his hands and clapped, a dull sound in the quiet room. "Too bad there's only about three people in town right now who would agree with you—or vote for you if you made that speech outside this room. And that includes McAllister."

"He can't vote, he's not a resident," Harriet corrected him.

"He owns property and pays taxes," Emily said, astounded.

"Needs to be his legal address for six months. It's on the books. Check for yourself," Harriet said with a shrug.

"Real estate values are going to take a nosedive if that project goes through. Have you thought about that?" Betty asked.

"That's not necessarily true." Emily had expected this from Betty, friend or not. "Luke dropped a package of information off for me yesterday, and I read it through last night. These centers are all over the country and don't appear to have any effect on property values, in the long run."

"Meaning five years from now?" Betty sat back and tucked her silk scarf into her jacket. "Honestly, Emily . . . be realistic."

"I know Charlie has gotten under your skin with this thing. He's rattled the entire town. But this isn't the only issue in the campaign. You've got to shift the focus somewhere else, where you can show him up," Harriet coached her.

"Get a little distance from this, Emily. It's an emotional issue, but it's not really that important," Warren argued in a more persuasive tone. "Is this project going to provide services to any of our residents? No. In fact, it's only made them angry. So what's the point of sticking your neck out?"

"Warren is right. This isn't the time to take the high ground. You'd be smarter to back off," Doris advised.

"You can beat Charlie now, and then help McAllister later," Frank added.

"I can't just sit back and say nothing for the next six weeks," Emily countered. "It's just not right."

"I'll tell you what's not right," Warren said. "We've all worked very hard on this campaign, given up our valuable time and energy. I thought we were a team. Now you want to drive right off a cliff and take the rest of us with you. Is that fair to us?" he demanded.

Emily didn't answer at first. She looked at the faces of the others, realizing they all agreed with Warren. She swallowed hard. Was she being selfish? Crumbling under Charlie's pressure, falling for his tricks?

Luke's project was not vital to the well-being of the village, that much was true. But the small-minded, negative spirit it had aroused was harmful and went against everything Cape Light stood for.

Why was that so hard to explain to them—and why did she feel so foolish and ineffectual trying?

"You need more time to think this over. You're worn out. It's been a long week," Betty gently suggested. "Why don't you have copies made of the information Luke gave you, so we can all look at it?"

Trying to give me a graceful way out, Emily thought. Betty was such a good negotiator. She knew how to hold a deal together.

"Good idea," Warren assented. He could see he had not really moved Emily from her position, but was willing to settle for this compromise. "You don't see the Rotary for almost two weeks. You have plenty of time to figure out what to say," he added.

Emily sighed. Just when she thought she had made her mind up and stood on solid ground, everything shifted underneath her again. But she didn't feel as if she had any chance of overruling them on this now.

"All right. I'll run off some copies on Monday and get it out to all of you," she promised. "We'll see what you think then."

After reviewing a few more routine matters, the meeting concluded. Everyone left quickly, looking drained and downbeat, Emily thought. As if she had already let them down.

ONE THING WENT RIGHT FOR EMILY THAT EVENING. DR. ELLIOT VISITED Lillian, so Emily was spared yet another confrontation with her mother. Instead, she finished up the housework she had put off all week and set off on a long run. But she wound up cutting it short. She felt so tired, weary down to her very soul. And empty, too.

She returned to the house, poured more food into the cats' bowls—they each seemed to be eating about twice their body weight per day—and got ready to go to bed. Out of habit, she picked up the Bible on her night table and opened it to the marked page. She read a chapter from Philippians and paused when she came to the words "I can do all things through Christ which strengtheneth me."

She tried to find comfort in the familiar words. But tonight they just didn't ring true for her. She didn't feel the resonance, down deep in her heart, renewing her and putting her back on track. The words on the page seemed to be just words, type on a page, the deeper meaning sealed from her. She couldn't penetrate their mystery or release their power to help her.

She closed the Bible and began to pray. *Dear God, why is everything so hard for me? Why is everything so confused? I can't seem to figure out what to do about anything. Everyone seems so disappointed in me—or angry. Or both,* she conceded.

What am I doing wrong here? What is the point of tying myself in knots to get reelected? Or arguing with my mother about Jessica and Sam at every turn? And even thinking about what happened with my baby—I feel as if I'm just banging my head against a wall. Nothing changes. I feel so stuck. Everything just seems so . . . futile.

Her litany of complaints sounded so empty and negative. She stared into the dark, the shadowy shapes of her room, simultaneously familiar and strange in the cool moonlight.

Even prayer wasn't helping her tonight. Where was her gratitude? Her perspective? Had she lost her bearings so completely that she had lost the thread of her faith as well? In her heart she knew she wondered why God wasn't helping her. She knew she doubted. Herself and God.

No wonder I'm alone, without a husband or family of my own, she thought. *No wonder I've never found my daughter. I don't deserve all that. I'm a hypocrite, with a lot of opinions and judgments about the way the world should be but no courage to act. Well meaning but ineffectual. Just like my father.*

Trying to please everyone, I've turned into a talking suit, a sellout, a phony. Emily felt the dark impulse to quit the election entirely. *I just can't do this anymore,* she said to herself.

She tossed in her bed and yanked the cover over her shoulder. But if she did lose, what did she have left? Nothing. An empty house and two cats. An invalid mother who was impossible to please. Her sister, God willing, would soon be married and immersed in her life with Sam. *A life that will make mine look even more barren in comparison.* Is that what she had to look forward to?

Sometimes she felt as though she wanted to run away and never come back. For a few moments, she allowed herself the guilty pleasure of imagining it. Then finally, she sat up to set her alarm clock. She had nearly forgotten.

Church tomorrow, with her mother. Lunch at the house on Providence Street afterward. Hour by hour, she would get through the day.

And then the next and the next after that. . . . She closed her eyes again, and her thoughts ran on as she tumbled into a colorless sleep.

CHAPTER TEN

RS. WARWICK. EMILY." TUCKER TULLEY NODDED in greeting as they entered the church on Sunday morning. Emily smiled back; for a split second she hadn't recognized him out of his uniform.

He handed each of them a program and led them to an empty pew. Her mother liked to sit in a front row, looking directly at the pulpit. Once they were settled, Lillian leaned over and whispered, "Where's Gus Potter? He always handles the left aisle."

"He's ill again. I think it might be pneumonia," Emily whispered back. "He's in the hospital, getting some tests. I heard they may have found some trouble with his heart."

"Really? I hadn't heard." Her mother looked down at her foot. "These new shoes are terribly uncomfortable. The left is rubbing my heel. You'll have to return them." Without further comment she opened her prayer book and began to read.

A typically compassionate reaction, Emily thought wryly. Then again, her mother wasn't in a very good mood today. She and Dr. Elliot had argued last night. From what Emily gathered, it was more than the usual intellectual fencing that seemed to be the basis of their friendship. This was different, a disagreement over whether the town should block Luke McAllister's project. Dr. Elliot was for the project and her mother, against it, of course. The argument had gotten so serious, he had left before dessert. "I was shocked," her mother had told her. Emily, however, was not surprised. The issue seemed to put the best of friends at odds.

Glancing over her shoulder, she saw Jessica walking into the church. Sam was sitting near his parents, and though there was space, Jessica didn't try to sit near him. Good grief, Emily thought, that's not a good sign. She had already decided that she wouldn't even try to bring her mother and sister together this morning. No one needed another round of that snub routine again.

Reverend Ben greeted the congregation and started the service. Though Emily tried to focus, her thoughts began to wander.

Her spirits had been so dark last night. This morning she felt more herself but somehow dull, as if everything inside her were going numb. Some part of her that had always fought and held out hope was giving up.

Then the Reverend Ben's deep voice caught her attention. Was it already time for the sermon? Her thoughts had taken her far away, but now she could hear what he was saying. ". . . and I was reminded of a simple proverb that rings consistently true. 'Actions speak louder than words.' "

Emily sat up a little straighter. She knew who said it, and when, as did most in the room. Where was Reverend Ben going with this? she wondered.

"The words stuck in my mind all week long," the Reverend continued. "And it occurred to me that God has told us the same. 'Actions speak louder than words.' Specifically, the kind of action he wants us to take in our lives every day. As we find in the gospel according to St. John, 'By this shall all men know that ye are my disciples, if ye have love one to another.'

"And again, in Corinthians you will hear the same, even more eloquently perhaps: 'And now abideth faith, hope, charity, these three, but the greatest of these is charity.'

"What does that mean—'the greatest of these'?" Reverend Ben paused and looked down at his notes, then back at his flock. "This is the key, the beating heart of being a Christian, the essential, identifying characteristic. This is the thing that all Christians must do . . . or must try to do. But is that it? you might ask yourself. Just to love one another?"

He nodded slowly. "Simple, right? Just one single request. It's like telling your children that you'll give them a thousand dollars a week allowance and all they have to do is make their beds. Or take out the garbage. That isn't very much at all for that great reward, is it?"

Emily listened keenly, watching the Reverend glance around at his audience. "Nothing to it, you say," he continued lightly. "And on a beautiful sunny day when your job is going well, the bills are paid, and there are no family problems on your mind, it's easy to love the world and everyone in it. To be cheerful, kind, generous, considerate.

"But does God say, 'Love one another when you feel like it. When you're in a good mood. When you've got the time'?" the Reverend asked. "Does he say, 'It's okay. You just do it when it's convenient for you. I don't mind.' Does the Lord tell us, 'Just love the people near and dear to you— your family and friends? Or the ones who give you respect and affection, the ones who agree with you? It's fine with me if you don't love, or even like, the others.' " The Reverend shook his head and continued. "Does the Lord say, 'It's fine with me if the rest of the time you're short tempered and angry, if you treat your neighbor with envy, contempt, suspicion, intolerance. . . .' "

Emily glanced over at her mother. Her gaze was fixed on the Reverend, but instead of the composed, thoughtful expression she usually wore when she listened to his sermons, her expression was a tight, sour frown.

" 'Actions speak louder than words,' " Reverend Ben repeated. "Let us pray today that the light of the Holy Spirit will fill our hearts and inspire us to be known by our acts, and our acts will reflect the Holy Spirit of love."

Emily watched Reverend Ben leave the pulpit, his eyes bright, a fine sheen of perspiration on his forehead. His words had stirred her, touching so many places in her life. But instead of stirring up more guilt and worry, something dark and heavy inside had subtly shifted. It wasn't that she now had an answer to the questions that plagued her. It felt more like a door swinging open just a crack, a thin shaft of light cutting through the shadows. It was the recognition that she needn't give up hope. She could find an answer.

Ben removed his vestment and hung it carefully in his office closet. Then cleaned off his glasses with his hanky. He was grateful that the Lord had done his part, sending both Jessica and Sam to the service. But seeing them sitting rows apart, with not even a glance exchanged, had caused Ben deep concern. Now he was going to try to do his part. He hoped his plan wouldn't misfire.

If only he had made headway with Lillian last week, he thought regretfully. But he hadn't. Now it seemed time to approach the problem from some other front.

Sam arrived first and stood in the doorway. "You wanted to see me, Reverend?"

"Come in, Sam. Take a seat," he said waving him inside.

Once Sam was seated he said, "Enjoy the sermon?"

"Yes . . . yes, I did," Sam replied. "It got me thinking. Not just about what's been going on in town. But about—a lot of things."

"Good, that's what I like to hear." Ben suddenly saw Jessica in the doorway. She paused as she noticed Sam.

"Please come in," Ben coaxed her. "And close the door. I don't think I need to introduce you to my other guest," he added as he sat down behind his desk.

"Hello, Sam," Jessica said quietly. She sat down in the chair near him but didn't look at him.

Sam looked at her, though, love and longing flashing in his dark eyes, Ben noticed. No, he was not too late. Not at all. This might not be as hard as he first expected.

He smiled gently at them, sending up a quick prayer that this meeting would help.

"I apologize for resorting to this—juvenile trick to get you together. But I wasn't sure that you would come if I asked you to meet with me as a couple." Sam and Jessica both studied the floor. "And that worries me," Ben said sincerely.

"It worries me, too, Reverend," Sam said. He looked about to say more, but glanced at Jessica and grew silent.

"Well, what's been happening with you two?" Ben pressed on. "I hear the wedding has been postponed. Is that true?"

Jessica nodded. "We're trying to work this out. At least I am," she added. "But Sam just doesn't understand what I'm going through, what I'm dealing with. He tells me I have to choose between him or my mother, when it's not that way at all."

"I love her," Sam spoke up. "I want us to be married. But I want to believe she'll have me with or without her mother's seal of approval. Is that too much to ask?" Sam was struggling to keep his patience. "I can't go for- ward if she's not one hundred percent sure. She tells me she's feeling pres- sure, she feels torn. Well, to me those are doubts. That's not one hundred percent sure."

"You've talked to your mother again, Jessica?" Reverend Ben asked.

"Yes. I went there last week. It didn't go well. I want to give her more time. But I don't know if she'll ever come around," she admitted.

"She may not," Ben agreed. "I feel your mother is wrong and will eventually regret the way she's behaving. But you may never get her blessings or approval on your marriage to Sam."

He paused, watching Jessica's reaction. Her eyes were downcast, her expression sad.

"I know that," Jessica said quietly. "But I can't seem to get past it. I just feel so—stuck. So backed into a corner."

"Who backed you in there, Jessica?" the Reverend asked.

"My mother," she replied, as if the answer were obvious. She glanced quickly to her right. "And Sam," she added.

"How can you even say that? This mess isn't my making." Sam turned to Jessica, his voice rising. But Ben met his eye and he quickly calmed down.

Ben gave them a moment, then turned to Jessica again. "Did you ever play tug-of-war?" he asked. She looked puzzled by the question but nodded. "Well, you're in a tug-of-war with your mother. One that you're not likely to win," he said. "But there is a way out of the game, a way to disarm your opponent."

"How?"

"Just let go of the rope." He paused for a moment. "Instead of battling with her, try to forgive her. Do you see what I mean?"

Jessica glanced at Sam for a moment, then turned forward again, settling in her chair with her legs tucked beneath her.

"You're probably right, Reverend," she admitted. "But would you at least give it one more try with me? Could you come and talk to her one more time with me? And maybe Emily could come, too."

Ben was not surprised by the request.

Sam did not look pleased, but he said, "One more try wouldn't hurt, I guess, if that's what you think you have to do."

"All right, call me later and we'll try to set up a time," Ben told Jessica.

"Thank you, Reverend," she said as she stood up. Sam stood up, too. He leaned over and shook Ben's hand. "Thank you for seeing us."

"Thank you for coming," Ben replied lightly. Since there was no mention of his subterfuge, he guessed they had forgiven him.

He watched them walk out, close but not touching. He could see the tension between them still—but also the love.

He straightened out his desk and gathered some belongings. Carolyn was expecting him home right away. Rachel and Jack were coming over.

Through the half-drawn curtain of his office window, he spotted Sam and Jessica again, out in the parking lot. They stood by Sam's truck, talking in an animated fashion, and Ben wondered if they were having a fight. He rubbed his forehead, worrying that he had been wrong to force them together.

Jessica went very still, staring up at Sam. He stared back at her a moment, then seemed to swoop down and surround her in a huge, hungry embrace, kissing her full on the mouth till her head tilted back and she nearly lost her balance.

Ben turned away, feeling embarrassed. They seemed to be . . . working things out, he thought. And Sam, at least, had taken the words of his sermon to heart.

HARRIET DeSoto STOOD IN THE DOORWAY OF EMILY'S OFFICE, A BUNDLE of folders under her arm.

Emily could tell by her expression that she had been standing there some time—long enough to have overheard the phone conversation she was having with Luke. Emily waved her in, focusing on Luke again.

"I've told him about the reaction here. I'm sure he'll agree to come," Luke said.

"Maybe he could ask some of the counselors to come along, too. They could describe the program in detail, talk about the kids who get help, answer any questions. That sort of thing."

"It might help," Luke agreed.

"Great, why don't we try for Wednesday night?" Emily said, glancing at her own calendar. "It's not much time to prepare, but I think it's important to do this as soon as possible."

"Absolutely," Luke agreed. "I'll call Dr. Santori and get right back to you."

When Emily looked up she knew from Harriet's expression that she'd figured out who Emily had been speaking to, but not what it was about.

"I've asked Luke McAllister to give a presentation to the town about his project," Emily told her. "He's inviting the program director to come down and help him answer questions."

"You did what?" Harriet stared at her. "I don't think that was such a great idea."

"Don't you see? As long as people don't know the facts, and what this program is all about, Charlie can say anything he likes. He's spreading all kinds of misinformation and making the situation look worse every day."

Harriet wouldn't meet her eye. She pressed her lips together, looking annoyed. "I'll tell you what's going to look bad. You sitting there, shoulder to shoulder with McAllister and the lot of them from Boston."

"This is going to help, Harriet." Emily sat back in her chair, sending a clear message that she wasn't going to be talked out of this.

"You might have checked with your campaign committee first," Harriet muttered.

"I knew you'd all disagree and try to talk me out of it." Emily put her reading glasses on and turned to her computer screen. "Besides, I have the right to call a town meeting. It's well within my authority as mayor."

"Enjoy it while you still can, I guess." Harriet dropped the folders she was holding on Emily's desk and stalked out of the office.

* * *

SOPHIE WALKED AMONG THE TREES, THE FALLEN APPLES CRUNCHING UNDER her rubber boots. She picked up what she could and tossed them into the wagon she pulled, her fingers moving clumsily in the thick work gloves. The blackbirds would help clean up the rest.

A stiff breeze blew and caught the top of the hillside, tossing the leafy branches of the apple trees that still hung heavy with fruit. The trees were like her old friends, their thin arms waving hello to her. She loved to walk among them. The smell of the fallen fruit sweetened the cold morning air. The musky perfume sunk deep inside, restoring her.

Stopping for a moment to catch her breath, she unbuttoned the top of her canvas barn jacket. It was an old one of Gus's, which didn't fit her badly, except for the sleeves that had to be rolled up. Pulling the wagon over the ground, bumpy with tree roots, was hard work. The load was growing higher. *What a waste,* she thought. *I could have made a hundred pies from all this fruit.*

She sat on the bench and looked out over the orchard. The mist was burning away, and she felt the warm sun on her skin. It was a deep pleasure to her, just to sit here in the quiet and look out at her land. She had been raised on the orchard, never lived anywhere else. She took it for granted, like taking air into her lungs or seeing the sunlight.

Now the load of spoiled apples looked to her like all the long days of every season that she'd taken for granted, just rushing through the hours unconsciously, as if it would never come to an end. Her children growing up from babies to adults while her back was turned, cooking something on the stove. She had seen her husband for the first time under these trees. She had been out here working in the spring, the boughs full of white blossoms and the smell of the flowers so heavy it would make her head ache some days. Her stepbrother Carl had brought Gus around. They had just gotten out of the army and both needed work. She had inherited the orchard and was running it all on her own. Gus was the handsomest man she had ever seen. The first time he smiled at her, she nearly fell off her ladder. She was twenty-nine, already an old maid and sure she would stay that way. She never thought Gus would be interested in her, especially since he was six years younger.

And now here she was, fifty years later, thinking that she never expected him to get sick first, either.

"Sophie! Hello—" She heard the Reverend call out to her from a long distance and saw him wave as he climbed up the hill from the house. She stood up and waved back, then picked up the wagon handle and headed down to meet him.

"Good morning, Reverend. Sorry I missed the service yesterday. Do you go out and track down all your missing sheep on Monday mornings?"

Ben laughed. "I'm hardly here to scold you, Sophie."

"I know that." She smiled. "Come on into the house. I've got some nice apple pie."

"I'll take some coffee. It's a bit early for me for pie," he said, patting his stomach. "I've barely had breakfast."

Sophie parked the wagon by the toolshed. She glanced at the Reverend over her shoulder. "You mean to tell me you never had pie for breakfast?" She shook her head. "You've lived a sheltered life, Reverend Ben."

He nodded, following her, and took off his hat as they entered. "No argument there," he agreed.

Sophie moved about the kitchen, heating the coffee and setting out cups. The Reverend sat at the table, watching her. She knew what he had come here to talk about. It was hard, though. Easier to keep her hands busy so her head didn't have to think too much.

"It's quiet here today," he said.

"It's always quiet on Mondays. Sometimes school groups come up, though."

"How are you managing alone out here?"

"All right." She nodded firmly. "I ran the place on my own before I married Gus, you know," she reminded him. She set a cup down in front of him and a plate with a fork and napkin, too. He always said he didn't want anything, then ended up enjoying it.

"I wouldn't do it again by myself, of course. I'm not planning on that, so you don't need to look so worried, Reverend."

He didn't answer right away. "Have you given much thought to what you will do? Once Gus is out of the hospital, I mean."

"I can finish up the picking season on my own. That's no problem," she said, pouring out the coffee. "Having Sam and the other men from church here was a blessing. If they come by again to paint, that will help me."

"I'll arrange it for you. No problem," Reverend Ben promised.

"I've been trying to persuade one of my kids to take the place over. You know, keep it in the family. They all love coming for a visit, but nobody wants to move back now. They're too involved with their own lives, you know. I raised them to know their own minds, so I really can't blame them."

"Very wise of you," Reverend Ben said.

"I guess we'll stay the winter. I hope it's not a bad one, either," she added, already feeling a chill in her bones from the memories of winters past—snow piled up to the windowsills and the ground hard with frost well into April. "I can take care of Gus and then we'll have to see," she said resolutely.

"Have you heard yet when Gus will be home?"

"The doctor says maybe next week. The infection is clearing, but they still want to watch him." She cut a thick wedge of pie and put it on the Reverend's plate.

"And what about his heart problem? How will they treat it?"

"They're only talking medications so far. They say he's too weak right now for an operation. He can't tire himself, of course. He has to slow down, live a different kind of life altogether," she said, sitting down beside him.

"That will be hard for him."

"Don't I know it. Hard for both of us," she said honestly. "I don't want to sell this place. I've been here so long, you would think I'd be rooted to the ground myself by now. I always thought I would die here," she said with a shrug. "It feels like it's just too late to move away."

The Reverend reached out and covered her hand with his. "It must be very frightening for you. I can't imagine it myself."

She nodded, swallowing a lump in her throat. "At least Gus and I will be together. That's the main thing now—that and getting him back on his feet again. Whatever comes our way in the spring, we'll face it together."

"You have Gus, you have your children. You have me, of course, and all your good friends in town," the Reverend reminded her. "And you have the Lord, Sophie. He knows you're frightened. Trust Him to help you get through this and show you what He has in store." He took a bite of the pie. "This is wonderful."

Sophie nodded. "Now you make me even sorrier that I missed the service Sunday." She saw him smile and then she smiled, too. "I know what you're saying, but I forget sometimes. That's why God set aside one day a week for going to church. To remind you of these things, right?"

"That's one way of looking at it."

"My mother always told us, 'Work hard, pray hard, and leave the rest to God.' That's all I can do now." She sat back, her lips set in a tight line. "People see me living up here on the orchard my whole life, and I guess they think, 'Poor woman. Up there with all those apple trees day in, day out. Why, she's barely set foot outside this town. Nothing very special has ever happened to her.' But lots of things have happened to me, Reverend, extraordinary things. Miracles, really, you could call them. Why, just the way Gus showed up here when I had lost hope of ever finding a husband. That was sort of a miracle, don't you think?"

"Yes, you could say that. Love is always a miracle, I believe."

"What I'm trying to say is, I've felt God's presence in my life. When I remember that, my faith is strong. I know I can trust Him to help us find our way now."

The Reverend smiled slowly, and leaned back in his chair, making Sophie feel as if she were his star pupil who had just worked out the answer to some particularly complicated equation.

When the Reverend got up to leave, Sophie went into her pantry and fixed a box for him, filling it with apples and squash, jars of apple butter, honey, and a fresh-baked pie. It was their usual routine, him refusing at first, saying it was too much, and her insisting until he accepted. This time he didn't argue as hard, she thought, and she saw a certain sadness in his eyes as he thanked her.

She pretended not to notice, though. She knew he was thinking that pretty soon, this too would come to an end. She didn't want to dwell on it anymore today.

She pulled on her jacket again and walked the Reverend outside to his car. The sun had rolled up over the hillside, warming the world in its wake, and Sophie felt eager to return to her work.

BEN SPENT A BUSY MONDAY, HIS VISIT WITH SOPHIE CROWDED OUT BY THE demands of his day. But she came to mind again that evening as he carried the half-empty carton she'd given him up to his own house. He had stored the jars of preserves and honey on the shelves of the church food bank, and given the pie and most of the apples to the church secretary.

There was still plenty left, though, he thought as he presented the box to Carolyn in the kitchen. "I was out at Sophie Potter's, and she gave me one of her care packages."

Carolyn was working at the sink, pulling apart a head of lettuce. She shut off the water, kissed his cold cheek, and quickly dried her hands on a towel. She didn't even spare a glance at the box, he noticed, as she brushed by.

"Look, a letter from Mark," she said, handing him a tan envelope with their address scrawled in a familiar slanted script. He slipped the letter out of the envelope, which had already been torn open.

He felt Carolyn watching him as he read it. It wasn't very long, but it was more conversational than Mark's last missive. This one described his life at the retreat, and how much peace he was finding in the beauty of the southwestern landscape. Then he asked questions about everyone in his family, especially Rachel.

Reaching the second page of the letter, Ben still wondered at Carolyn's happy, excited expression. So far he couldn't find any news from Mark that had inspired that reaction. Was she merely happy to hear from their son?

Then, near the bottom of the page, he read, "Coming here was good for me. It's helped me a lot to sort things out. I may come back to this retreat someday, but a month or so feels like enough for now. I'm thinking of heading back East to see you folks. But I'm not sure. There are other possibilities, too. I will be in touch soon and let you know." Finally he concluded, "Stay well. Love to all, Mark."

"He sounds good," Ben said, looking up at his wife.

"I thought so," Carolyn agreed. "More relaxed or maybe more secure. This is the first time he's said he might come home. Wouldn't that be something? To have him here for Christmas and Rachel's baby?"

"Yes, it would be." Ben could see that his wife was trying to control her anticipation but couldn't help hoping. "He doesn't say definitely, though," Ben cautioned her. "I don't think we should count on it."

"Yes, I know." She nodded, a swatch of thick blond hair falling across her cheek. "But I think it's a good sign."

"Absolutely," he agreed. He slipped the letter back into the envelope, feeling pensive. His visit to the orchard had put him in a strange mood today, melancholy and restless.

"Want to write him back tonight, after dinner?" he suggested.

"Yes, let's write him back right away. We need to let him know how much we want to see him. And that he doesn't have to be afraid to come home." She glanced at her husband quickly. "Afraid of us forcing some big confrontation, I mean."

"I understand," Ben said. "But I also think he might be ready to hear what we have to say." He started taking the apples out of the box, putting them in a blue ceramic bowl. "I think we need to let Mark know we want to talk things out finally, each of us taking responsibility, so we can truly make amends."

"I'm not sure we should tell him all that right now. We might scare him off," Carolyn said worriedly.

"Possibly," he acknowledged. "But it seems dishonest to me to have that hope for his homecoming and not tell him how we really feel. If Mark reacts badly, we'll just have to try again."

"No, Ben." Carolyn's voice was quiet, but Ben sensed a steel resolve beneath it. "You want to have everything out with him and heal the old wounds. You want to fix everything. And that would be a wonderful thing to do, but it may not be possible right now. Mark might not be ready for that."

"I realize—" Ben started.

"Hear me out," she insisted, cutting off his protest. "I don't want Mark to feel we're waiting here to pounce on him with some big reckoning. He won't come back if he thinks that. I know he won't. I'm his mother, and all I want is to see him again."

Ben met his wife's clear blue gaze, seeing a rare fierceness there. He knew what she said made sense. But up at the orchard he had felt time's keen blade pressed to his skin, the touch that reminds you life is so very short. He wanted to open his heart to his son. If they were ever going to set things right, he needed to be honest with him, and he wanted to start tonight.

But maybe that was the wrong approach, appeasing his own needs instead of considering Mark's—or Carolyn's, for that matter. Carolyn's hopes had been so high when he'd walked in the door. Now she was afraid. He didn't want her to feel that way—or to blame him if what she feared came to pass, he realized. This time they would try things her way. He owed her that much.

"I understand," he said finally. "Don't worry." He touched her arm. "Why don't you write back to him, and I'll just add a note at the end?"

She nodded and moved toward the table. "All right. I'll do it after dinner. We can take a walk and mail it."

The table was already set. Carolyn had put two low candles in the center. Her hand moved gracefully as she lit them. "Thank you, Ben, for letting me do this my way," she said.

She sat down and unfolded her napkin. She looked happier again, he thought. He reached over and squeezed her hand.

"I hope he does come back, dear. I hope you're not disappointed."

"We all would be," she pointed out.

He nodded. "Yes, of course." But he knew in his heart that her disappointment would be the greatest somehow. He wished he could protect her from that possibility, and he knew all too well that he couldn't.

ON WEDNESDAY NIGHT EVERY SEAT IN THE VILLAGE HALL AUDITORIUM WAS filled. Emily sat at a long table, shoulder to shoulder with Luke McAllister and the New Horizons Boston-area program director, Dr. Jim Santori. Two other members of his team were there as well, a psychologist, who counseled the kids in the program, and one of the teachers.

"Good evening, everyone," Emily began. "Since Luke McAllister's proposal to bring a New Horizons program to Cape Light is causing so much controversy, it seemed that it would be useful to have the facts, and to give you a chance to ask questions of the people who run this program."

Then she introduced each speaker and sat down to listen while Dr. Santori and the others explained the program.

"Since New Horizons started fifteen years ago, over five thousand young men and woman have attended," Dr. Santori began. "Most have either returned to school full-time or finished a GED and gone into our job training and placement program. We also make continued support available after their twelve-week stay at a New Horizons center.

"As you can see from the fact sheets handed out at the door, our success rate is measured in the number of residents who enter the workforce full-time by age twenty and remain employed and out of jail for five years. That figure is over seventy-five percent." Jim Santori paused. "Now, that may not sound to you like a picture-perfect record, but if we were playing baseball, we'd be batting .750."

"The Sox could use you next year!" Harry Reilly shouted out, drawing a laugh.

But Emily sensed that the tension in the room was high. She felt tense herself, waiting for the question-and-answer period to begin. She saw Charlie sitting a few rows back from the front, flanked by his campaign supporters. Dressed in a gray suit and tie, and tapping a pile of index cards on his knee, he looked primed to make another speech. Emily wondered how Dr. Santori and his staff would field those line drives.

Alice Gerber, a psychologist and social worker, and her colleague, Phillip Engel, a specialist in remedial education, each spoke about their role in the program. Alice offered a story about a boy who had dropped out of school at age sixteen and was picked up for shoplifting before his referral to the New Horizons center in Minneapolis.

"He graduated law school two years ago and has been working as an assistant DA in Minneapolis–St. Paul," she added proudly. "Which is not to say that all of our kids go to college or even should be pointed in that direction. But I think it's solid proof that our program really can work."

Emily watched the audience reaction carefully. She felt that the speakers from New Horizons were making a good impression. They presented the facts in a clear, professional manner, their dedication to the program unmistakable.

When it was Luke McAllister's turn to speak, he seemed nervous walking to the podium, his slight limp obvious as he moved across the stage. He had not dressed up for this moment in the spotlight, Emily noticed. Luke wore a black crewneck sweater and jeans with a worn leather jacket, looking every inch the outsider and not about to hide it. He was the take-it-or-leave-it type, she thought, and she liked that about him.

"Thank you for coming here tonight," he read from a sheet of paper. "I hope the presentations of Dr. Santori and his staff have given you more information about our plans. I hope the facts have answered your questions and helped to erase the fear that this center will ruin Cape Light."

He paused and took a sip of water. Then he looked directly at Charlie, who shifted in his seat. "I think most of you realize now, that's just not true," Luke said slowly.

He put the speech down and scanned the audience. Emily followed Luke's gaze and saw him find Sara, sitting in a seat near the front. Their eyes locked for a moment, then Luke continued.

"I know I'm an outsider here. There's a lot of talk around town about me, too. Some of it is even true," he added wryly. "I didn't come up here to purposely ruin your town, like some of you think. A few years ago I was a police officer down in Boston, trying to do some good for people. I can't be a police officer anymore, but I still want to do some good. You have a choice, too, about what you want to do.

"You can share the peace and purity of this place with other people—kids who maybe need it even more than any of you and are getting one chance to turn their lives around.

"This center isn't going to take anything away from any of you," he insisted. "It might even make you prouder to say you live here."

He stopped abruptly, seeming suddenly self-conscious of the emotional turn his words had taken. "Thank you," he said, and stepped away from the podium.

Emily took the microphone on the table. "I'll open the floor to—" She saw Charlie jump up and scramble to the microphone set up in the aisle. "—to questions," she concluded quickly.

"My question is for Dr. Santori," Charlie spoke up. "We heard a lot of nice stories about how these kids are ending up lawyers and doctors and model citizens after they go through your program. But not too much about where you find them. I'm hearing shoplifting, assault, suspended sentence because the kid's a first time offender—"

"What is your question, Charlie?" Emily interrupted.

"My question, Mayor, is who are we opening our doors to? A bunch of juvenile delinquents with no respect for the law, some who have already broken it and been caught red-handed."

"Not all of our referrals are from the court system," Dr. Santori replied. "Many are from the schools or social services."

"Okay," Charlie continued, "so every night seven out of ten are going to go to their rooms and do their homework. Meanwhile, the other three are maybe going to jump the fence and cause havoc around here."

The audience murmured, sounding as if they agreed with him.

Emily leaned toward the microphone. "That's still not a question, Charlie." She turned to Dr. Santori. "Can you speak to this point?"

"We'll always have some kids who don't follow our house rules," Dr. Santori admitted. "After three warnings, they have to leave the program. There are also some isolated incidents of problems in the surrounding neighborhoods with kids who leave the center without permission—"

"I thought so," Charlie said with satisfaction.

Oh, dear, Emily thought. That was just what they didn't need to hear.

"But these events are very few and usually minor," Dr. Santori concluded.

Everyone in the audience was talking again. Did anyone even hear him at that point? Emily wondered.

"How few?" Charlie challenged.

Dr. Santori glanced at his colleagues, clearly on the spot.

"I don't have specific numbers, but I would say that there's no significant rise in crime in the neighborhoods hosting centers."

"Really, why not? You have figures for everything else." Charlie waved the information sheet. "Of course he doesn't have the information. They don't want us to know the truth," Charlie said, glancing around for support.

"Address your questions to the speakers," Emily cut in. "And I don't think that accusation is fair or appropriate," she added.

She was about to say something stronger and more definitive when Warren Oakes caught her eye. He sat in the front row, red-faced and looking ready to explode. Emily couldn't tell if he was angrier with Charlie or her.

"Next question, please," she said, encouraging Charlie to step out of the way so that the next person in line could speak. Charlie didn't seem ready to give up the microphone, but then Betty Bowman stepped up. Wearing her cheerleader smile, she edged him out of position in a determined but ladylike fashion.

Emily watched her warily. Betty being her friend and supporter didn't mean that she was for the center.

"The fact sheet notes that real estate values are not affected in neighborhoods where there are New Horizons centers," Betty began. "Can you talk a little more about that, Dr. Santori? I'm a realtor here in town, and I know that's a big concern."

Thank you, Betty, Emily said silently to her friend. Give him something positive to talk about. Good move.

While Dr. Santori answered the question, Emily had a chance to get her bearings. Fifteen minutes left to the meeting and emotions were rising. She wondered if they would make it to the finish without another outburst from Charlie.

Emily looked down to see Lucy step to the microphone. Charlie turned around in his seat, scowling, but Lucy paid him no attention.

"I noticed the fact sheet says that kids might go out in the community and work for free, to get some practical experience. What kinds of work do they do?"

"I'll let Alice answer that," Jim Santori said, passing the microphone down the table.

"They won't find any jobs in a diner, I'll tell you that!" someone shouted out, evoking more laughter.

Looking positively livid, Charlie got up from his seat and stood next to his wife. Emily had a feeling that he would have happily dragged her away; the only thing stopping him was his fear of embarrassing himself.

"Thanks for bringing that up," the social worker said smoothly. "We sometimes do an outreach in the community, with our kids working on some project that will benefit the neighborhood. Like building a play-ground, for example, or cleaning up a park or a beach. Local businesses can also get an intern for a few hours a week, who would learn useful job skills."

"That sounds just lovely," Charlie interrupted. "They're going to come and build a new playground for us. Isn't that good news? But I'd like to get back to this crime question."

"Charlie!" Lucy protested.

"You said before that the rise in crime is insignificant," he went on, ignoring her. "Is that right?"

Dr. Santori's expression was wary as he said, "Yes, that's right. That's what I said."

"But insignificant . . . that's a relative term, don't you think?" Charlie persisted. Without waiting for a reply, he continued. "I mean, what's not so bad to you, doesn't mean it would be okay to us. If you're living in a city, where crimes are happening every five minutes, well, what's a few more per year? Meanwhile, we hardly have any crime going on here at all—"

"Except for jerks tossing rocks through windshields, you mean!" Luke shouted out, coming to his feet.

"You brought that on yourself, McAllister!" somebody else shouted.

"Go back where you came from, all of you," another voice called out. "What do we need this for?"

"We don't need it," Charlie answered. "We—"

"Wait just a minute!" Emily called out, trying to regain order in the room. "We're getting off the track here—"

"Not at all, Mayor," Charlie corrected her. "I think we just got to the real point."

The audience stirred, the noise level rising with so many people talking at once that Emily could hardly hear herself think.

She leaned forward to reply when Warren Oakes caught her attention. His face contorted in an angry scowl, he held up his wrist, pointing frantically to his watch, then slicing his finger across his throat.

Is that a signal to call time, or is he telling me I've just slit my own throat up here tonight? Emily wondered.

Emily quickly took the microphone. "That will conclude the meeting. Thank you all for coming. If you have any further questions, you can drop them off at the Village Hall, addressed to my attention, and I'll pass them on to Dr. Santori and his staff."

Dr. Santori said a few quiet words to his colleagues, then they all started collecting their papers and packing up to go. Luke sat there, looking frustrated and unhappy.

Emily barely had time to thank the guests for coming before they made a quick exit from the room. Her campaign advisers stood in a small cluster near the deserted speakers' table, but didn't approach her. Emily swallowed hard. She had acted against their advice, and now she would hear about it.

Luke still stood near and she turned to speak to him. His expression was so downcast, he barely met her eye.

"It got rough out there at the end," she acknowledged, "but I still think this meeting was a good idea."

"A good idea for Charlie Bates, maybe," Luke agreed with a sarcastic laugh as Sara walked up to stand beside him.

"People need time to take in the information," Emily said. "They need time to think and get used to new ideas."

"Sometimes people need someone to tell them what to think," Sara cut in. "Charlie is certainly doing his share."

"I didn't set up this meeting to get my opinion out," Emily said carefully. "I held it to get out Luke's information."

Luke glanced first at Sara, then back at Emily. "I guess we have to wait and see. Work on the cottages started on Monday, and we're going to keep at it. Thanks for trying."

"You're welcome," Emily said.

" 'Night," Sara said, and walked away with Luke.

Emily felt drained and misunderstood. She had thought a rational presentation of facts would encourage a rational response. Obviously, that wasn't the case. And she had thought holding this meeting would be a clear sign that she was trying to help Luke. But the look in Sara's eyes told her that she was wrong on that count, too.

CHAPTER ELEVEN

⌒

S ARA WATCHED THE DOOR AT THE CLAM BOX THE
next morning, knowing Emily would not stop in. But
still, she watched for her.

I was hard on her, Sara thought. *The meeting was her idea.
She was trying, at least. But then she sat up there all night, like a
stone lion, and didn't say a word in Luke's favor. Still afraid to
stick her neck out. Meanwhile, Charlie turned it into a pep rally.*

"Order up!" Charlie slapped the bell near the service
counter. "Sara, come and get your order," he called.

"I hear you—" she called back, half-ignoring him.

A customer was telling her what he wanted for breakfast,
and Sara suddenly realized she hadn't been listening.

"Sorry, how do you want the eggs?"

"I didn't ask for eggs. I want hotcakes, bacon on the side," he said, sounding annoyed.

"I got it." Sara whisked away his menu. "Be right back with your coffee," she promised.

She went to the counter to pick up her order and found Charlie arguing with Lucy. "It's not what a man expects from his wife, Lucy. You embarrassed me in public while I'm in the middle of this election. How could you go against me like that?"

"I didn't go against you. How many times do I have to say it? I was just asking a question."

Sara was about to escape with her order when she noticed it was missing a side of hash browns. She didn't need another annoyed customer this morning. The tips were bad enough around here. She felt self-conscious listening to Charlie and Lucy argue, but she needed her hash browns and didn't quite dare to interrupt.

"Your innocent question made me look like a fool," he went on.

As if he needed any help doing that, Sara thought.

"I don't know what's gotten into you lately, but it's got to stop," he warned Lucy. "Do you hear me?"

Sara thought Lucy was going to burst into tears for a moment. Then her face got a tight, determined look.

"I can get up and speak in a meeting if I want to. The world doesn't revolve around you—"

"You're wrong and you know it. You just won't admit it, as usual," he grumbled. "Here's your order," he said, grudgingly setting a plate of pancakes on the order bar. He suddenly caught sight of Sara. "What do you want?"

"I need some potatoes on this," she said, shoving the plate toward him. He scowled and dumped a scoop on the dish.

She pulled the plate back. "She has a right to ask a question, Charlie," she said impulsively. From the corner of her eye, she caught sight of Lucy, who hadn't walked away yet with the pancakes. Lucy slowly turned, watching Sara and Charlie.

Charlie stood with his hands on his hips. "Who asked you? As a matter of fact, I think you're the one who's been filling my wife's head with all these wild ideas. All this lunacy started when you came to work here."

"That's ridiculous. Lucy wanted to go back to finish school for a long time. She didn't need me to talk her into it."

"Ridiculous? I don't think so. You're the troublemaking type, just like your misfit friend, McAllister. He is your friend, isn't he?" he challenged her. "I saw the two of you leaving the meeting last night. You were the only one in there who would talk to him."

"A lot of people there agreed with him, Charlie," Sara shot back. She was too angry now to be cautious. "They might have said so, too, if you weren't hogging the mike all night."

Charlie's face got beet red. "You're fired! Do you hear me?" he shouted at her. "As of—right now!"

Sara stared at him a minute and was surprised to realize she felt only relief. "Fine with me," she said, reaching for her apron strings.

"Hold on—" Lucy moved forward and took hold of Sara's arm. Sara turned to face her, and she felt a stab of guilt. Lucy looked so woeful, as if she were stranded in some hostile place and Sara's was the last familiar face.

"You can't let her go like that," Lucy said, still holding on to Sara's arm.

"Oh, yes, I can," Charlie insisted.

"Okay, then, who's going to take care of the customers at night? Billy's got his hands full cooking, and you want me home stuffing envelopes, making phone calls, driving all over town to drop off this and pick up that. You say I don't help with your campaign, but the bottom line is, I can't be in two places at once. I can't take care of all your campaign stuff every night and watch the kids and work here, too, while you're out making a speech or having a meeting or—"

"All right, all right." Charlie put his hands over his ears. "You made your point, Lucy. She can stay. But no more back talk," he said sternly, looking at Sara. "I'm still the boss here."

Sara swallowed hard but didn't say anything in reply. She was more than half-sorry that Charlie reversed himself, but glancing at Lucy, she felt she couldn't walk out on her friend.

"You're going to stay?" Lucy asked, "Right?"

"I'll stay," Sara told her quietly. "For a while, at least."

She turned and carried the plate of eggs and potatoes away, feeling a curious sense of triumph. Nothing's really changed, she thought. But it sure felt good to stand up to that blowhard.

LUKE WORKED HARD BESIDE SAM AND DIGGER FOR THE REST OF THE DAY, pushing himself to keep up with them and to keep his worries at bay. Finally, as the sun went down, Sam and Digger packed up and headed back to town.

Luke walked slowly back to his cottage, his limp more pronounced. His bad leg ached. His whole body ached, actually. He thought he was in shape, but he hadn't done any hard physical work like this for years now. *It's going to take me a while to get up to speed with Sam and even Digger,* he realized. But he was satisfied with the progress they had made in only four days.

That at least was something, he thought. And he would have a visit from Sara tonight. Last night she said she would stop by with some dinner from the diner for them. That was something else good to look forward to.

By the time Sara knocked, he had showered and changed his clothes. He was happy to see her. It was the first time he had really smiled all day, he realized. He had an impulse to kiss her hello, or even hug her, but he held back.

"Hey, how are you? What did you bring me to eat?" he asked, taking the white take-out bags from her hands.

"Now, there's a typical guy greeting," she said, slipping off her jacket.

He laughed and put the bags on the countertop. "You're right. I'm sorry. How was work today? Sell a lot of clam rolls?"

"Charlie fired me. But Lucy made him take it back."

Sara met his startled gaze. "I'm not even sure if I'm happy about that part yet."

"He fired you? Because of me?"

"Your name did come up. But that was after I called him on hogging the mike last night at the meeting. And he thinks I'm a bad influence on Lucy."

"He's a jerk. You ought to go in there tomorrow and quit."

"I would, but I feel bad for Lucy."

"You're loyal, Sara, I'll say that for you." He pulled some plates out of the cabinet and set them on the table, along with some silverware. "So, according to the Clam Box grapevine, did last night's meeting help us or hurt us?"

Sara shrugged. "It's hard to tell. Charlie and his friends aren't exactly neutral. But I saw people really listening when you spoke. I think you showed a lot of commitment. And courage," she added.

The word *courage* caught his attention. Did she really think that? He turned and grabbed the take-out containers. For some reason, he didn't want her to see how much her praise affected him.

"Here, let's eat. I'm starved," he said as he put the cartons of food on the table.

"Listen, I've got an idea," Sara said. "Why don't you write a letter to the *Messenger*? You could rebut Charlie's claims and say everything you wanted to say last night. I'll help you," she offered.

Luke sat back. "I'm not sure you know what you're offering. It would be more like you doing all the work. Believe me, I'm no writer."

"That's okay. Just tell me what you want to say, and I'll put it all together."

He thought for a moment. "Okay. Let's do it. I can't see that I have anything left to lose."

"No," Sara agreed with a grin. "You don't."

*   *   *

EMILY PUSHED HERSELF UP THE BIG HILL BEFORE THE TURN TO EMERSON Street. Today the weather was warmer—a brief flash of Indian summer in the midst of winter's approach—and she was jogging in running shorts and a sweatshirt. She felt the burn in her legs and lungs but kept going, focusing on the rhythm of her breath.

Saturday, finally. It had been a long week, but somehow, she had made it through. Now afternoon sunlight illuminated the red and gold leaves on the trees that lined the road. She loved the autumn—except this year. The election and the problems with Jessica's wedding were taking the joy out of it for her.

Though Reverend Ben had gotten Sam and Jessica talking again, Emily was still worried about them. Jessica still had not set a wedding date. *At least I'm getting her out today to look at gowns,* she thought.

Wandering around shopping malls and trying on bridesmaids' dresses was the last thing Emily felt like doing—she actually dreaded it—but she knew she had to keep Jessica focused on the wedding. Besides, the evening promised to be even tougher. Her campaign committee was meeting at Betty Bowman's.

As she reached the top of the hill and turned on to Emerson, Emily slowed her pace. A moving van was parked in front of Dan's new house. He was moving in today. She'd forgotten all about that. She jogged up to the house and stopped, looking around for him. One of the movers stepped out of the truck, carrying a pile of boxes. "Coming through here," he grunted.

"Oh, sorry. Is Dan around?"

Dan emerged from the garage. "Looking for me?"

"I forgot you were moving in today," she replied as he walked toward her. "Congratulations."

"Thanks, I think." His hands were dusty, and she spotted another streak on his cheek and had the impulse to brush it off, but didn't quite dare.

"No wonder I put off moving for so long," Dan said. "It's such a pain. I didn't think I had so much stuff. I'd say about half of it could have been thrown out and the other half given to charity."

"It always seems to be more than you thought," she agreed.

He looked different to her, wearing jeans and a worn blue flannel shirt with a green T-shirt underneath. His hair was messed up, too, and somehow the casual, unkempt look made him seem all the more appealing.

"So, what do you think?" he said, framing the small bungalow with his hands. "I know it's not much, but looks like I'm stuck with it."

"Oh, it's not that bad," she said, gazing at the squat little cottage. "The color isn't right, though. I think you should paint it off-white and put up some shutters, dark green maybe."

"I can see that," Dan replied, squinting at the house. "But I'll have to leave the home improvements for my son, Wyatt. I doubt I'll be living here long enough for any major changes."

Oh, right. Dan was sailing off to tropical climes, and Wyatt would be living here.

"When is Wyatt coming?"

"Looks like early November now. It would be great if he could help me with the campaign coverage. I could use a hand right now, with all the controversy about McAllister's center."

Emily couldn't help laughing. "Wait a minute. Aren't you the guy who was complaining to me about a dull race?"

"Well, you've livened it up enough now. Stop any time you like," he suggested with a smile.

"If only," she said. "Thanks, by the way, for printing Luke's letter this morning. I'm sure my phone will be ringing off the hook on Monday."

"Poor Emily. Sorry about that. But I couldn't resist." He crossed his arms over his chest and took a long, appraising look at her. So long, in fact, it made her feel self-conscious.

"It was a good letter, don't you think?"

"Very well written," she admitted. "I think it should help his case. He was shouted down so badly at the meeting."

"Yes, he was," Dan agreed. He paused, looking thoughtful. Did he think she could have done more to help Luke that night?

"Actually, Luke told me Sara Franklin helped him with the letter," Dan said. "His ideas, her writing."

Of course, Emily realized. It sounded a lot like Sara when she thought about it. "She polished up that piece I gave you on the substation, too. I think she's good, don't you?"

"Yes, very good. I could give her some work at the paper if she wants it."

"I'll let her know. I think she'll be happy to hear it."

Sara would be pleased, Emily thought. And at least I can tell her about that.

"Would you like to come in?" Dan asked suddenly. "I have a pizza sitting around in that mess somewhere. Probably dropped a box of books on it. And I can offer you a glass of water, but we'll have to search around for the glasses," he added with a grin.

"I'd love to," she said truthfully, "but I've got to get going. I'm supposed to meet my sister in a little while. Some other time, though, okay?" she added.

He met her gaze. "Absolutely. You'll be tired of seeing me in no time."

Guess again, she silently corrected him. She tried to ignore the warm light in his eyes and smile, but couldn't quite.

"Ready with the couch," a mover grunted, swinging one end of a long brown sofa past the two of them. "Where do you want it?"

"I'll be right in." Dan turned to Emily, looking torn.

"Sounds like you're needed," Emily said. "See you."

"Yes. See you soon, Emily. Thanks for stopping by," he called as he started off to follow the workmen.

She turned and walked the rest of the way home. Dan Forbes was a puzzle to her. Even when they didn't agree, she felt so relaxed with him, so much herself. Which was not the case with most men she met. Was he interested in her? He seemed to be lately. Or was he just being friendly?

She was bad at reading those kinds of signals, always had been. Either she missed the message entirely or made too much of it in her mind.

But with Dan, there seemed to be more there. Not just flirtatious games. Something real—or with the potential to be real. *So near and yet so far,* she thought with a sigh.

Emily opened her front door and went inside, then tossed her keys on the hall table.

Get a grip. The man smiled at you. End of story. Besides, it can't go anywhere if he's sailing off into the sunset in a few weeks. The most you can hope for now is a few nice postcards with palm trees, she advised herself wistfully.

She yanked off her jogging shoes and started to get ready for her shopping date with Jessica.

"WHEN YOU ANNOUNCED BACK IN AUGUST, WE HAD BATES BEAT, FOUR TO one. Look at this poll." Warren passed around a handout he had prepared. "If the election were held tomorrow, there's no saying who would win."

Sitting in a comfortable armchair in the middle of Betty's living room, Emily stared down at the handout. One of Warren's telephone polls, which probably amounted to Warren phoning six of his closest neighbors. Of course, Warren acted as if he were Gallup and CNN rolled into one, his information infallible. For once, though, Emily wasn't skeptical of his results. She didn't need a survey to tell her she was in trouble.

"Monday is October one," he reminded her. "We can still win this, Emily. But we all have to really bear down now."

"The problem is that that McAllister issue just won't go away," Harriet said. "Did you read that letter of his in the *Messenger*? As if that town meeting wasn't enough."

"I think we've all learned our lesson from that meeting," Warren said, looking straight at Emily. "The New Horizons Center is not what we're going to talk about."

"Oh, come on," Emily said. "We've all known each other too long to be playing games. When I speak to the Rotary next week, should I just act as if the elephant is not in the room?"

"You don't have to ignore it, Emily," Warren said. "Just come out against it."

Emily felt a jolt. Everyone in the room was quiet.

Betty breezed in from the kitchen, holding her silver coffeepot. "Anybody need more coffee?" she asked brightly.

Nobody said anything for what seemed to Emily a very long time.

"I can't do that," Emily said finally. "It's not the way I really feel. I think the center is a good idea, and I think you already know that."

Warren pulled off his reading glasses in disgust. "I give up! Can anybody talk some sense into her?"

Doris, Frank, and Harriet all avoided Emily's gaze.

But Betty placed the coffeepot on a silver tray and sat down next to her. "I know how you feel, and I respect you for it. We all do, even if we don't agree," she added. "But the feelings in town are already so strong against this center, Emily, that I don't think anything you do or say can change it."

"And it's only going to get worse," Doris predicted in a grim tone. "I heard some kids from this program are coming from Boston next week to work on the construction."

"They are?" Harriet looked shocked. "How did you hear that?"

"Molly Willoughby. Luke hired her to cook a big welcoming dinner when they arrive on Monday night. That's her day to clean for me, so she told me when she called to cancel," Doris noted.

"Charlie will jump all over this," Frank said with a groan.

"The point is, it's out of your hands," Betty went on. "It's gone too far.

Can't you see? . . . Is it really worth handing Charlie the election over a lost cause?"

Emily met her friend's gaze. Betty had a clear way of looking at things, a simple way. Weighing the costs and benefits, pluses and minuses. Why throw good money after bad? Why lose an election by championing a lost cause?

The problem was, Emily didn't see it that way. Not in her heart. She shifted restlessly, then got up from her chair.

"Don't worry. I'll figure out something to say to the Rotary Club," she promised.

"But not in favor of McAllister, I hope." Warren's tone held a warning note Emily resented.

"Oh, please don't, Emily," Doris added. "Betty's right. There's nothing to gain here."

"You'd be a fool to try," Harriet said, her eyes narrowing. "And I never thought I was supporting a fool."

"Well, what's it going to be?" Warren asked impatiently.

Emily swallowed hard. This was it. Stand up against them—or watch them all walk out on her.

"Okay," she said. "While the race is going on, I won't support Luke's program."

She saw them exchanging looks of relief. Once again she had backed off, she realized. It was the sensible, politic thing to do. And it made her feel hollow and cowardly.

"SO, YOU LIKE CAUSING TROUBLE FOR YOURSELF, DO YOU?" DR. ELLIOT STOOD at the bottom of the ladder, peering up at Luke through his gold-rimmed spectacles.

Where in the world did he come from? Luke wondered. *And what was he talking about?* "Wait a second, I'll be right down."

As he came to the ground, he saw a copy of the *Messenger* in Dr.

Elliot's hand. It was Saturday's edition, opened to the editorial page, where the letter he and Sara had written appeared.

"Oh, that." He rubbed the back of his neck with his hand. "I just wanted to set the record straight, that's all."

"You did a good job of it, too. But you have enough on your plate without defending me as well." Ezra gave him a curt nod. "I appreciate it, is what I came to say. It was good of you."

Luke felt embarrassed by Dr. Elliot's gratitude. "It's okay. It was nothing, really," he said, bending to pick up a hammer.

The property was filled with activity now that six teenagers from the program had arrived—two girls and four boys—along with two counselors. Sam had put them all to work, and the place had turned into a bona fide construction site. Hammers pounded and an electric drill started up.

Ezra glanced around. "It's gotten busy as a beehive around here. Where did you find all the help?"

"Those kids are from the program," Luke explained. "There's a lot to do. We're renovating the cottages as bunks. And we're going to add a main building on that empty property back there, with classrooms and a common room, for lectures and group activities. So we need to dig the foundation soon, before the ground freezes."

"Sounds like a big undertaking," Ezra said soberly. "I hope all this effort isn't in vain."

So do I, Luke nearly replied, but he didn't even want to recognize the possibility of failure.

"We have the permits. There's no legal way they can stop us." He met Ezra's thoughtful gaze, sounding far more certain than he actually felt.

"Luke, something's happened! You'd better come," Digger suddenly appeared, running toward them from the other side of the property. "An accident. One of the kids."

Luke dropped the hammer and started running. Dr. Elliot followed. On the other side of Luke's cottage they saw a tall boy sitting on the ground. Sam and one of the counselors were beside him. Sam was wrapping his shirt around the boy's arm. Blood seeped through the thick layer of cloth.

Luke felt sick at the sight, images of the shooting at Delaney Street flooding his mind. He stopped in his tracks, trying to get his bearings.

Dr. Elliot rushed forward. "What he'd do, cut himself?" he asked, kneeling down next to the boy.

"Yeah, it's pretty bad, too," Sam said. "It's my fault. I should have kept a closer eye on him."

"No, it's not," the boy said. "You told me not to touch the machine, and I did it anyway."

"All right, we'll figure that out later. Keep the pressure on it. And get it elevated." Dr. Elliot glanced over his shoulder at Luke. "Let's get him inside. Somebody needs to go out to my car and get my bag," he said, pulling out his car keys. "It's parked down on the drive, under the big tree."

One of the other boys trotted forward. "I'll go," he volunteered. Dr. Elliot nodded at him and handed over the keys.

"Okay, get him up," he said to Sam and the counselor.

As they helped the boy to his feet, Dr. Elliot touched the boy's shoulder. "You're going to be all right," he assured him. "What's your name?"

"Derek. Derek Wilson."

"All right, Derek Wilson. Let's go inside and I'll take a look at the damage." Dr. Elliot led the way into Luke's cottage. "Let him sit at that table, under the light. I'll wash my hands. Somebody bring me some clean towels, will you?"

The doctor's bag soon arrived and he got to work, cleaning the wound and talking practically nonstop to his patient.

"I knew a Derek once in school," Dr. Elliot was saying as he prepared a syringe for a tetanus shot. "He wasn't nearly as tall as you. Sort of a runty fellow, like me. But he was quite strong. Once we were hiking around in that marsh over there, and I fell into some quicksand." He jabbed the boy's arm with the needle. Derek blinked but didn't say a word. "Well, Derek found a birch sapling and pulled me right out. . . ."

As Luke stood by watching, he couldn't help but be amused by the doctor's rambling conversation, which seemed to be the perfect distraction for his young patient.

A short time later Derek's cut was sutured and covered with a gauze bandage.

"I'll be back in three days to check on him. If the cut starts to look red or puffy around the stitches, call me right away," Dr. Elliot instructed Luke.

"Thanks for helping me," the boy said.

"No problem. It could have been worse. If you don't know how to use a tool, stay away from it until you learn," he added curtly.

"I hear you, Doc," Derek said with a nod.

Luke noticed Dr. Elliot's surprised smile. "I'll see you in a few days. We'll talk some more."

The counselor led Derek back to his cottage to rest. Luke watched Dr. Elliot roll down his sleeves and pack up his medical bag.

"You sure showed up at the right time."

"Yes, I did, didn't I?" Dr. Elliot agreed. "If you have an emergency, feel free to call me. Otherwise, you'll need to drive these kids to the Southport ER. That could be a problem."

"Yes, it could. Thanks for the offer."

"That's all right. I've got nothing better to do," he admitted.

He snapped the bag shut and looked up at Luke. "That boy is bright. A good kid, too. He didn't even fuss when I stitched him up. He's got a heap of trouble stacked against him, though," the doctor added, shaking his head. "He told me he's been in five foster homes in the last three years. He ran away from the last one and was picked up for vagrancy. The real shame is, that's probably just the half of it."

"No, the real shame, Doctor, is that compared to some of the other kids in the program, Derek had it easy."

Dr. Elliot slipped his jacket on. "I'm sure that's true. Meanwhile, narrow-minded blowhards, like Charlie Bates, think they know it all and don't have a clue."

He opened the door to let himself out. "You're doing a good job here. Keep it up."

Luke smiled at him. "Thanks, Doctor. See you soon."

ON TUESDAY MORNING EMILY ARRIVED AT THE PEQUOT INN AT A QUARTER to eight, right on time for the Rotary Club's monthly breakfast meeting.

The members smiled and shook her hand as they entered, and Emily greeted most by name. She had dressed carefully in one of her best suits, a slim gray skirt and belted jacket. She even put on makeup and extra lipstick. On the outside, at least, she seemed the perfect candidate—poised, polished, and well prepared.

The room filled up, but she waited by the door for Warren. Standing alone in the inn's lobby, she slipped her speech out of her purse to sneak a look. It was mainly her stump speech, dressed up a bit for this group. It listed her accomplishments during the past three years and described her goals and the special talents she brought to the job of mayor.

Toward the bottom of the page, Warren had penciled in a few "suggestions" to address the New Horizons "problem." Emily had revised and rewritten the section dozens of times. Coming out against the project would never sit right with her, no matter how she phrased it.

But I promised them I would, she reminded herself.

Emily turned abruptly and pushed through the door to the ladies' room. She ran the cold water and wet a paper towel. Then sat down in a chair, the towel pressed to her head, her eyes closed. She felt very ill. It has to be nerves, she told herself, though it felt like something much worse.

It wasn't like her to be nervous or upset before an appearance, certainly not before a little breakfast speech like this one. She had given speeches with jet lag and the flu, and once did a TV interview an hour after having a root canal. She was a trooper.

But here she was, rattled and dizzy and about to lose the little that was in her stomach.

What are my alternatives here? Give the speech as is, even though the words will stick in my throat as I come out against the center—and then read all about it in the next edition of the Messenger. She had spotted one of Dan's stringers. *Or I could be honest and say I support it—and then take the heat from Warren and the others.*

Neither of her choices seemed the right one.

What could she do? She checked her watch. They must be looking for her. Feeling desperate, she closed her eyes and began to pray. *Dear Lord, please take pity on me. What should I do?*

A sharp knock sounded on the door. "Emily, are you in there? . . . Are you all right?"

It was Warren. She took a deep breath and ran her fingers through her hair. "I'm fine. I'll be right out," she called back.

She stood up and smoothed out her skirt. The nearby window was small and high—but not an impossible escape route, she thought wryly.

She turned, forced one foot in front of the other, then opened the door slowly. Warren stood there, looking annoyed and nervous. "Are you all right?" he asked again, his tone impatient.

She swallowed hard and began to nod her head, then felt—overwhelmed. As if she might scream or faint. Or both.

Emily leaned forward, whispering in his ear. "I can't do this. You have to make some excuse. Tell them anything. I don't care."

He pulled back and stared at her. "What do you mean? You're not giving the speech?"

She shook her head and slipped her purse strap over her arm. "I can't do it. . . . I don't feel well. I have to go."

"You can't just run out like this, Emily." He grabbed her arm. "They're all in there, waiting for you. What am I supposed to say?"

Emily pulled away from his hold. "I don't know," she said honestly. "You're so good at putting words in my mouth. I'm sure you'll come up with something."

Before Warren could reply, she swept past him and out the door, into the bright morning sun. She quickly got into her car and headed toward the village, her thoughts whirling. What had she just done? Had she lost her mind altogether? She'd never done anything like this before in her life. . . . Well, practically, she amended, thinking of the way she ran off with Tim right after high school.

But that was different.

Warren will be livid and the rest of my committee not much happier. How am I ever going to face them?

What was happening to her?

Emily turned down Main Street, but when she came to the Village Hall, she kept on driving. She drove all the way down to the harbor and the green. She parked the car and sat there a minute, then got out and started walking on the nearest path, with the water on one side and the green on the other.

The green and town dock were quiet, except for a few dog walkers and women pushing strollers. Emily walked to the farthest bench and sat down. The day had started off sunny, but now clouds were gathering, blocking the sun. *It's going to rain. Just as well,* she thought. *We need some rain. Everything is so dry.*

Sea birds dipped and dived around the pier, and the wind that lifted their wings chilled her. She hugged her arms around herself and took a deep breath. She didn't want to start crying, right here, sitting on a bench in the park, but she felt tears in her eyes when she blinked the wind away.

"Emily . . . are you all right?" Emily heard the voice and felt the light touch on her shoulder almost simultaneously.

She looked up and saw Reverend Ben standing beside her, the collar of his jacket turned up against the wind.

"Is there something wrong?" he asked, sitting down next to her.

"Hello, Reverend." Emily felt embarrassed, and wiped her eyes with the back of her hand. "It's nothing, really. I'm okay," she said automatically.

"You know, it's all right to ask for help sometimes," he said gently. "You don't have to carry the world on your shoulders—though you do a very good job of it most of the time, I will say."

She gave him a weak smile in answer, but couldn't say anything more.

"What is it? Something with your mother?" he persisted.

"No." She shook her head. "I was supposed to give a speech this morning, and I just couldn't. I walked out on them. It was awful, really. I shouldn't have done that."

He sat back, regarding her. "Doesn't sound so horrible to me. You're under a lot of pressure. Anyone can see that. Don't be so hard on yourself all the time, Emily. Nobody expects you to be perfect."

"Perfect?" Emily sighed. "Lately, it seems I can't do anything even half-right. Everyone is mad at me, or disappointed, or both. Everything in my life is going haywire. This election, Jessica's wedding, dealing with my mother." She cut herself off abruptly. "It's just a big mess, that's all. I feel so—drained."

"Have you prayed about this? Have you asked God to help you? He will, you know."

Emily sighed again and stared out at the water. Could she admit to Reverend Ben that even her faith had failed her lately?

"Yes, I have prayed, Reverend. At least, I've tried. But I don't know. . . . It hasn't seemed to help. I feel as if I don't know whether I'm coming or going. I don't even really care about winning the election," she admitted quietly. "But I'm afraid to lose. My life is so empty. What do I have to look forward to?"

The Reverend regarded her thoughtfully. "What do you want to look forward to Emily? What is it you're really thinking of?" he gently challenged her. "Marriage? Children?"

Emily stared at him, then shook her head. "If it hasn't happened by now, it's not very likely."

"Anything can happen, Emily. You know that. Nothing is impossible for God."

She let out a long breath. The water looked so dark now, with the sun behind the clouds. The waves in the harbor were rough and choppy.

"Do you think God is punishing you for giving up your baby? Is that what you've been thinking all these years?"

Emily turned to him. "No, not at all." She looked away again. "I think I've probably been punishing myself," she admitted bluntly.

"Yes, probably," he agreed. "It doesn't have to be that way, you know."

"It doesn't seem to go any other way for me, Reverend, even after all this time. How can I be happy with someone and start over again, after what I did? It always gets in the way. I don't think I'll ever get married again. But maybe I can find my daughter. After the election I'm going to try," she confided. "This time I won't give up so easily."

"All right," Ben said. He reached over and touched her hand. "I hope you do find her. But even finding your child won't solve this completely for you, Emily. You can find her and still not forgive yourself."

"Why should I? It was wrong, the deepest kind of betrayal—of my baby, my husband, and even me." Emily fought to keep her voice steady. "It was the worst thing I've ever done, Reverend. I can never forgive myself."

"But you must," Reverend Ben insisted. "Can't you see? Yes, it was an error in judgment, a mistake. You were young and grieving after losing Tim. Your mother pressured you to do as she wanted." He held his hands out to her, imploring. "It doesn't even matter how it happened. That isn't important."

"Isn't it?" she asked. She knew the Reverend was trying to help her, but she felt numb to his words, numb to everything.

"God understands, and *He* forgives you, unconditionally," the Reverend assured her. "But when you refuse to forgive yourself, you put yourself above Him. Do you think you know more than God, Emily?"

"Uh, no, of course not." She shook her head, clasping her cold hands in her lap. "I know what you're saying, Reverend. And I want to believe it. I just wish I could feel it deep inside, in my heart."

"Then open your heart to it, Emily. Think with your heart instead of your head," he advised. "True forgiveness is beyond reason. It's not something rational or granted because the other person is willing to admit they've done wrong. God grants it unconditionally, and absolutely. And this is how we must forgive each other. And ourselves."

Emily thought about it. Her mother would never admit she had done anything wrong when she had insisted that Emily give up her daughter. If what the Reverend was saying was true, then God had already forgiven her—and Emily needed to do the same. *Rational or not, it probably makes more sense than waiting for Lillian to apologize,* Emily thought wryly.

The Reverend smiled at her, as if he could sense her emotions shifting. "You know, it's often said that God never closes one door to happiness without opening another. But sometimes we sit staring at that closed door for so long that we don't even see the other."

Seeing herself so clearly in the image, Emily had to laugh. "I'll try to remember that one."

"If it's marriage and children you want, it's not too late for you," he added quietly. "You're only what—forty? Forty-one?"

"Forty-two," she corrected him.

He shrugged. "Women are having babies these days at your age and older all the time. And there are many ways to have a family. All things are possible for God, you know. You must never underestimate Him."

Emily couldn't answer. Was that what she really wanted, all this time, and had been denying herself? Pushing it away, because she felt so undeserving and scared?

She would need time to absorb all this, to consider Reverend Ben's advice, especially his words about forgiveness. But as she turned to him again, she did feel much better. Ready at least to get off the bench and return to work.

She stood up and looked down at him. He regarded her with deep concern.

"Have I helped at all?" he asked.

"Yes, very much." She gave a deep nod. "I'm going to think about what you've said, Reverend."

"Yes, think about it. Pray about it, too," he added. "Hold on to your faith, Emily. God is always there for you. Let Him help you figure this out, for once and for all."

CHAPTER TWELVE

❧

*A*LTHOUGH IT WAS NEARLY FIVE IN THE AFTER-
noon, the sun was still bright and strong, Luke
noticed as he drove his 4Runner down the sandy road that led
to Durham Point Beach. It was an uncommonly long beach for
this part of New England. He had always loved the way it
looked at this time of day with its high, cliff-like dunes and the
wide flat shoreline at low tide. The smooth wet sand took on a
silvery sheen in the afternoon sun. He could remember running backward across it to spy on his own footsteps when he
was a kid, amazed at how quickly they vanished with the next
wave that rolled in.

The beach was practically empty, too. The kids from the
program would have it all to themselves. And there would be no
potential for "incidents" with villagers who opposed the project.

"Okay, we're here, guys," he said, coming to a full stop. Without another word, the three teenagers who sat in the backseat pulled open the doors, jumped out, and ran toward the shoreline. A van driven by one of the group's counselors, Paul Delgado, pulled up alongside Luke's 4Runner. The doors of the van slid open, and the rest of the group ran out to join their friends.

Calling out and waving their arms and hands, tugging off sneakers and socks while still in motion, the crew was quite a sight. Luke laughed out loud as he walked around his truck to meet Paul and the other counselor, Leah.

"I must be getting old. I can barely remember having that much energy," Luke marveled.

"They've been dying to get to this beach," Leah said.

"But I think it was a good thing to save it until the end of the week. A reward for all their hard work," Paul added.

"I need one, too," Luke said. "Why don't you take them for a walk to the lighthouse? It's really a sight. I'll hang out here and get the food ready."

"Good plan," Paul replied as he trudged toward the kids through the sand beside Leah. "They'll be bugging us about dinner in no time," he predicted. "I hope we brought enough."

"Me, too," Luke said. The only real challenge so far this week was having enough food on hand. The group of teens seemed to eat endlessly. Luke knew he was the same way at that age, but watching it every day was still amazing. Today, to be safe, he had packed enough to feed a small army—hamburgers, hot dogs, pickle chips, rolls, potato chips, soda, juice, ice cream, and cookies, plus yogurt, carrot sticks, and granola bars.

He flipped open the tailgate and pulled out the bag of charcoal and blankets. Then stood back, shocked.

Where was the cooler? He stared at the empty cargo area and slapped his head with his hand. *What a dummy. How could I forget the food?*

He slammed the tailgate closed and stepped out in front of the truck, cupping his hands around his mouth to shout. "Hey, Paul, I have to go back. I forgot the food! Can you believe it?"

Paul nodded and waved at him. "Okay, man. See you later."

Luke jumped back in his truck and swung out of the parking lot. It was a short drive back to the cottages, walking distance really, if you were in the mood. He always walked it when he was a kid—a quick trip down to the beach in the morning and a slow, itchy walk home, feeling sunburned, his clothes full of sand.

He smiled at the memory, feeling again that he did the right thing by coming here. Even by trying to start this center. When the kids arrived on Monday, he braced himself, expecting the worst. But nothing too bad had happened. Sara even reported that talk in the diner was starting to die down, though Charlie was doing his best to keep things stirred up.

But Charlie had his own motives, and maybe people were starting to see that, Luke thought. Besides, now that the kids were actually in Cape Light, perhaps people realized that the reality of New Horizons wasn't anywhere near as dire as Charlie Bates's hysterical predictions. Sara had also told him she heard a group in the diner talking about his letter to the editor and sounding as if it had swayed them.

As the signs for Cranberry Cottages came into view Luke checked his watch, wondering if Sara was home. Maybe he could convince her to go back to the beach with him.

He drove down the gravel road to the cottages and parked his truck. He didn't see Sara's car, but he did notice Sam, struggling to get a long ladder into the bed of his truck.

Luke walked over to help him. "Here, let me give you a hand." Luke grabbed a step on the long ladder and pushed hard. "I thought you already left."

"I would have," Sam said, "but I can't find Digger. He was working on the cottage right next to me, then he wandered off again."

Luke stepped back and brushed off his hands. "Maybe he went clamming. It looked like low tide out there."

"Maybe he did," Sam agreed, slamming his long metal toolbox into the truck bed. "He ought to have told me, though."

Luke was not surprised. When the clamming urge struck, Digger would look up suddenly, drop his tools, and walk right off the job. It was as if the old man mysteriously sensed just when the tide was low enough for good clamming. During the past week he had wandered off a few times without telling anybody. Sam was used to it but still got annoyed at times.

"I didn't see him walking on the Beach Road, though," Luke remarked. "Maybe he went back to town?"

Sam was about to reply when suddenly they heard shouting. It was the old fisherman, calling for help from the other side of the property.

"Digger!" Sam said. With a look of alarm on his face, he started running.

Luke followed, unmindful of the pain in his leg as he pushed himself to keep up.

He soon caught sight of Digger, not far from Sara's cottage, waving his arms and his jacket and shouting something unintelligible. At just about the same moment Luke realized he smelled smoke. He stopped in his tracks and gazed around, then spotted flames covering one wall of the cottage closest to Sara's.

Digger had turned around and was trying to beat out the flames with his jacket. Sam reached him first and pulled him back, but the old man was doubled over coughing and seemed unable to catch his breath.

"I'm going to call the fire department!" Luke shouted. He burst into the nearest cottage, where a few of the kids were staying. He called in the fire, then grabbed a fire extinguisher from the kitchen wall on his way out.

The pain from his leg had gone from a dull throbbing to an insistent stabbing, and Luke wanted desperately to rest it, but he refused to give in to his pain. Instead, he forced himself into a hobbling run and returned to the fire.

He twisted open the fire extinguisher's pin and directed the foam at the flames, hoping he could at least stop the fire from spreading.

The foam helped a little, he saw, but he didn't have enough of it. He needed serious reinforcements. A line of flames was creeping perilously close to Sara's cottage. *Where are the firefighters?* he wondered frantically, his ears straining for the sound of sirens.

Sam had pulled Digger away from the heat and smoke, but the old man was still coughing heavily and struggling to get his breath.

"Easy now," Luke heard Sam say to him. "Just stay calm. Try not to talk—"

But Digger shook his head, hacking as he struggled to say something. He gasped, pointing to Sara's cottage.

Luke turned just in time to see Sara running toward it. "Sara, no!" he shouted as she pushed open the door and ran inside. "Get out of there!"

He dropped the extinguisher and ran after her. Was she crazy?

Luke pushed her door aside, his heart sinking as thick, black smoke poured toward him. He couldn't see a thing. He dropped to his knees and crawled through the dark cloud, the smoke stinging his eyes and throat. "Sara? Answer me, please!" he rasped.

He felt his way across the living room. The floor felt hot, and the smoke was getting thicker. It hurt to breathe. He wasn't sure how much longer he could keep going. But the one thing he knew was that he couldn't leave her in here.

Coughing, he made his way down the short hall toward her bedroom, then bumped against something—her body, stretched out on the bedroom floor. He knew he couldn't risk standing up—the smoke would asphyxiate him and neither one of them would get out—so he grabbed hold of the collar of her shirt and, still crawling, began to drag her out of the cottage.

She was dead weight, and the insistent pain in his leg intensified—shooting up his spine—as he struggled to get her outside. All he could think about was Sara. She didn't make a sound, or react in any way. He wasn't sure she was even breathing.

God, no. Don't let her die. Please help her, he silently prayed.

He couldn't see anything, so it was with a sense of shock that he felt a change in the temperature and realized he had reached the door. He gave Sara one last hard tug, and they both tumbled out into the cool air.

For what seemed an endless moment, Luke doubled over coughing and retching. His eyes were tearing from the smoke. His throat felt as if it had been rubbed raw. But he got to his feet, lifted Sara into his arms, and carried her a safe distance from the fire.

He laid her down on the ground and crouched beside her. Beneath the greasy smoke stains, her face was very pale. He quickly felt for her pulse. It was weak, but at least she had one.

"Thank you, God," he whispered. "Thank you. Thank you. Thank you."

Was she breathing? He leaned closer. Just barely. He tipped her head back and quickly began mouth-to-mouth resuscitation.

After three breaths he paused, waiting to see if she was breathing on her own. No, nothing. He felt his heart clench and started again. One, two, three, four, five more breaths. He waited.

"Come on, Sara. Breathe. *Please* breathe," he muttered, wanting to slap her lovely pale face back to consciousness. Or maybe just hold her and cry.

He bent to her again. One, two, three . . .

Then finally he felt her lungs fill on their own and pulled back. She moaned and tossed her head. Then her eyes opened, and she struggled to sit up, coughing.

Luke put his arm around her. "Just relax. You're okay. Don't try to talk," he told her, hugging her a bit closer.

He heard the screaming sound of fire engines, coming down the Beach Road, toward the cottages.

The first truck arrived and pulled up behind Sara's cottage. A team of firefighters jumped off and began unreeling the long black hose. Moments later a thick jet of water streamed out, dousing the flames, but causing even more smoke to fill the air.

Luke crouched down next to Sara, his arm still around her shoulders. "The ambulance is here," he told her. "I'm going to get one of those guys to take a look at you."

Sam and the EMS crew had already started to tend to Digger. Sara looked over at them and shook her head and coughed again. "I'm okay. Really . . . sorry. That was dumb. . . ."

"*Dumb* isn't the word for it. Were you trying to kill yourself?" He tried not to shout at her. He gripped her arms, not knowing whether he wanted to shake her or hug her.

"No!" she said, managing to sound indignant through a fit of coughing.

But before he could ask her why she ran into the smoke-filled cottage, an EMS worker rushed over to them. "How are you doing?" he asked as he knelt down by Sara.

"Okay . . . I think," she answered, though the effort made her cough again.

"Let's see." He fitted a stethoscope to his ears, then asked Sara to breathe while he listened to her lungs. He quickly fitted an oxygen mask over her face, which was attached to a small canister he carried. "Here, you need this. Try to relax and breathe normally."

"How is she?" Luke asked anxiously.

"She'll be okay. But she needs to go to the hospital so we can check her lungs and make sure there's no damage from the smoke inhalation. You stay here with her a minute, and then we'll get her into the ambulance," he instructed.

"No!" Sara sputtered, looking frightened. "I don't want to go to the hospital."

"It's okay," Luke told her in a soothing voice. "They just want to check you out. I think it's a good idea." He rested his hand on her shoulder. "Don't worry. I'll stay with you the whole time, I promise."

Sara's expression relaxed a little, and she nodded. But she also looked relieved that he'd promised to stay with her, he thought. Which was just as well. He met her gaze and held it. There was no way she was getting rid of him now.

FRIDAY EVENING FOUND EMILY SITTING AT HER COMPUTER, WORKING ON A letter to the editor for the *Messenger*. She paused, reviewed what she'd written so far, then with a frustrated sweep of her mouse, erased all of it.

This is going to be harder than I thought. Please God, she prayed silently, *help me out here. Please send me the right words.*

She stared at the blank screen a long moment. Reverend Ben's advice seemed to echo back at her. "Think with your heart, Emily, not just your head."

Okay, I get it. Maybe that's what I have to do here. She raised her hands over the keyboard again, considering how to start.

The phone rang then, breaking her concentration. Who could that be? There were just too many people she didn't want to talk to right now. She reached over to turn the volume on the speaker down—and stopped as she heard the voice of the fire chief, Ed Rhinehardt.

"I tried you at home and there was no answer, so I thought I'd leave a message here as well," he said. "There's been a fire at the Cranberry Cottages—"

Emily grabbed the receiver. "I'm here," she said. "What happened?"

"We got a call about five o'clock. Sent out two trucks and the ambulance. The fire seems to have started in a pile of building supplies. It caught on one of the cottages but was contained pretty easily. We're not sure of the cause yet. Lots of smoke, though."

"Was anyone hurt?" she cut in, thinking first of Sara. Then all those kids . . . and Luke McAllister, of course.

"Luckily the place was practically empty—" Ed's reply made her sigh with relief. "Everyone had gone off to the beach for a barbecue. Digger Hegman and Sam Morgan were still there, working. Luke McAllister called it in. Digger was the one who saw it first. They checked him at the hospital for smoke inhalation, but I think he'll be all right."

"Thank God," Emily said sincerely.

"They brought Sara Franklin in, too," he added, making Emily bolt up in her seat. "But I heard they looked her over and sent her home. It was just a precaution."

"That's good to hear." Emily still felt worried, though. She didn't care if Sara was mad at her. As soon as she hung up with Ed, she would call Sara or maybe even go out to the cottages and see if anyone was there.

"What are the damages? Is the place still livable?"

"Not too bad," Ed said. "I guess they'll have a better idea tomorrow. I don't think anyone went back there tonight. Too much smoke. McAllister said they would find rooms for the night at a motel on the highway. They're going to have a hard time cleaning up. A lot of lumber and roofing material was ruined—either burned or got doused. I don't think any more work is going to go on up there for a while. Which may have been the idea," he added thoughtfully.

Emily knew exactly what he meant. This was more than a rock tossed through a windshield, and yet she couldn't accept the idea that anyone in Cape Light would commit arson. Still, she knew what she had to do. "I'll get a hold of Jim Sanborn," she said. "I think we should all meet right now and talk about this."

"I had a feeling you would say that. Just give me a few minutes to get cleaned up. I'll be right over."

Emily called the police chief at home and caught him at the dinner table. He hadn't heard about the fire yet, but agreed that they had to meet immediately. "I was afraid something like this was going to happen," he said right before he hung up.

The two men arrived at her office at practically the same time. Ed quickly filled them in on what they knew so far about the fire's origins. It wasn't much.

"By the time we put it out, it was too dark to really see anything," Ed said. "We'll start the investigation first thing in the morning. We have a guy on the squad who has a lot of experience with arson. I think we should team him up with one of your men," he said to Chief Sanborn.

It was the first time anyone in the room had mentioned the word *arson*, and Emily felt her heart sink at the implications.

"I understand what you're saying, and I know you have to investigate," she said, "but I have to tell you that I can't believe this fire was started deliberately. Charlie may have everyone all riled up and frightened about the New Horizons Center, but I just can't see anyone here going to such extremes. The idea of someone from this town setting fire to the site—it's unthinkable."

"I hope you're right," Ed Rhinehardt said. "And I'm very glad no one was hurt. Now we have to make sure that no one gets hurt in the future. So we'll investigate this situation from top to bottom, and we'll find out what really happened."

The two men left a few minutes later, and Emily picked up the phone to call Luke and Sara. But where would she find them? There were dozens of motels and inns between the village and the hospital in Southport. She couldn't try them all, she realized. It would take hours.

She set the phone back in place and took a moment to think. She would have to catch up with them tomorrow. The best help she could offer to Luke—and the only olive branch she could offer to Sara—was to finish this letter.

Sitting here, working on a letter that voiced support for the center and then hearing about the fire, had been the strangest coincidence, Emily realized. Certainly this latest event made the letter seem even more urgent.

Whether or not the fire was set deliberately remained to be seen. But the fact that both the police and fire departments suspected it was arson said something to her. If there was enough toxic feeling in this town to even suspect a resident of arson, surely it was well past time for her to take a stand.

If her campaign committee deserted her, so be it. If these were the compromises she needed to make to succeed in politics, then she didn't need a career in politics. If she lost the election, it might be a blessing in disguise. Something else would come along to fill her days and give meaning to her future.

God will open a new door for me, she told herself as she began to steadily type away, *if I would only stop staring at the closed ones. . . .*

EMILY STOOD AT THE GLASS DOOR TO THE NEWSPAPER OFFICE, HOLDING A brown manila envelope containing her letter. She had expected to shove the envelope into the mailbox for Dan to find first thing in the morning. But even though it was nearly eleven P.M., all the lights were on and Dan Forbes was still working at his computer.

The office was a large open space. Half a dozen desks, each topped with a computer terminal, filled the center of the room. A long table that held several printers and fax machines flanked one wall, and bookshelves filled with reference books lined another. An artist's layout board and tools were tucked away in a corner. The decor was spare: whitewashed walls and a few front pages mounted in thin black frames. An egalitarian, no-frills atmosphere for a no-frills guy, she thought.

She knocked on the glass and Dan looked up, surprised to see her, she thought.

He came to the door quickly and swung it open.

"I didn't think I'd still find you here. I just wanted to drop this off," she said, handing him the envelope. He looked down at it curiously.

"It's a letter to the editor, supporting the New Horizons Center," she explained.

He started to say something, then stepped aside and opened the door for her. "Come in a minute."

She followed him inside, where he sat on the edge of a desk. "You heard about the fire, I guess," he said.

She nodded. "I had a meeting with Ed and Jim tonight, just after the fire trucks returned." She dug her hands in her pockets. "It's funny because I was staying late at the office to write this when Ed called me. Then I really had something to write about."

He gave her a long hard look. "I knew you would do it."

The confidence in his voice made her feel good. She hadn't really been so sure herself.

"Took me long enough," she admitted. "But at least I got off the fence. It was getting uncomfortable up there."

"I can imagine," Dan said. "But now your camp is going to make it uncomfortable down here."

"I'll just have to deal with it. Why don't you read the letter, see what you think," she added. "You might not even want to use it."

"I can't imagine that," he said, opening the envelope and pulling out the letter.

Emily felt nervous watching him scan the pages. It was grueling to have someone read your writing right in front of you, especially Dan.

He lifted his head, his expression impossible to read. "This is wonderful. Honestly. It's direct, well informed, and right from the heart."

"You think so?" she asked, not quite believing him.

" 'The people of Cape Light have never been mean-spirited,' " he read aloud. " 'Helping others, giving them the benefit of the doubt and a second chance if necessary—those are acts that have always typified the people in this town. What have we become if we give in to fear and prejudice, if we ignore the facts and let panic override the spirit of compassion?' "

Dan smiled at her. "I'm not saying people are going to change their minds overnight about this whole mess. But this is going to make a dent, Emily. I almost guarantee it."

"I hope so," she said sincerely. "It made me feel better to write it, but that wasn't really the point. Do you think you can fit it into tomorrow's edition?" she asked hopefully.

"Tomorrow?" He glanced at his watch and shook his head. "I'm sorry, Emily. I already ripped up the entire layout to fit in the story about the fire. I just sent it into the printer, and he's probably working on it right now."

"That's okay. I knew it was a long shot," she said, feeling disappointed.

"It will be in Monday's edition for sure. No matter what," he promised. "Besides, if I redo the layout again, I'll feel obliged to include the wise insights of one Charlie Bates on the cause of the fire."

"Charlie? What did he have to say?" Emily asked curiously.

"He called here tonight, claiming one of the kids from the program set the fire, and the whole thing just proves that he was right when he predicted that the center will ruin the village."

Emily felt her jaw drop. "Are you going to print that?"

"We couldn't reach you for a quote, so we had a good excuse to bag it." He smiled, looking like a schoolkid who had played a trick behind the teacher's back and gotten away with it. "Equal time for the candidates, you know."

"Saved by the old 'equal time' rule . . . but no one even called my office for a quote."

"I know. What if you had picked up? Then we would be stuck printing Charlie's baloney, too."

Emily had to grin. "You'd better stop right there. I thought you were this hard-nosed, objective newsman. You're ruining your image."

"Yes, well . . . there's a lot you don't know about me, I guess."

"There's a lot you don't know about me, either," she countered quietly.

"I already suspected that," he said.

Dan crossed his arms over his chest and looked at her a long moment, and she felt—better. As if she had redeemed herself in his eyes. Not up on a pedestal, by any means. But then again, a pedestal put you at a distance from people, and she liked being down on the ground, closer to him.

The phone rang, breaking the silence. Dan walked over to his desk to pick it up. "Could be the printer with a problem. You may need to cover your ears," he warned.

"I'd better go, then. Thanks again for taking the letter."

"Thank you for bringing it to me, Emily," he said sincerely. He turned and put the phone to his ear, and Emily let herself out the door.

She wished the letter were going to appear in tomorrow's paper. Somehow Monday didn't seem soon enough. But the fault was partly her own for waiting so long to take a stand. It would have to do, Emily reasoned.

LUKE MADE HIS WAY THROUGH THE LABYRINTHIAN CORRIDORS OF THE Southport Hospital and finally found Digger's room. It was Saturday morning, and visiting hours had just begun. Digger was already sitting up in bed, wearing white-and-blue striped pajamas and drinking what appeared to be an ice-cream milkshake out of a big red plastic cup.

Not hospital food, Luke thought, noting the name of a local fast-food stop on the cup.

Luke entered and smiled, a bunch of flowers in hand. "Hello, everyone," he said.

"Hi, Luke." Digger paused just long enough to greet him.

The Reverend Ben stood on the other side of Digger's bed, facing the door. He met Luke's eye and nodded.

Grace Hegman and Harry Reilly were hovering over the patient with their backs to the door, and didn't even turn to glance at him.

"I know he asked you for it, Harry. But it's really not good for him," Grace said to Harry Reilly as she regarded her father with an exasperated expression.

"The man nearly died yesterday. He can at least have a milkshake if he wants it," Harry argued.

"Oh, my, you can't win." Grace sighed to herself. She leaned over and smoothed the sheet over Digger's chest. Then she turned to see Luke. "Oh, hello, Luke. I didn't even hear you come in." She walked over to him and took the bouquet. "I'll get some water for these. Look, Dad, Luke brought you some flowers."

Digger paused another second. "Very pretty. Thank you," he said to Luke.

"How are you doing today, Digger?" Luke asked.

"I'm fine," he said. "The doc will probably let me go this afternoon. Nothing wrong with me. It was just a precaution. They need these beds for sick people, you know, not malingering old men. From the way Grace has been acting, you would think the Reverend was here to write my epitaph."

"You can hardly blame her," Harry said, sitting down on the edge of Digger's bed. "You put a good scare into her last night. I shouldn't have even brought you that milkshake, come to think about it."

"If you were a real friend, Harry Reilly, you would have brought me my pipe and tobacco pouch," Digger countered. "That's another reason I want out. No smoking in this dang place, that's for sure."

"What did the doctor say about your pipe, Digger?" the Reverend asked. "Don't you need to give your lungs a rest?"

Digger made a pouting face, which made him look a great deal like a gnome, with his long whiskers and knitted cap.

"My lungs are having a rest right now. They're resting so much, they're bored to tears," he grumbled. "And just for the record, I inhale more smoke blowing out the candles on my birthday cake these days than I did in that fire."

Luke smiled but felt a pang of guilt. Digger was making light of it, but Luke had seen him doubled over, gasping for breath the day before. He hated to think that Digger was hurt working on his project.

Grace returned, carrying a glass vase filled with the flowers. "Aren't these pretty," she said again. "I'll put them by the window, Dad. They're very cheerful."

"Yes, indeed. Unlike yours truly," Digger complained, crossing his arms over his chest. Luke wasn't sure if Digger was really cranky or just hamming it up. Maybe a little bit of both, he decided.

"Cheer up, Digger. You said it yourself—you'll be out of here in no time," the Reverend reminded him.

"Here, let's play some checkers," Harry suggested. "That will take your mind off your troubles."

He picked up a board and a box of checkers from the side table near Digger's bed and began to set up the game.

"Are you going to stick around and cheer me up all day, Harry?" Digger asked.

"I'm here for Grace," Harry bantered back. "She needs someone to keep you in line, looks like to me."

Luke met the Reverend's glance, and they both softly chuckled.

"Who wants to play the winner?" Digger asked, looking hopefully at Luke.

"Sorry, I've got to get going. I just wanted to make sure you were okay."

"I'm fine, young man," Digger assured him in a hearty voice. "Maybe something dreadful could have happened to me. But it didn't," he pointed out. "There's no sense in worrying about things that didn't even happen, is there?"

"No, I guess not," Luke agreed.

Digger nodded. "Fine, then. You start cleaning up. I'll be back on the job the day the building starts again," he promised.

"We won't start without you," Luke promised. He said good-bye to Digger and then to Harry and Grace.

"I'd better go, too," the Reverend said. "I'm glad to see you're feeling better, Digger. I know it's hard to be stuck in bed. But go easy on Grace and Harry," he pleaded in a humorous tone.

"I'll let Harry win a few games," Digger said, eyeing the checkerboard. "I don't want his feelings getting hurt."

Luke and the Reverend left the hospital room together and walked to the elevator. "It's good to see Digger making such a quick recovery. I was worried about him," Luke said.

"He's quite amazing. I'm sure he will be back on the job site in no time," the Reverend replied.

The elevator reached the lobby and the two men got out. Luke stared straight ahead. "I didn't want to say anything up there, but I'm not sure there will be a job for him to come back to. I spoke to Dr. Santori last night. He was concerned. There's no proof that the fire was arson, but the police aren't ruling it out. Dr. Santori thinks there might be too much opposition in the town to carry on."

The Reverend stopped walking and faced Luke, looking very concerned. "I can see why he would feel that way," he said slowly. "How do you feel about it?"

"Terrible," Luke admitted with a shrug. "I guess I had some strange idea that the negativity was dying down and the worst was over. I believe in this project. I really want to make it happen. But I don't want anyone to get hurt over it. Thank God, no one was seriously hurt yesterday. What if the kids had all been there? What if it had happened at night?"

The Reverend reached out and touched his arm. "Frightening scenarios, I agree. But like Digger said, there's little to be gained by worrying about things that didn't happen. You're shaken up. You may not be seeing things clearly right now, you know."

"I realize that," Luke said. "But I'm not sure anymore if Cape Light is the right place for the center. What if this *is* harassment and it continues? I don't think I could handle having it on my conscience if someone really got hurt."

"Give it time," the Reverend advised. "Why don't you wait for the investigation and see how that turns out before you make any major decisions?"

"We can't really do anything more until that's over with and we clean up," Luke replied. "The kids can help, I guess, but that's not the kind of work they came here to do. I've been thinking of sending them back to Boston for a while."

"That's too bad. I'm sure they'll be disappointed," Reverend Ben said. Then he stopped walking and touched Luke's arm again. "I have an idea for you. An inspiration, actually," he added. "What if this group of kids works at the Potter Orchard for a while? Gus is just home from the hospital, and I know he and Sophie could use the help. It's not just keeping up with the orchard, either. Since Gus's health has gone down, the entire place needs fixing and painting. There's plenty of work over there, believe me."

"That a great idea," Luke said, his spirits lifting for the first time all morning. "I can check with Dr. Santori. Do you think the Potters will agree?"

"I can almost guarantee it. I know Sophie felt very positively about the center, and knowing her, she'll probably offer to put them all up in her house as well." The Reverend glanced at his watch. "As a matter of fact, I was going to stop there this afternoon. I'll talk to Gus and Sophie about it and call you later. I'm sure they'll be thrilled with the idea."

The solution was almost too good to be true, Luke thought. It would also buy him some time. "Let's see if we can work this out. Thanks for the help, Reverend."

"Don't thank me." Reverend Ben shrugged. "I've found the Lord is amazingly efficient sometimes, answering two prayers with one solution."

* * *

LUKE LEFT SOUTHPORT FEELING HE'D AT LEAST SOLVED ONE PROBLEM THAT morning. He wasn't looking forward to facing the mess at his property, but it had to be done. Going back this first time would be the hardest, he told himself. It would get easier after that.

Sara would be back by now, too. He had spoken to her briefly, before he left to see Digger, and she told him she wasn't planning on going to work today. Just as well, he thought. She needed the day's rest, and he wanted to have a long talk with her.

When he reached the cottages, he found a police car and the fire chief's car in the lot. Chief Rhinehardt, two of his men, and a police officer were examining the area where the fire had presumably started.

Ed walked over to greet him. "We'll be here awhile, rooting around. It would probably be best if the others don't come back right away," he told Luke.

"I understand. I'll keep them out of your way," Luke replied.

"All right, then. We'll keep you informed," Chief Rhinehardt said. He turned to go back to work, and Luke turned toward Sara's cottage. He had seen her car in the lot and caught sight of her silhouette as she moved past the curtained windows.

He stepped up to her door and knocked, then vividly recalled crawling through smoke yesterday and finding her limp body on the floor. He swallowed hard and pushed the image aside. The worst didn't happen, so no sense worrying about it, he told himself. Still, when he spotted her familiar smile through the window, he felt a wave of relief all over again and gave silent thanks that she had made it through unharmed.

"How are you doing?" he asked once he got inside.

"Oh, I'm okay. How's Digger?"

"He looks fine. He might be out of the hospital by tonight."

"That's good," Sara said.

He watched her moving around the kitchen. She looked nervous and a bit tired, he thought.

"What are you up to?" he asked, following her. "I thought you were going to rest today."

"Just trying to clean up a little. There's this black sooty stuff all over everything." She held up a sponge that was black on one side. "I admit, I am domestically challenged, but this stuff just won't come off."

He took the sponge out of her hand and put it down on the counter. "Come here a minute," he said, leading her over to a seat in the living room area. "I need to talk to you."

She looked at him curiously but sat down beside him on the couch.

"Listen, I just need to know something," Luke said. "Why did you run back in here with all the smoke yesterday? What in the world was so important?"

Sara looked straight at him for a moment, then turned away. "It's personal," she said quietly.

"Yeah, well whatever this personal thing is, it nearly killed you." He ran a hand through his dark hair. "I'm sorry, Sara," he said in a gentler tone. "I don't want to sound angry at you. Mostly, I'm just so grateful you weren't hurt. Still, I can't help wondering."

She turned back to him, her eyes downcast. "You're right. You deserve to know." He saw her take a breath. "I had to get my journal . . . but I guess I dropped it when I passed out. I found it this morning on the bedroom floor. It was fine," she added, looking over at him.

"Your journal? That was it?" He stared at her, sensing this wasn't the entire story.

She got up and walked across the room. "There was something else, too. Here, I'll show you." She opened a book on the kitchen table, took out a photograph, and handed it down to him. "This is what I really came back for," she said. "This picture."

Luke took the photograph and studied it. He could tell by the man's hairstyle and clothes that it was taken years ago, maybe in the late seventies. So it couldn't be a boyfriend. . . .

"I don't get it," he said honestly. "Who is this?"

Sara sat down next to him again and looked over at the picture. "He was Emily Warwick's husband—my father, Tim Sutton."

Luke felt dumbfounded. He didn't know what to say.

He swallowed hard. "Emily Warwick is your *mother*?"

Sara nodded. "My birth mother. She gave me up for adoption right after I was born. I don't really know why."

He stared at her. "That's why you came here. To find her."

"You're the only one who knows," she said, her voice barely audible.

"Wow," was all he could manage to say. The revelation was—overwhelming. But so much about Sara that had puzzled and confused him suddenly made sense.

"But you came here in May," he realized, thinking back. "Why haven't you told Emily Warwick who you are?"

She shrugged and shook her head. "Afraid, I guess. I know that sounds amazingly dumb."

"It doesn't sound dumb," he said. "But it has been a long time."

"I don't know. . . . There always seems to be some reason why I don't do it." She pushed a thick lock of hair behind her ear. "When I first got here, I was surprised she was the mayor. I thought she wouldn't be happy to have her long-lost daughter pop up after all this time. I thought I ought to get to know her a little. Then once I made up my mind to tell her, the election campaign started. I knew if I told her now and Charlie Bates found out, he would find some way to use it against her. This election is important to her. If she loses because of me, maybe she'll hate me."

"Come on, she won't hate you," Luke countered. "She'll probably think finding her daughter is a lot more important than winning the election."

"That's what I thought, too—for a while. But I've been disappointed in Emily lately," Sara admitted. "I used to really like her. But the way she's acted about the center has really surprised me. She just takes the easy way out. Maybe that's why she gave me up."

She looked at the photo again, then tossed it on the side table with an expression that made him think she was about two seconds away from bursting into tears.

He reached out and touched her shoulder. "Maybe that is true," he agreed. "Nobody can answer those questions for you except Emily. You ought to ask her."

"You think so? Even before the election?"

"Why not? It's never going to be the perfect time, Sara. If you tell her before the election, you might find out what she's really made of. Either way, you'll never feel settled inside unless you tell her. No matter what the answers are, or what Emily is really like, it's better to know."

Sara sighed. Instead of answering, she moved closer to him, and he slipped his arms around her, tucking her head under his chin. It was more of a comforting hug than anything else, he knew, but he loved the feeling of holding her close.

Sara needed looking after and he was happy to do it, he realized. He had come here a few months ago, bitter and angry, not wanting to get involved with another living thing. Now here he was, the self-appointed guardian of this strange but wonderful girl.

She pulled away a bit and tipped her head back to look up at him. "By the way, thanks for saving my life yesterday."

"Don't mention it," he replied with a small smile.

He had the impulse to kiss her, but then she slipped out of his grasp and the moment was lost.

Sara got up, walked back to the kitchen, and started cleaning again.

"Listen, Sara," he said, following her, "I don't think you should even bother with this mess. I think you should move off the property. It's not safe here for you anymore."

She took a moment to consider what he said. "What about the kids in the program? If they're coming back, why can't I?"

"They might not be coming back here. I have to speak to Dr. Santori later today. Looks like they'll either go back to Boston, or maybe work at the Potter Orchard. The Potters really need some help, and Reverend Ben is trying to arrange it."

"Oh . . ." Sara looked surprised. She put the sponge down and wiped her hands on a towel. "That would work out well for everyone."

"Yes, it will. And it will be safer," he added. "I really think you should go, too. I don't want you in danger, Sara."

"But where will I go?" she asked. "I'm not even sure how long I'll be staying in Cape Light. I don't want to go back to some tiny hotel room."

"I'll help you find something nice," Luke offered. "Plenty of places around here rent month to month. We can go into town and start looking today." She sighed but seemed unconvinced, he thought. "Hey, I'm your landlord, remember? Do I have to throw you out?" he threatened in a firm but teasing tone.

He saw the corners of her mouth turn down as she tried not to smile. "If you put it that way, what choice do I have? I really don't like leaving you all alone here, though. Maybe you should move, too."

"No, I don't think so," he said right away.

Her suggestion made sense, but he felt a gut reaction against it. *I may have lost some ground,* he realized, *but I'm not ready to give up on this place yet.*

Sara walked past him toward the bedroom. "I guess I'll change my clothes, and we can go apartment hunting," she said.

"I've got some phone calls to make. Come knock on my door when you're ready."

He pulled open the door and stepped outside. Two firemen and a police officer were still picking through the charred rubble.

He nodded to them and walked to his cottage. *What have I done?* he asked himself. *Sara's secret was the only thing holding her here. Once she confronts Emily, she'll probably go back home.*

But this is something she has to do. She has to resolve it, one way or the other. It's important to her and I have to help her. She might leave once she confronts Emily. But it will always get in the way between us if she doesn't.

EMILY WALKED QUICKLY TOWARD THE VILLAGE HALL, TRYING TO IGNORE the slight knot of tension in her stomach. Her campaign committee had been surprised to hear from her on a Saturday morning, but they all agreed to come to a meeting, even though she had been deliberately vague about her agenda.

This meeting was going to be tough, despite her resolve. She had known the men and women on her committee for years and would still have to face them daily despite today's fallout.

But it had to be done, Emily reminded herself. Things had gone too far in the wrong direction.

They were all waiting for her when she arrived, seated at the meeting table in her office. Only Betty offered a small welcoming smile.

"Sorry I'm late," Emily apologized as she took a seat. "Here, I'd like you to read this. It's going to appear in Monday's paper, but I wanted to let you all know in advance."

She passed out copies of her letter to the editor, then braced herself for their reactions.

"Wait, this is just too much," Warren muttered. He began to read aloud. " ' . . . That is why I support Luke McAllister's initiative to bring the New Horizons program to Cape Light. Let's put our fears aside and look at the facts, which clearly show that the center is not a danger to Cape Light.

" 'We are very fortunate to live in such a beautiful place. But is it really ours alone to share or not share? Where does this biased spirit end—with setting up checkpoints at the road into town, so we can control who's allowed to enter?' "

Warren stopped reading and tossed the letter on the table in disgust. "Thanks a lot, Emily. I'm sure that will do wonders for the campaign."

Emily had expected him to come out swinging, and wasn't surprised. She sat up straight and put her hands flat on the table in front of her. "All of you already know how I really feel about this issue. I had to come out for it. I couldn't face myself otherwise."

"Did you consider us for one minute when you gave this to Dan Forbes?" Warren demanded. "All our hard work for you, all the hours we've spent on this campaign? Did you even think of calling any of us up to talk this over before you did it?"

"I never thought of calling you, Warren. I knew you would try to talk me out it," she returned bluntly. Then, looking at the others, she said, "I appreciate the time that you've all given to my campaign. No question. But supporting a candidate is not just about me. It's about ideas, plans, and values. If you don't agree with this position and don't support it, then you're working for the wrong candidate. It's that simple."

Warren pushed his chair back and got up. "I've had enough. I'm gone."

The room was silent as they all watched him leave.

Emily sat back in her seat. Her pulse was racing, but she felt clear, determined. "All right . . . who else?"

The members of her committee were glancing at one another uncertainly. Emily found herself looking at Harriet, who wouldn't meet her eye. She knew Harriet had her grievances. Would she follow Warren?

Suddenly Doris Mumford stood up and picked up her purse and jacket. "I'm sorry, Emily. It's nothing personal. I still think you're a better choice than Charlie. But I just don't agree with this center issue, so I guess it's best if I go."

"All right, Doris. No hard feelings," Emily assured her.

Doris nodded, then, without looking at the others, quickly left the room.

Betty cleared her throat. Was she going to leave, too? Emily wondered.

"This is quite a letter," Betty said. "I guess if you had called me, I would have told you not to write it, too," she admitted. "But I have to say, I realize now that in my heart, I *do* agree with you. It may not be the politically smart thing to do, but I for one feel good supporting someone who is willing to stand up and say what needs to be said. What *should* be said."

"Even if I'm waving the banner of a lost cause?" Emily gently chided her.

"Especially since you are. I know I wouldn't have the guts to do it," she replied.

Emily smiled. Betty's words meant a lot to her.

"I'm in," Frank Hellinger said simply. "You're still the best ticket in town, no question. Warren takes this stuff too personally. How about you, Harriet?" he added.

Harriet sat back and took a deep breath. She looked at Emily. "I would do things differently in your shoes. I don't make any secret about it, either. But on the whole, I still support you and want to see you back in this office come next January."

Emily was surprised. She had thought that Harriet would leave with the others.

"I hope I will be, too," Emily replied. "Now, let's get to work."

By the time Emily got home that evening, she felt exhausted but still on edge. She went for a long jog, and felt herself unwinding as she made the turn back to Emerson Street. She glanced wistfully at Dan's house as she ran by. The windows were dark, his driveway empty. She wondered where he was. But it was Saturday night, she reminded herself, when most people have a social life.

Well, good for him, she grumbled to herself as she opened her front door.

She heard a vehicle pull into her driveway and turned. It was Sam's blue truck. She stood on her doorstep and watched as he got out and came toward her.

"Sam . . . is everything all right?"

"I need to talk to you, Emily. It's about Jessica," he said, his expression serious.

"Sure. Come in." She opened the door all the way, and he followed her into the living room. "Is this about the wedding?"

"What else?" He began to pace in front of the sofa, too agitated to sit down. "I was just with your sister. I finally got her out to the house, to do some work. We haven't been there much since we decided to put off the wedding."

Not good, Emily thought. She hadn't realized that.

"We had another fight about setting the wedding date." He turned to her. "Has she ever asked you to come with her and Reverend Ben to talk to your mother?"

"Uh, no, she hasn't," Emily said honestly. "Is she going to?"

"Jessica said she needed to give it one more try before she sets the date. Meanwhile, she's terrified of facing your mother again. So here we are, totally stuck on square one."

"I see." Emily sat down on an armchair, facing him. "I'm sorry to hear that. I thought things were going better after you met with Reverend Ben."

"So did I," Sam said, sounding confused—and terribly disappointed, she thought. "Your sister just doesn't understand how I feel. I want to set the date or call the whole thing off."

He means it, too, Emily thought, feeling a chill.

"Have you told her how you feel—just that way?" she asked.

"I've told her every way I can think of," Sam replied grimly. "I don't know what to do next. I wanted her to go with me tomorrow to look at a new place for the wedding. My dad knows people in the restaurant business, and he has a friend who runs this great inn, out in Spoon Harbor. They even have our date open—someone else just canceled. But Jessica wouldn't hear a word about it. She said November nineteenth is way too soon, and she couldn't possibly be ready." He sighed and sank down onto the sofa. "Well, it's not too soon for me. I'm starting to think she'll never be ready. She either wants to marry me or she doesn't. I'm not going to beg her."

His angry tone surprised her. Sam was normally so easygoing, Emily never imagined he had a temper. Was this about Sam trying to control things? she wondered. No, she realized at once. His pride was hurt; he thought Jessica was rejecting him.

"I'll talk to her," Emily promised. She stood up and looked up at him. "Don't worry. Jessica loves you."

"I thought she did. But I'm not sure anymore if that's going to be enough."

"Let me see what I can do," Emily said. "I'll call her tonight."

"Thanks." He suddenly looked embarrassed. "Sorry to burst in on you like this, Emily. But I didn't know what else to do."

"I'm glad you came to see me. Really," she assured him as she walked him to the door.

If anyone could talk some sense into Jessica, she could, Emily thought unhappily. Who would know better what her sister was about to throw away?

CHAPTER THIRTEEN

*J*ESSICA . . . WAIT," EMILY CALLED SUNDAY MORN-
ing from the bottom of the steps of Bible Community Church.

Jessica turned to look at her sister. Warily at first, Emily
noticed. Then, when she realized Emily was alone, she smiled.

Emily quickly caught up with her and kissed her hello on
the cheek.

"Where's Mother?" Jessica asked.

"She didn't want to come out today. She thinks she's coming down with a cold and didn't feel up to it. I'm going to see
her later, after we have lunch."

Just as she promised, Emily had called her sister a few minutes after Sam left. But instead of mentioning Sam's visit, she
invited Jessica out after the church service. It was a perfect fall

day, and Emily was looking forward to an afternoon away from the village.

They walked into the church and took seats. Emily glanced around for Sam, but only saw his mother and father, sitting in their usual seats. They cast a strained smile at Jessica, and she smiled back, but Emily could read the tension in the brief exchange.

Jessica turned around and paged through her book for the opening hymn. She sang in a clear strong voice, and Emily realized she had hardly ever heard her sister sing in church before.

Jessica's faith had grown so much since she returned home. Sam was the one who initially drew her back to church. Now, despite their troubles, her faith continued to grow. *She's become a real example to me,* Emily thought.

But I am trying to get back on track again, Lord, Emily silently explained. *Please help Jessica and Sam. And help me to help them.*

A short time later Reverend Ben stepped up to the pulpit, and Emily found herself sitting up straight and even feeling a bit apprehensive about what he might say this week.

But his tone was gentle and conversational as he started off with an anecdote about two women who went to the opera together. ". . . One was sighted and one was blind," he explained. "They sat side by side, in the same row of the theater for the entire performance. When the show was over they compared notes, as theatergoers will do. The sighted woman was very disappointed. She criticized the costumes and scenery—not to her taste at all. The soprano, she thought, was not very pretty and rather old for the part. The male lead was too short, she said, and didn't look anything like a prince. It ruined the romance of the story for her. . . ."

Where in the world was he going with this one? Emily thought. At times Reverend Ben came up with some very unique anecdotes to illustrate his points. She suddenly wondered if there ever were two opera-loving friends such as this.

But then his story drew her in again, as he continued. "The blind woman, however, had thoroughly enjoyed the evening. She said it was the most wonderful performance she ever attended. She found the voice of the soprano as clear and pure as an angel's, and the tenor's rendition of the romantic arias had brought tears to her eyes. She told her friend she would remember this night for the rest of her life and thanked her endlessly for taking her along."

He paused, looking out over the congregation. Emily heard a cough and then a nervous, restless stirring.

"Whom are we most like, do you think? The sighted woman or the blind one? We pass through this world so distracted by the material 'wrapping paper,' we're entirely blind to the beauty within one another. We're deaf to the heavenly voices—and the sparkling pure spirits that each one of us possesses.

"No wonder we're suspicious and intolerant, critical and judgmental. Treating each other without sympathy and charity. The blind woman saw the performance the way God sees each of us. Not the costumes and backdrops, the unattractive imperfection of our bodies—and even our personalities. But the pure light within."

He paused for a moment and looked down at his notes. He stroked his beard in an absentminded gesture. When he raised his head again, Emily saw a harder, more determined expression.

"There is unrest and anger in this village right now. No denying it," he said firmly. "But maybe if we make the effort, we can step back a moment and look at one another 'blindly.' When we strive to recognize the same spirit in each other that shines within ourselves, we see the affinity, not the differences. We see the touch of the divine Creator and we are . . . humbled. That, my friends, is the beginning of seeing Heaven here on Earth."

Good job, Emily thought as she watched the Reverend step down from the pulpit. *Would it help, though?* she wondered.

* * *

"I THINK THIS MUST BE THE TURN." EMILY SLOWED HER JEEP AND PEERED AT the sign that poked through some hanging branches. "I can't see the name of the road, though. What do the directions say again?"

Jessica checked the piece of scrap paper with Emily's scrawled directions. "Right on Scudder Lane, I think. . . . I can't really read your handwriting. The water must be that way, so you ought to make a turn over here, I guess."

"Have you been here before?" Emily asked curiously.

"I don't think so. But I can tell we're in Spoon Harbor. Sam brought me to a restaurant on a dock around here for our first real date," she added, glancing out the window.

"Really? I didn't know that," Emily murmured as she steered the vehicle down the narrow lane. *That makes it even better*, she thought.

"Who did you say recommended this place?" Jessica asked.

"Uh . . . somebody. I can't remember who," she fibbed. "But I heard that they have a great brunch. I really wanted to get out of the village for a change."

"You've had a tough week," Jessica said sympathetically. "I bet you want to run away to Australia, or something."

"It wasn't my first choice, but it did make the short list," Emily replied with a laugh.

They soon found the inn at the end of the curving lane, and Emily was secretly pleased to hear Jessica's gasp. "This is lovely. Look at the flowers—the landscaping is gorgeous!"

"Very pretty," Emily agreed, trying not to smile.

They pulled up on a curved drive, and Emily gave her car key to a valet. A long white limousine pulled up next. The doors opened, and a bridal party began to get out.

"I guess they have weddings here," Emily said as they passed through the entrance.

"Yes, I guess they do. I wonder if the food is any good?"

Emily didn't reply at first. "We'll soon see," she said as the hostess approached them.

They were seated in the main dining room near a long wall of windows that framed a view of gardens and a pond. The room was spacious and sunny, the tables set with heavy starched linens and fine china.

"Look, a gazebo," Emily pointed out. "I'd love one in my yard, but it's way too small. You have room at your house, though. It would look great right in front of the pond. Maybe that's what I'll get you for a wedding present."

Jessica didn't look up from her menu. "We haven't been working on the house much lately," she admitted.

Emily didn't answer right away. Then she said, "Yes, I know. Sam told me."

Jessica stared at Emily for a moment, her expression unreadable. *Is she angry?* Emily wondered.

"When did you talk to Sam?"

"Last night. He dropped by my house. I think he had just been with you, as a matter of fact." She paused, letting the information sink in. "He told me that you had another argument. He was very upset."

Jessica sat back. "I was upset, too. He's just been pressuring and pressuring me—"

"He loves you. He wants to marry you. For goodness' sake, I wish somebody like Sam was pressuring *me* to get married," Emily added, in a half-joking manner. *Now, where in the world did that come from?* she wondered, but had no time to follow the errant thought.

Jessica's face had gone pale. "When we spoke to Reverend Ben, Sam agreed that I could try to talk to Mother one more time," she said, her voice defensive.

"I know he did," Emily said. "But it's been what—two or three weeks? Time is passing, Jessica. You haven't tried to see her, and frankly, I don't think anything would be changed by it. Mother's never going to give in on this. I think you have to accept that now . . . and go on with your life."

Jessica didn't answer. She sat sullenly, studying the pattern on her china plate.

"Jessica, I don't mean to be hard on you, but I can't just sit by and watch Mother ruining everything. Look at me," Emily implored her. "No husband, no children, a microwave dinner, and two cats to come home to every night. Is this how you want to end up ten years from now?"

Jessica reached over and touched Emily's hand, looking close to tears.

"Sam told me he won't wait any longer. He means it, too," Emily went on. "Is it worth losing him? Because that's what's happening."

Jessica swallowed hard and gripped her hands together. Emily's heart shifted. Had she finally gotten through to her?

"I don't want to lose him," Jessica said, her voice breaking. "And I don't know what to do."

"Call him. Ask him to meet you here," Emily said, pulling out her cell phone. "I think he'll be happy to."

Jessica took the phone in hand. "Right now?"

"Just do it," Emily prodded her. "You and I can check out the food while we're waiting for him. Then maybe you two can find somebody to talk to about the wedding. I happen to know that they have the date you wanted free."

"They do? How do you know that?"

"Uh . . . somebody told me, I don't remember who," Emily mumbled. She pushed her chair back and got up. "You call Sam. I'll give you some privacy. I'm going to check out the buffet. It looks yummy—and I think I'm ready to ditch that awful diet," she added happily.

JESSICA AND EMILY WERE STILL AT THEIR TABLE, FINISHING A SECOND CUP OF coffee when Jessica noticed him standing at the entrance to the dining room. Jessica waved at him and felt a bit better when he smiled at her.

But as he strode toward her, she felt herself go tense with worry. What if they argued again and he walked out—this time for good? What if they really couldn't work this out?

"I wish you wouldn't run off right away," Jessica admitted to Emily.

"I don't belong here now. You two have to talk this out alone." Emily patted her hand. "As far as I'm concerned, the wedding is on. I'm going to start working on the bridal shower right away. Call me later, but I don't want to hear differently," she warned.

Jessica bit her lip and nodded.

"You're going to be fine," Emily whispered as Sam approached. "Just remember how much you love each other."

"You're one in a million," Jessica told her, finally smiling. "If we have a girl first, I'm going to name her after you," she said impulsively.

Emily's eyes brightened. "I'd love that," she said sincerely.

Sam stood near the table, his gaze lingering on Jessica.

"What are you two smiling about?" he asked curiously.

"Baby names," Emily admitted, rising from her chair. "Good to see you, Sam. But I've got to run," she said, picking up her purse.

Jessica could tell Sam understood perfectly. "Good to see you, Emily—and thanks," he added.

Emily smiled, but only said, "You two ought to take a walk out in the garden. I think you can go right through that door."

Jessica glanced at Sam, feeling her heart beat so loudly she was sure he could hear it. "Want to?" she asked.

"Sure, why not?" He pulled out her chair and she stood up.

As they walked together toward the exit, he took her hand, surprising her with the affectionate gesture. She glanced up at him, and his mouth tipped in a half smile.

"This place is very pretty," she said when they got outside. "You're the one who found it, right?"

"My father suggested it. He knows the owner." They followed a path that led around the small pond. Though the landscaping and flowers were far more manicured here, Jessica was suddenly reminded of the walk she and Sam took the first time he brought her out to his house—the house they were now going to share as man and wife. It had started to rain that day, she remembered, and he had kissed her.

He was so quiet. Was he remembering it, too?

"Listen," Sam began. "I owe you an apology. I think this all started that night you got the phone call about the job. I'm sorry I was eavesdropping. I couldn't help it."

"I didn't really care. I wasn't trying to hide anything from you."

"I know that. It's just that the whole thing made me feel like . . . well, like maybe your mother is right," he admitted.

"What?" Jessica stopped, not quite believing what she had heard.

"I don't want to feel as if I'm limiting you, Jessica, making you give up opportunities or the kind of life you really want. I don't want you to have regrets about marrying me—and sometimes it sounds as if you already do," he confessed.

It hurt to hear him say that, but Jessica felt as though she finally understood why this was so hard for Sam.

"My mother is not right, not about anything concerning our relationship," she said flatly. "I have no regrets about passing on that job or any other, Sam. It was never an issue for me."

He stared down into her eyes and didn't say anything. "You're sure about that, really?"

"Absolutely," she said emphatically.

She turned away and looked out at the pond. Two swans floated by. One ducked its head, hunting for food, and the other beat its wings against the water.

"I'm not going to try to see my mother again," she said with finality. "Ten more visits won't change her mind. I have to face that." She turned to face him again. "If she won't come, she won't come. What more can I do?"

He stepped toward her, his warm gaze enfolding her in a sympathetic light. "I know this is hard for you. Don't think I don't know that," he assured her quietly.

"I'm trying my best now to forgive her, like Reverend Ben said," Jessica confided. "Maybe after we're married, she'll give up and come around."

A slow, tentative smile spread across Sam's face. Her future husband really was so handsome, Jessica thought. She was definitely a very lucky woman.

He took her hand and pressed it to his lips. "Does this mean you'll meet me on November nineteenth on the altar at the Bible Community Church?"

She nodded, feeling tears of joy and relief well up in her eyes. "I'll be waiting for you," she promised.

"No, I'll be honored to be waiting there for you. But not too long, I hope," he said, pulling her close for a long, slow kiss.

"YOU'LL NEVER GUESS WHO STOPPED BY TO VISIT ME TODAY," LILLIAN SAID. Before Emily could guess, her mother filled in the blank. "Sara Franklin. I haven't seen her in a while."

Emily sat with her mother in the living room, a typical Sunday night scenario, she thought. For once the noisy TV set was off. Emily had made them both some tea, and Lillian sat sewing new buttons on an old cashmere cardigan. Lillian's eyes were still good enough for fine sewing, her fingers nimble and steady.

"She told me that she's moving to an apartment in town. A few blocks from here, on Clover Street."

"Really? I'm glad to hear that. I didn't think she should stay at the cottages anymore."

"Not since the fire there. I agree." Lillian snipped a thread with her scissors. "She's moving in on Tuesday. I told her she could take a few things from the attic if she wanted. It's a lot of old junk up there, quite frankly, but some of it might be useful to her," her mother said with a shrug.

"That's good of you," Emily said, surprised by her mother's generosity. Lillian usually clung to her possessions tenaciously, no matter how old or worn. The sweater she was working on, for instance, Emily thought. The gray cashmere had been fine once, but was now not even worth the investment of new buttons. It was more suited to the charity basket, or even the trash bin. But try to tell her mother that . . .

"Of course, she wouldn't tell me why she stopped coming by, just said she's been busy. Busy, busy, busy. Everyone is so busy these days," Lillian added in a mocking tone. "Busy with nothing, if you ask me. In my day we just called it living."

"I think Sara's been upset with me about something," Emily offered. "Maybe that's why she hasn't been by lately."

"What does she have to be upset with you with about?"

"She was disappointed when I didn't come out right away in support of Luke McAllister."

"Oh, that—" Lillian waved her hand in disgust. "We had a long debate on that topic. You know how that girl likes to argue," Lillian said, rolling her eyes.

"Well, I agree with her actually. I wrote a letter to the editor supporting the project. It should appear in tomorrow's paper," Emily replied evenly.

Lillian's stared at her in shock, dropping her sewing into her lap. "Why in the world did you ever do that?"

"Because it was the right thing to do, Mother," Emily said simply.

"The insane thing to do, you mean. You've handed Charlie Bates the election. I guess you just don't want to be mayor again after all." Lillian picked up her sewing and shook her head.

"Not that badly."

"Well, I don't mind saying I think that center is an awful idea. For once I agree with that fool Bates."

"You know what they say, 'Politics makes strange bedfellows,' " Emily remarked lightly.

Her mother looked up at her over the edge of her half-moon reading glasses. "Very funny." She turned back to her sewing and clipped off a thread with her scissors. "Did you see your sister in church today?"

"Yes, I did. In fact we went out together afterward." Emily paused. "The wedding is on again. Same date as before. Jessica and Sam have made up and booked an inn for the reception in Spoon Harbor."

Lillian didn't lift her head, and Emily wondered at first if she had even heard her. Then she noticed how her mother's hands shook as she placed the sweater in her lap and laid the needle and thread aside.

"Thank you for sharing the unhappy news. I'm not coming, so don't even bother to ask me."

"I wasn't going to ask you," Emily replied honestly.

Her mother stared at her for a long, tense moment. "Don't give me that smug look of yours, Emily. I know what you're thinking."

"I'm thinking that I feel relieved that Jessica and Sam will be very happy together."

"Dear me. If you lose the election, you can always get a job writing greeting cards. You have a real talent for it," her mother snapped.

"Now, there's a useful suggestion. I hadn't thought of it," Emily said, willing herself to remain calm under fire.

"You can't fool me. I know why you did this. You just wanted to get back at me," her mother charged.

"What do you mean, get back you?"

Her mother gave a long, aggrieved sigh. "It makes no difference to you if your sister marries Sam Morgan or the Man in the Moon. But you know it pains me to see her throw her life away. So, you encouraged her, helped them patch things up—just to hurt me. Just to punish me for your own mistakes."

Emily felt her face get hot and red. "I just want to see Jessica happy. I don't want to see her end up like me, with nothing."

"And who's fault is that? It's certainly not mine," Lillian insisted, shaking her head. "You make me out to be a monster. A cold, unfeeling mother who gives no thought to her children. I know that's what you really think of me, don't deny it."

"I would never say you were unfeeling, Mother," Emily replied carefully. "Can't you see that if Jessica doesn't marry Sam, she'll be heartbroken and so will he? And she may never fall in love or have that chance again. Can't you see that when you forced me to give up my child for adoption, I was horribly shortchanged?"

"Forced you? Whoever forced you? I certainly didn't. And what were the alternatives at the time?" Lillian challenged her. "What kind of shape were you in when I came down to Maryland, Emily? No money, no job, living in a cheap apartment. Laid up in the hospital after that husband of yours crashed the car and killed himself, with not even enough money in the bank to give him a proper burial. . . . I still say he must have been drinking, though I'm sure you'll deny it—"

"You can stop right there, Mother," Emily interrupted her. "I've heard this all before."

"Why stop? We're just getting to the good part," Lillian said with false cheer. "And so, sick as you were, you had a baby. Premature, complications. It's amazing the child survived. And you cried like a little girl to keep it, as if it were a dog or a cat and needed no more care or thought than that. As if you, with no money or education, not to mention maturity and common sense, had the wherewithal to raise a child."

"I could have taken care of my baby."

"Not without our help, you couldn't have. And why should we have gone the limit for you? After everything you did to us, the way you disrespected our wishes and ran off with that—that layabout fisherman. I think it was very good of your father and me just to bring you home again. And after your father died, I found a way to keep you in college until you finished your degree—to give you a decent future, a chance to make something of yourself. Was that the act of an unfeeling mother?"

"What about me keeping the baby and coming back here to live? Didn't that ever occur to you?" Emily asked in a strained tone.

"Why should I have done that? It was bad enough you ran off to Maryland. Most people didn't even believe you had gotten married. And they wouldn't have believed it, either, if you had come home alone, with an infant in your arms."

"That's enough. More than enough," Emily retorted. "My husband was killed! I was a widow!"

"Well . . . we know that. But that's not what people around here would have believed."

"You know," Emily said slowly, "sometimes I think that with the exception of marrying Father, everything you have ever done has been motivated by what people will think of you. There's nothing more important to you, is there?"

"Why do I even waste my breath arguing about this with you?" Lillian asked, ignoring her question. "If I hadn't done what I had, you never would have become mayor in this town, I'll tell you that much."

"Yes, my life would have been different," Emily agreed. "Not nearly so empty." She sighed and ran her hand through her short, thick hair. "I'm sorry, Mother, but sometimes I don't think I can ever forgive you."

Lillian's eyes widened in outrage. She started to stand up, then sat down again, holding the arms of her chair for support.

"Whoever asked you to forgive me? I refuse to be blamed for your great mistake, your great unhappiness, Emily. You have no one to blame for it but yourself. I did what I thought was best at the time, for you and for the rest of the family. My conscience is clear, dear girl. You signed those papers. I certainly did not."

When Emily didn't reply, she added, "It's yourself you can't forgive, Emily. Not me."

Emily couldn't answer. Her mother's indictment was chilling.

And yet Reverend Ben had said the same in a far more gentle manner. Was her mother right?

Emily felt completely overwhelmed by emotions. She felt herself starting to cry and knew that she couldn't stay in her mother's house another minute. Brushing back tears, she stood up, knocking her teacup off the coffee table. She watched it roll under the sofa without bending to pick it up.

"I-I've got to go," she stammered, then rushed out of the room.

"Emily? . . . Emily? . . . Oh, for goodness' sakes. Why must you always be so emotional?" Emily heard Lillian mutter as she grabbed her coat and purse in the foyer.

Emily slammed the door shut and ran down the path to her car.

It was ironic to hear her mother accuse her of being too emotional when she felt as if she had spent years hiding her emotions, carefully pushing them beneath the surface, and pretending they didn't exist. She, who was so careful to always act coolly and rationally, was being accused of being too emotional!

It would almost be funny, she thought, if she weren't weeping.

"WE'RE PRETTY SURE WE FOUND THE CAUSE OF THE FIRE," CHIEF RHINE-hardt reported over the phone on Monday morning. "Can we meet with you?"

"Yes, of course," Emily replied. "Come over right away."

Twenty minutes later Jim Sanborn and Ed Rhinehardt entered her office. Ed turned and closed the door. "Well, here it is," he said, reaching into his pocket. He withdrew a plastic bag that contained the charred remains of a pipe.

It was the second plastic bag of evidence tossed on her desk in two weeks, more than she'd seen in three years.

"It's Digger's," Jim said. "It's got to be. He's the only one who's been anywhere near that property who smokes a pipe."

"Besides," Ed added, "I recognize the long curly handle."

"Yes, I see what you mean." Emily sighed and sat back. Even she recognized the pipe. "Are you sure this was the source of the fire?" she asked. "He didn't happen to drop it, unlit perhaps, where the fire occurred?"

Ed shook his head. "No, that's not the way it happened. You can read these things in the debris, especially in a relatively small fire that was contained and put out quickly. It was all right there—like an open book," he added, glancing up at Jim Sanborn.

"I feel terrible about Digger," Emily admitted, "but I am so thankful it wasn't arson."

Ed gave her a weary smile. "I know exactly what you mean."

"How do you want to handle this, Emily?" Jim asked.

Emily massaged her temples. Despite her relief at learning that the fire wasn't caused by arson, knowing that Digger started it presented a whole new set of problems.

"It was an accident," she said, thinking aloud. "And fortunately no one was hurt. So I don't see the point of going public with this and embarrassing Digger and Grace. Can we simply declare the fire an accident and say the cause was unknown?"

The two men looked at each other.

"That's fine with me," the police chief said. "But we need to tell McAllister. He deserves to know the full story."

"We also have to tell Grace and Digger what we've found," Ed said.

"We all love Digger, but somebody needs to keep a closer eye on him. We can't have him wandering around, sending the village up in blazes because he's gotten so absentminded."

"No, of course not," Emily said quietly. She suspected that Digger would be devastated when he learned the true cause of the fire, but Ed was right. They had to tell him.

"I'll go out to the property today and talk to McAllister," Jim said. "He should be happy to hear that it wasn't arson."

"I'm sure he will be," Emily replied. She planned to go out to the cottages herself this afternoon to see Luke and Sara.

The news would make a big difference to Luke, she was sure. It was already lifting a layer of despair from her own heart. She felt deeply grateful that no one in Cape Light had been so hateful. This could work out yet, she thought hopefully.

IT WAS JUST AFTER TEN ON MONDAY MORNING. SARA WAS PACKING UP HER books when she heard Luke at the door. She raised her eyebrows, surprised. He was supposed to go down to Boston today to meet with Dr. Santori and discuss the future of the program.

"Hi, I thought you left," she said, opening the door.

"Soon," Luke said.

He was dressed up, she noticed, or as dressed up as Luke got. He was wearing a dark tweed sports jacket, black corduroy pants, and a gray V-neck sweater over a pale blue tailored shirt.

He had an odd look in his eye, Sara thought, excited and wary at the same time. "The police chief just came by to see me," he told her. "He said it wasn't arson."

"Really? That's great!" Sara exclaimed. "What was it, then—an electrical fire?"

Luke looked away. "If I tell you, you can't tell anyone," he warned her.

"I promise. Heaven knows, you have the dirt on me," she reminded him.

"It was Digger's pipe. He must have dropped it in the pile of supplies next to that cottage. Just an accident. The town is going to keep Digger's name out of it. The official story is an accidental fire, cause unknown, okay?"

"Got it." She nodded. "But you must be relieved to hear it wasn't someone from the village, trying to destroy the program."

"Of course I am," Luke said. "I knew people here were upset about the center—but I never thought they would resort to arson. I'm glad I was right."

"How are the kids doing at the Potters'?" Sara asked. Luke and Sara had helped the six teenagers and their counselors move to the Potter Orchard yesterday. Sophie had seemed so delighted to see them, you would have thought they were part of her own family.

"Paul says great, so far. The kids are going to paint all the outbuildings, starting with the barn. That should keep them busy until Thanksgiving," Luke predicted with a grin.

"Well, they'll have to come back here once the work starts again. Some of them at least."

Luke glanced quickly at her, but didn't say anything, an uneasy look in his gray eyes. "How's the packing coming?"

"Fine. It isn't all that much."

"That's what you say." He pushed one of the boxes with his booted toe. "What do you have in there, bricks?"

"Books."

"Figures. I hate helping brainy women move. It throws my back out for weeks."

Sara smirked at him, but didn't say anything. *How many women have there been in his life?* she wondered, feeling a surprising flare of jealousy.

She busied herself with packing a box of spices and canned goods, avoiding his eyes. She was falling for him. There was no getting around it. The last few weeks they had gotten closer and closer until it was hard to imagine what life around here would be like without him. She knew that once she moved into the village, they wouldn't see each other as often. She would miss him; she almost did already.

"Well, I guess I'd better go." Luke glanced at his watch. He was nervous; she could tell from the sound of his voice. "The meeting isn't until two, but you never know with the traffic."

"Sure. You never know. Are they still saying they don't want to go through with it?"

"I don't know. I spoke to Dr. Santori on Saturday night, when everything was settled with the Potters. That's when he asked me to come in. He said they just want to talk, but I have a feeling they're going to put me on the spot. The controversy in this town is no secret. I even had some reporter from the *Boston Globe* calling me about it."

"The *Globe*? What did they want to know?"

"I don't remember. I hardly spoke to her. It was part of some feature story, I guess. Who knows if half this stuff ever gets into print? The point is, everyone at New Horizons is wary about this village now. Even though the fire wasn't arson, I don't know if I can convince them not to pull out."

"I think that ought to be a pretty compelling argument," Sara said.

Luke shook his head. "It may not be compelling enough. I think I'm starting to look disorganized, out of control. I probably should have written up some new proposal or plan, but I didn't have the time."

Sara moved closer and touched his arm. "I think you will convince them," she said. "And I don't think you need a new plan. You just need to remember the old one—how excited you felt when you first told me you wanted to do this. You were practically jumping out of your skin," she reminded him. "Think about that on your drive down to Boston."

He looked at her a minute and then smiled. "Okay, I will." He paused, as if wondering if he should say something more, then he added, "I guess I'll pray about it, too."

"You pray?" She didn't mean to sound so shocked. As if he just admitted he could flap his arms and fly out of the room or something. She hoped she hadn't offended him, but he just laughed.

"Yeah, I do." He nodded.

"I don't see you go to church much."

"Not so much, no," he agreed. "From time to time, though. I like Reverend Ben's sermons. He's a smart guy. Ever talk to him?"

"Once or twice in the diner."

"He's helped me a lot since I got here," Luke said. "And praying— well, praying is like talking to God. I think it is, anyway. It's like writing a letter, except you're writing a letter to God. . . . Ever try it?"

She shook her head. "I guess I do pray once in a while. But only when things seem so desperate and black, I feel really panic-stricken. That's not being religious," she added with a slight shrug. "If I were God, I'd probably get annoyed at people like me, who only call you when they need a favor."

Luke's smile broadened, the light of his gaze warming her. "I'll have to tell the Reverend you said that. He could probably use it in one of his sermons."

She wrapped a jar of spaghetti sauce in a sheet of newspaper and placed it in the box. "All right, I'll try it sometime. Instead of writing in my journal, I'll write a letter to God. How will I know if he writes me back?"

Luke smiled at her and straightened his jacket, preparing to go. "You'll know," he promised her.

SARA CONTINUED HER PACKING FOR MOST OF THE MORNING, STOPPING only to eat a bite of lunch while standing over the kitchen counter. She had downplayed it when she told Luke it wasn't much to move, she realized, looking at all the boxes lined up near the door. His back *was* going to be out for weeks. It was amazing how much a person could accumulate in four short months. And she hadn't even tackled the mound of papers and books on the kitchen table yet.

She heard a tapping sound on the glass of her front door. It was much too early for Luke to be back. Was it Lucy, stopping by to say hello? she wondered as she turned to the door.

She stopped for a moment as she recognized Emily through the glass. Then she crossed the room and pulled open the door.

"Hello, Sara. May I come in?" Emily asked politely.

"Uh . . . sure." Sara opened the door and stepped aside. "Hi. How are you?" she asked stiffly.

"I'm fine." Emily looked at her with a slight smile. "But I wasn't caught in a fire on Friday. Are you feeling any ill effects?"

Sara shrugged. "It was nothing, really. I'm okay."

"I came here on Saturday, but no one was around," Emily replied.

"I was in town, looking for a new place."

"Yes, my mother said you found an apartment on Clover Street. When are you moving?" she asked with interest.

"Tomorrow. Luke's going to help," Sara added. She saw a certain look in Emily's blue eyes at the mention of Luke's name.

"I didn't know you and Luke were such good friends," Emily said, clearly trying to be tactful. "No wonder you were so upset with me about not coming out more strongly for his program."

"Yes, no wonder," Sara said tightly. She stared at Emily a moment, then picked up a pile of books from the table and dumped them in a box.

"Is Luke around? I wanted to see him, too. I didn't see his truck."

"He's gone to Boston. To see Dr. Santori and the New Horizons people. He's probably arguing his heart out right now, so that they won't shut down the program," Sara reported bluntly.

"Oh . . . I see," Emily said after pause. "He's in a tough spot. I hope it works out for him."

Sara stared at her for a moment, surprised at the white-hot anger simmering inside her. She could feel her cheeks flush with hot color. "How can you say that?" she asked harshly.

Emily's eyebrows shot up. "Say what?"

"How can you just stand there, sounding so nice and concerned, when all this time you didn't do a thing to help Luke? You didn't say anything or take any kind of stand against Charlie and all the others who were against this center." Sara could hear her voice rising with anger, but she couldn't stop herself. "People would have listened to you, but you wimped out, Emily. Just the way you must have wimped out when you gave me up for adoption!"

Emily stared at Sara with her mouth hanging open. "When I—what did you say?"

Sara took a step back. She pressed her hand over her mouth, as if trying to push back her confession. Impossible. It was out now. She turned away from Emily's searching gaze, feeling breathless, as if she had run a marathon. Her pulse was hammering, and she felt a little sick and a little exhilarated all at once, as if she had tapped into a vein of strength she hadn't known she had. She took a long, steadying breath.

"Emily, you're my mother. My birth mother, I mean," she forced herself to say.

Emily blinked. Her complexion drained of all color, and her skin turned white and bloodless as snow.

"*You?* . . . Sara? Is this true?" She took a shaky step toward her. "I don't dare believe it."

"Believe it," Sara said more forcefully than she intended.

Moved to tears, Emily rushed forward and put her arms around Sara, but Sara felt stiff and wooden and couldn't respond. She felt Emily pull back, sensing her distress.

"I'm just so shocked," Emily said quietly. She wiped tears from under her eyes with her fingertips. "So over—overjoyed, I mean. Forgive me. I didn't mean to overwhelm you."

She reached out and tentatively touched Sara's hair. Then let her hand drop away.

One part of Sara yearned to melt into Emily's embrace, to put her head on her mother's shoulder and cry her heart out and be comforted.

But another part felt incredibly angry, so angry she could barely see straight. Sara felt shocked as the anger surged through her, taking over and rushing out.

"Why? Just tell me that. That's all I really came for," she asked. "Why did you just—dump me like that? Didn't you want me? Or was it just the easy way out? Like this problem with Luke and your election?"

Emily pulled back, looking suddenly smaller, as if she had somehow retracted into herself, Sara thought.

"Nothing can compare to that decision, Sara. Hardly this election," Emily said bitterly. "Giving you up was the biggest mistake of my life. I've thought about you and regretted it every single day since."

"Then why did you do it?" Sara repeated, refusing to be put off.

"My husband, Tim, your father, died in a car accident right before you were born. I was in the car, too, and there were injuries. You were born prematurely and I was . . . sort of a mess. Even younger than you are now. I wanted to keep you. I only saw you once, but you had been inside me for nearly nine months. I already loved you." She swallowed hard and wiped her eyes with a tissue. "My mother came down to help me. I didn't have any money or even a job at the time. . . . Adoption seemed like the right choice, the best choice for you. It was a weak moment for me, a confused time in my life. I didn't really know what I was doing, what I was giving up."

Emily's tone had started off in its familiar, reasonable pitch but now sounded desperate, as if she were pleading with Sara, her pride entirely forgotten.

"So, your mother talked you into it? Was that it?"

Emily met Sara's gaze. Then she looked away and rubbed her forehead.

"No, that's not how it happened. Not really." She took a long, shaky breath. "I blamed her for a long time, but I was wrong. I can't blame her anymore, because I'm the one who did it. It was my own mistake.

"I tried to undo it," she went on, her voice trembling. "I looked for you. But the adoption was closed. The best I could do was leave information in case you wanted to find me."

"That's how I found you," Sara admitted. "Right now, though, I'm not so happy I bothered."

"Sara, please, don't say that. I'd give anything . . ." Emily's voice trailed off. "Please try to understand the way it happened. I was really very young. I didn't realize—"

"You already said that," Sara cut in. "You think you can—"

Sara felt a lump in her throat, blocking her words. She heard herself gasp and realized she'd burst into tears. She turned and pulled open the door, then ran out of the cottage and down the path to her car.

"Sara, please, wait. . . ." Emily called, running after her.

Sara didn't look back. She got into her car and started the engine. As she shifted into gear, she saw Emily standing nearby, watching with a sad expression, her eyes and cheeks wet with tears.

She's too late, Sara thought. *Too late.*

EMILY HESITATED FOR A MOMENT, THEN CLIMBED IN HER CAR AND FOL-lowed Sara. She drove out to the Beach Road, where she thought she caught sight of Sara's white hatchback rounding a turn.

Emily pressed down hard on the accelerator. The fact that she was speeding barely registered. She took the curves of the road heedlessly, her concentration narrowed to one blazing thought: She had to find Sara.

Where did she go? Emily asked herself. Had she turned off someplace? Most of the turnoffs were private roads that dead-ended at houses.

Emily went down a few of those roads, but Sara's car was nowhere in sight. Finally Emily found herself heading into town and driving down Main Street. Maybe Sara went to the diner to talk to Lucy. They were close friends, Emily reasoned.

She parked her car and started walking down the street at a fast pace. Then suddenly she found herself running, overwhelmed by a feeling of urgency. She raced down the street, her open coat flapping around her legs. She hardly noticed the cold or the strange stares as she wove around people on the sidewalk.

She was panting as she pulled open the door of the Clam Box and stepped inside. She spotted Lucy at the counter, flipping through some receipts. Thank goodness, she thought. She wasn't sure she could deal with Charlie now.

"Is Sara here?" Emily asked.

"No, she took the day off to do some packing. She's moving tomorrow," Lucy explained calmly.

"Yes, I know that. . . ." Emily shook her head, finally catching her breath. "I mean, did she come by just now?"

Lucy gave her a puzzled look. "No, I haven't seen her."

"Thanks." Emily turned and slipped out the door, feeling Lucy staring at her back.

Out on Main Street again she walked quickly, looking around in all directions for Sara. *Would she have gone down to the harbor or the green?* Emily wondered. She picked up her pace, straining her eyes to see down to the waterfront. *Did she turn around without me seeing and go out to the Point?*

Sara was all packed up to move tomorrow, Emily remembered. *Would she just take off and go back to Maryland without even giving me a chance to explain things to her?*

The possibility froze Emily's heart.

At the dock and on the green there was no sight of Sara. Emily felt bleak and deflated. She turned and found herself standing in front of the church. The door was open and she went inside. *Just to sit down for a moment and catch my breath,* she told herself.

Golden light streamed through the stained-glass windows. It was so quiet, she could practically hear the sound of her own heartbeat.

She knelt down in the last pew and folded her hands. *Thank you, God, for answering my prayers and sending my daughter to me. She is a wonder, a miracle. But what's going to happen now? I know I told you that even if I only saw her for five minutes, it would be okay. But I was wrong. I do care, God. I do want more. Please give me some time with her. Help her to forgive me. Is there a way? I don't know how, but surely you can find one.*

Please forgive me, Lord, for ever doubting you, she added. *Help me to stay strong.*

She sat for a long while with her eyes closed, her head bowed on her hands. When she picked her head up, she felt strangely refreshed, almost as if she had been asleep.

She sensed someone nearby and turned to see Reverend Ben, who stood in the aisle, watching her.

"What is it Emily? You look awful," he said bluntly.

Emily got up off her knees and sat down in the pew. "Sara Franklin is my daughter. She just told me. She came to this town to find me."

"Sara?" He stared at her amazed. "All this time she's been here and never told you . . . but why?"

Emily bit her lip. This was hard to talk about, even with Reverend Ben. "I don't know. Sara didn't say. We didn't get that far," she added, feeling overwhelmed again. "She's so angry with me. I tried to explain how it had happened, how sorry I was for the mistake I made and the wrong I did to her. But she—" Emily shook her head. "She didn't understand. I'm afraid she's so angry, she'll just leave here and go back home again."

Reverend Ben sat down next to her. "You can find her and try again. Just try to persuade her to wait and not just rush off. If she won't see you again, maybe you should write her a letter," he suggested.

"Yes . . . I guess I could. I could tell her how it was for me back then. It's so hard to describe, though. . . . She'll think I'm exaggerating, or making it up just to convince her." Emily paused, her thoughts racing, then she felt a glimmer of hope. "I just remembered. I used to write in a journal back then, almost every day, just like Sara does. I still have it. I could give it to her, have her read it. It's all there—what I went through when I was deciding what to do, all my thoughts and feelings. She would have to see that it was genuine."

"Absolutely," Reverend Ben agreed. "That's an excellent idea, an inspiration."

"Yes, yes, it is," Emily agreed, smiling weakly through her tears. "Thank you, Reverend." Emily leaned forward and gave him a tight hug. "Thank you for talking with me."

"I didn't say anything, really," he admitted. "You're the one who thought of it."

"God reminded me. I'm sure of it." She got to her feet. "I'll get it and bring it to her house right away."

"Good luck, Emily," Reverend Ben said to her as she left him. "I'll pray for you. And for Sara."

"Thank you, Reverend. I need it."

A short time later Emily drove back to the cottages and parked her car. She saw lights on in Sara's cottage and guessed she had returned.

She walked up to Sara's door, knocked softly, and waited, feeling a tightness in her chest that made it hard to breathe.

Maybe she'll see it's me and not answer the door, Emily thought. But just as she was about to write a note and leave her package on the doorstep, the door opened.

Sara stared at her, her eyes hard.

"You don't have to talk to me," Emily said quickly. She pushed the large envelope that held the journal into Sara's hands.

266

"You came a long way to find me and went to a lot of trouble. Please don't leave until you read this. I know it's hard to believe what I told you, about the past. I know the way I acted about Luke's project disappointed you. Frankly, if I were you, I'd be angry, too. But if you read this, I think it will answer some of your questions and doubts. Don't do it for me. Do it for yourself."

"What is it?" Sara asked warily.

"My diary. I kept one back then. This book is from the months when I was expecting you . . . and later, after Tim died and I had to decide what to do."

Sara didn't react at all, and Emily felt her heart sinking. Was she making it worse? Should she just leave now and give up? No, she couldn't do that.

"You said you wanted to know why," she reminded Sara.

Finally Sara reached out and reluctantly took the envelope from her. "I don't owe you anything, and I'm not promising I'll read this," she warned.

"Fair enough," Emily said. She was dying to ask if Sara planned on leaving, but she forced herself not to say any more.

"Thank you, Sara," she said quietly. "No matter what you think of me, I'm still glad you found me. I still feel this is a blessed day in my life," she added, not daring to meet her daughter's eyes.

Sara didn't reply. She stood by the door as Emily turned away, then Emily heard the door snap closed.

CHAPTER FOURTEEN

*W*HAT IS THIS SUPPOSED TO BE?" LUKE MUTTERED to himself as he drove down the gravel road to his property. "A surprise party?"

The hard rain on Wednesday night had left puddles in the rutted road that splashed the sides of the Toyota as he sped up.

Sam's blue truck, Dr. Elliot's Buick, and Paul Delgado's van stood side by side in the parking area behind the cottages. Sam and Digger were unloading ladders, long planks of fresh lumber, and rolls of roofing paper. Three kids from the program hung around near the truck, looking as if they were waiting to be told what to do.

Dr. Elliot was the first to see him. He walked toward the Toyota as Luke came to a stop.

"We've been waiting for you, McAllister. Sam thought he should start unloading, though."

Luke peered down at the doctor as he hopped out of his truck. "Where did all that stuff come from?"

"Sam picked it up someplace. Bought on account—on account of the work here has got to start again, you know," the doctor quipped.

Luke didn't know what to say to him. "That's my call, I think, Doctor," he said finally.

"May be. But what are you waiting for, exactly?" Dr. Elliot persisted. "We heard that you got the okay from Santori on Monday to keep going."

"That's right." Luke said. He wondered where the group had heard about his meeting. That was the problem with a small town. It was hard to keep any secrets.

"So, what do you say?" the doctor pressed. "It's a fine day—the weather cleared up nicely, no wind, either." He tipped his head back to survey the sky. "You won't find a better one."

"The weather's great," Luke conceded, "but people in this town are still against us. Even Emily Warwick changing horses in the middle of an election hasn't done too much to help our side."

"Yes, that letter she wrote was extremely supportive—and at great risk to her own career. I have to hand it to her," Ezra remarked, shaking his head. "But I get your point. You're afraid to go ahead again. You're scared."

The doctor's choice of words nettled him. "Not scared. I'm just trying to be realistic. Maybe this center doesn't have a chance here, even if I force it through."

Luke suddenly realized that all the activity around him had stopped. Sam stood up on the truck bed, looking down at him. Digger put down the long black metal toolbox he was carrying. Luke felt seven pairs of eyes fixed on him.

"Maybe you're right, and the center doesn't have a chance." The doctor surprised him by agreeing. "But you won't know that unless we keep going. If we quit now, you're the one who called it off." Dr. Elliot paused, letting his words sink in. "Do you really want to run and abandon this thing half done?"

The word *run* struck a bull's-eye. Run, like everyone said he did the night he was caught in the shoot-out. Luke tasted something bitter and metallic at the back of his throat and shook his head to clear it. He wished everyone would just stop staring at him. But he knew they were waiting for him to make the decision and tell them to start work or quit.

Luke looked up and cleared his throat, finding his foreman's voice. "Okay . . . get to it, then. You all know what we have to do," he said curtly.

The others looked briefly at each other, then returned to what they'd been doing, as if a "freeze frame" button had been pressed and now the movie was turned on again.

Luke released a long breath and glanced at Dr. Elliot. "Did you organize all this?"

Dr. Elliot nodded. "Purely selfish motives. I'm looking for a little part-time job here once the buildings are up and things get rolling. See any possibilities for me?"

"I'll see what I can do," Luke replied, matching the doctor's wry tone.

Luke had the impulse to thank him for the timely kick in the pants. But he brushed the thought aside, his feelings too close to the surface.

He opened the back of his truck and took out his toolbox. There would be time for thanks later, he thought. Ezra Elliot was going to be around here for a while.

SUNDAY MORNING AFTER THE SERVICE, EMILY STOOD IN LINE BEHIND HER mother as the congregation exited. Reverend Ben made a point of shaking hands with everyone who waited in line, taking time for a private word with each. When Emily stood beside him, he took her hand. "Any word yet from Sara?" he asked quietly.

Emily shook her head. For nearly a week she had barely slept or been able to eat or focus on her work. It seemed all she had done was wait and wonder about Sara.

"She's still in town," Emily said in a low voice. "She's moved to the village, I know that. I just don't know what to think—about the other thing."

"I'm praying for you, Emily." He pressed her hand between his own.

"Thank you, Reverend. So am I," Emily said sincerely.

Her mother had stepped away to chat with friends from the museum board. As Emily approached she pinned her with a curious stare. "What was that little tête-à-tête all about?"

Emily didn't know how to answer that. She wasn't ready to tell her mother about Sara and certainly was not about to have that conversation in the middle of the church vestibule.

But before she could reply, Lillian spoke again. "It was about your sister and Sam Morgan again, right? I don't want to hear another word about them, so don't even bother."

"All right. Let's go, then," Emily said. Taking her mother's arm, they proceeded out the wide arched doors of the church.

THE SUN SANK INTO A BANK OF PURPLE- AND ROSE-TINTED CLOUDS. THE damp air off the water felt colder, and it was almost too dark to read the scrawled, rushing handwriting that covered the pages.

Sara had found it hard to decipher at first. But by now she had read the book through twice. At first, very hurriedly, scanning the lines, as if afraid to really hear the voice inside the words.

Then she put it aside for a few days, trying hard not to think about it, not to let the voice in, using her anger and pain like a door to keep it out. But this morning she had taken it out again and started reading. Slowly this time. Now here on the beach with Luke at the end of the day, she still wasn't done. She glanced down at the page, checking the date. April 3, 1979.

The baby kicked me today, a strange, fluttery feeling. I could barely believe it. I made Tim try to feel it, but I'm not sure he did. She feels so strong. I know it's a girl; I just have the feeling. I love her so much already. I can't wait to see her, to hold her. I imagine how she'll feel, lying right on my chest. I was reading today how babies like to rest near their mother's heartbeat. It comforts them. I'll keep her there, close to me. I talk to her, too, sometimes. Tim heard me the other night. He thought it was funny at first, then he started to do the same thing—talking to my huge stomach in bed.

I've been trying to pick out a name, but it's so difficult to choose. I want to find something really special for her. Not like Emily, so drab and ordinary. She won't be like that at all, I'm sure of it. . . .

Sara paused and stared out at the sea. A sudden flare of light illuminated the horizon. She looked down at the book again and flipped ahead. The top of the page read May 5.

Tim is dead. I have to keep writing that out, saying it out loud. It won't sink in. I can't believe it. How can it be? I don't remember the accident. Only just a second before. The look on Tim's face. His arm swung out to hold me back, then—just blackness.

They say it was two days ago. I've been unconscious. I've lost a lot of blood, but my baby is all right. They think so, anyway.

I'm so worried about her. Something feels—wrong. I can't lose her, too. She has to be okay. Tim . . . Tim, what am I going to do without you? I don't think I can live. But I have to. The baby needs me. She's all I have now. Thank God, she survived. Thank God. If I had to hear she was gone, too . . .

There was another line or two on the page, but so blurry Sara couldn't make out the words. She turned the pages, moving through Emily's past. Finally she found the page she was looking for.

It would be the best for the baby, Mother keeps telling me that, night and day. "Best for the baby. You have to think about her now." She says I'm being selfish, horribly selfish. A bad mother already. Not putting my feelings, my needs aside for my child. But doesn't she need me, her own mother? She's not even born yet. I can't let her go. She's part of me, my flesh and blood. Part of Tim.

That's why Mother can't stand it. Why she won't let me keep the baby and bring her back home. She wants to punish me for running away with Tim. She doesn't want to be reminded of him. She thinks I can give up my child, go back home, put on my old clothes waiting in the closet, and take up my life again, as if none of this ever happened. As if I never loved Tim and was his wife. As if I never carried this child inside of me. I can't do it. I won't. She can't make me.

If only Emily had had someone to help her, anyone to take her side against Lillian, Sara thought. She might have even had a chance if she hadn't gotten ill again, but a few pages later, the voice became far less defiant, sadder, and worn down. The date was May 19. Her own birthday.

I wish I could die. I'm sick again, a high fever. They can't find the infection. I'm so scared. The baby is in danger. She's not right. They won't tell me, but I know it. I keep falling asleep. I need to stay awake, to guard her. They said a few more hours, and they will take her out with a C-section. I'm afraid they're going to take her away from me. Mother won't let me bring her home. I begged Daddy on the phone, but all he said was that he thanked God I was alive and would be home soon. He won't go against her. He won't help me. What will I do? There's a hole inside me now. Tim, I need him. Last night I heard him come into the room. I heard his voice right next to me. I reached out to touch him. Hallucinating, Mother said. . . . The doctor is here. With my mother. I guess it's time. . . .

"Sara? How can you see anything?" Luke stood next to her, his hands sunk in his front pockets.

She looked up at him and blinked. "It got dark. I didn't notice."

He crouched down and sat in the sand beside her. "Are you crying?"

She shook her head. "No, the wind got in my eyes, that's all."

She looked down at the diary and carefully closed it.

"What do you think now?" he asked her.

She had so many thoughts, so much welling up inside, like the high-rising waves washing in on the shoreline.

"I think Emily really tried," Sara said carefully. "She had a lot against her. I don't know what I would have done if it had happened to me."

"What are you going to do now?" Luke asked.

"I want to go see her. Will you take me there?"

"Right now?"

She nodded. He looked at her for a moment, then leaned forward and cupped her head with his hands, pressing his lips to her forehead.

"All right. Let's go."

Sara put the diary away in her knapsack and took Luke's hand. He pulled her up from the sand and twined his fingers through hers as they walked up the beach.

At the end of the point Sara saw the lighthouse, its thin beam sweeping across the dark sky. The sight stopped them in their tracks for a moment, and Sara felt the light pass over her. She glanced at Luke, recalling how he had told her that he prayed. She looked out at the dark sea.

God, if you're out there, please help me talk to Emily. This is so hard. I don't know how to begin. . . .

EMILY DIDN'T HEAR THE DOORBELL AT FIRST. IT WAS MONDAY NIGHT, AND she was running water in the tub for a bath. She leaned over and shut off the faucet. Yes, that was the bell. Her bath would have to wait. She walked quickly to the stairs.

"Coming," she called out. As she passed the window, she looked but didn't see Sara's car. Her secret hope instantly deflated.

She pulled the door open, then stood back. Her breath caught in her throat.

"I hope I'm not bothering you. Is this a bad time?" Sara asked.

"Come in. Come in." Emily swung open the door, her eyes hungrily fastened to Sara. She knew she had repeated herself.

Calm down, slow down, she chided herself. *You don't know what she's come for. Maybe to tell you she's going back to Maryland.*

"Come into the living room," she said, showing Sara the way.

Sara stood next to the sofa, but didn't sit down. "Did you just go running?" she asked.

Emily realized she was still wearing her jogging clothes. She touched her hair with her hand. "Yes . . . cold out," she added, thinking she sounded nervous and inane.

She had been running a lot the last few days. And taking a lot of hot baths. Anything to calm her down from the wait. But now Sara was here. Finally.

"Here . . . let's sit down," she suggested.

Sara sat in an armchair and Emily sat on the sofa. Sara opened her knapsack and took out the diary. She placed it on the coffee table. "I wanted to return this to you."

Emily felt as if she couldn't breathe. "Did you read it?"

"Yes . . . I read it twice."

Emily waited, aware of the sound of her blood rushing in her ears.

"You went through a lot." Sara added hesitantly, "It was a lot to lose your husband like that. I can see how scared you were." She paused.

But it wasn't enough, right? Emily nearly said.

"I can see it now. How it happened. You didn't really want to give me up, but somehow, the whole thing was just too much for you to handle. I can see that." Sara nodded to herself. "The part where you wrote about how much you already loved me, even when I was inside you and you hadn't even seen me yet . . ." Sara's eyes filled up with tears and her voice trailed off. "I believe you did."

"But I still do. I never stopped, Sara. The time, the distance . . . It never mattered at all that I never saw you. That I never knew you." Emily heard her voice breaking and realized that her eyes were stinging. Any second now she was going to burst into tears. Embarrassed, she covered her mouth with her hand and stared at the pattern of the upholstery, struggling to get control.

As she stared down, willing herself not to cry, Sara suddenly rose from the chair and sat on the couch beside her. Sara put her arms around her, and Emily could hardly believe it. She felt frozen for a moment, in shock. Then she hugged Sara back, squeezing her eyes shut. This time Sara didn't pull away but leaned toward her. Emily pressed her cheek to Sara's hair.

"Can you ever forgive me? Not now, I know it's too soon. But some-day maybe?"

Sara pulled back and sighed. "I'm trying," she said. Then finally, "I do."

Emily hugged Sara close again. *Thank you, Lord. Thank you from the bottom of my heart. I don't need another thing in my life now that I have her again.*

A short time later they sat in the kitchen and Emily happily served Sara a sandwich and a cup of tea.

"What do you like in the tea? Here's sugar, lemon, milk." She put everything on the table.

Sara smiled at her. "Emily, sit down. You're making me nervous. It's just me, remember?"

"I know. I know." Emily sat down across from her and took a sip of tea. "Sara, I need to ask you about something. I'm trying to figure out the best way to let everyone know about this—this wonderful change in my life. Normally, the gossip mill in this town would just take care of it in an hour or so. All I'd have to do is tell Harriet DeSoto or Lucy Bates," she said wryly. "But I was thinking maybe I'd just tell Dan to run something in the paper. . . ."

"But what about the election?" Sara protested. "This is going to be terrible for you. I think you should wait."

"Wait? I've waited twenty-two years." Emily laughed in disbelief. "I don't need to wait any longer to tell everyone about you. Do you really think I care so much about being mayor?"

"You don't have to do that for me, really. I don't want you to," Sara insisted. "What if you lose because of that—because of me? I'd feel awful about it."

"I would never think that way, Sara. You're too important to me. Besides, I think I've learned my lesson about taking the middle of the road."

"But you like being mayor. You're good at it," Sara argued. "I want to be part of your life, Emily, but not mess it up for you. . . . How else can I say it? Please don't do this," Sara nearly begged her.

I'm not listening to her, Emily realized. *I have to really stop and listen. Is this my first lesson in being a mother?*

She reached across the table and touched Sara's hand. "Sara, don't worry. I'll wait and think this over some more. I won't do anything without talking to you first, okay?"

"Thank you," Sara said, looking enormously relieved.

"I've already told Reverend Ben about you, but he won't tell a soul.

I've told Jessica, too. She was very, very happy," Emily added. "She's always liked you."

"I like her, too." Sara put both of her hands around her mug. "What about Lillian? Did you tell her yet?"

Emily shook her head. "I was waiting to see what you were going to say after you read the diary."

"She'll be surprised," Sara said.

"To say the least," Emily agreed. This was going to be difficult. There was no telling how her mother would react, and Emily couldn't stand the idea of Sara being caught in Lillian's bitter crossfire.

"Don't worry," Sara said, as if reading her mind. "I already know Lillian. I've seen her at her worst."

"Not quite," Emily assured her. "But you have some idea." She stirred a spoonful of sugar into her cup. "We'll figure it out."

"Listen," she went on as an idea occurred to her. "If you're not in a rush to get back home, would you like to see some pictures? I have an old album around here someplace with photographs I took of me and Tim while we were married. I may even have one of me when I was pregnant— out to about here." She gestured with her hand.

"That's hard to imagine," Sara said honestly. "Get them out, I want to see them."

"No problem." Emily got up and went into the den. She found the album easily, where she knew it had been sitting for years, wedged in the bottom of a bookcase.

"Here it is," she said as she returned to the kitchen.

Sara was standing next to her chair, rummaging through her knapsack. "I have one to show you, too," she said.

She pulled out a photograph and handed it to Emily. It was of Tim, a picture Emily vividly remembered taking in late winter, a few months before his death.

"Where did you get this?" Emily asked curiously.

"I found it. Up in Lillian's attic. It was in a box of old books." Sara sat down again. "I know it wasn't right to take it without asking. But I knew it was my father—and I couldn't very well ask Lillian."

"No, you couldn't have," Emily agreed. She finally looked away from the photo and smiled at Sara. "You look a lot like him, you know. Around the eyes, and you have the same-shape mouth." She reached out and lightly touched Sara's cheek.

She sat down again and sighed, giving Tim's photo one last lingering look. Then she pushed it across the table to Sara. "Here, you keep this. He's part of you, too."

"Yes . . . I know," Sara said, taking the photo carefully in her hands. She looked back at Emily. "Tell me about him. What was he like?"

Emily slowly smiled. She rarely had the chance to talk about Tim. Even thinking about him made her feel sad and wistful, but also fortunate to have been loved once by such a wonderful man. Finally she had the chance to share him with their child. *Don't worry, darling. She'll really know you when I get through,* she promised him.

"Well, for starters," she told Sara slowly, "he would have gone absolutely crazy over you. He would have loved you very, very much. . . ."

WHERE HAS THE DAY GONE? REVEREND BEN WONDERED. HALF-PAST THREE and he was just sitting down to lunch. The Clam Box was empty, the midday crowd long gone, and the Early Bird Special contingent not yet arriving.

Am I falling into that category already? he wondered vaguely. He opened the *Messenger* and checked the headline story—a hot debate at the school board meeting over the food service contract. *Thank you, Lord. Just about two weeks left to the election. Do you think you could keep it quiet around here until then, please?*

He had thought long and hard about his sermons the last few weeks, pushing himself to speak to the spiritual issues without further stirring up the political situation. He wasn't sure if he had helped any. Sermons, even the best, were like rain, taking a long time to seep into the ground and reach the roots of the problem.

Was it a minister's place to get involved in an election? While he had his personal preference, publicly he tried to remain neutral. *No, I can't take sides in political issues,* Ben told himself, though some clergymen saw the question differently. But in this matter, the moral and even spiritual threads had become so tangled in the political, it was not only hard to stay out of it, but at times he felt it his duty to jump in.

"Grilled cheese with bacon and tomato, right?" Lucy checked as she dropped off his order. "And here's your coffee." She settled down a mug.

"Thank you, Lucy." Ben spread a napkin on his lap and picked up half his sandwich.

"Anything else?" Lucy asked, balancing her tray on one hip.

The Reverend glanced up at her. "Well, I could use some company," he said, sensing she needed to talk. "Can you sit for a minute or two?"

"Oh, sure," she said eagerly. She slipped into the seat across from him. "All the ketchup bottles and salt shakers are full, so I don't even have to bother with that."

It was amazing to him what some people had to worry about, the multitude of trivial concerns that made up the average person's day. But Lucy had larger concerns today, he guessed from the way she nervously twisted a lock of her hair.

"I bet you'll be glad when the election is over," he said.

"I'll say. If Charlie wins, that is. If he doesn't . . . well, I don't even want to think about it."

"The paper says the race is too close to call," the Reverend replied.

"I know. That's what everyone says. But don't tell Charlie that. He keeps saying he has the momentum. Like a rock, rolling downhill, gathering no grass—or whatever the expression is."

"No moss, I think you mean," the Reverend corrected her with a grin.

"No remorse, in my husband's case," Lucy countered. "I think his tactics against Emily and Luke McAllister have been just awful. I'm not saying he had anything to do with that rock, and they know the fire was an accident," she hastened to add. "But when I see the way he acts trying to get elected, I don't like it, Reverend. It's as if he's a stranger to me, honestly." She looked up at him, wide-eyed.

"That doesn't sound good, Lucy," the Reverend replied in a serious tone.

"Charlie says the same thing about me," she replied defensively. "He says ever since I started school again, I'm like a different person and he doesn't know what got into me. As if he's waiting for me to get over the flu or something."

"I see," Reverend Ben replied. He pushed his plate aside and took a sip of coffee.

Lucy had come to him several times over the summer with issues about Charlie and their marriage. He had counseled her as best as he could—with mixed results, it seemed. She had started college in September. But it appeared now that their problems and her grievances went deeper than that.

"Reverend, sometimes I really feel as if our lives are—are going in different directions. Charlie has never been the easiest man to be married to. But at least I always felt we were on the same wavelength, wanted the same things out of life. But I don't know now. I'm not so sure," she added in a sad and worried voice.

"Have you thought of going to a marriage counselor? Or coming to see me together maybe?" he asked.

"I've thought of it. I even told Charlie we had to go after the last big fight we had. But he said he was way too busy to waste time sitting in some shrink's office, listening to me complain about him when he could do the same thing for free, right in our living room. Now, that was a mean thing to say, don't you think?"

"He's not being very reasonable or respectful to you," the Reverend had to agree.

"He's under a lot of pressure now," Lucy offered. "This election has really got him worn out."

Count on Lucy to come to her husband's defense, the Reverend thought, *no matter how vehemently she complains about him.*

"That goes without saying. I imagine it's a great strain on both of you."

"I know we need some help. We can't keep going on this way for very much longer," she said in a cautious tone. "I think the kids are starting to notice, too. They get so . . . so quiet sometimes, like they're trying to be invisible. Charlie Junior just burst into tears the other night at the dinner table, over nothing. I don't want them to feel bad like that."

"There's just a little more than two weeks left to the election," Reverend Ben reminded her. "Charlie is too focused on the race right now to deal with anything like this. I think you just have to wait it out a little longer. Why don't you resolve to see a counselor after, win or lose," he suggested. "Would you like to make a date with me right now?"

Lucy sniffed and straightened up in her seat. "It will be hard for the both of us to get out of here together, though—"

"Now, now. No excuses, Lucy. You can manage somehow."

He took his calendar out of his breast pocket and flipped the pages to November. "How about November twelfth, say, eight o'clock? That will give you both a week to recover from Election Day."

"I need a year, but that's okay. I'll write it down, too," she said, ripping off a guest check from her book and noting the appointment on the back. She folded the slip of paper and stuck it in her pocket. "Thanks, Reverend. I hope I can get Charlie there."

"You work on him, Lucy—I'll work from my end."

She nodded and stood up. "Thanks. We sure could use some prayers."

* * *

REVEREND BEN DID NOT GET HOME UNTIL NEARLY ELEVEN O'CLOCK that night. He had visited a parishioner in the hospital, then stayed late in his office, catching up on paperwork. Now the house was quiet and dark, except for the small lamp in the hallway Carolyn always left on for him. He didn't call out, in case she was asleep, and entered the bedroom quietly.

The white Bible, which she'd had as long as he'd known her, was open on her lap. She looked asleep. But before he could tiptoe over and turn off the light on her end table, she blinked and smiled at him.

"I must have dozed off. . . . I didn't even hear you come in."

"That's surprising, since I just rattled every cracker box in the house."

He bent over the bed and kissed her hello on the cheek. She smelled like floral soap and toothpaste, a familiar combination.

"Didn't you have any dinner?" she asked with concern.

"A late lunch. A very heavy late lunch," he corrected himself. "I'm all right. What I need is a good night's sleep." He sat on the edge of the bed and took off his shoes, feeling Carolyn watching him.

"I left something for you on your chest. A letter from Mark," she said.

"Really?" He sat up and ran his hand over his beard. "What does it say?" he asked eagerly.

"You can read it. It's pretty long. For Mark, I mean," she replied. He could tell from her tone that it had not been the answer they hoped for. Still, Carolyn sounded all right; maybe the news was not that bad.

He walked over to his dresser and found the envelope which had been addressed to both of them, then he slipped out a two-page letter.

His son could be eloquent when he put his mind to—or maybe his heart into—it. Ben could not help but be touched by the opening of the letter in which Mark was clearly making an effort not to hurt them. But while Mark acknowledged their eagerness for him to come home, he said he had changed his plans. Ben felt his heart drop as he continued reading.

. . . Coming back East just doesn't feel right for me now. I hope you can understand. The monastery was a good place for me to clear my head. I'd like to keep this feeling for a while. I'd like to be in an even quieter place where I have time and space to think and just—be. A friend of mine is living on a ranch in Montana and invited me to come out there and work with him. I've always heard that part of the country is a beautiful, wild place, and I've wanted to see it.

I'm sorry to disappoint you. Maybe I shouldn't have mentioned coming home at all if I didn't know for sure. But I will be back someday. You know that. Probably sooner than any of us think, right? Until then, I think of all of you often and hope that you are well. Please give my love to Rachel and wish her the best of luck with the baby. With love, Mark.

"He mentions Rachel here at the end," Ben noted, his eyes still fixed on the letter. "I don't think he realizes how soon the baby is due, do you?"

Carolyn put her Bible on the table next to the bed. "I'm sure we mentioned it. But he's not ready to come back." She sighed. "It's not the end of the world, I guess, if Mark comes in the spring or even the summer. At least he sounds as if he's been thinking about it, too," she said hopefully.

"Yes," Ben agreed. "It sounds as if he's thinking about a lot of things." He went over to her and sat on the edge of the bed. "Are you very disappointed?"

She nodded and Ben could see she was trying not to cry. "I guess I got my hopes up. He didn't realize, I guess, what it meant to me. To us," she added, her voice thick.

Ben took her hand in his and studied it. She had such fine hands, perfect for the piano, still supple and strong. "No, he didn't realize," he said, believing it. Mark didn't understand half of what they felt for him. What child did?

But it did seem cruel somehow to dangle that prize, then snatch it away. He felt disappointed—and angry. But he wanted to focus on Carolyn. Her mood had been so even lately, so upbeat. Would this news push her into a tailspin?

She sighed and leaned back on the pillows. "Rachel will be disappointed, too. She was in bed today with another cold—or just plain worn out. I couldn't really tell. I stopped by to see her and . . . I don't know . . . she looked just awful. So pale and drawn."

"What about Jack? Isn't he helping her?" Ben asked as he undid the buttons of his shirt.

"I asked her the same thing. She said Jack has been doing practically everything around the house, but she feels exhausted. Her ankles are swollen, too," Carolyn said. "I made her just sit in one spot all day and keep her feet up."

Ben heard the worry in her voice. Carolyn wasn't the worrying type normally. But this was different—her only daughter having their first grandchild. Yet, in a way this was good, he realized. It gave her something to focus on besides Mark.

"The end of the pregnancy can be very hard for some women," he said. "Maybe she should stop working now. Or at least, cut back her hours."

"I told her that, too. She has cut back to part-time, but I'm afraid that's not enough."

"Come on, dear. She'll be fine," Ben assured her. "The baby will arrive, and we'll forget all about Rachel's swollen ankles. That's always the way."

Carolyn crossed her arms over her chest, not looking comforted at all. "I suppose I'm worrying too much," she admitted. "It's hard for me to see her like this, though. I can't wait until the baby is here, safe and sound."

"Me, too," he agreed.

"Then maybe Mark will come home," she added wistfully.

Ben didn't reply. He leaned over and held her.

CHAPTER FIFTEEN

$\sim$

"*S*ARA, I'M SO HAPPY TO SEE YOU." JESSICA PULLED OPEN her front door before Emily and Sara even had a chance to knock.

As Sara walked in, Jessica hugged her close, then quickly stepped back. "I'm sorry . . . I couldn't resist. It's silly, really, isn't it? It's like I've never met you before, and I just saw you the other day in the Clam Box—but I didn't know," Jessica tried to explain.

Emily watched Sara shyly smile at her aunt. "I know what you mean. It's sort of strange for all of us, I guess."

"But strange in a good way," Jessica pointed out.

"Absolutely," Emily agreed.

Emily told Jessica about Sara the night she found out. During that tense, awful period while she waited for Sara to read the diary, it was Jessica who was her greatest comfort. Emily would always be grateful to her sister for that. And for taking Sara into her own heart with such warmth and sincerity.

"What time did you tell Mother?" Jessica asked Emily.

"I said around eight. She thinks I have a late meeting."

"We have a few minutes, so come into the bedroom," Jessica said, walking ahead. "I want to show you both something."

Emily followed her sister, with Sara trailing close behind. In the center of the bed lay a large, flat carton, a scrap of dark blue velvet peeking out from one end. The bridesmaid gowns had come. Emily felt unexpectedly excited.

Jessica flipped open the lid and pulled out the gown. She held it up against her body. "It's great, isn't it?" she said. "Look, they changed the sash to the darker satin, just as we asked, and took off those ugly beads around the neckline."

It actually looked better here in Jessica's bedroom, Emily thought, than it did in the dressing room of the store, which had been bursting with dresses in all shapes, sizes, and materials.

"Even Molly didn't complain," Jessica said. "And she loved the coordinating gowns for Lauren and Jill."

"I think we made a very good choice," Emily agreed, feeling pleased. The wedding was really starting to come together.

"It's very pretty," Sara added. She reached out to touch the velvet. "I love the color."

Emily and Jessica glanced at each other. Jessica took the dress and held it against Sara. "Oh, look at that . . . it's perfect for her. She'll need a smaller size, though."

"She'll look gorgeous in that. With her hair up maybe," Emily said with an affectionate, tender look at her daughter. She bunched up Sara's long ponytail and held it up behind her head.

"Very elegant," Jessica agreed.

Sara glanced at them, confused. "You're just kidding, right?"

"Would you be one of my bridesmaids, Sara?" Jessica asked sweetly.

"Oh . . . I couldn't. Really," Sara said, looking self-conscious.

"Oh, please do it. I would just love it if you would. And Sam would love it, too!" Jessica exclaimed.

Emily watched Sara struggling with the question. She could understand why Sara might feel shy or hesitant. She also knew that she would be so proud and happy to follow her daughter down the aisle.

"Please, Sara? I'd love for you to be there with us, like a real family," Emily said softly.

"I won't take no for an answer," Jessica insisted with a smile.

Sara pursed her lips and looked down at the dress again. "Okay. If you really want me to."

"I really do. You can't know how much," Jessica said. She hugged Sara close for a moment, then glanced at her sister, smiling over Sara's shoulder.

Emily swallowed back a lump in her throat. She had not felt this content in a very long time.

EMILY'S GOOD FEELINGS LINGERED, BUOYING HER UP AS THE THREE WOMEN walked up the path to Lillian's house. Emily paused before knocking on the door. "Now, please remember, Sara—" she began.

"I know. She's liable to get nasty, and I shouldn't take it to heart," Sara replied in a rote tone.

Emily had to grin. Was she sounding so much like a mother already?

"All right. Sorry if I sound like a broken record."

Sara leaned over and gave her arm a squeeze. "Why don't you knock so she knows we're here?" she suggested gently.

They waited only a few moments before Lillian appeared. "What is this?" Her sweeping glance took the three of them in.

"I thought you were bringing me some groceries, not another contingent to badger me about this wedding."

"I have the groceries, Mother." Emily raised the white plastic bag like a peace offering. "Why don't you let us in?"

Lillian stepped aside, grudgingly allowing them to enter. She shut the door and turned to Jessica. "Well, look who's here—the bride to be. How nice to see you again, Jessica," she said in a chilly formal tone.

"Hello, Mother," Jessica said mildly. Lillian stared at her, but when Jessica didn't say anything more, she made a frustrated sound in her throat and headed for the living room.

"Hello, Lillian," Sara said, catching her grandmother's attention.

Her mother seemed confused to find Sara there and yet, not unhappy, Emily noticed. As she carried the groceries into the kitchen, she could still hear their conversation.

"Sara, how are you? I expected you last week, to go through the things in the attic. But maybe you'd forgotten."

"No, I didn't forget. I'm sorry I didn't call, though. I did get a little busy."

Lillian nodded. "Yes, a little busy. Everyone is so busy these days—too busy to call or stop by."

Emily came back in the room. Her mother was staring at Jessica again, but Jessica ignored her.

"Why don't you sit down, Mother? We need to tell you something," Emily began.

"Why do I have to sit down? Is this bad news?"

"No, I don't think so," Emily said sincerely. "But it will probably surprise you."

Lillian stood up tall, as if to defy Emily's suggestion.

"Well? What is it?" she demanded curtly. "The three of you look like the proverbial cat who ate the canary. I'd like to be in on the joke, too."

Emily rested her hand on Sara's shoulder as she gazed at her mother.

"This is my daughter, Mother. Your granddaughter." She paused, waiting for her mother's reaction.

Lillian blinked. "What do you mean, your daughter?" she asked harshly. "How could that be?"

"Sara is my daughter, the child I gave up for adoption down in Maryland," Emily explained calmly. "She came up here in May to look for me—but she just told me a little over a week ago."

Lillian narrowed her eyes and her mouth trembled. She shook her head, as if to say "No," then turned around and took firm hold of the chair behind her. "I think I will sit down, after all," she said on a long breath.

"Are you all right?" Jessica asked with concern, walking toward her.

"Don't you dare fuss over me," she warned her youngest daughter. She swallowed hard and lifted her head. "I don't believe her," she said flatly, glancing at Sara. "She must be . . . some sort of imposter. You're a fool to believe her," she warned Emily.

Emily felt her temper rising but struggled to control it. "Don't be ridiculous, Mother."

"Really? Has she shown you any proof of this at all?" Lillian demanded. "This happens all the time, you know. I've read about it. She'll be asking you for money next, mark my words."

"Mother, please, stop right there," Emily said. She felt Sara touch her arm and turned to her. Sara shook her head, as if to say, Don't bother. I'm okay.

Emily had expected something like this, but it was hard to take, nonetheless. She forced her voice to an even pitch. "After all this time and all I've been through over this, Mother, I hoped you would at least try to be understanding."

"I understand this," Lillian said slowly. "Whether she's really your child or not—and that, to my mind, remains to be seen—you will entirely ruin your chances for reelection if you allow word of this to get out." She paused, her cheeks flushing with emotion. "You would be a fool to do that, Emily. A genuine fool, if you ask me."

"As if I have something to be ashamed of," Emily said with a long exasperated sigh. "Look at her," Emily demanded, pointing to Sara. "She's a wonderful young woman. A living, breathing miracle. My child," she said in happy astonishment. "This is the greatest thing that ever happened to me, Mother," she added quietly. "Can't you understand that?"

Lillian gave Emily a hard look, then her cold glance moved to Sara. "Why did you ever come up here? There's nothing to be gained from these—reunions. Doors are closed for a reason."

Emily moved forward to reply, but Sara stilled her with a touch on her arm again. "I don't think so, Lillian," she replied quietly. "I didn't come here to cause anyone trouble. I think you know that, too."

Lillian glared at her, then looked away. "Oh . . . just get out, all of you. I'm tired. I've had more than enough of this."

Emily glanced at Jessica. The worry in her sister's eyes mirrored her own.

"Okay, we'll go now," Emily said. She met her mother's gaze. "Do you need anything?"

"Not from you, Emily. You've given me a granddaughter tonight. I'd say that's more than enough."

"DAN, I NEED TO SPEAK WITH YOU." EMILY MET DAN AT THE FRONT OF THE newspaper office, just as he was opening up. He glanced at her curiously as he unlocked the door.

"All right, Emily, come on in."

He closed the door behind them, then dropped his briefcase near his desk. "What is it?" he asked quietly. "You look upset."

"It's nothing bad—something very good, actually." She turned away from him, gathering her thoughts. She had carefully planned what she wanted to say to him, but now that he was staring at her that way, it was making her forget.

"Charlie Bates has decided to drop out of the race?"

She smiled. "Even better for me, I'd say." She saw his eyebrows go up a notch. He sat back on the edge of his desk, his gaze fixed on her.

"This is something you're going to hear about," she said. "And rather than have you weed through a tangle of gossip, I thought you should hear the real story from me."

Dan crossed his arms over his chest. "All right. I'm always up for a good story."

"Well, let's see—" Emily was finding it hard to begin. "I was married right after high school. I eloped, actually. Did you know that about me?"

"Yes. I think I did," he said, looking curious about where this was going.

"My husband—his name was Tim Sutton—he died in a car accident. We were married not quite two years. After he died, I came back here to live. I went away to college, actually, and came back after that."

Dan's expression turned serious. "I didn't know you were a widow. I'm sorry. That must have been terribly difficult."

"Yes, it was. I was pregnant. I had the baby about two weeks after . . . after the accident," she said, pushing herself to continue. She felt his steady gaze bearing down on her, and she willed herself not to look at him.

Now for the very hard part. The big admission. Her dark secret. She knew she shouldn't worry about what Dan might think when she told him, and yet she did. Somehow Dan's opinion of her had become very important.

"I gave the baby up for adoption. I'm not proud of that. I'm quite ashamed, in fact, but at the time it seemed like the right thing to do." She took a breath and then gave him a brief version of why she gave up her daughter, never really spelling out her mother's role in it.

Dan listened sympathetically, then asked, "Why are you telling me this now?"

Emily felt her heart lift as she said, "Well, what's happened now is that my daughter has found me. It's Sara," she said, meeting his gaze again. "Sara Franklin."

"Sara . . . the waitress?" He suddenly came to his feet.

Emily nodded and smiled. "Uh-huh. Isn't she wonderful?"

Dan looked astounded. He shook his head as if he felt dizzy or couldn't see straight. "That's an amazing story, all right." He looked at her again. "When did you find this out?"

"A couple of weeks ago. It took us a while to get things sorted out," she said with a breathless sigh. "But it's working out well, so far. I know it will take time for us to build a real relationship," she added, on a realistic note. "But we're working on it. Day by day."

"Good for you," Dan said. He met her gaze for a long moment, and she could see he felt sincerely happy for her. "What about the election?" he asked in a quiet, knowing tone.

"I've given this a lot of thought. Sara didn't want me to reveal our relationship yet. She asked me to wait until after the election," Emily explained. "But I spent the last twenty-two years pretending I didn't have a child. I can't do that any longer."

Dan nodded. "You know Charlie's going to find out about it."

Emily gave him a weary shrug. "I'm sure he will."

"He'll use it if he can," Dan told her. "But I can assure you that the *Messenger* is not going to aid and abet him in that."

"I didn't think you would," Emily said. "I trust you." She did trust him, she realized. He was her friend, and maybe something more than that, too. Even if there was no real future in it, she felt close to him.

She met his gaze again. "I believe I would be a better mayor than Charlie Bates, and I still want to be mayor. But I know now that there is a limit to what I will do—or not do—to win. If I lose, then it wasn't God's plan for me to be mayor again. I've prayed for years to find her, Dan," she confessed, though she knew he wasn't religious and might not fully understand.

"This is a miracle to me. I won't deny or hide my daughter's existence another day. My first priority now is Sara, and building our relationship. Everything else comes after that."

"I'm very happy for you, Emily. Honestly." He smiled down at her and reached out to touch her arm. For a moment, she thought he was even about to pull her close in an affectionate hug. But then he suddenly stepped back.

"I know that," she replied. She pushed her hands deep into her pockets. There didn't seem to be anything more to say.

"All right then, time to get to work, I guess," she said.

He walked her to the door and opened it for her.

"You're not the only lucky one, you know," he said quietly. "She's lucky you turned out to be the one she's been looking for."

Emily felt herself nearly blush. "You think so?"

"I know so."

"Well . . . thanks. I'm just about terrified of being a parent," she confessed. "It's not as easy as it looks, and it doesn't even look very easy."

He laughed. "You're going to do just fine. I'd say you're doing better than average already."

"I SPOKE TO MY PARENTS LAST NIGHT," SARA TOLD LUKE. SHE STARED OUT AT the water and hugged her knees to her chest.

"Really? How did it go?"

Sara sighed. "Sort of mixed, I guess. They were happy to hear I finally told Emily the truth, and my mom especially felt sorry for Emily when I told them about the diary. . . ."

"But what?" Luke prodded her.

She shrugged. "Well, now they're wondering why I'm still staying up here. My dad just doesn't get it. He's an accountant, and he sees things very logically."

"An accountant, huh? I didn't know that." Luke leaned back and crossed his long legs. "What's your mom do? Does she work?"

Sara realized she hadn't told him much about her family. "She teaches

English at the high school in our town. She's a good teacher. All the kids love her," Sara said proudly.

Luke glanced over and smiled at her. "That makes sense."

"They wanted to come here and meet Emily. And take me home, I guess," she added making a face. "But I talked them out of it."

From Luke's suddenly alarmed expression, she could see she had struck a nerve. But he didn't say anything at first. "I guess they're just concerned about you."

"As always," she replied with a sigh.

"What did you tell them? I mean, about going back?"

Sara shrugged. "Just that I needed more time with Emily. They seemed to understand after a while. At least, they said they did."

Luke didn't reply. He shifted, leaning back on his elbows and looking down the long stretch of white sand. "The beach is empty today. We have the entire place to ourselves. And the ocean," he added.

"It's fine with me. I felt so—so weird this week," Sara picked up a handful of sand and let it drift through her fingers. "Everyone is staring at me or something. I've gone from 'that dark-haired waitress, good old what's-her-name' to an instant celebrity—Emily Warwick's daughter."

"Come on. It's not that bad. I think you're just feeling self-conscious right now. It will die down in a few days."

Luke reached into a nearby paper bag and tossed a hunk of bread out toward the birds. They screamed and dived for it, the noise mirroring Sara's jagged nerves.

She sighed. Their bike ride to the beach had been a good idea. Luke had repaired her bicycle and tuned up his own. The ride from the cottages had been long enough to burn off some stress but not exhausting. Sitting out on the empty beach with the clear, wide open sky above made Sara feel as if she'd gotten very far away.

The sun felt warm on her skin, even though she was glad she wore a heavy sweater under her denim jacket. She tilted her head back, and closed her eyes.

Luke had been nice to take the afternoon off from work and bring her here. He even packed them a lunch. If she went back to Maryland, she would miss him, she thought. She opened her eyes and found him watching her.

"What are you thinking about?" he asked.

"Nothing. I'm glad the work at the cottages started again."

"Yeah, so am I. So far, so good, right?" he said, looking at her quickly. "We're going to break ground for the new building next Monday. It's all set. I've got real heavy equipment coming. A bulldozer, a crane, and a dump truck."

She sat back, impressed. "That's exciting. Can I watch?"

"Sure, if you want to." He smiled at her. Then he looked serious again. "How is it at work for you? Charlie must be impossible now."

"Well, yesterday, once the news got around, it was pretty awful," she admitted. "He sat there all afternoon, calling Emily a liar to anyone who would listen. And I called in sick today," she added with a shrug.

"Sick of Charlie Bates, you mean. It's turning into an epidemic around here." He rubbed his chin. "I guess you have to quit."

"Yeah, I know I do now." She brushed some sand off her hands. "Another reason to leave this place, I guess, if I don't have a job."

Luke glanced at her. He tossed more bread to the birds, throwing this chunk very fast and hard until it nearly reached the water.

"But what about Emily? She'll be upset. She's just found out about you. And she's put her whole campaign on the line over this," he reminded her.

Sara nodded, her long hair blowing across her face. "I know. I don't really want to go now. My folks will have to understand."

Luke stared at her. She couldn't tell what he was thinking. She reached over and touched his face with her hand. Her fingertips rested lightly along the thin white scar that ran from the corner of his eye to the middle of his cheek. The mark had looked so ominous to her the day she first met him. She didn't even notice it anymore.

Luke didn't say anything or move. He just sat there looking at her, his eyes locked on hers. Finally she let her hand drop away.

She gazed out at the water again, trying to follow one wave from out on the horizon into shore, the way she used to when she was younger.

"If I stay, will you come with me to Jessica's wedding?" she asked him suddenly. "I'm going to be a bridesmaid, and she said I could bring a date . . . did I tell you?"

"No. I guess you forgot." He smiled very slowly at her. "Wearing a gown and all that?"

"Uh-huh. But probably not so much *that*," she corrected.

"What color?" he asked, surprising her.

"Blue. Dark blue velvet. The top is sort of—satiny."

"Hmm. Sounds very pretty," he said in a half-teasing tone. She could tell he was trying to picture her in it, and it made her embarrassed. "I don't have to wear a tux or anything like that, do I?"

So, he was going to take her, she realized.

"Uh, no. I don't think so. A suit should be okay."

"I have one of those—somewhere," he said, making her smile. He held out his hand to her. "Okay, it's a date."

The first real one they had ever had, she realized.

She put her hand in his. It felt strong and warm, his fingers and palm covered with callouses. She shook it, staring into his eyes and saw his slow smile, then felt him tug her closer. Her eyes closed and they kissed. His lips tasted salted and sweet all at once, and she felt herself smiling against his lips even as the kiss deepened.

She just really liked him. He made her happy.

The gulls cried shrilly overhead. One brave and battered-looking bird dipped down and pecked at the brown paper bag they had carried their food in.

Sara and Luke suddenly broke apart, the nearness of the gull startling them. "Oh . . . goodness, watch out," Sara said, putting her hands to her head.

Luke jumped up and waved his arms wildly.

"Thanks a lot, buddy! I'll do the same for you sometime!" he yelled. His shirttails hung out the back of his jacket, flapping in the wind. "That's the last time you get any bread from me, pal."

Sara sat back and laughed, covering her mouth with her hand. Yes, the perfect escort for the wedding.

THIS ISN'T GOING TO BE AS HARD AS I THOUGHT, SARA REALIZED AS SHE walked up to Charlie early the next morning. It was seven-fifteen. The diner had just opened and there was hardly anyone there yet.

"Charlie, can I talk to you a minute?" Sara asked him.

"What is it?" He glanced at her over his shoulder, turning over a pile of hash browns on the grill with a huge metal spatula. She could live without smelling those onions every morning, that was for sure.

"I can't work here anymore. I guess I can stay until Saturday if you really need me."

She knew she should have given him more than three days' notice, but she hoped he wouldn't even take her up on that much. It would be hard to stick it out, she thought.

"Well, well. I was expecting something like this." He put the spatula down and wiped his hands on his apron. "I guess that now you found out you're a Warwick, you're too good for us. Isn't that it?"

Sara heard Lucy gasp behind her. She hadn't even realized she was standing there.

"Shush up, Charlie. You know that's not it," Lucy defended her. She glanced at Sara, looking sad, Sara thought, but understanding, too.

"Let her go, then. The end of the day is fine with me," Charlie said, tossing up his hands.

"I don't want you to, of course," Lucy added, turning to Sara.

"I know," Sara said regretfully.

"Women—" Charlie shook his head in exasperation. "She's quitting her job, Lucy. Sticking you with a bigger load of work, I might add. She's not going off to war."

Lucy glared at her husband's back but didn't reply. "I'm happy you found your mother, Sara," she said quietly. "I'm not surprised to hear it's Emily Warwick," she added. "I always knew there was something special about you."

Sara reached out and squeezed Lucy's hand. "Thanks, Lucy. I'll be around. We'll still see each other," she promised.

Lucy nodded, looking as though she might cry. Sara felt badly about leaving her. But she knew now, finally, that she really had to.

"Of course we will." Lucy nodded and dabbed her nose with a paper napkin. "I'll still be bugging you to help me with my homework, I know that."

"Anytime," Sara promised.

"Get back to work, you two," Charlie scolded them. "The orders are stacking up over here like flights over Logan." He peered at a guest check. "Who's got the egg sandwiches and the pancakes?"

"Mine, Charlie." Sara stepped up to take the plates.

"Well, get it out of here," he snapped.

Sara framed a tart reply in her head, then thought, why bother? In a few hours she would be out of the Clam Box forever.

"HOW WAS WORK TODAY? I'M ALMOST AFRAID TO ASK," EMILY SAID AS SHE headed her Cherokee toward Southport.

Emily had insisted on taking Sara to the bridal shop there to order her gown for Jessica's wedding. Sara knew she could have done it by herself, but Emily had seemed so excited to go with her, she couldn't refuse. *A real mother-daughter thing*, Sara thought, glancing at Emily. *She's trying so hard, which I never expected.*

"It wasn't that bad today," Sara finally answered. "I quit."

"You did?" Emily looked about to say more, then stopped herself and turned her gaze back to the road.

"I've been thinking about it for a while. It wasn't just because of the news about me and you."

"All right." Emily sighed. "I guess it's all for the best."

"I think it was," Sara agreed. "I might get a job at the library. I spoke to the head librarian on my way home today. It would only be part-time, but I can probably find something else, too."

Emily didn't answer right away. "Maybe you could get a job on the *Messenger*. Dan liked that letter you wrote for Luke, and the one you edited for me about the substation."

"Really? What did he say?" Sara was surprised and pleased. Dan didn't seem like the type who was free with his compliments.

"He said he thought you were a good writer," Emily told her. When Sara glanced at her in disbelief, she added, "I can call him tomorrow for you, if you like."

"That's okay," Sara said. "I'll call him. . . . But, thanks, Emily. That's really good to hear."

"You know what they say, one door closes, another opens." When Sara glanced at her, Emily seemed to be smiling at some private joke. But Sara didn't ask her to explain.

ON MONDAY MORNING SARA GOT UP EARLY AND DROVE DOWN TO THE cottages. Luke and his crew were going to break ground today for the new building. Everyone was excited, and Sara had even brought along a long strip of ribbon and some scissors. When Luke wasn't looking she planned to tie the ribbon between some trees and make him cut it. A silly gesture really, but he deserved a little ceremony, she thought, for the way he had fought for the project and carried on after the fire.

She parked her car next to Sam's truck and walked toward the group assembled at the new building site. Just as Luke had promised, there was a big red dump truck parked there and a yellow tractor with something on the front that looked like a big claw to scoop up the earth. The men standing around all wore yellow hard hats, even Luke, she noticed.

But as she drew closer to the group, she realized that the voices she heard were not just shouting directions at each other, preparing to work. They were angry. Especially Luke, who was having an argument with an older-looking man in a plaid wool jacket with a shirt and tie underneath. Sara recognized him from the Village Hall but couldn't recall his name.

"Look, this is totally bogus. I have a permit. Signed by the mayor!" Luke shouted.

"You didn't read the fine print, my friend. You had ten business days to file the plans."

"I filed the plans," Luke argued back, sounding pushed to the edge of frustration. "Look around your office, Farley. Check under the doughnut box. I filed the plans."

Sam rested a hand on Luke's shoulder, holding him back.

"Look, what is this about?" Sam asked in a calm voice. "Nobody is ever held to that ten-day limit, Ray. If they were, half of this village would be vacant lots."

Ray Farley cleared his throat. "I don't make the rules. I just work in the permits department."

"And happen to be a chum of Charlie Bates," Luke added bitterly.

"Look, McAllister, get it through your thick head." Ray Farley jabbed the air with his finger. "You're shut down. There isn't going to be any new construction going on here, so you ought to tell those drivers to go home and save yourself some money. If you break ground on this site, you're breaking the law. If you don't understand that, the next time I'll come back with a police officer and maybe he can explain it to you."

Sara felt her body grow tense as she watched Luke glare at Ray Farley, then stalk around in a circle, his fists balled at his sides. Finally he pulled off his yellow hard hat and tossed it on the ground.

She felt so bad for him. She wanted to run over and put her arms around him, but felt shy with everyone else watching. *There must be something we can do,* she thought. And then she knew. *We'll call Emily,* she decided. *Maybe she can straighten this out.*

EMILY STARED DOWN AT THE TWO SETS OF PAPERS THAT SAT ON HER DESK, Luke's original building permits and the Stop Work order he had been presented with that morning by Ray Farley.

Sara and Luke sat in the two chairs across from her, waiting tensely for her reaction.

Dear Lord, can you turn this pencil into a magic wand for me . . . just for five minutes, she prayed. She shook her head. *No, I didn't think so.*

She sighed heavily and sat back in her chair.

"Look, this order is valid, even though no one has put this ordinance into use since it went on the books. I wish I could just override it somehow, but I can't," she admitted, feeling her heart drop as both Sara and Luke's expressions fell.

"Sure, thanks anyway," Luke said curtly.

Sara didn't say anything. Emily could see she was trying to be understanding. Still, Sara had turned to her, expecting her to be Super Woman—and oh, how she wanted to be.

"The only thing I can do is bring it before the town council." The idea was a long shot, but the only possibility that occurred to her. "The next meeting isn't until—the last week in November," she said, checking her calendar.

"Too late to help us. The ground will be frozen like rock by then," Luke said. He shook his head in disgust. "The board at New Horizons is going to pull out. This is just another sign of the town's resistance. I don't think I'll be able to talk them out of it this time."

"I didn't even think of that," Emily admitted. "Well, then, we won't wait. I'll call an emergency meeting for this Wednesday night. Can you hold off the foundation until then?" she asked Luke.

He nodded, looking grateful. "Sure, no problem."

"Okay, then. Let's do it." Emily said firmly. "We all know where this is coming from. It's time I showed up Charlie's underhanded tactics for what they are."

"But what will you say?" Sara asked. "You already said the Stop Work order was valid."

Emily rubbed her forehead with her hand. "I don't really know," she said. "Something will come to me," she added hopefully.

Sara and Luke glanced at each other.

"All right. We'll be there," Luke promised.

"Thanks, Emily," Sara said.

"Don't thank me yet," Emily replied cautiously. But Sara just smiled at her, as if to say, *I know you can do it.*

Emily smiled back, feeling her stomach twist with tension. She had to do something. She had to pull this one out of the fire. But how? she wondered pensively. How would she manage it?

Emily sat at her desk and squeezed her eyes shut. She felt a headache coming on and massaged the bridge of her nose, fighting it off.

Lord, I really need your help. Not just because Sara is depending on me, but because it's the right thing to do, the right choice for the town to make. Charlie's tactics have muddied the waters so much by now, it's hard for most people to see this clearly anymore. Please help me make it clear to them. Please don't let it be too late.

ON TUESDAY NIGHT, JUST PAST MIDNIGHT, EMILY SAT IN THE VERY SAME place, in a similar state of mind. Just slightly more desperate. Since meeting with Sara and Luke on Monday, she had worked on little else than her presentation to the town council for tomorrow night's meeting. But despite her hard work and prayer, she still felt ill prepared.

She stared at the computer screen, her eyes burning, then sat back and blinked—not quite believing it when she saw Dan Forbes standing in the doorway of her office. *That's how I get when I have too much coffee,* she thought vaguely.

"I saw the light on, but I couldn't quite believe you were still here," he said, proving that he was indeed real. "You work too hard, Emily," he greeted her as he walked in.

"That habit will be easy to mend, once the voters get through with me," she countered. "I can't quite figure out what to do after my career in politics, though."

"Oh, you've got time," he said lightly. "Getting ready for the meeting tomorrow night?"

She nodded and sighed. "I'm trying. I don't have much ammunition, though," she admitted, standing up. "So far, I'm counting on firing blanks and hoping they jump back."

Dan smiled and tossed the manila envelope he'd been carrying on her desk. "Try that. I was going to drop it off as a surprise for you, but I'm glad I found you here. Open it carefully. It's definitely live ammunition."

She glanced at him curiously, opened the envelope, and slipped out what looked like a fax transmission. It was a newspaper article from the *Boston Globe*, set in type, but missing the photo insert. "Coastal Town Battles Change and Benevolence," the headline read.

Emily scanned the text quickly; her glasses slid down her nose, but she didn't bother to push them back up. The article was about Cape Light and the opposition to the New Horizons Center. It showed the town in a very poor light, mean-spirited and biased against newcomers.

She felt confused at first. Why had Dan given this to her? Then she thought about it a moment. Yes, she could use this. It was definitely live ammunition.

She took off her glasses and looked up at him. "How did you get this?"

"A friend of mine at the *Globe*. I heard she was doing an article on the New Horizons controversy. I called in a favor and got an early copy."

"That was good of you," she said slowly. "But not very objective."

He smiled. "Sorry to ruin my image, again."

"I'm not sorry you did," she said honestly. It was hard to look at him suddenly. He had tossed her a lifeline when she really needed one.

"Thank you," she murmured, so quietly she wondered if he could even hear her. Then impulsively she stood up on tiptoe and kissed his cheek.

Dan stood very still for a moment, then turned his face to hers and put his arm around her waist, pulling her close. His mouth brushed hers tentatively at first, then he really kissed her. She closed her eyes and felt herself melt against him. She felt breathless—and swept off her feet. She wasn't sure how long they stood there, kissing. She felt as if it could have gone on and on.

But suddenly an irritating sound broke into her consciousness, the bleat of a cell phone.

Dan stepped back, releasing her. He looked disoriented for a moment. "Mine or yours?" he asked, glancing around.

She felt embarrassed and ran her hand through her hair. "Umm, yours I think," she said.

He nodded and reached into his pocket to pull out his phone. "Yes?" he said. "Oh . . . Wyatt. Where are you? . . . All right. Let me call you back in a few minutes. I'm in the . . . in the middle of something here," he said slowly, avoiding Emily's gaze. She noticed a faint hint of color slip into his cheeks. ". . . Okay, I will."

He clicked off and slipped the phone back in his pocket. "My son, on the West Coast. He always forgets the time difference."

Emily smiled and nodded. Wyatt, who was coming to take over the paper when Dan left town in December, she thought wistfully.

"Well, guess I'd better go," he said awkwardly, lingering by the door.

"Thanks again, Dan," she said sincerely.

"That's all right. What are friends for?" he added with a slight smile as he left her.

Was that a message? she wondered. A postscript to the kiss? Oh, well, she already knew the fine print: No expectations, no future there.

But Dan had proven himself to be a good friend, she thought gratefully. If nothing else.

ALTHOUGH THE MEETING WAS ANNOUNCED WITH VERY SHORT NOTICE, THE auditorium at the Village Hall was filled on Wednesday night. The setup was typical of an ordinary town council meeting. The council, along with Emily, sat at a long table on a raised platform in the front of the hall. A podium and a microphone were set up in front of the table, so residents could address the town officials.

However, the setup was the only thing ordinary about the meeting, Emily thought as she looked at the audience. The room was tense and quiet as Charlie addressed the council, nearly shouting into the microphone.

"It's a valid Stop Work order, in accordance with the laws of this village. The mayor can't start writing new laws to suit herself. Or help her friends," Charlie added harshly.

Emily leaned forward and spoke into her own mike. "Speaking of friends, Charlie. I would like it to go on record that Ray Farley is part of Mr. Bates's campaign advisory committee. I'd also like to note that since this ten-day time limit was written into the books, it has been enforced to stop construction"—Emily glanced down at her notes—"*once* in twenty years. On the other hand, it has been ignored, totally, by the building inspectors . . . oh, approximately twenty thousand times."

"That's ridiculous," Charlie argued back at her.

Emily pushed her voice to the limit to talk over him. "It's perfectly transparent that Mr. Farley, who sides with the faction in this town that opposes the New Horizons Center, has used his office and this arcane ordinance to obstruct Luke McAllister's legal rights and to further the cause of his candidate of choice, Charlie Bates. This is politics, clear and simple. Dirty politics, I should say."

"Of course you'd say that. The work is stopped, fair and square," Charlie insisted. "There's nothing dirty about this. And plenty of people in here are relieved to hear about it."

Joe Clark, a member of the town council, took the mike, looking irritated. "Pipe down, Bates, we can hear you," he said. "You don't have to shout your head off. Now does anyone else want to speak?" he asked the audience.

Emily's glance fell on Sara and Luke, sitting together in the front row. She thought for a moment Luke would get up and address the issue. But he didn't. He looked at her a moment, then down at the ground, one hand gripping Sara's.

He's depending on me, Emily realized. *They both are.*

"I have something more to add," Emily said. She stood up, holding the article from the *Boston Globe.* " 'Coastal Town Battles Change and Benevolence,' " she read aloud. She held it out for all to see. "That's about us, folks. An article that's going to appear in this week's *Boston Globe.* Here, let me read you a little of it."

She held the article in front of her, and started to read aloud. "A quaint, picturesque Main Street, complete with gaslights and well-preserved storefronts dating back to the 1800s, Cape Light is a place out of time. A town invented to fit the adjective *charming,* it would seem to any visitor, the perfect day trip by car or even boat from the bustling urban scene. But since a former Boston police officer, Luke McAllister, has tried to establish a learning center and retreat for disadvantaged city teenagers on property he owns there, another face of Cape Light has reared its head—the ugly face of a biased and mean-spirited population, suspicious of newcomers, terrified of change. The term *provincial* at its very worst . . ."

Emily glanced out at the audience, judging the effect of her words. "Want to hear more?" she asked.

"That's enough for me," someone in the audience called out.

"Is this for real?" another voice asked. "I'd like to read it with my own eyes."

"Me, too," another person spoke up.

"Betty, would you pass out those copies now?" Emily asked. "If you'd like to read this for yourselves, Betty Bowman has some copies in the back of the room."

Several people got up and moved toward Betty. Charlie looked flustered. "Big deal. The *Boston Globe*," he said. "Who cares what they think? They're not living here. They don't know what's really going on."

"You're right, they don't know what's going on," Emily agreed. "They don't know the real Cape Light. Cape Light is a place where people live together as neighbors, good neighbors. It's a place where people work hard and believe that everyone should have a chance for a good life. It's a place where we pull each other through the hard times. Those are our ideals, and they are the spirit of this town. We are not provincial or mean-spirited bigots, and this is the time to prove it." She swallowed hard and shook her head. "Whether or not I am reelected is not important. What is important is our town, the town we all love. We never want to be ashamed of it."

"Come on now," Charlie blustered at the microphone. "Let's not get all sentimental over this."

But before Charlie could continue, Emily saw a few residents rise and approach the microphone, their copies of the article in hand. This time Charlie was forced to step aside and let them speak.

"I have to agree with Mayor Warwick," Doris Mumford said. "Revoking the permits seems too much like political shenanigans to me. I think we should stop fooling around and let this center in."

Emily noticed that Jack Anderson was the next in line for the microphone, and his wife, Rachel, stood right behind him.

"I think we need to give more attention to the real facts," Jack said. "There's no evidence that crime rises or real estate values go down. But kids do get a chance to get back on track and have decent lives. How can we have pride in our town if we won't give kids that chance?" he asked.

Rachel took the microphone next. "As some of you may have noticed, I'm going to have a baby soon," she began with a smile. "And I don't want to bring this child up in a place that's ruled by fear. One of the reasons we live in Cape Light is that we believe it's a good place, filled with good people. That's the home I want for my family. Isn't it what you want, too?"

"That's right. I agree with the Andersons!" someone else shouted out.

Sophie Potter took the microphone, smiling. "So do I," she said. "And I would like to tell you all that I have had those kids living in my house and helping me and Gus out for the last two weeks. As far I'm concerned, we're very lucky they're here. I will always be grateful to them."

"They're good kids," Digger Hegman called out. "Good workers, too." A few people began to clap, and Emily felt herself relax a little. Finally, it seemed, the tide was turning in her favor.

"I move to vote," Harriet DeSoto declared. "All in favor of renewing Mr. McAllister's building permits, say aye."

Four of the five council members raised their hands. "Aye," they said in unison.

"Wait a minute—" Charlie called out.

"All not in favor, say nay," Harriet continued.

"Nay," the remaining voice said bitterly. It was Art Hecht, Emily noticed, one of Charlie's key supporters.

Charlie stood staring with his mouth partially open, like a man who has just narrowly missed a train and is watching it chug down the tracks away from him.

"This meeting is adjourned," Emily said gratefully, banging her gavel.

She suddenly caught sight of Dan, standing at the very back of the room. He got up immediately and made for the aisle. Rushing off to write his story, she guessed. Then he paused a moment, caught her eye, and nodded. She lifted her chin and smiled at him. *Thank you, friend,* she thought.

Thank you, Lord, she added.

She gathered up her papers, feeling drained but happy. Sara and Luke stood waiting for her. She walked over to them, smiling.

"You were awesome, Emily," Sara said.

"Well . . . thanks," Emily replied. *Awesome. She called me awesome. I can die happy now,* Emily thought giddily.

"That was great," Luke added. "Really. I didn't know what was going to happen there for a while," he admitted. "Where did you get that article? That reporter called me weeks ago. I forgot all about it, figured they never printed it."

"Oh, I have my sources," Emily said lightly. "Why don't we get out of here? It's getting a little stuffy," she suggested, hoping to distract them. She couldn't tell them about Dan.

Outside Luke suggested they go to the Beanery to celebrate. But Emily begged off. "Thanks, but you two go without me," she said, not wanting to intrude. "I'm really beat."

"Are you sure?" Sara asked her.

"Positive."

"Well, good night, then, Emily," Sara said. She leaned over and gave Emily a quick hug.

Emily was caught by surprise for a moment, then hugged her daughter back. She smiled into her eyes. "Good night, dear. I'm glad it all worked out."

"Me, too," Sara said sincerely.

Emily stood at her car a moment, watching Sara and Luke walk arm in arm down Main Street.

Thank you, Lord, for your help tonight, she silently said. *It was . . . awesome.*

"WHAT'S THIS?" JESSICA ASKED, UNFOLDING THE LAYERS OF WHITE TISSUE paper. "Oh, a nightgown—oh, my goodness, it's gorgeous," she gushed. She held up the peach silk fabric for the rest of the women to see.

"Oh, that is beautiful," Betty agreed. "Look at that lace. It must be handmade."

"I love the color," Suzanne Foster said. "It matches the walls in your bedroom."

"Sam won't notice," Sophie predicted, drawing laughter from the other women.

Emily listened in contentedly as she set up the cake and coffee. The bridal shower was a small gathering, about a dozen women altogether, most from the village plus a few friends of Jessica's from Boston. Rachel Anderson couldn't come at the last minute because she wasn't feeling well, but everyone else who had been invited was there.

Jessica hadn't even mentioned their mother, and Emily believed she was now resigned to Lillian's absence.

Although the party had been put together in a rush, it had turned out to be a very nice evening, Emily thought. Molly had helped with the food, which everyone raved about. Molly's daughters, Lauren and Jill, who were going to be junior bridesmaids, were also there. They were so sweet, Emily thought. They had been staring adoringly at Jessica all night.

But for Emily the best part was that Jessica had gone out of her way to make Sara feel welcome, and Sara seemed completely comfortable. Though she tried to be laid back about it, Emily couldn't help showing her off proudly. Sara was a wonder to her.

She caught sight of Sara now, sitting near Jessica, handing her the gifts and keeping track of the cards. Her adoptive parents had to be fine people, Emily thought wistfully. She had asked Sara a little about them and had privately thanked God for putting her child in the hands of such a loving, responsible couple. One day, Emily thought, she would have to thank the Franklins in person for taking such good care of her child.

The phone rang in the kitchen. Emily picked it up and immediately recognized Reverend Ben's voice. "Hello, Emily. May I speak to Carolyn please?" he asked.

He was either in a hurry or greatly distressed, Emily thought. "Yes, of course, I'll get her for you," she said.

She called Carolyn to the phone and couldn't help but overhear her conversation.

"Hello, Ben," Carolyn said curiously. She paused and Emily saw her face grow alarmed. "Oh, no—when did that happen? Are you at the hospital with her now?" she asked anxiously. "All right . . . tell her I'll be right there. Yes, don't worry. I'll be fine."

She hung up the phone and turned to Emily. "Rachel has been rushed to the hospital in Southport. She's bleeding and they're having trouble getting it to stop—" Her voice faltered and Emily took her hand. It was ice cold.

"Here . . . sit down a minute," Emily urged her. "You're too upset to drive, Carolyn. I'll take you to the hospital."

"Oh, no . . . you couldn't. You're the hostess. You can't leave your own party," Carolyn protested, ever the gracious Southern lady. "I'll be fine."

"Don't worry. I'll take her," Sara offered.

Emily looked up and realized she must have been in the room awhile.

"Would you? That would be wonderful, Sara," Emily said, feeling relieved.

"Don't worry, it's no trouble, Mrs. Lewis."

Carolyn sighed and looked up at her. "Thank you. That would be a great help," she admitted. "I'll just run and get my coat."

A few minutes later Emily walked them both to the door. "Please call me when you can and let me know what's happened." She gave Carolyn a quick hug. "I'll be praying for Rachel and the baby. We all will," she promised her.

Carolyn nodded. She looked too overwhelmed with worry to reply. "Good night, Emily," she said squeezing her hand. "I must go."

Bless them, Emily thought as they hurried down the drive. Then she sent up a quick prayer that Rachel's child would be as healthy and completely wonderful as her own.

CHAPTER SIXTEEN

❧

By the final days of October only the weather-toughened fishermen and hardiest weekend sailors ventured out on the cold, choppy water. The harbor near the Village Green was nearly empty of sailboats and cruisers. The tall trees on the green had gone gold, rusty red, then brown. Most of the branches stood bare now, shifting against a stark blue sky in a chilly breeze that marked the start of New England's fierce, legendary winter moving in.

But though summer's glories were long faded and winter's pristine beauty still a few weeks off, the villagers of Cape Light saw fit to give the season its due, celebrating with an annual Harvest Festival on the first Saturday of November.

It was Emily's favorite town event. As she walked toward

the green on Saturday morning, she was pleased to see so many people out early, making their way to the fair.

"Good morning, Mayor," a passerby greeted her.

"Hello, Emily," a neighbor said as she walked by.

She smiled and waved back, enjoying the attention. She still felt good about standing up to Charlie Bates in the town council meeting on Wednesday night. It was hard to say if the open confrontation and the position she had taken would cost her the election. But if it came to that, she still felt certain that she had done the right thing.

I may very well not win the election on Tuesday, she told herself. *But I'm going to enjoy every minute of my last big "fling" as mayor today.*

At the edge of the green Emily paused and surveyed the setup, an ambitious project that had started a few days ago. The tree-shaded lawn was filled with tables, booths, a few gaily colored tents. Rows of folding chairs stood in front of the gazebo's bandstand, where workers were setting up microphones. The candidates were scheduled to give a speech later, the last big event of the campaign before Election Day.

Emily wondered what Charlie would say today. Would he still press the issue of Luke's center, or had he finally abandoned that tactic? She only hoped he wouldn't retaliate with some trick that was even dirtier. She turned toward the green, pushing thoughts of Charlie Bates out of her mind.

The farmers' market was breathtaking and looked even more picturesque to Emily this year than usual. Or maybe she was getting nostalgic in advance? She wasn't sure, but she wished she had a camera as she wandered from booth to booth. There were bushels of apples and cabbages, mounds of pumpkins and autumn-colored squash in every shape and variation imaginable, bunches of orange carrots and deep purple eggplant, wheels of cheese and cartons of eggs gathered only hours ago. A bushel of russet potatoes caught Emily's eye, and she bought a few along with a bunch of chives and a wedge of sharp Cheddar.

Sometimes a stuffed baked potato made a perfect dinner, Emily thought as she strolled away with her purchases. *It would be hard to get away with that menu if I had a family or even a husband,* she reminded herself. *There are advantages to living alone.*

Another table held red and gold mums and pots of feathery purple-and-white kale. Beside it was a booth filled with colorful dried bouquets, bunches of fragrant herbs, racks of hand-dipped candles, and jars of fresh honey.

She stopped and picked up a bayberry wreath for her front door, then on impulse bought a second one to give to her mother. Since visiting her mother with Sara, Emily had only spoken to Lillian a few times by phone—brief, tense conversations. Her mother insisted she didn't want visitors and was having her groceries delivered. Emily wondered how long her mother would cling to this attitude. Probably straight through to November nineteenth, Jessica's wedding day, she thought wryly.

As if on cue, Emily heard her sister's voice nearby. "Oh, those wreaths are pretty. We ought to get one for our front door."

Emily turned to see Jessica and Sam strolling her way. They wore identical paint-spattered sweatshirts, jeans, and baseball caps. Emily guessed they were taking a break from working on their house.

Jessica greeted Emily with a quick hug. "What are you doing here? I thought you would be up on stage by now, announcing things."

"I probably should be. I just snuck over early to do some shopping."

"Same here, I'm afraid," Sam said, glancing at Jessica and raising his eyebrows.

"Oh, shush." Jessica gave her fiancé an affectionate poke in the ribs. "I haven't bought a thing."

"Yet," Sam finished in a knowing tone.

Jessica smirked at him, then couldn't help smiling.

"I just narrowly escaped a major purchase of lawn sheep," he confessed to Emily. "An entire flock of them. We don't even have a lawn yet."

"Lawn sheep?" Emily turned to Jessica. Her ever-tasteful sister buying lawn sheep? She must have the prenuptial jitters real bad, Emily thought.

Jessica shrugged. "They were really cute. But Sam is right. We need to focus on the major things now. We only have two more weekends until the wedding."

"I know. I'm counting the days," Emily said happily.

"Me, too," Sam agreed. He put his arm around Jessica's shoulder and gave her a tight hug.

Then with Jessica's head tucked under his chin, he glanced at Emily, his eyes sending a silent thank-you for helping them get back together. She smiled in return, then looked away. She felt happy for her sister and Sam, but she also knew that in a way, she had done it for herself, as much as for them.

Without releasing Jessica, Sam glanced at his watch. "Fifteen more minutes of browsing, then we have to get back to the house. You promised, remember?"

"Yes, boss," Jessica agreed with a contented sigh. She gave Emily an apologetic glance. "We've got to run. Looks like we'll miss your speech today."

Emily grinned. "That's okay. You've heard most of it before."

Jessica kissed her. "Good luck. I'm sure it will go well."

"I'll give it my best shot," Emily promised. One last chance to win over a few more votes.

Emily heard the sound of horses' hooves and took a quick step back to make way for a hay wagon full of bright-eyed children. One small, beautiful beaming face waved down to her, and she waved back.

Why waste time worrying about Charlie on a beautiful day like today? Thank you, God, for reminding me.

Up on the gazebo, the high school band was beginning a medley of Broadway show tunes, an ideal backdrop for the happy crowd, Emily thought.

She turned to a long row of booths that displayed handcrafted work—wood carvings, woven rugs and mats, and pottery. A quilt caught her eye that she thought would make the perfect wedding gift for Jessica and Sam. But as she walked closer to examine it, Emily was distracted by the sound of Sophie Potter's voice.

Sophie stood at one of the demonstration tables nearby, with a small but intensely interested audience gathered around her.

Emily moved closer to listen in. ". . . Now the beauty of this type of crust is that you don't have to fuss, rolling it out with a pin. It's more like cookie dough. So you can just take a hunk like this, and flatten it out in the pan, like so. . . ."

Her fingers moved in a swift, able fashion, Emily noticed, as she pressed a wad of the buttery-colored dough into a large round tart pan. Emily caught sight of Gus, sitting on a stool just behind his wife, smiling proudly. He looked a little pale, Emily thought, not his usual robust self. Still it was good to see him up and about, enjoying the day.

"Maybe you want to arrange some slices on top in some nice design, like a spiral or a star," Sophie went on. "Then a little more sugar and spice mix on top and a few pats of butter, and into the oven. Bakes about forty-five minutes," she concluded, wiping her hands on a cloth.

She turned and whispered something to Gus, who reached into a carton, then handed her a pie. "Thank you, dear. That's my husband, Gus. He married me for my cooking, no matter what he says otherwise." The group responded with a laugh. Then she held up a baked apple tart and her audience emitted a collective sigh.

Emily stood back, watching as Sophie served slices of the tart onto paper plates, and Gus magically produced more pies from the carton. Emily also noticed a couple near the table who appeared to be videotaping Sophie's performance. She knew right away from their clothing and haircuts that they weren't locals. The woman wore a leather jacket, slim-fitting jeans, and big sunglasses. The man wore a baseball-style satin jacket and a black cap turned backward, and he was holding a heavy-duty video camera, the kind that professional newspeople used.

The couple moved closer to her, and Emily overheard their conversation. "Get a shot of her dishing out the pie, Kyle. Can you move in closer? I want the design she made with the apples."

Suddenly Sophie looked up and seemed to realize that she was being filmed. She held a slice of apple tart out to the woman. "Care for some tart?" she asked politely.

"I'd love some, thank you," the woman replied with a smile.

"How about you, fella?" Sophie asked the cameraman. She eyed his video equipment but didn't ask any questions.

"Sure, thanks." He put his camera down on the table and took a slice of tart.

"We've been watching your demonstration, Mrs. Potter," the woman told Sophie. "We've filmed it, actually. It might be on the news tonight, part of a segment we're putting together on autumn fairs in the area."

"Oh, how nice," Sophie said, sounding pleased. She folded her hands across her aproned stomach. "Hear that, Gus? We might be on the news."

"You don't say?" Gus got up off his stool and stood beside his wife, eyeing the strangers. "What channel?"

"Channel five, WKPR. I'm Nina Miller, a producer there. I really enjoyed your presentation, Mrs. Potter, and I wondered if you would be interested in doing the same type of thing in a studio setting for a show I'm putting together. This would be just a preliminary taping, sort of a sample for my boss."

"You want to film me in a studio making a pie?" Sophie asked in disbelief.

"Well, making a pie, weaving a basket, making some soap, maybe?" Nina asked hopefully.

"Sure, I can do that. I also make honey and beeswax candles. I keep bees, you know," Sophie offered.

Nina looked remarkably pleased to hear it. "Oh, you do? That's wonderful. We could really do something with bees."

"You want to put Sophie here on TV? Like on one of these cooking shows?" Gus cut in.

"Quiet down, Gus. The girl is just talking," Sophie said to him, looking a bit embarrassed.

"First we need to do a pilot. The sample show," Nina explained. "Then I'd need approval to tape a few segments. But the concept is already on the board for next season, and I think Mrs. Potter would be just perfect as the hostess."

Sophie suddenly seemed to be standing a few inches taller, Emily noticed, with her head high and shoulders proudly squared.

"What will you call it?" Gus asked eagerly.

"We were thinking of something like, *A Yankee in the Kitchen—New England Cooking and Crafts.*"

Gus clapped his hands together, his eyes shining. "That's perfect. It's got my Sophie's name written all over it. Don't you think so, honey?" he asked his wife.

"Calm down, dear. One step at a time," she reminded him. Still, Emily could tell she was excited.

"I'll bet you'll be paying her nicely for this, too," Gus added pointedly.

"If it all works out, the salary will be attractive, I'd think." Nina Miller smiled again and handed Sophie a business card. "Here's my number. I'm going to show this clip around, and I'll call you sometime next week. Where can I reach you?"

"Potter Orchard," Sophie and Gus replied simultaneously. They looked at each other, and the young woman laughed. "Maybe there could be a part for Mr. Potter on the show, too," she suggested.

"You can call me Gus," he said brightly. "And you take this pie. The phone number is right on the box, and your boss can have a taste, too. That film might make him hungry."

"Thanks, I'll do that." Nina Miller took the box, then slipped on her sunglasses again and glanced at her cameraman. "Kyle, let's just get a shot of that band before we go," she said. "Nice meeting you both. I'll speak to you soon."

"Nice to meet you, dear. I'm going to think of some ideas for your show," she promised.

As the television producer and cameraman walked away, Emily caught Sophie's eye. Sophie waved at her to come closer.

"Did you hear all that? That girl says she thinks I could be on TV. She says she's a TV producer, though she hardly looks out of high school. *A Yankee in the Kitchen.* That would be me," she said in a hushed but elated tone.

Emily smiled at her. "You'll be absolutely wonderful. Move over, Martha Stewart."

"It's all just talk for now." Sophie patted Emily's arm. "But it would be fun," she added, her eyes twinkling.

"It would sure be a big help to us," Gus pointed out bluntly. "If you got on this television show and they paid you some good money, we wouldn't need to give up the orchard."

"Yes, that's right," Emily realized. She turned to Sophie. "I do hope this works out for you, Sophie. It could be the answer to your prayers."

"Yes, it just might be." Sophie nodded, looking suddenly thoughtful. "We'll have to wait and see if this is what the Lord has in store for us, right, Gus?"

Gus nodded sagely. "Yes, we'll have to wait and see," he agreed. "Of course, if it all comes about, you're going to have to share those recipes of yours. Nobody's going to have a cooking show with secret recipes," he warned her.

Emily struggled not to smile too broadly as she watched Sophie process this troubling issue.

"Oh, dear . . . I suppose you're right. I have a lot to think about here, all of a sudden, don't I?"

A woman pushing a stroller stepped up to the table. "Excuse me, am I in the right place for the apple butter demonstration?"

"Yes, you are, dear. I'm just about to set up for that," Sophie assured her. "Here's a nice slice of apple for your baby. Just let me take the skin off." She handed the woman an apple chunk. "It's a handy thing when they're teething."

"She is teething," the young mother admitted. "I never tried apple, though—"

Emily saw her chance to say good-bye. "I'll see you later, folks. You have a good day."

"You, too, Emily," Sophie called out to her. "I'll be listening for your speech later."

Emily waved and turned toward the gazebo, decorated with bunches of corn stalks, pots of mums, and huge pumpkins. On the stage the American flag waved at one corner and the flag of Massachusetts at the other. The Cape Light High School band was just winding up its performance with a rousing rendition of "Oklahoma," and the rows of folding chairs were now almost filled. She spotted the town council members gathered to one side of the stage, and knew it was almost time for her appearance.

TWENTY MINUTES LATER EMILY STOOD BEHIND THE PODIUM, DELIVERING her speech to the crowd. A small voice in her head kept reminding her this could very well be her last public address as mayor. But she couldn't think about that now. She had to go forward, hoping for the best. She truly believed she was a better choice than Charlie Bates and hoped that her speech would touch the hearts and minds of her audience.

She held the pages of her speech in front of her but instead of reading the familiar words, she found herself studying the audience. Her closest supporters—Betty, Harriet, and Frank—sat in front-row seats. In the row behind them she saw Felicity and Jonathan Bean smiling up at her with encouraging expressions. Digger Hegman sat between Harry Reilly and Ezra Elliot. Suzanne Foster and some of Jessica's coworkers from the bank sat in a row near the back. All of them seemed familiar and dear to her. Then Emily spotted Sara, standing alone under a nearby tree. On impulse, she put the notes aside and spoke from her heart.

"I think you all know my positions by now," she began, her voice sure and steady. "I said everything I needed to say at last Wednesday's meeting. But what I want to say to you today is *thank you.* I had a wonderful time being your mayor during these last three years. It has been a pleasure and an honor."

She paused and took a breath. "Thank you for your time, and remember, get out there on Tuesday and vote. I have complete confidence that whoever you choose will be the best mayor for Cape Light."

She nodded and stepped back from the microphone. The audience responded with strong applause, and Emily felt an unexpected wave of hope. Maybe she had a better chance on Tuesday than she had thought.

She glanced over at Sara, who stood closer now and was clapping vigorously. Emily met her daughter's eye and Sara smiled. Emily smiled back, feeling warm inside.

Emily stepped down from the platform and took the seat that had been reserved for her in the front row between Betty and Harriet. Betty leaned forward and patted her shoulder. "Good job, Emily," she whispered. "I think they appreciated that."

"Yep, it was short and sweet," Harriet said. "You got my vote."

"Thanks, that's saying something, Harriet," Emily whispered back, suppressing a smile. She kept her eyes forward and sat up tall in her seat.

Charlie stepped behind the podium, a sheaf of papers rattling in his hand. He somehow looked both nervous and full of blustery ego, Emily thought. And a bit uncomfortable in his blue suit, white shirt, and bold red tie.

At the opposite end of the front row, Emily saw Lucy Bates and their boys, their eyes glued to him. He's a lucky man, Emily thought. She knew how badly he wanted to be mayor, but wondered if he realized how many blessings he already had in his life.

Charlie's speech started off as Emily would have predicted, reminding the voters how his family stretched back many generations in the village, and how his experience as a businessman qualified him to run the town. Emily had heard him speak before during his campaign and recognized familiar words.

But when his address took a new, unexpected turn she sat up with interest. "Everybody has a dream. My dream has always been to be mayor of Cape Light," he stated solemnly. "This village is a paradise to me, the only place I'd choose to raise my family, to grow old alongside my wife, and to be buried someday, up on that hill overlooking the harbor. I could travel the whole world and find no better place. I am dedicated to this town, watching over it like a father watches over a beloved child. Like Grace Hegman watches over her garden," he added, inspiring a few smiles.

"If you make me your mayor, sometimes we may very well disagree. But you could search the world over and you wouldn't find a man—or woman, for that matter—more dedicated to this town. Or one who will work harder, giving one hundred and ten percent of his effort to the job. And you won't find anyone who holds the title higher or who holds the dream of winning that trust closer to his heart."

Emily couldn't quite believe it, but hearing Charlie's heartfelt words and watching the open, unguarded emotion on his face, she felt a lump in her throat and tears in her eyes. *He wants to win this election more than I do,* she realized. *And in some strange way, maybe he even deserves it more.*

"I thank you for your time and consideration," Charlie concluded politely. He nodded his head a few times and gathered up his papers. "Like the *present* mayor said," he added in a jaunty tone, "don't forget to get out there and vote."

After the speeches the audience began to disperse. Emily spotted Dan over the heads of the milling group. He was talking with his photographer and one of his reporters. As she stood there wondering if she should say hello, he looked up and smiled at her. A slow, warm smile that gave her butterflies in the pit of her stomach. She smiled back, thinking he was about to come toward her. But then the photographer pointed at something on the far end of the green, and they walked off in the opposite direction.

Just as well, Emily thought. She wasn't sure if she was ready to face him yet. She hadn't seen him since the town council meeting on Wednesday night, hadn't spoken with him since Tuesday—the night he dropped off the *Globe* article and they kissed.

She felt herself practically blushing just thinking about it. It was really so silly. Such a little thing. Nothing to make such a big deal over. *Get a grip, Emily,* she coached herself.

She looked up and suddenly faced Sara.

"What you said up there, it was really moving," Sara told her. "It really felt as if it came from your heart."

"It did," Emily admitted. "I know I just passed up my last chance to give a 'vote for me' pitch, but somehow it was what I really wanted to say." She glanced around, finding she didn't really want to talk about the campaign anymore. "Are you enjoying the fair?"

"It's great. I've already bought so much stuff, I can hardly carry it all back to my apartment." Sara held up two full shopping bags. "My mom loves this handcrafted stuff. I picked up some mugs and these great baskets." Sara opened the top of one bag so that Emily could see.

At the words *my mom,* Emily had felt a small pang. *But I'm your mom,* she had wanted to say. But of course, she knew in her heart that although she was technically Sara's mother, she was not her *mom*—and would never be.

She gazed into the bag and forced a smile as she looked back up at Sara. "It's a very pretty set. I'm sure she'll love it."

Suddenly she wondered if Sara had made plans to return to Maryland. Was that why she was buying gifts for her mother?

"I guess I'll save this stuff for Christmas presents," Sara said. "I never do anything like that, but the mugs might break if I try to mail them."

Emily felt relieved, but couldn't help worrying. She knew that Sara was trying to work out a delicate balancing act between two mothers. "Have you spoken with your parents lately?" she asked in a tentative tone.

Sara nodded. "I finally called them last week and told them that I had spoken with you, and how that all went." Sara avoided Emily's gaze for a moment. "They sounded really happy for me," she added. "So, that was nice."

"They sound like wonderful people," Emily said sincerely. She hesitated a moment, then added, "I'd like to meet them someday."

Sara looked surprised. "Sure. That would be . . . good. They would like to meet you, too. My mother, especially. She asked a lot of questions about you."

"I get a generally good report, I hope?" she joked.

Sara smiled. "Generally, yes," she replied with a grin. "Better than that, actually," she admitted. She looked self-conscious and picked up her shopping bags again. "I'd better get going. I start my new job at the library this afternoon."

"That's great," Emily said. "It should be more interesting for you than the diner."

"In some ways. The pay isn't great. No tips," Sara noted with a shrug. "But I will get first crack at the new books, so that's a plus."

"Definitely," Emily agreed. "Did you speak to Dan Forbes yet?"

"No, not yet," Sara said. "I just haven't gotten the chance."

Her expression made Emily think Sara was scared to approach him. Emily's first impulse was to offer to handle the situation for her. Then she caught herself. She didn't want Sara to feel smothered or pushed. This was something she had to deal with on her own.

"I was just wondering," Emily said. "Oh, I nearly forgot. The bridal shop called and said your gown should be in on Monday. I can take you after work to pick it up."

"Won't you be busy Monday with the election?"

"By Monday night there won't be anything left for me to do but stress out. It will be the perfect distraction," Emily told her. "Besides, I want to make sure it fits you right. And we still have to find you some shoes."

Emily had persuaded Sara to let her pay for whatever she needed for the wedding. It seemed the least she could do. Emily wished she could do more of—everything, actually. Though that impulse was totally unrealistic, she realized. But there would be time, she kept telling herself. Opportunities would come up in the future, to help Sara with graduate school perhaps, or maybe even with Sara's own wedding.

"Oh, the shoes," Sara replied, cutting into her thoughts. "I nearly forgot. Sure, if it's not any trouble for you. Monday would be fine. I'll be working at the library so I can come over to your office when I'm done."

Emily agreed to the plan and then watched as Sara ambled away, her shopping bags loaded with gifts for her *real* mother.

Well, at least Sara would definitely be here until Jessica's wedding. Maybe she ought to just be grateful for that, and willing to wait and see what happened next.

ON HER WAY HOME FROM THE HARVEST FAIR, EMILY took the long route and stopped at her mother's house. She climbed the porch steps and rang the doorbell. It was late afternoon and she saw one lamp lit in the living room and heard the sound of the television. She waited a few minutes, then pressed the bell again, wondering if her mother was asleep. Or was something really wrong? She realized that Lillian had missed her speech today, which was very unusual for her. *It's probably because she's still furious with me,* Emily told herself.

At last Emily saw the corner of the living room drape pulled back for an instant, then close again, and she knew her mother was fine.

Still, she stood waiting. Lillian did not come to the door. Emily considered going in with her own key, then decided not to. Although she worried about her mother isolating herself like this, Emily realized that she was angry, too.

She couldn't get past Lillian's cold, derisive reaction when she told her about Sara.

It's hard to forgive her for that, Emily thought, *though I'm trying my best. And it's hard being caught in this place, stuck between anger and concern.*

Lillian obviously didn't want to see her. Though this couldn't go on forever, it seemed to Emily best right now to just let her have her way. *Let her have some time to feel what it's really like to be cut off from her family,* she thought as she walked down the porch steps and headed for home. *If she really needs something, I'm sure she'll break down and call me.*

Later that night, though, Emily dialed her mother's number. When the machine picked up, she left a brief message. "Hello, Mother, it's Emily. I wondered if you wanted me to pick you up for church tomorrow. You can call me back tonight, or in the morning if you like. I'll be leaving here at the usual time, around nine." She waited a moment, picturing her mother standing near the phone, listening. "All right, maybe you went to bed early. Give me a call if you need anything," she said finally.

Lillian didn't return her call on Saturday night or the next morning. Emily wondered if she should call again. She finally decided not to, but she did wait until nearly half past nine before leaving the house.

She arrived at the service late and slipped into a seat in the back row. She saw Jessica and Sam sitting together with Sam's parents a few rows up ahead. Gus Potter had returned to his post as usher of the pulpit side, wearing his gray tweed sports coat and a burgundy wool vest. While he did not look completely recovered, he did look bright-eyed and cheerful, and Emily was pleased to see him back.

As she listened to Reverend Ben's sermon, she felt odd to be sitting there alone, even though there were many weeks when Lillian did not feel well enough to attend the service. But this Sunday Emily knew her mother had deliberately missed the service in order to avoid her company, which somehow made it feel different.

The Reverend Ben cleared his throat. " 'Forgive us, Lord, as we forgive those who trespass against us,' the Lord's Prayer says. But I've sometimes thought that prayer, as beautiful as it is, has been written backward," he said. "Or at the very least, the author has made a huge assumption. I really think the directions should be more like, 'Dear Lord, please let us forgive each other the way that *you* forgive us.'

"You see, because the Lord is so much better at this business of for-giveness than we mere mortals could ever hope to be, we're the ones who should be modeling His method, not the other way around. The Lord for-gives us unconditionally. He doesn't need to sit and think it over, with-holding His compassion, His mercy, and His grace. He doesn't cling to his grudges, like we do, reliving them daily, reminding himself how He was hurt or cheated, or disappointed by someone as frail and flawed as we are. He forgives and wipes the slate clean. That is true forgiveness, the pure, ideal spirit of amnesty we must try to extend toward each other."

He paused and looked down at his notes a moment, then smiled. "I once heard it said that 'Everyone in this world is walking around, chewing on something that just won't go down,' and sometimes, my friends, it does ring very true to me," he said over a smattering of laughter.

"It's a rare person who does not carry around some grudge, small or large, some onerous bit that won't go down. But how many of us find that as we approach middle life and even later, we are carrying around a load of grudges, like a big bag of rocks, slung over our shoulder. The wrongs the world has done you—parents, siblings, friends, coworkers, neighbors—oh, so many wrongs that we righteously cling to. It takes a lot of energy to carry that bag around with you, doesn't it? It doesn't really make much sense, either. . . . So, why do we do it? We drag it along, letting it pull us down when we can be lifted up. When we can follow the Lord's example and forgive—and let go."

He stood quietly for a moment and pushed his spectacles up on the bridge of his nose. "As I leave you today, I suggest that you select even the smallest pebble in your collection and consider how you can let it go."

Emily swallowed hard. It felt as if the Reverend had been speaking directly to her about the situation with her mother. She glanced down at her prayer book, but didn't really see the words. Yes, she would like to be free of this bag of rocks she dragged around. It was really an enormous nuisance.

But true forgiveness was very difficult and seemed so very elusive to her. *Maybe I just need to try harder,* Emily thought as she automatically came to her feet for the next hymn. *Maybe it will be easier for me, now that I've found Sara.*

When the service ended, Emily left church through the front door, stopping to greet the Reverend.

"Wonderful sermon, Reverend," she said sincerely.

He smiled and took her hand. "Thank you, Emily. I usually save that theme for the holidays. But for some reason it seemed fitting for today. . . . Where's your mother? Not feeling well?"

"Well, she's not speaking to me right now. Because of Sara," Emily explained briefly. "I guess that's why she didn't come to church today."

"Ah, that's a pity, though predictable, I guess," he said thoughtfully. He rubbed his cheek a moment, thinking. "I'll stop by and visit her during the week," he promised. "She needs some time to work this out."

Emily nodded. "Yes, she needs time. It was a shock for her." She paused, then added, "I'm going to think more about your sermon, Reverend Ben—and what you said to me in the park that day."

He smiled, his eyes bright with kindness. "Good, Emily. Think and pray," he suggested.

"How is Rachel doing? I heard that she's still in the hospital," Emily added.

"Her doctor wants to keep her there for a few days. They stopped the bleeding, but she's still in danger. They've diagnosed the condition as something called placenta previa. It's not uncommon, I understand, but in Rachel's case it's rather severe."

"Oh, I'm so sorry," Emily said. "How is the baby?"

Her heart fell when she saw the grim expression on the Reverend's face. "They're still not sure. She lost a lot of blood. They've taken a sonogram and think the baby is all right, but these tests can only tell you so much. We really won't know until the child is born," he reported honestly. "We're hoping for the best, of course."

"Of course," Emily agreed sympathetically. "Tell Rachel I said hello and wish her the best. I'll be praying for her and the baby."

"Thank you, Emily. It's a comfort to know that so many prayers are being said for her right now."

Emily said good-bye to the Reverend and left the church, thinking that she couldn't imagine what he and his family were going through right now. She knew she wasn't much of a cook, but maybe she'd make a casserole today and take it over to their house. When someone was in the hospital, it was always a help if you didn't have to bother about shopping and cooking dinner. She decided she would send Rachel flowers at the hospital, too.

Reverend Ben had done so much for her over the years, she wished that right now there was something more she could do. Emily promised herself that no matter how busy or tired she felt later today, she would set aside some time to pray for all of them. She knew that the Reverend and his family would appreciate that effort most of all.

SARA STOOD AT THE DOOR AND KNOCKED HARDER. MAYBE THE DOORBELL wasn't working, she reasoned, and Lillian hadn't heard her. Then she heard a shuffling sound and knew that her grandmother was standing on the other side.

"Lillian? It's me, Sara," she announced boldly. "I know you're in there. I can hear you breathing."

Sara couldn't actually hear her grandmother breathing, but she thought the remark would be irresistible to her.

"I'm sure you cannot because I'm practically not breathing at all. Down to my last breaths, actually. I'm sure of it. And I don't feel like having visitors, so please go away."

"I'll only be a minute. I have something for you," Sara coaxed her.

"Leave it by the door, I'll get it later," Lillian called back.

"Come on, Lillian. That isn't very good manners," she countered, thinking that would get her. "One doesn't ask a visitor to leave a gift without even opening one's door," she added, imitating her grandmother's instructive tone. "Unless of course, you're not quite decent. . . ."

Sara listened for a long moment, but didn't hear any reply.

Then she heard the sound of the door latch clicking, and the door magically swung open. Lillian stood to one side, neatly dressed, as usual, in a silk blouse and a long, pleated wool skirt and sweater set, her reading glasses hanging from a chain around her neck.

"I'm quite decently clothed, as you can see. And you may come in . . . I suppose," she said crisply.

As Sara entered, Lillian directed, "Go on into the living room. I was just doing some mending."

Sara did as she was told and sat down in the middle of Lillian's high horsehair sofa. The thick upholstery had a silky finish that made her feel as if she were going to slide off the cushion.

Lillian walked into the room slowly and settled herself in her large armchair. "Well, what brings you here? Did Emily send you?" she asked bluntly.

"No, she doesn't even know I came." Sara reached into the shopping bag she had brought and took out a box. She handed it to Lillian. "There was a fair on the green yesterday. I bought this for you."

"Really?" Lillian seemed surprised. She stared at the box a moment before opening it, as if she feared something might jump out, Sara thought.

"It isn't much," Sara said suddenly.

Lillian looked up at her. "Then why bother?"

Sara laughed at her. "I thought you might like it. Why don't you open it and see."

Lillian sighed and undid the ribbon, then lifted the lid on the box. She took out a white ceramic planter filled with potting soil and stared at it.

"A pot of dirt. You're right, it isn't much, is it?"

"It's an amaryllis, or it will be once you water it for a while. The bulb is planted in there, and there's a card in there somewhere with instructions on how to grow it."

"I know how to grow an amaryllis," Lillian assured her, looking at the planter again with interest. "They are lovely flowers, very dramatic. I haven't had one for years. My husband would bring me one every year around this time, and it would bloom by Christmas. . . . Did I tell you that?" she asked suspiciously.

"Uh, no. I don't believe you ever did," Sara said honestly.

Lillian sat back and sighed, holding the pot on her lap with two hands. "Well, thank you. You need to start them in a dimly lit spot, as I recall."

The entire house was so dimly lit that that shouldn't be a problem, Sara thought. "How about that little table near the bookcase?" Sara suggested.

"Yes, that will be good to start," Lillian agreed. She handed Sara the planter. "Put it there for me, please, and I'll take care of the watering later."

Sara carried the planter to the designated spot and then returned to the sofa. "Oh, I almost forgot, I have a book for you, too, from the library—the new Margaret Haywood. It just came in."

Lillian took the book in two hands and blinked in surprise as she gazed down at the cover. "Well, well. If I had known you had this in your bag of tricks, I definitely would have opened the door sooner," she admitted.

"I'll remember that next time," Sara said with a laugh.

"How did you get hold of this? I read it was just published."

"You have connections at the library now. I started working there on Saturday."

"Did you really?" Lillian put the book in her lap. She stared at Sara, looking genuinely pleased. "That's news. It's about time you quit that dreadful job at the Clam Box. I always thought that was very much below you."

"Well, thanks, I think," Sara replied, recognizing Lillian's backhanded form of praise.

Lillian put on her glasses and examined the book. *"Error Messages,"* she read the title aloud. She peered over her glasses at Sara. "What do you suppose that means?"

"It's a computer term. When the program has made a mistake, you get a little screen—"

Lillian held up her hand to signal a stop. "That's quite enough, thank you. I know nothing about computers and prefer to pass on in ignorance." She frowned at the book. "Have you read this yet?"

"No, I haven't, so don't take too long with it. I can only have it for two weeks."

"All right. I shall put the book I'm reading aside and get to this one right away," Lillian said eagerly. "She's quite a good writer. This won't take me very long."

"Good, after I read it, we can talk about it," Sara said.

"Argue about it, you mean," Lillian corrected her. She cast Sara a half-scolding look and pursed her lips. "Gets the blood moving, I suppose."

"Yes, it does," Sara agreed, smothering a small laugh. Once they got into a debate about a book they had both read, neither could ever concede to the other. *Maybe I'm more like Lillian than I want to admit.*

"Well, thank you for the book, Sara. I could use the diversion. I haven't had much company lately," she complained, with a theatrical sigh.

"Have you tried opening the door when someone knocks on it?" Sara asked bluntly.

Lillian glared at her and gathered her sweater closer.

"No need to be snide, young lady. You don't know what it's like to be old and alone. You've no idea."

You think you've been deserted by your daughters, but the truth is, you've driven them both away, Sara wanted to say. But she caught herself, knowing that would be too much. She had come to make peace today, not alienate her.

"Emily is very busy right now with the election coming up on Tuesday," she said finally.

"Emily has lost her mind lately, if you ask me." Lillian nearly spat out the words. "She's going to lose this election to Charlie Bates, I'm certain of it. I'm not even sure I'm voting for her and I'm her mother. It will be her own fault, too. She won't be mayor much longer, and she won't be so infernally *busy* all the time. Then we'll see."

Lillian sounded as if she wanted Emily to lose the election, Sara thought, just to prove a point.

"What will we see?" Sara asked quietly. "Whether or not Emily is mayor again, everyone respects and admires her. I respect and admire her. She's a very unusual person."

Lillian fixed her with a cold stare. "I'm glad you're both so pleased with each other. Now, if you don't mind, I'd like you to go. Visitors can be tiring when one is accustomed to being alone."

"Sure, I understand," Sara said lightly as she got up from the couch. "Let me know when you're done with the book. I'll come and pick it up."

Lillian nodded. She shifted uneasily in her chair, avoiding Sara's gaze. "All right, I will. Maybe you can have some tea next time."

"Yes, maybe I will," Sara replied. "Don't bother to get up, I can let myself out. Good-bye now."

"Good-bye, Sara," Lillian said evenly. "And thank you for the presents."

Sara smiled. "Okay, see you," she called back to her grandmother. She let herself out and closed the heavy door behind her. It had been a good idea to visit Lillian on her own, Sara thought. No matter what her grandmother said, Sara believed that deep down inside, Lillian really did like her.

CHAPTER SEVENTEEN

✎

"Any news?" Betty swooped into Emily's office, carrying two pizza boxes and a large paper bag.

"Not a word since the last report. The suspense is killing me." Harriet sat at the meeting table, her head in her hands. Emily could not remember seeing the older woman so dispirited.

Election night was always pure torture, but this one seemed even worse than the one before, Emily thought. Perhaps because the outcome was so uncertain. It was nearly ten at night; the polls had been closed for two hours. Huddled in Emily's office, her loyal supporters looked wrung out and exhausted.

"This is a squeaker, all right," Frank agreed. He had been unable to sit still and had just about worn a hole through the rug, pacing back and forth in front of the desk. "I keep feeling like I want a cigarette. Then I remember I quit five years ago," he offered with a faint laugh.

"Good for you. I'm about to start," Harriet said with a sigh.

"Here, have some pizza," Betty offered, flipping open one of the boxes. "I have some paper plates and napkins here, too," she added, opening the bag.

"That actually smells good." Frank finally stopped pacing and walked over to the table. "Care for a slice, Emily?"

"Uh . . . no, thanks." Emily stood up. Even though she hadn't eaten any dinner tonight, the smell of the pizza was not appetizing. "I think I'll get some air," she said, grabbing her coat from the back of her door. "I'll see you in a few minutes."

Her stalwart companions cast her looks of concern. For a moment she thought Betty might offer to come with her, but finally her friend just smiled. "Take a break. That's a good idea. If anything exciting happens, I'll send Harriet out to find you."

"Thanks a lot," Harriet said with a grunt. "Just don't disappear on us. It won't be long now," she warned.

"I know." Emily nodded and left. That was just what she was afraid of suddenly—that it wouldn't be very long before she heard she had lost.

She walked quickly down the dark corridor and left the Village Hall. She turned and started walking down Main Street. It had been a long night of waiting. Too long.

Jessica and Sam had stopped by earlier to give her a reassuring hug, and Sara and Luke had come by to cheer her on, which Emily had truly appreciated. Even Reverend Ben had called from the hospital, where he was visiting his daughter. Her mother, of course, had not called all day, but Emily had expected that. There had been other calls and visitors, too, friends from around town and supporters in Village Hall.

Still, the hours had gone so slowly, especially these last two. She had sat in her office, picturing the men and women of the board of elections, tally-ing up the votes. They would be done soon—and that was worse somehow.

Now that she was nearly at the end, she wished she could stop time. And maybe never know. The last report from the vote counters had said that the race was too close to call, a dead heat. Suddenly her heart was filled with a frigid certainty that she had lost the election.

She put her hand to her temple and shook her head, as if trying to shake the thought loose. "Oh, I hope not," she murmured out loud.

"Emily, are you all right?"

She looked up and realized she had nearly walked right into Dan Forbes. Talking to herself out loud, no less. He stood staring down at her, his curious, concerned expression shadowed by the streetlight.

"Dan, I'm sorry. I didn't even see you there," she said, taking a quick step back.

The corner of his mouth lifted in a half smile. "I said hello. I guess you didn't hear me. You have other things on your mind tonight, understand-ably."

She nodded, forcing a halfhearted smile. "No word yet. They say it's neck and neck."

His sympathetic look was nearly her undoing. "What is that Emily Dickinson poem . . . something about Hope being the thing with feath-ers—"

" 'That perches in the soul, And sings the tune without the words, And never stops at all . . . ' " Emily quoted from memory.

"I should have known you would be a Dickinson fan," Dan said.

"Are you kidding? I was a teenage girl with literary leanings, growing up in New England, and I happened to be named Emily. Believe me, it was unavoidable."

Dan laughed. "Come on," he said. "Let's take a walk. It will do you good."

He took her arm and fit it comfortably through his, and Emily had no choice but to fall into step with him. His gesture probably didn't mean anything, she told herself, just a friend offering support. Still, it felt very nice to walk along with him like this, his strong body leaning protectively toward her, their steps evenly matched. Even nice enough to distract her for a moment from the election returns.

"I was just coming by to see how your group was doing," Dan told her. "When will you hear, do you know?"

"It won't be long now," she said. She'd tried hard to hide the anxious note in her tone, but knew it had sounded all the same.

She noticed they were coming up to the Clam Box and slowed her steps. "I'll bet Charlie is in there with his whole gang right now."

"Yes, he is," Dan reported. "Doing the same thing you are."

"Well, we have that in common, at least," she replied. She glanced up at him. "I've already faced the fact that I might lose this." She paused and took a breath. "It won't be the end of the world."

"No, not at all," Dan assured her. He stepped aside and faced her. "Not at all," he repeated. "This was a tough campaign. You made some hard calls."

"Yes," she said. "I don't regret anything, either. It's not that. . . . It's just that I really love this job," she confessed. "I like being mayor. I think I'm really good at it, too. It will be hard to give that up."

Dan stared down at her, looking thoughtful, admiring, and guarded, all at once. He took her hands and held them in both of his own. "You are good at it," he agreed. "Confidentially, I hope you pull it out. But whatever happens—win or lose—I know you'll accept it gracefully. Because that's who you are."

Emily felt warmed by his words and honored by his compliment. "Thanks . . . off the record, of course," she added with a small smile.

For the briefest moment, as Dan stared down at her, she thought he might lean forward and kiss her. But then he seemed to change his mind and stepped back abruptly, dropping her hands.

"Emily! . . . Emily! Come back . . ."

Emily heard someone down the street shouting her name and turned to see who it was.

Frank Hellinger was half-running, half-walking down the sidewalk toward them, his hands cupped around his mouth, like some reluctant town crier, she thought.

"Returns are in . . . they just called . . . you won!" he shouted. "You won!"

She felt a wave of shock and happiness so strong her knees nearly caved in. "I—I don't believe it," she whispered under her breath.

"Emily, you won!" She felt Dan's hand on her shoulder and turned to face him. "Congratulations!"

She swallowed hard, feeling she might cry.

"Thanks . . . I can't quite believe it."

Then they moved toward each other, automatically it seemed. She felt Dan's strong arms go around her and nearly lift her off her feet, and she felt free for a moment, pressing her face against his shoulder and hugging him back.

Finally they parted and she stared up at him, feeling practically dizzy. "Come and celebrate with us," she offered.

"Love to, but I have to write the story." He glanced quickly at his watch. "I'll call you later for a quote."

"I'll be waiting," she said with a smile.

He waved and rushed off in the opposite direction. Emily dug her hands in her pockets and turned toward the Village Hall. She saw that Frank had walked back to the building, where Betty and Harriet waited. They were outside without coats, standing in the clear chilly night, and each one held an "Emily Warwick for Mayor" sign and waved it in the air.

"Yay, Emily! Hurray for Emily!" Their shouts of joy echoed down the empty street, shattering the night's stillness.

Emily waved to them and quickened her pace, glancing for a moment over her shoulder at the Clam Box, where she was sure a very different scene was unfolding.

As she reached the Village Hall, her supporters ran down the steps and embraced her in a group hug. "We did it! We did it!" Harriet chanted. She broke away from the group and waved her hands wildly in the air.

"Oh, Emily. I'm so happy!" Betty cried. "I knew you'd win."

"I didn't," Harriet admitted. "But you did, my girl, fair and square!" Harriet clapped her hands together gleefully. "Bates will demand a recount, I'm sure. But he won't get anywhere with that."

"Won it by a nose," Frank chimed in. He shook his head and hitched up his pants. "By a nose," he repeated.

More by the grace of God, Emily added silently as she smiled with relief at her companions.

Thank you, Lord. Thank you for giving me another chance at this. I'll really do a good job, I promise.

"Gosh, I wish I had a big fat cigar," Frank said wistfully. He grinned at Emily again and shook his head.

Lucy watched Charlie as he paced up and down the dark living room. She sat with her hands clenched in her lap, not daring to speak or barely breathe, as if waiting for a terrific storm to blow past their little house.

"There's going to be a recount, I'll tell you that much," Charlie insisted harshly.

"Of course, you ought to ask for a recount. It was a close race. There might have been—some mistake," Lucy said, though she secretly felt sure that there had not been a mistake and that Charlie had indeed lost. Still, if it helped him tonight to hold out some slim hope, then so be it. It seemed the kind, if not the totally honest, thing to do.

"You can bet there's been some mistake. Emily Warwick's got friends on the board of elections, you know. Good friends, friends who would add a few in her favor, or lose a few of mine."

Lucy felt herself losing patience. "Oh, come on now, Charlie. It's the board of elections. They're not going to do something like that—"

"There you go again!" Charlie said, turning angrily toward her. "How do you know what the board of elections is likely to do, Lucy? How would you know that?"

She swallowed hard, alarmed by his angry expression. "I'm just saying that I think you can trust them."

He shook his head, his mouth turned up in a bitter smile. "You can never just take my part, can you? You always have to question and argue and go against me."

Lucy felt her stomach drop, as if she'd been standing in an elevator that had missed a few floors. "That's not true. That's not true at all," she insisted.

"Of course it is, Lucy," he countered. "Ever since you started talking about college, ever since I starting running in this election. I talked about this for years—how I was going to run for mayor—and you knew how much it meant to me. But you had no interest in my campaign and helping me win this election."

"How can you say that to me?" Lucy came to her feet, feeling winded, as if she'd run a long race. "I worked night and day on that campaign. I did whatever you asked me to do—running errands for you, sticking flyers in mailboxes, calling people until my finger got sore from punching the numbers. I covered for you in the diner whenever you asked me to—"

"Sure, you did some here and there, but not like a wife who was really going all out to see her husband win. You stood right up in a town meeting and spoke against me. When people see that a candidate's own wife doesn't care if he gets elected, well . . . why would they even vote for him?"

"Charlie, please. I know you're disappointed but—"

"But nothing," he cut in. "Can't you even hear yourself talking? Why, just five seconds ago, you were sticking up for Emily Warwick, telling me she and her buddies down in the Village Hall wouldn't rig an election. Well, I'm saying they would and they did. But you just can't take my side, can you? You're so independent now, you can't stick up for your own husband."

"Charlie, I can't believe you," she said, shaking her head.

Lucy turned away from him, her thoughts whirling. A few minutes ago she had felt so much sympathy for him. No matter how bad things had been between them lately, she still felt devastated by his loss. Even now, some rational, objective part of her knew that Charlie was only lashing out because he hurt so much inside. *He isn't thinking straight,* she told herself. *He'll feel sorry for saying these things tomorrow.*

But the old Band-Aids that had held their relationship together through so many marital battles just wouldn't stick tonight. She pressed her hand to her lips, as if to hold back the words that were rising up inside.

"That's all you have to say to me—you don't believe me?" he goaded her. "Well, I don't believe you, Lucy. This is not what a man expects of a wife. I need support and interest. I need a helpmate, not another kid to put through college."

She couldn't hold it back any longer. "You lost that election because people didn't vote for you, Charlie. You didn't lose because it was rigged or because I didn't help you enough. People didn't vote for you," she repeated in a low, harsh tone. "Maybe they didn't like your opinions or the way you shout people down, but you lost fair and square, and you're too self-centered to even see the truth."

"Lucy, that's enough!" Charlie shouted, jabbing the air with his finger.

Lucy felt scared all of a sudden and cold. She rubbed her arms, even though she was wearing a long-sleeved sweater. She had an awful feeling that they had just slid into some dark, terrible place that they might not get out of.

Charlie stood there staring at her. His face had gone from beet red to a pale, sickly white. He picked up a candy dish. It was one of her favorite pieces of china, and she didn't have many. He stared at it a moment, as if he'd never seen it before and wasn't quite sure what it was. Lucy put her hands to her mouth and sucked in a breath. She knew she must have made a sound because he looked up at her, then back at the dish with a grim expression. He threw the piece of china to the floor with all his might. Lucy gave a small sob as it burst into pieces.

Charlie took his jacket from the chair and pulled open the front door.

"Where are you going?" she asked, her voice shaking.

"Out. I'm going out," he said, without turning to look at her. "Thanks for all your help tonight. You've been a big comfort to me."

Lucy rubbed her forehead as she watched him disappear through the front door. She felt tears pressing at the back of her eyes. Part of her wished him good riddance, but a deeper part of her believed he was right. She hadn't been any comfort at all on the hardest night of his life.

I'm not a very good wife, she thought wearily. She went to the kitchen closet and pulled out the broom and dustpan. Then she swept up the broken china, worried that the boys would come down tomorrow barefoot.

It was hard to be Charlie's wife lately, she thought. And yet it was equally hard to imagine any other life for herself. She loved raising her boys. She didn't even mind being a waitress so much, most of the time. But she needed more. She needed school and the way it made her feel more alive, more interesting.

Chilled, she walked into the kitchen to make a pot of tea. She was surprised to see her hands trembling as she filled the kettle, set it on the stove, and turned on the burner.

For the first time she truly considered the possibility of leaving Charlie. The practicalities of it, not just a soothing daydream. Where would she live? She and the boys. They'd have to come with her, of course. Rents were so high. Maybe her mother would take them in.

She would have to give up school and find a new job, but that would be the least of it. The worst part would be the children. It would devastate them, and when she came face-to-face with that ultimate truth, her unhappiness didn't seem as unbearable.

She thought of the appointment she'd made to see the Reverend. It was one week from tonight, she realized suddenly. Could she get Charlie to go with her? She hadn't even told him about it yet. She had been waiting until after the election.

But now did not seem to be a better time to ask him to start counseling. If anything, it seemed worse. Lucy shuddered as she thought of the scene they just had.

It would be better to wait a few weeks, she decided. Maybe once Charlie had some time to get over his loss, she could talk to him about it. She would just have to call the Reverend and explain.

Dear Lord, please help me, Lucy prayed, squeezing her eyes closed. *I don't know what to do. I don't want to leave Charlie. Please help our marriage be good again. Please show us the way.*

When she opened her eyes, she felt tired, too tired even for a cup of tea. She shut off the burner. It was nearly two A.M. Somebody had to get up soon to open the diner, and it didn't look as if it was going to be Charlie, Lucy thought as she dragged herself up to bed.

BETTY INSISTED ON THE PARTY. "I'VE BEEN PLANNING THIS FOR WEEKS. I knew you would win," she claimed. She held out a guest list for Emily's approval. It was written on a yellow legal pad and looked to Emily about two feet long.

"You don't really have to go to all this trouble," Emily said again. "Just having you and Harriet and Frank with me last night was plenty."

"Oh, please, Emily. Don't be silly. You have to celebrate what you can celebrate in this life. You won. It's your day."

"You're a good friend, Betty," Emily told her. "I want to thank you for all your help during the election. I couldn't have made it without you."

"Of course you would have. I didn't do much," Betty replied, brushing off her comment. "Actually, I learned a few things from you, Emily," she admitted. "When that whole issue about the center came up, I thought you were smart to lay low and avoid getting involved. Then when you did defend it, I thought, Gee, now that's a dumb move. Why is she doing that? You know how I hate to be on a losing team," Betty added.

They'd known each other since high school, and Emily did know how Betty hated to back a loser.

"Then something you said in one of those meetings changed my mind. I realized this isn't just a game or even a business deal. There are real principles involved. I never thought I'd admire anyone for making a totally dumb move, twice. But that's what happened." Betty shrugged and smiled, as if still surprised at the realization.

Emily felt a little taken aback by her friend's admission. "Well, thanks. The truth is, I was floundering there for a while. But it all turned out okay in the end."

"Yes, it did, didn't it? I ran into Warren this morning on the street." Betty's smile grew wider. "I know it's awful to say, but I loved digging it in a bit with him. I invited him to the party, though, and he'll probably come. I think he wants to stay on your good side."

"Good old Warren. We'll patch things up, I'm sure," Emily said lightly. "If you want to stay in politics, it helps to have a short memory."

"Just about total amnesia, from what I can see," Betty agreed. She slipped the list in her purse and rose to go. "Well, see you tonight," she said with a grin. "Seven o'clock. Don't be late."

"I'll do my best," Emily promised, though they both knew she would probably be late for her own funeral.

"Oh, be late if you have to." Betty said from the doorway. "You're the guest of honor. You ought to make a real entrance."

Emily just laughed. She was looking forward to the party. Betty was right. It was time to celebrate. And she had a lot to be thankful for.

EVEN THOUGH SHE HAD DONE HER BEST, EMILY DIDN'T ARRIVE AT BETTY'S until well after eight. There were so many cars on the street, she had to park nearly a block away.

The front door was open, and the foyer and living room so filled with guests she could hardly wedge herself into the crowd. It looked as if Betty had invited the entire town—and more than half had shown up. Despite Betty's plan of Emily making a grand entrance, hardly anyone noticed Emily slipping through the throng.

"Emily, when did you get here?" Betty pushed a few guests aside to greet her with a hug. "Here, have a canapé," she said, and before Emily could answer she handed her a paper plate with what looked like a crabcake. "The very last one. I was saving it for you. In about five minutes there won't be a scrap of food left. I never expected such a turnout," she confessed.

"There are a lot of people here," Emily agreed.

"Wait right here. I need to make a call for a delivery. I can't have a party without any food," Betty said, looking alarmed.

Emily nodded and her friend disappeared. She looked at the crabcake and set the dish down on a nearby table.

She turned to find Warren Oakes regarding her with an ironic expression. "Congratulations, Mayor," he said.

"Thanks, Warren," she said simply.

Warren shifted nervously, then scratched his head. "I didn't think you'd do it," he admitted.

"So I noticed," she replied with a slight smile.

"Well, you showed me," he said in a good-sport kind of voice. "I know you'll do a very fine job, as you've done the last three years. No doubt in my mind about that. If you need my help at any time, I hope you'll call on me."

He held out his hand for a conciliatory shake, and Emily met his gaze. She had thought she would feel bitter toward him, but she really didn't. They just had different views of the world, and he was still a valuable ally in town. Betty had been right about the amnesia. She could feel it setting in.

"Yes, I will," she replied, shaking his hand. "Thanks for the offer."

Emily mingled, wandering through the crowd and receiving hugs, handshakes, and even kisses at every turn. Jessica had already stopped by her office to congratulate her that morning, but she was there tonight with Sam, who greeted Emily with a huge hug.

"You did it," Sam said. "We knew you would."

"Of course she did. That's my big sister you're talking about," Jessica said, smiling widely at Emily.

"She had some dirty weather there," Digger acknowledged, nodding at her. "But she kept her balance, stayed the course. She's worthy, all right."

"Thank you, Digger," Emily said, realizing she had just been compared to a boat. "How are you feeling?" she asked, thinking again about the fire.

"I never felt better," Digger insisted. "I'm working again for Luke McAllister down at the construction site. Good of him to have me back, all things considered. Harry wants me at the boatyard, too," he said, nodding at his friend, who stood nearby with Digger's daughter, Grace. "I've got more work than I can handle. I'm in demand," he boasted.

"Good for you." Emily felt relieved to see Digger so lively and obviously in good health.

All of a sudden she spotted Sara entering the room. Sara smiled and waved at her. She wasn't very far away, but there were so many people between them, Emily felt frustrated trying to make her way through the crowd.

Finally they reached each other. Sara gave Emily a hug, then pulled back and handed her a bouquet of roses.

"These are for you, Emily. I wanted to get you something . . . but I didn't know what."

"Sara, they're beautiful. Thank you so much," Emily said, gazing down at the flowers. The gift meant a lot to her, more than Sara would ever realize.

She looked up at her daughter, smiling. "I'm glad you came. It's so crowded. Can you believe it?"

"Everyone wants to wish you well. They're happy for you."

Emily glanced around. After the last few weeks, it was hard to believe, but yes, they really were happy for her.

"Hello, Emily. I just wanted to congratulate you," a voice behind her said. Emily turned to see George Parker, the principal of the high school. "Is this your daughter?" he asked, smiling at Sara.

"Yes, this is Sara Franklin," Emily said, feeling proud to introduce her. "Sara, this is George Parker. He's the principal at the high school."

"Nice to meet you, Sara." George Parker glanced from daughter to mother and back again. "She has your eyes," he told Emily.

"Do you think so?" Emily said, feeling pleased by the compliment. She met Sara's gaze and smiled.

"Maybe," Sara agreed with a laugh.

Once George had left them, Emily felt suddenly awkward. She wasn't sure if Sara was comfortable hearing someone say they looked alike. Emily thought Sara looked more like her father, but there *was* something about Sara's eyes that resembled her own.

"I'm going to look for some water for these roses. I'll be right back," she told Sara.

"Okay, see you later. Oh, there's Jessica and Sam. I think I'll go over and say hello," Sara said as she drifted away.

Emily made her way to the kitchen, clutching the roses close to her body, like a fullback pushing toward the goal line.

Betty's kitchen was empty. Emily breathed a long sigh of relief in the open space, then looked around, wondering where she would find a vase or container. She pulled open a few cupboards and found a large plastic pitcher. Perfect, she said to herself as she filled it with water. She stood at the counter and placed the flowers in the vase, then wondered if she should add a teaspoon of sugar. Isn't that what people said to do with roses? Or maybe she ought to wait until she got them home.

"And I thought I was being so original," a voice said behind her. "You must have gotten about ten bunches of these so far."

She turned to see Dan standing just inches away, holding out another bouquet of roses. His was yellow.

"Not quite, only this one and yours," she replied, smiling at him. "And I do think that yellow *is* original," she added.

"Just the right thing to say. You ought to be in politics."

"Thanks." She smiled again, feeling suddenly self-conscious with him. "I think these will fit together. I don't want to forget them," she said, putting the second bouquet into the pitcher alongside the first. "Sara gave me the red ones."

"She did? How thoughtful." His expression brightened slightly. Did he look—relieved somehow? she wondered. No, that was silly, Emily told herself. He didn't think that much about her. He was just being nice.

"Has it sunk in yet? You looked pretty shocked when I saw you last."

"Yes, I was." Emily laughed and shook her head. She remembered how he had taken her arm and walked with her. Kept her from strolling right into the traffic, probably. He was standing very close, and she had to tip her head back to look up at him. "I was a real mess, wasn't I? Sorry about that."

"Don't be silly. I sort of like you like that," he admitted. "I know I'm getting the real deal. Not everybody around here does, I imagine."

"They don't see me falling apart at the seams every twenty minutes, if that's what you mean," she said. "But you seem to catch me at it pretty often lately."

He smiled at her, as if they shared a secret. "Well, that just shows you're comfortable around me, Emily. I take it as a compliment."

She sighed. "You're a very nice man, do you know that?"

It seemed so silly to say, but she really meant it. Dan looked uncomfortable a moment and gave a nervous laugh. "I have my moments. Don't let it get around, though. It will ruin my image."

"I never really thanked you for that article," she added quietly. "I don't think I'd have won without it."

"Of course you would have." His expression turned serious for a moment. "I wasn't sure at the time it was the right thing to do, but I couldn't quite resist."

"And what do you think now? Any regrets?"

"No, none. I guess I let my impartial, all-too-human side take over . . . but maybe I just feel comfortable around you."

"I'll take that as a compliment," she replied, smiling up him.

He smiled back, then reached out and cupped her cheek with his hand. When he moved toward her, she closed her eyes and her hand moved up to rest on his hard shoulder. His mouth met hers in a tender, lingering kiss that was different from the last time. This one was slower, less urgent and surprising, but still amazingly exciting.

Emily felt his arms around her, pulling her even closer for a long, deep moment. Then suddenly he lifted his head and looked down at her. "I'm not sure why I keep doing this," he said slowly. "I mean . . . I know why . . . but . . ." He touched her face again and smiled briefly.

She saw the regret in his eyes. He didn't really need to say more.

He sighed and stepped back, his hand falling to his side. "You know, my son, Wyatt, is coming soon. Next weekend. I'll be leaving a few weeks after that."

"Yes, I know. Your sailing trip," she said, managing to keep her voice smooth and even.

He stared at her, as if he didn't know what to say.

"Listen, Emily . . . I think you're great. You might be the greatest woman I ever met. But the timing is just all wrong here."

"I know." She forced a smile. "It's all right. Really," she assured him. "We'll always be friends, Dan. That's good, too. Right?"

"That's very good." His gaze still looked serious, but the corner of his mouth turned up in a small smile.

He reached out and took her hand and gently pressed it between both of his own. She gazed up at him, feeling sad and wistful, yet resigned. She had feelings for Dan. More than she wanted to admit. But if this wasn't meant to be, she could accept it, Emily thought. She had made a new resolution not to sit staring at closed doors. She had to have faith in what the Lord had in store for her.

EMILY THOUGHT OF DAN OFTEN DURING THE NEXT FEW DAYS, BUT TRIED not to let the situation get her down. Jogging past his house on Saturday afternoon, she saw an unfamiliar car in the driveway. California license plates, she noticed. His son, Wyatt, had finally come. So, that was the end of that.

Not that "that" had ever been much. A friendship mixed with a mild flirtation was the sum total. But Dan had been honest with her, and she ought to be grateful to him. She couldn't go moping around over something that hadn't even happened. It had been good just to feel attractive to someone again, she realized. Just to feel her heartbeat quicken when a man caught her eye and smiled at her, as if they shared some private knowledge and didn't need to talk at all. She hadn't felt that way in a very long time.

So, maybe Dan moving in and out of her life like this was just a reminder, she thought. Just as Reverend Ben had said, it wasn't really too late for her.

At least she had Sara now. Emily's mood brightened with that thought as she showered and dressed. She was going to pick up Sara soon for one more trip to the mall before the wedding and didn't want to keep her waiting.

On Monday night the gown had not fit Sara properly and had needed a few adjustments. The sash was wrong, and a large, silly bow had been added to one shoulder. Emily and Sara had actually laughed together when she tried it on. So now they were down to the wire with the wedding next weekend. Didn't it always go this way? Though Emily wasn't a shopper, she didn't really mind. The shopping trip gave her another excuse to spend time with Sara.

Half an hour later Sara got into the Cherokee. "The dress had better be right this time," she said, sounding weary. "I never realized getting married was so much trouble."

"Well, if you want a big wedding with all the trimmings, it is," Emily replied as she started driving again. "There's always the no-frills route."

Sara glanced at her. "That's what you and my father did, right? You eloped."

Emily nodded, her eyes still on the road. "We were married at the courthouse in Newburyport, right before we left for Maryland."

"Were you scared?" Sara asked her.

Emily thought for a moment. "More like extremely excited. As if I were about to jump off a cliff—but I knew there was a trampoline down there somewhere. I guess I just loved your father so much, I felt very sure that it was the right thing."

Sara smiled a little and glanced out the window. "I've had some long relationships, but I never really felt that way about anyone."

"When you do, you'll just know. It's worth waiting for," Emily promised.

"You were lucky," Sara said, glancing over at her. "I think some people wait their whole lives and never feel that way."

Emily nodded. "We didn't have much time together, but I know what we had was very rare. It's hard to explain," she said, searching for the right words. "It was like a deep, sweet well that I could always draw on. Even long after Tim was gone. Even now. It really helped me to keep going . . . especially after I gave you up."

Sara glanced at her, but didn't say anything more. Finally Emily reached over and touched Sara's hand for a moment, then the sign for the mall came into view, and she turned at the entrance.

"Here we are, at long last. Saturday night at the mall. Who could ask for anything more?" She sighed theatrically, making Sara laugh.

They were both relieved when the saleswoman produced the gown, minus the bow, and it fit Sara perfectly. After the bridal shop, they browsed in a few stores and then picked a quiet restaurant for dinner.

"I've been so busy with the election, I haven't even taken care of a wedding gift yet," Emily confessed. "I was thinking of getting them a gazebo. I thought they could put it somewhere near the pond."

"I bet Jessica would love that."

"It could be from both of us, if you like," Emily suggested. "Unless you wanted to get something on your own."

She watched Sara's expression carefully, wondering if she had assumed too much. She felt as if she walked a fine line with Sara. She understood that it would be this way for a long time; still, she couldn't help feeling frustrated by it. She loved her so much and wanted to be close to her.

"I picked something up for them already," Sara said carefully. "But thanks for offering."

"That's okay. No problem," Emily said. She glanced back at her menu. But she felt Sara watching her, as if she had more to say but was wary for some reason. Emily suddenly felt nervous.

"I'm happy you won the election," Sara said slowly. "Relieved, actually. I was waiting to see what happened. I told my parents I couldn't make any plans to come back until I knew."

Emily felt as if the floor had just dropped out beneath her. Now she knew why Sara looked so nervous. She knew this question had to be faced sooner or later, but she was hoping Sara would wait until after the wedding.

"Well, if it means you'll stay here longer, I can still concede to Charlie," she replied, trying to strike a light tone though she actually felt like crying.

"Emily—" Sara met her gaze, tilting her head to one side. "My parents are upset. They try not to say so, but I can tell they feel as if—as if I've abandoned them or something. Especially my mom," she added.

"Yes, I'm sure this is hard for her," Emily said, imagining herself in the place of Sara's adoptive mother.

"I really like it here. I like my job at the library. I even spoke to Dan Forbes about a job at the newspaper. But I'm not sure now if I can stay. My parents think I should just come home and keep up with you through visits and phone calls. That sort of thing . . ."

Her voice trailed off, and Emily could see how hard it was for Sara to tell her this. And to figure out this problem.

She hadn't even mentioned Luke McAllister, but Emily knew that the two shared a special relationship, something that was more than just friendship at this point. Leaving him would be hard for her, too.

Emily reached across the table and covered Sara's hand with her own. "I don't know what to say to you, dear," she admitted honestly. "I can hardly stand the idea of losing you now, when I just found you. But I know you have a family and a life in Maryland that's important to you. . . . I'm very new at being a mother," she forged on. "I really want to do and say the right thing here. You know how I feel, but I don't want to pressure you to stay. Whatever you decide, I want it to feel right to you."

Sara lifted her gaze finally and smiled at her. "You're doing okay so far."

"I never really thanked you for finding me," Emily suddenly realized. "How you came so far and waited so long. That took a lot of courage. I'm not sure if I could have done it." She squeezed Sara's hand. "If you decide to go, I may not have another chance to tell you, so I want you to know how proud I am of you. The way you turned out. You're so smart and mature and talented. I think you're absolutely perfect in every way."

"Emily!" Sara was blushing now.

"Please, let me finish," Emily said, her voice getting thin. "No matter where you go, back to Maryland or wherever, I'll always be there for you.

You'll always be the most important thing in my life. I know it can't happen overnight, and it's sometimes still very hard for us, but I love you truly, Sara, and I want to be—" *A real mother to you*, she nearly said, but she stopped herself.

"—I want to be part of your life. I want to have a special relationship with you. Can we try for that?"

Sara nodded. "I think we can," she said softly. "I have a wonderful mother, and what you and I have will be different. But it can be just as important—and loving."

Sara looked as if she was about to cry, and Emily felt overwhelmed, too. She leaned over and put her arms around Sara, giving her a hug.

"Sara, you can't know what you mean to me," she confessed quietly. With a sigh, she finally pulled away again, then reached into her handbag for a tissue.

"I can't leave before the wedding, of course," Sara assured her. "Jessica is counting on me, and I really want to be there."

"And the store finally got the dress right," Emily pointed out, feeling slightly encouraged.

"I don't want to hurt my parents," Sara said again. "But maybe I'll wait to decide until after the wedding. I'm just not sure what to do."

"Well, give it a few more days, then," Emily suggested. "Maybe now that we've talked about the problem, it will be easier for you to figure out what you need to do."

"Maybe," Sara agreed, looking relieved. "It was on my mind a lot."

Emily had an impulse to pray for Sara to stay on, then decided it would be selfish to ask God to grant her that favor. She prayed instead that Sara would make the right decision for herself, the one that would be best for her well-being. Then she realized that was what a good mother should do, and she felt quietly satisfied.

CHAPTER EIGHTEEN

*T*HE WEEK BEFORE JESSICA'S WEDDING FLEW BY. JESSICA and Sam were so busy getting their new house ready that Emily barely saw her sister once the final countdown began. The couple had already moved in all of their furniture and belongings. But on Friday there was still plenty of unpacking and putting away to do, and Sam was preoccupied with last-minute painting and repairs. After a moderately panicked phone call from her sister, Emily decided to take the day off to help.

"Good, I'm glad you're here," Jessica greeted her as soon as she walked in. "Come into the kitchen. I haven't unpacked a thing. Sam just got the cabinets finished last night," she said, sounding a bit frantic.

"Don't worry. You'll have plenty of time to put things away after the wedding," Emily reminded her.

Jessica glanced at her. "Right, just what I want to do on my honeymoon—unpack boxes."

Emily reconsidered her statement. "Yes, well, you have a point." She tugged open a box and found a pile of cooking pots inside. "Just tell me where you want this stuff. I'm here for as long as it takes."

They worked steadily all day, barely stopping for a break.

Finally, when it was dark outside, they each flopped down in a chair at the kitchen table.

"Thank you, Emily," Jessica said. "I can't believe how much we got done. Sam will be amazed."

"The only thing that's missing is your new toothbrush in the bathroom," Emily teased.

"Since I'm spending the entire day tomorrow at a beauty salon in Southport, the toothbrush will have to wait," Jessica said. "One less thing to worry about. Speaking of which . . . have you seen Mother at all lately?"

"No, I haven't," Emily admitted. "I keep calling and dropping by, but she won't speak to me. Sara has visited her, though, a few times, and so has Dr. Elliot. And you know that Reverend Ben went to see her."

Emily and Jessica had both spoken with Reverend Ben the other night at the wedding rehearsal. He reported that he visited Lillian last week, but she barely spoke to him. Not about Sara, or the wedding.

"Everybody says she's just fine, so I guess we shouldn't worry." Jessica sighed and examined her hands, which were chapped from all the housework.

"I think she is fine, but how are you?" Emily asked her sister quietly. "Have you been thinking about her and the wedding again?"

Jessica shrugged, then nodded. "A little, I guess. It's hard not to," she added, glancing up at her sister. "But I'm keeping my eyes on the finish line. I'm not going to lose Sam over this. She's the one who made me choose, and my choice is marrying Sam."

Emily released a long breath that she hadn't even realized she was holding. "All right, then, good for you. On with the show!"

She rose from her seat and grabbed her jacket off the chair.

"Why don't you stay and have some dinner with us?" Jessica offered.

"I'd better get going. I just want to get into a hot tub and soak for a while. I'll need until Sunday to look halfway decent."

"Go on . . . you'll look great, as always." Jessica reached out and gripped her sister's hand. "You've been a pal, Emily. I couldn't have made it without you."

"Don't get all mushy on me now . . . please?" Emily teased her. She playfully patted her sister's head. "Just do me a favor, and don't get married or move again for a while. I'm exhausted and I'm getting too old for all this hard work."

"Deal," Jessica promised.

"See you on Sunday, Bride," Emily called as she started toward the back door. "I'm coming by to help you get into your gown, right?"

"I'll be there," Jessica promised.

Emily closed the back door and smiled to herself. She peered up at the soft blue- and rose-tinted sky, and the first pinpoints of starlight above.

She could hardly wait for Sunday. . . .

FOR ONCE IN MY LIFE I'M READY ON TIME, EMILY THOUGHT HAPPILY AS SHE drove toward Jessica's house on Sunday morning at half past ten. They were due at Bible Community Church by eleven forty-five. The ceremony was scheduled to start at noon. Sara was going to meet them at the church, so Emily didn't have to worry about picking her up.

It was a perfect fall day, fair and even on the mild side for mid-November in New England. Emily found that she felt quite comfortable with just the satin shawl from her gown around her shoulders as she walked up to Jessica's door and rang the bell.

Jessica opened the door dressed in her robe, but all her makeup was done and her hair was fixed beautifully as well, half pinned up in back and half flowing down over her shoulders.

"Goodness, you look beautiful already," Emily declared.

"Oh, come in, come in. I'm so nervous," Jessica confessed.

"Look—my hands are shaking." She held out her hands, which were, in fact, trembling slightly.

Emily gripped them and smiled. Ice cold, too.

"Great manicure," she said brightly. "Don't worry. It will all be over soon. Come on, let's get the gown on. You can't go to the church in your bathrobe."

In the bedroom Jessica slipped into her gown, and Emily worked on fastening the back, a row of satin-covered buttons. Then there was a train to attach and the buttons on the sleeves. It was a gorgeous gown of cream-colored satin with a slightly off-the-shoulder shallow neckline and touches of crocheted ecru lace that gave the classic style a Victorian touch.

Jessica looked devastatingly lovely, Emily thought. Just like a bride from a picture book. She sat at her dressing table, and Emily helped her put on her headpiece, a simple garland of fresh flowers with a shoulder-length veil attached.

"Well . . . all set, I guess," Jessica said, sounding breathless. She glanced at the small clock on the dressing table. "The limousine should be here any minute."

Emily sat in the chair next to the dressing table and opened her purse. She took out the dark velvet jewelry box, opened it, and set it on the dressing table.

"Here are the pearls. Remember? I said I would save them for you."

Jessica picked up the necklace, then set it down again.

"I really want to . . . but I can't." She looked up at her sister. "I'll go against Mother today and marry Sam, but I can't wear the pearls. It just wouldn't feel right without her consent. Isn't that silly?"

Emily looked at her a moment. Then shook her head. "No, I understand." She took the jewelry case back, closed it, and slipped it back in her purse.

The doorbell rang and they knew the limo had arrived.

"Are you ready?" Emily said.

Jessica nodded. She smoothed down her sleeve and gave her reflection one last check in the mirror. "Ready as I'll ever be."

BY THE TIME THEY ARRIVED THE CHURCH WAS FILLED, ITS FRONT STEPS AND railing decorated with white ribbons and flowers. Molly Willoughby and her daughters waited anxiously in the vestibule, and they all shrieked with delight when they caught sight of Jessica.

"Oh, don't you girls look gorgeous," Jessica said to her two new nieces, giving them each a careful hug.

"You look like a princess, Jessica," Jill, Molly's younger girl, said in awe.

"We all look pretty good, if you ask me," Molly cut in. She smiled at Jessica and handed her a bouquet. "Nice flowers, too."

Emily thought Jessica should go wait in the little room off the vestibule, reserved for the bride. But she was too excited and didn't seem to care if Sam saw her before she walked down the aisle. "That's just a silly superstition," she scoffed when Emily mentioned it.

Dr. Elliot was there as well, since Jessica had asked him to give her away. He had on a brand-new suit, Emily noticed, a navy blue pinstripe with a gray satin vest and a pale yellow satin bow tie. He stood to the side, quiet and calm, as if he did this sort of thing every day.

Almost all the seats in the church were taken, though a few stragglers were still arriving. Organ music filled the sanctuary, and a soft golden light filtered in through the arched windows. The altar and pews were decorated with more white ribbons and flowers, and the subtle fragrance reached all the way to the back of the church.

Emily could see Sam and his younger brother Eric, who was his best man, standing tall up at the altar. Sam looked handsome and restless as he glanced to the back of the church.

The Reverend Ben appeared from a side door. "It's time to start. Are we all here?"

Jessica glanced at Emily. She knew they both had the same thought, wishing their mother would somehow miraculously appear at the last minute.

Then Emily looked around and felt a tightness in her throat. "Sara . . . isn't Sara here yet?"

Everyone started talking at once, but no one had seen her. She wasn't at the church. Luke had arrived separately and sat with the Hegmans and Harry Reilly.

"Luke hasn't seen her, either," Dr. Elliot said. "He was waiting for her to come, then he finally gave up and sat down."

"She must have gotten held up somewhere," Jessica said. "We can wait," she offered, glancing at Emily.

Emily could tell her sister was nervous and just trying to be considerate. She checked her watch. It was already a quarter past twelve.

"Let's wait a few minutes," Emily suggested. Jessica nodded, and the others stood around, chatting quietly.

Emily stood by the open church door, watching the street for Sara's car. She pulled her shawl around her shoulders.

What had happened to Sara? Did she have car trouble—or, God forbid, an accident? Wouldn't she have called about that? She couldn't have left for Maryland, could she? Emily thought with a cold knot of dread in her heart. It was understood that she would stay until the wedding. *At least, that's what I understood.* But maybe Sara's parents had pressured her or there had been some emergency that called her home.

Still, I can't believe she would have left without saying good-bye. There's got to be an explanation.

Emily felt her mind spinning off in all directions at once. Maybe Sara was held up somewhere with a flat tire or something, she consoled herself. No need to go running off the deep end. *She'll be here any minute. She wouldn't just break a promise like that.*

Emily glanced at her watch again. Five, ten, fifteen minutes had passed. Her spirits sank. The worst scenario seemed possible.

Finally she turned to Jessica. "We'd better start," she said. "I don't think Sara's coming."

"What do you mean? Did she say something to you?"

"I don't know. . . . I think she may have gone back to Maryland," Emily admitted. She sighed and Jessica squeezed her hand.

"Let's just wait a few more minutes," Jessica said.

Emily shook her head. "It's all right, Jessica. Let's go ahead."

Jessica finally nodded and then walked over to Reverend Ben. She whispered something to him, and he glanced with concern at Emily. Then turned to the group and got them in order again.

Emily took her place at the back of the procession, just before Jessica and Dr. Elliot.

She heard the first notes of the wedding march begin and felt her stomach jump with nerves. Molly's daughters started walking slowly down the aisle, and everyone in the church rose, turning to look at them.

Then Molly started walking and Emily followed.

Suddenly the heavy wooden door of the church flew open. Emily turned at the sound and felt her heart nearly stop beating.

Sara stood there, smiling. Then she held the door open wider and Lillian appeared. She paused for a moment, then slowly walked into the church, looking very well turned out in an ice-blue silk coat and dress ensemble perfect for the mother of the bride.

Emily stood there, speechless.

"Mother," Jessica gasped. "You're here."

"So I am." Lillian glanced at Sara. "That girl would not take no for an answer. She takes after you, Emily. Very headstrong."

Sara came to stand beside them, and Emily leaned over and gave her a hug, then planted a kiss on her hair. "More like you, Mother, I'd say," Emily replied.

"I think you've finally met your match, Lillian," Dr. Elliot chimed in.

Emily saw her mother cast a cool glance at Dr. Elliot, but she didn't respond. She turned instead to Emily. "Where are the pearls? They're not at the bank. Have you lost them?"

"Of course not. . . . I have them right here." Emily retrieved her purse and pulled out the velvet box.

Her mother took it from her, opened it, and took out the necklace.

"Come here, Jessica. Let me put this necklace on you. You can't get married without pearls. It's practically . . . unheard of."

Emily lifted her sister's long hair aside as Lillian fastened the necklace. She noticed her sister blink back tears, but her lips formed a shaky smile.

Jessica stood back and touched the pearls at her throat, then she glanced at her mother. "Thank you." She leaned over and gave Lillian a brief kiss on her cheek.

Her mother looked surprised and even touched, Emily thought, then she quickly squared her shoulders and turned away.

"Who will escort me to a seat?" Lillian asked, gazing around.

"I will," Reverend Ben said. He stepped up and offered Lillian his arm. "I'm headed in that direction again anyway," he added with a small smile.

Emily nearly laughed, but her mother's solemn expression stopped her.

The organ music started again, and everyone in the wedding party gathered at the back of the church and prepared for the procession once more. Sara stood in front of Emily this time. When it was Emily's turn, she followed automatically, feeling almost in a dream as she put one foot in front of the other.

She had expected Jessica's wedding to be lovely, but this was beyond her wildest imaginings. Everything felt right, for the first time in years.

The wedding party took their places at the altar, and the bride and groom stood before Reverend Ben and joined hands. A hush fell over the gathering as the Reverend raised his hands and began to speak.

"We are gathered to celebrate the marriage of Jessica and Sam, who have chosen to promise themselves to each other in the presence of God and in the company of those who love them," Reverend Ben began.

"As they begin their journey together, we are called upon to rejoice in their happiness, to be patient when they make mistakes, to help them in time of trouble, and to remember them in our prayers."

He paused and glanced at the bride and groom who stood before him, holding hands. "God's gift of human love is among the most precious and glorious we can experience here on Earth. Through this love, man and woman come to know each other with mutual care and companionship. Jessica and Sam have been blessed with this gift, and today we rejoice in this gift for them.

"They acknowledge that there may be bumps in the road ahead," the Reverend continued solemnly. "Yet they trust that the God who brought them together and brings light out of the darkness will also smooth the way. As they pledge themselves to each other today, let our hearts be filled with new joy and allow God's grace and light to illuminate our lives, even as these two lives are joined as one and made anew today."

Jessica and Sam exchanged their vows and rings. Then they leaned together for their first kiss as husband and wife, and the church filled with applause.

The organ music started again, loud and resounding, and Emily marched back down the aisle in the wake of the happy newlyweds, the many familiar, smiling faces on either side of the aisle blurred by her tears of happiness.

THE INN AT SPOON HARBOR HAD BEEN THE PERFECT CHOICE AFTER ALL, Emily reflected as she sat and watched couples dancing in the soft candlelight. The table settings were elegant, the flowers luxurious and fragrant, and the food delicious, receiving high reviews from even the Morgan clan.

Funny how things worked out, she thought. After all the ups and downs, her sister's wedding couldn't have turned out any lovelier.

Emily spotted Sara sitting alone and walked over to her. "Have you been enjoying it?" she asked.

"Absolutely," Sara said. She nodded toward Luke, who was across the room, talking with Digger. "Luke's having a good time, too. It's a great party."

"Yes, after all," Emily agreed with a happy sigh. "Tell me, how did you ever get my mother to come to the wedding? That was amazing."

Sara shrugged and smiled. "I think deep down, she really wanted to come. And she adores attention, somebody making a big fuss over her."

"Tell me about it." Emily rolled her eyes.

Sara laughed. "Once I got her to admit that she actually had a dress in mind to wear and we located it, the rest wasn't too hard."

"Not too hard? You ought to win the Nobel Prize or something," Emily remarked. "For a minute there I really thought you just weren't coming. I was afraid you'd gone back to Maryland without telling me."

"I wouldn't do that, Emily," Sara said.

"Well, it did cross my mind that maybe you were afraid to tell me face-to-face, but I also couldn't really believe that you would just take off like that. Still, if you had, I would have understood," she admitted.

Sara looked touched by Emily's admission. "I did speak to my parents," she said.

Emily held her breath. This was it. "And?"

"We had a long phone call. I'm going home in a few days—but only for a short visit, over Thanksgiving weekend. I'm going to see them and get some more clothes and things. Then I'm going to come back."

Emily felt as if her heart had just about stopped beating for a minute. Then she felt her body sag as all the tension suddenly drained out again.

"You're coming back . . . to stay here longer, you mean?" she asked, making sure she heard correctly.

Sara nodded. "My parents say they understand. They want to come and meet you sometime."

"I would like that very much," Emily replied, though the thought partly terrified her.

"Besides, Dan Forbes gave me a job at the paper. It would be hard to pass that up, and my parents thought it was a good opportunity for me, too. I'm just correcting copy at first, but I'll get to write some stories, too, pretty soon, I think."

"Oh, that's great." Emily felt a surge of pure happiness. Good old Dan. She would have to thank him for helping her once again, it seemed.

"I think his son has come to run the paper," Emily added.

"Yes, Wyatt. We met the other day. . . . Oh, and Dan had an accident. Did you hear?"

"An accident? No, I didn't hear a thing about it. What happened?" Emily asked in alarm.

"He was doing something on his boat, getting it ready for his trip or something, and the boom hit him. He fell and broke his arm and leg. He's basically okay, but I don't think he's going anywhere for a while," Sara added, shaking her head.

"When did this happen?"

"Yesterday morning. I'm surprised you didn't hear about it."

"I was out all day, getting ready for the wedding. Nobody mentioned it to me today, either." Emily sighed. "Poor Dan. He must feel awful."

"Well, at least he has Wyatt there to take care of him," Sara pointed out. "It would have been tough if he were all alone."

"I'll have to go by and see him," Emily said. She suddenly realized that this meant Dan was not sailing off into the horizon after all. Or not as soon as he had planned.

Yes, she would definitely go by and visit him. Maybe even tomorrow.

Sara suddenly stood up and took her hand. "Come on, Emily. Jessica's going to toss her bouquet."

"Oh, I can't do that. You go ahead up there if you like."

"Come on. Get moving. Betty is up there, front and center," Sara goaded her. She tugged at Emily's hand until she had no choice but to follow.

Emily sighed and stood at the back of the group of women, trying to slip away from Sara's watchful eye. She had her back to the group and was tiptoeing back in the direction of her table when suddenly Jessica's bouquet landed at her feet. She automatically leaned over and picked it up, not quite sure for a moment what had happened.

Then she turned and faced a clutch of surprised-looking women. Molly stood at the center of the group, and crossed her arms over her chest.

"Oh, for pity's sake . . . that was fixed," she grumbled.

Emily felt amazingly silly holding the bouquet and looked around for someone to take it from her.

"Good strategy," Sara said coming up beside her. "I never thought she would throw that far down field."

"Here . . . do you want this? This is a mistake," Emily replied.

"It's yours, Emily, no avoiding it." Sara pushed the flowers back at her, grinning mischievously.

The music started again, and couples moved out to the dance floor. Luke came by and smiled at Sara. "Care to dance?"

"Sure," she said, leaving Emily. "I didn't know you could do this slow stuff," she remarked, moving into Luke's embrace.

"I really can't. I just sort of—sway. And then kind of—shuffle."

"Okay. I can go with that," Sara said agreeably, trying to match his rhythm. She suddenly remembered the problem he had with his leg and thought it was good of him to dance with her at all.

"You look great in that dress," he said admiringly.

"Thanks." She glanced up at him. "You told that me before, you know."

He laughed. "Well, you still look good. What can I say?" They danced for a few moments, then he added, "I nearly thought you stood me up back at the church."

"When I was late getting Lillian, you mean?"

He nodded. "I thought you went back to Maryland," he told her.

"So did Emily," Sara replied. She turned away from him for a moment, realizing how much her presence meant to both Emily and Luke.

"So, what's the story? Are you going back soon?" he asked quietly.

"Uh, yes and no," she answered. "I'm going down for a visit with my family. Then I'm coming back here. I got a job on the *Messenger*."

"You're kidding, right?" She shook her head as he pulled back and looked at her, a smile slowly spreading across his face.

"Wow, that's really great. Sara Franklin, Ace Reporter."

"Try Ace Copy Editor," she replied.

"That still sounds good to me," Luke said. She felt him hold her just a bit tighter and swirl her for a second. "I'm glad you're not really leaving. I didn't like that idea at all."

She looked up at him and he gazed down at her, his gray eyes looking soft and tender. "Oh" was all she could manage to say.

"You really helped me all these weeks, Sara. I wouldn't have come this far without you."

"I didn't do anything," she said.

"Yes, you did. You helped me just by being there. You helped me by needing *my* help sometimes, I think. If you know what I mean."

"You're doing great now. Your plans are all going to work out, Luke."

"I know. But I would have missed you so much," he confessed. "It wouldn't be the same without you here." He took a deep breath and practically stopped dancing, but still kept his arms around her. "I know it's too soon to say what will happen between us, and I know you're not ready yet for a real relationship. But I hope that you'll give me a chance when you are . . . that you'll give *us* a chance. I really think there could be something great there."

Sara felt thrilled to hear Luke's softly spoken confession. She couldn't pull her gaze away from his, but couldn't find the right words to reply, either. "I didn't want to leave you, either," she finally admitted. "I thought a lot about that. Not just about Emily."

He hugged her close, and she pressed her cheek against his shoulder. "Do you still worry that I'm too young for you?" she asked.

He slowly eased away, his mouth turning up in a small smile. "Actually, I've been thinking maybe you're *too* mature."

Then the music stopped and the singer in the band announced it was time for the bride and groom to cut the cake.

Luke stood beside Sara, still holding her hand as they watched. Jessica met her eye and sent her a warm smile, and Sara smiled back. The wedding was almost over, she realized. The hours had flown by. When she was first invited, she had dreaded attending; she agreed only for Emily. But now she knew she would have been foolish to miss it. It had been a very special day for her. She was starting to feel like part of the Warwick family.

EMILY DROVE HER MOTHER HOME AFTER THE WEDDING AND HELPED HER into the house. Her mother was so tired that she didn't even argue when Emily offered to help her get undressed and into bed.

As her mother sat on the edge of her bed in her nightgown, Emily hung up her fancy dress and matching coat. "This is a beautiful ensemble. I don't think I've ever seen it before."

"Of course you have. I had it made in Paris. Your father and I took a trip there for our fifteenth anniversary. It was a fairly famous designer—what's his name . . ."

"That was over thirty years ago, Mother," Emily cut in. She stared at the dress and coat in amazement. "I guess I'd forgotten."

"Truly good clothes never go out of style. I've always told you that."

Emily turned to her. "I'm glad you came today. It meant a lot to Jessica. You did the right thing, Mother."

Her mother sat up a bit straighter and untied the sash on her robe. "I did what I thought I should do. I still don't approve of Sam Morgan, and I don't require your approval, either," she said curtly.

"Sara persuaded you, though," Emily noted.

"Yes, she did. She's a very persuasive young lady. She ought to go to law school."

"She has a job on the *Messenger*. She might turn out to be a reporter. At least she's going to be in town a while longer."

"Yes, she told me." Lillian swung her legs up on the bed and slipped under the covers. "I can see you're pleased."

Emily met her gaze. "I know you are, too, even if you won't admit it. Sara told me she's been visiting you."

"Yes, she has. What of it?"

"I'm glad you're finally accepting her. She is your only grandchild, you know."

"Don't you think I know that? We have our own relationship, Emily. It doesn't have anything to do with you," Lillian pointed out.

"Well, whether it has to do with me or not, I'm still relieved that you haven't shut her out. I really don't know what I would have done if you had, Mother," Emily admitted.

"What you would have done? What do you mean by that?" Lillian pushed herself back against the pillows and folded her arms over her chest.

"It would have been very difficult for me. I've waited over twenty years to see Sara again. I'm not sure I could have stood it if you didn't accept her." Emily paused. "I've thought about some things that you said, Mother.

I'm finally willing now to let the past go. But I'm not willing to have any-one destroy what I've found in the present."

Lillian glanced up at her, then folded her hands in her lap, as if resigned to some new idea.

"I did what I did and I believed it was for the best. The best for all con-cerned. I thought that you would go on with your life, Emily. That's what I would have done." She glanced up at her daughter and nodded firmly. "But you're different from me, clearly. You've been brooding about it all these years, obsessed with it. I never realized until just recently how much—pain it still gave you."

"Yes, I was stuck back there. But now Sara is here and I can move on." She sat down on the edge of the bed and sighed. "There's been so much time lost, though. I can never get that back again."

Lillian nodded thoughtfully. "No, you can't put spilled milk back in a bottle. What's done is done. I'm glad that your daughter found you. She's a fine girl."

Emily turned to her mother, feeling shocked by the admission. It was as close to an apology as she would ever get, she realized.

"Thank you. I think she is, too. Very fine," Emily agreed.

Lillian leaned back and yawned. "I'm very tired now. I need to rest. This has been a most exhausting day."

Emily took her cue and got up from the bed. She shut off the lamp on her mother's bedside table, then leaned down and kissed her dry cheek. Lil-lian surprised her by reaching out and squeezing her hand, then surprised her even more when she did not let go.

"Good night, Emily," she said quietly.

"Good night, Mother," Emily whispered back. She stood there hold-ing her mother's hand, releasing it only when she saw her mother's eyes close and heard the slow, heavy breathing of her sleep.

* * *

REVEREND BEN WAS OFTEN INVITED TO A WEDDING RECEPTION AFTER HE performed a ceremony, but even if he joined the party, he usually didn't stay the entire evening. But Jessica and Sam were different. He felt very close to both of them and privy to the ups and downs of their romance, so it had seemed fitting that he and Carolyn had stayed to the very last dance.

But by Monday evening he was feeling the effects of his late night out and walked up to his doorway with heavy steps. The house was dark. Carolyn wasn't home yet from Rachel's, he realized. Then just as he put the key in the door, her car pulled into the driveway.

He opened the door and waited for her. She hurried up the path, carrying a large basket of laundry. She looked weary, too, he thought, but happy.

"Here, let me take that for you," He grabbed the basket and leaned across to give her a hello kiss.

"Just put it in the laundry room, dear," Carolyn instructed. "I'll get to it later."

"How was Rachel today?" Ben asked, taking the basket.

"She's coming along, getting her color back. She was allowed to get out of bed a little today, but I made sure she didn't overdo it," Carolyn added as she hung up their jackets on the coat tree in the foyer.

"I'm glad you're going there every day, Carolyn," Ben said as she joined him in the kitchen. "Rachel needs someone to make sure she rests and follows the doctor's orders."

"Don't worry. I'm watching her like a hawk," Carolyn promised. She sat at the table and leafed through the mail. "I'm just so relieved that the danger is over. She has another doctor's visit at the end of the week, but it's just routine. They're practically positive now that the baby is fine. Thank God," she added sincerely.

"I'll say Amen to that," Reverend Ben added. "Practically every pregnancy has some crisis, when you stop to think about it. Let's pray this was ours, and now all we have to look forward to is that wonderful baby being born in a few weeks."

"Yes, it won't be long now. I hope I'm not too exhausted by then to enjoy it, though," Carolyn said. "I think I'm just tired tonight from the wedding. But it was lovely."

"Indeed. I enjoyed every minute of it. It was wonderful to see Emily and her daughter together in the wedding party, wasn't it?"

"Oh, yes. She's been through so much." Carolyn shook her head. "Emily looked positively thrilled, I'd say."

"She's made a whole new start these past few weeks. In just about every way," he added thoughtfully. "So, what's for dinner? Shall we get a bite in town? You look too tired to cook tonight."

"That's sweet of you, but just let me check the freezer. I think Emily sent over a casserole when Rachel was in the hospital. Maybe we can have that."

Carolyn reached into the freezer and found the covered Pyrex dish. She took it out and removed the foil, then stared down at it on the countertop.

"What do you think?" she asked her husband dubiously.

He looked at the frozen dish as well and didn't reply for a moment. "What is it?"

"I'm not sure." Carolyn moved closer and gave the food a sniff. "I'm sorry . . . I just can't tell." She laughed and glanced at him. "Shall we try it?"

He picked up the foil and covered the food again. "Emily is a lovely woman. A wonderful mayor, too, I'd say. But she's not much of a cook."

"Good intentions, though," Carolyn added.

"The finest," Ben agreed. He turned and picked up his car keys. "Unfortunately, I'm a bit too hungry to dine on good intentions," he added with a laugh. He lifted his arm with a flourish, gesturing for her to proceed him. "After you, dear," he said gallantly.

"Thank you, sir. Don't mind if I do." Carolyn grabbed her jacket and purse in the foyer and then considered the melting mystery casserole. She would send the empty dish back to Emily with a grateful, carefully worded note. When you were a minister's wife such gestures came with the territory.

WYATT FORBES HAD DAN'S SMILE, EMILY THOUGHT, AND THE SAME SQUARE-shaped face and blunt chin. But he stood a few inches taller with a lankier build, his hair dark brown and worn in a shaggy style.

"Come on in. My dad is in the den. Just warning you, he's in a real foul mood," he added with a grin.

"So I've heard," Emily replied.

Then she saw Dan, sitting in a wheelchair. She had heard all about the injuries to his arm and leg yesterday, but no one had mentioned the black eye or the cut on his forehead.

"Oh, dear, you look awful," she burst out, then instantly regretted it.

Dan laughed and touched his sore eye with a fingertip. "Oh, this, you mean. . . . You should have seen the other guy."

Emily sat down in a chair next to him and gave him the gifts she brought, a book—a famous newscaster's biography—and a box of fancy chocolates.

"Thanks. I've been wanting to read this," he said, holding up the book.

"But you didn't have the time?" she asked cautiously.

He shook his head. "You got it. I do now, I guess."

"How did it happen?"

"I'm still not sure," Dan admitted. "A line on the mainsail tangled, so I went up there to straighten it out. No big deal. But I stupidly forgot to secure the boom, and it swung around and knocked me right off my feet. It would have been better actually if I had fallen overboard, but I fell into the boat. Right on my head," he added, rubbing a lump above his brow.

"Did you black out?" Emily asked with concern.

"For a few minutes, I guess. I'm lucky I wasn't out on the water.

Tucker Tulley happened to be on the dock and saw the whole thing. He got help right away."

"I'm so sorry, Dan." Emily reached over and squeezed his shoulder. "You must be so disappointed about your trip."

"*Disappointed* is not the word for it," Dan said darkly. He let out a long, harsh breath that made Emily feel as if she were sitting next to a restless tiger.

"How long will you have the casts on?" she asked quietly.

"Six to eight weeks, depending," he replied glumly.

"Until the end of January?"

He nodded. "That's right."

"Well, you can still go then, can't you?"

"I guess so. Provided I'm not in an insane asylum." He glanced at her and she nearly smiled, but when she saw the unhappy look on his face, she didn't dare.

"Oh, it's not so long," she tried to console him. "It will go by quickly."

"No, it won't, Emily. It will go by very slowly," he argued back. "And I'll definitely go mad stuck in this stuffy little house all day." He sighed again and pressed his palm flat against the arm of the wheelchair. "Sorry for being so horrible. I don't mean to sound angry at you. . . . If I can manage to be more civil, will you visit me sometimes?"

Emily felt her pulse quicken at his question—and at the light in his gaze when he looked at her.

"I think I can manage that," she said slowly.

"I know you're always so busy," he added apologetically. "And you work awfully long hours."

"This is a new administration," she told him. "Nine to five, all the way. . . . Do you play chess?"

His expression brightened. "I used to. I even have a board and some nice alabaster pieces around here somewhere."

"Dust it off. I'm quite good," she promised.

"So am I," he replied with an appraising glance.

He sat back in his chair and sighed, then slapped the side of the long cast on his leg. "Ah, me. You just never know what's going to happen, do you?"

"No, you never do," she agreed. "You realize that you really know something about life when you know that you just don't know anything. Know what I mean?"

He smiled. "It's scary, Emily. But I actually understand what you're saying."

Emily laughed, then she felt suddenly self-conscious and looked away, her mind and emotions whirling.

Well, Lord, I'm just sitting here watching and waiting and not knowing anything at all, Emily thought. *I thought You closed this door on me, but looks like the wind—or something—blew it open again.*